THE BEGUM'S MILLIONS

THE

WESLEYAN

EARLY CLASSICS OF

SCIENCE FICTION

SERIES

General Editor

Arthur B. Evans

Cosmos Latinos: An Anthology of Science Fiction from Latin America and Spain
   Andrea L. Bell and
   Yolanda Molina-Gavilán, eds.

Caesar's Column:
A Story of the Twentieth Century
   Ignatius Donnelly

Subterranean Worlds:
A Critical Anthology
   Peter Fitting, ed.

Lumen
   Camille Flammarion

The Last Man
   Jean-Baptiste
   Cousin de Grainville

The Battle of the Sexes in Science Fiction
   Justine Larbalestier

The Yellow Wave:
A Romance of the Asiatic Invasion of Australia
   Kenneth Mackay

The Moon Pool
   A. Merritt

The Twentieth Century
   Albert Robida

The World as It Shall Be
   Emile Souvestre

Star Maker
   Olaf Stapleton

The Begum's Millions
   Jules Verne

Invasion of the Sea
   Jules Verne

The Mighty Orinoco
   Jules Verne

The Mysterious Island
   Jules Verne

H. G. Wells: Traversing Time
   W. Warren Wagar

Deluge
   Sydney Fowler Wright

THE BEGUM'S MILLIONS

JULES VERNE

Translated by

STANFORD L. LUCE

Edited by

ARTHUR B. EVANS

Introduction & Notes by

PETER SCHULMAN

Wesleyan University Press

Middletown, Connecticut

Published by

Wesleyan University Press,

Middletown, CT 06459

www.wesleyan.edu/wespress

The Wesleyan edition of *The Begum's Millions*

© 2005 by Wesleyan University Press

Translation copyright © 2005 by Stanford L. Luce

All rights reserved

Printed in the United States of America

The illustrations in the novel are by
Léon Benett and appeared in the original French
edition of *Les Cinq cents millions de la Bégum*.

Library of Congress
Cataloging-in-Publication Data
Verne, Jules, 1828–1905.
[Cinq cents millions de la Bégum. English]
The Begum's millions / by Jules Verne ; translated
by Stanford L. Luce ; edited by Arthur B. Evans ;
introduction and notes by Peter Schulman.
p. cm. — (The Wesleyan early classics of science
fiction series)
Includes bibliographical references.
ISBN 0-8195-6796-5 (cloth : alk. paper)
I. Luce, Stanford, 1923– II. Evans, Arthur B.
III. Schulman, Peter, 1964– IV. Title. V. Series.
PQ2469.C49E5 2005
843'.8—dc22   2005046203

5   4   3   2   1

CONTENTS

A Note on the Translation, *ix*

Introduction, *xiii*

The Begum's Millions by Jules Verne

1   Mr. Sharp Makes His Entrance, *1*

2   Two Friends, *13*

3   A News Item, *26*

4   Divided in Two, *36*

5   The City of Steel, *48*

6   The Albrecht Mine, *66*

7   The Central Block, *79*

8   The Dragon's Lair, *89*

9   Absent without Leave, *105*

10   An Article from *Unsere Centurie,*
     a German Journal, *117*

11   Dinner at Dr. Sarrasin's, *130*

12   The Council, *136*

13   Letter from Marcel Bruckmann to
     Professor Schultze, Stahlstadt, *148*

14   Preparing for Combat, *150*

15   The San Francisco Stock Exchange, *156*

16   Two Frenchman against a City, *165*

17   Explanations at Gunpoint, *174*

18   The Kernel of the Mystery, *183*

19   A Family Affair, *190*

20   Conclusion, *195*

Notes, *197*

Bibliography, *221*

Jules Gabriel Verne: A Biography, *253*

About the Contributors, *262*

A NOTE ON THE TRANSLATION

This new translation of *The Begum's Millions* by Stanford Luce is the first modern English translation of an important but often neglected Jules Verne novel, *Les Cinq cents millions de la Bégum* (1879). The two previous English translations both date from 1879. The first, an anonymous translation titled *The 500 Millions of the Begum,* was published by George Munro in New York; the second, *The Begum's Fortune,* was published in London by Sampson Low from a translation by W. H. G. Kingston, who already had several Verne translations to his credit: *The Mysterious Island* (1875), *Michael Strogoff* (1876), and *The Child of the Cavern* (1877).

Although not surprising given the overall poor quality of nineteenth-century English translations of Verne's works, neither of these two early translations of *Begum* was very faithful to Verne's original text. For example, the names of many of the principal characters were altered: in one, the name of the Alsatian hero Marcel was changed to Max and, in the other (even more perplexingly), he was called Mureel; his young friend Octave was renamed Otto; the love interest Jeanne became Jeanette; and even Herr Schultze himself lost the final "e" of his name—necessitating a translator rewrite of a crucial passage in the denouement of the story in chapter 18.

One also finds in these English translations a large number of errors and abridgments, many of which severely compromise the integrity of Verne's narrative. For instance, in the following passage, note how the translator has altered both the style and the meaning of Verne's characterization of Dr. Sarrasin when the good doctor is first given the news of his huge inheritance:

> Dr. Sarrasin was thunderstruck. For a moment, he remained entirely speechless. Then, feeling a bit guilty about his temporary lapse of critical reasoning and being unable to accept as proven fact this dream straight out of the *Thousand and One*

Nights, he replied: "But after all, sir, what proofs can you give me about this story, and what led you to find me here?" (Luce trans. of Verne original)

Dr. Sarrasin sat petrified—for some minutes he could not utter a word; then, impressed by a conviction that this fine story was without any foundation in fact, he quietly said: "After all, sir, where are the proofs of this, and in what way have you been led to find me out?" (Kingston trans., Sampson Low, p. 8)

Even worse, consider the following mistranslation where the literal-minded translator bungled Verne's metaphor of Paris as a competitive social arena (*la grande lutte parisienne*) by sending the hero to a wrestling match instead:

Marcel Bruckmann was one of those outstanding young champions, both spirited and discerning, that Alsace sends forth every year to fight in the great battlefield of Paris. (Luce trans. of Verne original)

Mureel Bruckmann was one of those valiant champions which Alsace is in the habit of sending every year to Paris, to contend in wrestling. (trans. anon., Munro ed., p. 3)

Defying the simplest logic, these translations often twist the story's meaning to say the opposite of what Verne wrote. The following description of Herr Schultze scornfully dismissing the utopian project of his French rival is quite typical:

This enterprise seemed absurd to him and, to his way of thinking, was destined to fail since it stood in opposition to the law of progress which decreed the collapse of the Latin race, its subservience to the Saxon race, and, as a consequence, its total disappearance from the surface of the globe. (Luce trans. of Verne's original)

This enterprise appeared to him to be absurd and in his opinion should not be allowed to go into effect, as it was opposed to the laws of progress: it decreed the overthrow of the Saxon race and, in the end, the total disappearance of it from the face of the globe. (anon. trans., Munro ed., p. 7)

For well over 100 years, English-language readers of Jules Verne have had to struggle with inaccurate, incompetent, or ideologically skewed translations of his *Voyages extraordinaires,* most dating from the nineteenth century. There is no doubt that Verne's literary reputation suffered as a consequence. The year 2005 marks the centenary of Jules Verne's death, and it seems an especially appropriate time to celebrate Verne's legacy by publishing a faithful version of his first cautionary novel, *The Begum's Millions.*

LES
500 MILLIONS DE LA BÉGUM
par
JULES VERNE

DESSINS
par
Bénett

INTRODUCTION

"Without him, our century would be stupid," the novelist René Barjavel once wrote.[1] From the magical aerial adventures of the balloonists in *Cinq semaines en ballon* (1863, *Five Weeks in a Balloon*) to the underwater discoveries of Captain Nemo, Verne has never ceased to stimulate the imagination of readers from every point of the globe. It is no small wonder that Verne, according to UNESCO, ranks fourth among the "most translated authors in the world" (behind Walt Disney Productions, Agatha Christie, and the Bible).[2] Verne's famous — if not apocryphal — statement "Whatever one man can imagine, another will someday be able to achieve" has been an inspiration to many who have looked to his works as a beacon for progress and wonder. Alas, one can read that quote with another message in mind as Verne's visions in *The Begum's Millions* (1879) — such as Stahlstadt, the horrifying protofascist state, or Schultze, its megalomaniacal leader — have come true all too often in our own cataclysmic twentieth century. As I. O. Evans remarks, the novel "contains some of Verne's most striking forecasts. He was probably the first to envisage . . . the dangers of long-range bombardment with gas shells and showers of incendiary bombs. . . . He regarded other developments as even more disquieting than such weapons: the attempt of German militarism to dominate the world and the rise of a totalitarian state, rigidly directing its people's lives and infested by political police."[3]

Indeed, when a string of relatively happy tales — such as *Voyage au centre de la terre* (1864, *Voyage to the Center of the Earth*), *De la Terre à la lune* (1865, *From the Earth to the Moon*), and *Le Tour du monde en quatre-vingts jours* (1873, *Around the World in Eighty Days*) — is interrupted by as frightening and enigmatic a text as *The Begum's Millions,* Verne's traditionally upbeat image as a lover of progress and technology must be questioned. Despite Dr. Sarrasin's declaration that the millions he is inheriting will go exclusively toward Science and the building of a utopian community

—"the half billion that chance has placed at my disposal does not belong to me, but to Science!"—*The Begum's Millions* is an extremely cautionary tale, which features Verne's first truly evil scientist, Herr Schultze, and stands as the only one of his works to present both utopian and dystopian visions of society. Whereas Verne's friend and publisher Pierre-Jules Hetzel had steered him away from writing grim dystopian novels in favor of more cheerful adventures after he rejected Verne's first—and recently rediscovered—novel *Paris au XXème siècle* (1994, *Paris in the Twentieth Century*), *The Begum's Millions* ushers in a more pessimistic period in Verne's writing that will reach its peak in his last novels, such as *Maître du monde* (1904, *Master of the World*), in which Robur, the once visionary and poetic inventor of the helicopter-airship *The Albatross*, becomes a psychotic megalomaniac who seeks to take control of the world through his new invention, *The Terror*. Curiously, as if to remind his readers of the terrible lesson of *The Begum's Millions*, Schultze is alluded to at the very beginning of *Robur-le-conquérant* (1886, *Robur the Conqueror*), when Robur's mysterious airship is mistaken for the huge missile-satellite that Schultze had launched into orbit and that circles continuously around the Earth.

That Verne painted more sobering pictures of the world later on in his career comes as no surprise, however, for readers of his early novel *Paris in the Twentieth Century,* in which he portrays a stifling hegemony in a Paris of the 1960s where creativity is frowned upon while greed and business reign. It took over a hundred years for *Paris in the Twentieth Century* to find the light of day because Hetzel had rejected it for being too drab and depressing. Perhaps an older Verne, grown weary of the world's wars and out-of-control capitalism, could no longer suppress the more cynical inclination that was growing within him.[4] As he would write to his brother, "All gaiety has become intolerable to me, my character is profoundly altered, and I have received blows in my life that I will be unable to recover from" (August 1, 1894).[5]

Although different in many ways from his earlier endeavor, *The Begum's Millions* remains one of Verne's most intriguing and exciting novels. And it came at a time (after France's humiliating defeat to the Prussians in 1870) when Verne's young and older readers alike desperately wanted a moral boost. Who better than Verne to lift the morale of a nation in dire need of inspiration? Certainly the Nazis were aware of the novel's potential power to stir an enemy nation when they had it removed from German libraries during World War II. Similarly, as the Germans began remilitarizing the Ruhr in the 1930s, Gaston Leroux knew that *The Begum's Millions* could serve as a "wake-up call" for his countrymen, when he referred to Verne's novel at the beginning of *Rouletabille chez Krupp* (1933, *Rouletabille at Krupp's*). As France urgently required a reminder of the horrors of World War I, Leroux warned of another Schultze rising on the other side of the Rhine. When one of his characters dismisses reports of a new German secret weapon similar to the one Schultze creates in *The Begum's Millions,* "But that's a Jules Verne yarn you're telling me there, my dear genius . . . I read it when I was in school! It's called *The Begum's Millions!*," the narrator feels compelled to interject: "We live in a time when all of Jules Verne's imaginings — on earth, in the air, and beneath the seas — are being realized so accurately and so completely that one can no longer be surprised if that novel enters the realm of reality as well!"[6] Alas, if only Verne *could* have been wrong in his predictions for *The Begum's Millions,* perhaps our twentieth century would not have been so bloody! Yet, just as Verne had been prescient in his description of Stahlstadt, the evil "City of Steel" of the novel, he hardly seems to endorse his utopia in the end either, as it too is a state governed by constraints and obsessions.

When asked by a reporter toward the end of his life if he believed in "progress," Verne could only give a rather "Zen" response. As *The Begum's Millions* demonstrates, progress can be a very subjective term indeed. "Progress toward what end?" Verne asked, before answering:

Progress is a word that can be abused. When I see the progress the Japanese have made in military affairs, I think of my novel

The Begum's Millions, one half of a colossal fortune went to the founders of a virtuous community, while the other half went to the followers of a dark genius whose ideal was expansion through military force. The two communities were able to develop within the possibilities made available through modern science—one aiming for harmony and knowledge, the other going in a different direction altogether. And so, in which direction will our own civilization go?[7]

While, unfortunately, only the future will be able to answer Verne's question, history has already decided the direction that the twentieth century has gone. And one can only hope that the twenty-first century will heed the warnings contained in works such as *The Begum's Millions* and evolve toward a more harmonious, peaceful world.

The Novel within the Novel: The Story Behind *The Begum's Millions*

How did Verne get the idea for *The Begum's Millions*, a novel that is traditionally seen as a "turning point" in his work, as he slowly began to shift from being a sunny optimist to a guarded pessimist? In fact, the story surrounding the novel's origins would be worthy of a novel in and of itself.

The first version, which was originally called *L'Héritage de Langévol* (*The Langevol Inheritance*), was written by a certain Paschal Grousset, a Corsican author, reporter, and revolutionary who wrote under numerous aliases such as Philippe Daryl, Leopold Viray, and Tomasi, but was best known as André Laurie, a pseudonym he used to write a series of successful young adult adventures. Grousset led an exciting and colorful life in his own right. He had been sent to prison in 1870 for attacking Pierre Bonaparte with his friend Pierre Rochefort but was released six months later during the Second Empire. Soon after, he fought alongside the Paris Commune, was arrested once again, and was sent in 1872 to a penal colony in Noumea, New Caledonia, from which he escaped with his friend Rochefort in a daring and perilous breakout. After living in the United States for a while, he went to London where he wrote *The Langevol Inheritance.* Through the auspices of the abbé de Manas, who served as his agent, he managed to sell his manuscript to Hetzel for 1,500 francs in a series of clandestine transactions, since Grousset was still a wanted man. In turn, Hetzel asked Verne to rework and rewrite the novel, as it had some serious flaws. Hetzel knew that Verne's "magic touch" would be able to make the novel into a success. Grousset/Laurie would go on to ghostwrite two other novels under this arrangement: *L'Etoile du sud* (1884, *The Southern Star*), set in South Africa and originally called "The Country of Diamonds," and *L'Epave du Cynthia* (1885, *The Salvage of the Cynthia*), for which Laurie was finally able to share credit publicly with Verne because the Communards had been pardoned and he no longer needed to stay in hiding.

Verne's Imprint

Although Laurie was delighted and honored to have his manuscript be a part of Verne's *Voyages extraordinaires,*[8] Verne thought the book needed a lot of work and proposed several changes in his correspondence with Hetzel. As Verne describes it himself, he considered *The Langevol Inheritance* to be both unbalanced and unrealistic:

> Above all, I have to tell you that in my opinion, the novel, if it is indeed a novel, is in no way complete. The drama, *the conflict,* and consequently *the interest* are absolutely missing. I have never read anything so poorly put together, and at the moment when our interest could be developing, he suddenly drops the ball. There is no doubt about it, the interest is in the conflict between the cannon and the torpedo;[9] and yet one is never launched and the other doesn't explode. It's a complete failure. *L'abbé*[10] drives me crazy with his new weapon system,

which I'll discuss later, and I don't see anything working at all. This is a big mistake as far as the reader is concerned.[11]

Among Verne's many comments to Hetzel about what was wrong with the original manuscript, he said that he was especially concerned with the passages he thought were not believable or accurate. From a purely narrative point of view, he did not believe that the contrast between the French utopia, which he referred to as "The City of Well Being" and the Steel City worked because Verne thought that Laurie's French city was really too *American*. Verne complained that "[The City of Well Being], which is hardly described at all except as part of a journal article, which is very boring, does not seem like a French city to me, but an American one. That Dr. Sarrazin [*sic*] is really a Yankee. A Frenchman, as opposed to a German, would have operated with more artistry than that" (*Correspondance*, 289). Moreover, in the same letter, Verne refers to the City of Well Being as "that Franco-American" city rather than the nationalistic French one. He also had harsh words for what he considered Laurie's awkward scenes, such as Marcel's death sentence and subsequent escape from Stahlstadt, which "should have been superb" but remains "pathetic," as well as the episode of little Carl in the mines, which Verne thought was tedious because he had already written similar scenes in the *Les Indes noires* (1877, *The Black Indies*). Without mincing his words, Verne remarked: "I have never seen such sheer ignorance of the most basic rules of novel writing" (289).

Verne was most concerned, however, with the scientific accuracy of the novel. As someone who researched every detail of even his most extraordinary of *Voyages extraordinaires,* he was appalled by what he considered to be Laurie's lack of understanding of the mechanics inherent in the weapons he was discussing. Since Verne thought that the novel's main focus was on Schultze's giant cannon and missile, he had little patience for any sloppiness on Laurie's part:

If *l'abbé* proves one thing, it is that he doesn't know what a cannon is, and that he is unversed in the simplest rules of ballistics. I've spoken to some competent people about this subject! It's just a *rag of absurdities,* from top to bottom. Everything has to be redone. Not even the invention of an asphyxiating gas shell is new. Can you see Mr. Krupp reading this novel. He would just shrug his shoulders! That we mock the Germans, so be it, but let's not let them mock us even harder. Believe me, when I imagined the cannon in *The Moon,*[12] I stayed within the realm of what is possible, and I said nothing that was not exact. Here, everything is wrong, and yet, that's what is at the heart of the novel (290).

Verne goes on to repeat his claim that all of Laurie's descriptions were mathematically and scientifically erroneous and further criticizes the absurdities of the plot, which he felt ended too abruptly: "It is as though it were being performed on stage and the hero had been hit on the head with a chimney in order to clumsily end the play" (290).

For his part, Hetzel was stunned at Verne's harsh criticism: "I knew that there would be parts of the novel that you would want to bypass or that would really bother you as you came across them. But I didn't expect this complete demolition" (293). Yet, Hetzel, in his continuing role as fatherly mentor and pragmatic editor, was nevertheless able to nudge Verne into reconsidering this project for reasons that Verne might have overlooked in his first reading of the novel. In terms of the narrative, for example, Hetzel urged Verne to see the novel in political and philosophical terms rather than simply scientific ones. For Hetzel, the crux of the story was centered on the notion of the two cities: a totalitarian state revolving around an all-powerful tyrant, and the other, a free, open society based on reason and democracy. "The cannon is everything in the first state," Hetzel remarked, "the torpedo is just an *in case of* in the second" (292). Hetzel was especially fascinated with the political structure of Stahlstadt and disagreed with Verne's assertion that the ending, in which Schultze is frozen just as he is about to launch a devastating attack on France-Ville, was too sudden. As Hetzel explains, when Schultze accidentally auto-destructs, it is an "explosion of both the machine and the man. Everything dies with him, precisely because of that abuse of the concentration [of power in the hands of one individual]. It's the despotic ideal that collapses, that necessarily had to abort, and that logically aborts. Not because a brick falls on his head, but because, in that system, *the brick is inevitable and logical*" (292).

Hetzel also disagreed with several other narrative points that Verne critiqued in the original version. While Verne thought that Marcel's initial entry into Stahlstadt was boring, and his escape ludicrous, Hetzel maintained that they were both important, and that his entry into the evil city, far from being tedious, was essential. While agreeing that the manner in which Laurie presented his ideas needed a great deal of improvement, Hetzel argued that Marcel's penetration into Stahlstadt could be not only effective but also crucial to the novel as a whole. "On the contrary," Hetzel maintained, "[Marcel's entry into Stahlstadt] was the part that seemed to me the most worthy of what readers might consider to be particularly Vernian" (292). While Hetzel also pointed out some of Verne's other criticisms that he disagreed with, such as the scene of little Carl in the mines ("As for the episode of the little worker —which is just one episode—it can't harm the novel at all because it's quite nice—and let me add that it existed in its own right, without any changes, in the first manuscript [of *The Langevol Inheritance*] which preceded *The Black Indies*" [292–93]), he ultimately gave Verne carte blanche to do as he pleased: "If, after all of this, you conceive of an entirely different book that would be better and in which the premise reduced to a question of science would be more apt to give you a good story [. . .] the abbot's book would be no more than a fifth wheel in the carriage of your affairs" (293). In an odd sort of coda to his letter, Hetzel felt obliged to condense his ideas into two sentences, which underline the intensity of the nationalistic Franco-German dialectic that would be at the core of Verne's novel: "Summary: Germany can break up by too much force and concentration. France can quietly reconstitute itself by more freedom" (293).

While Verne and Hetzel would exchange further letters regarding the technicalities of the novel, each of them made certain compromises that enhanced the final version. Verne, for example, dropped his obsession with the scientific veracity of the cannon and the missile, and ended the novel with Schultze's accidentally asphyxiating himself in his laboratory just as he is preparing an even more lethal attack against France-Ville (Verne was insistent on this point, much to Hetzel's delight as he thought it made the text more Verne-like). Although Verne initially wanted to drop the romantic side story of Marcel and Jeanne, which he thought added nothing to the novel, Hetzel persuaded him to include it in at least a perfunctory manner because he considered Marcel too important an opponent to Schultze not to be sufficiently fleshed out as a character. While there are no traces of Laurie's original version (besides its ending, which has been published in the *Bulletin de la Société Jules Verne*), [13] it was apparently presented in two volumes, which both Verne and Hetzel agreed to condense into one. The only other point of contention between Hetzel and Verne revolved around the novel's title, which Verne thought "said nothing" about the story. Verne juggled several titles in his mind, in fact, in order to arrive at the best "philosophical" definition of the novel: "*Parisius* or another title like that would work well, but it would have to be in contrast to *Berlingotte* or another—which is hardly possible. I would like a title along these lines: *Golden City and Steel City, A Tale of Two Model Cities*" (301). Hetzel, for his part, suggested *Steel City* (as Verne thought it was more interesting than Good City), but was not convinced that the title could stand on its own. He finally arrived at *The Begum's Inheritance* but not without reiterating that the fundamental thesis of the novel had to be grounded on the idea that "steel, force, do not lead to happiness" (302). In the end, what counted the most for Hetzel was that the novel be true to the Vernian spirit and that no one should suspect that another had written it. "Finally, my dear friend," Hetzel wrote, "it all rests on the idea of not publishing a book that would appear to the public as a book that you could have written but in fact didn't" (296).

Although *The Begum's Millions* did not turn out to be one of Verne's most successful novels financially, it nonetheless proved to be one his most potent. But did the majority of Verne's readership consider it to be sufficiently *Vernian*? According to Charles-Noël Martin, *The Begum's Millions* sold only 17,000 copies as compared with most of his previous novels, which averaged around 35,000 and 50,000 in first-run sales.[14] Hetzel himself sensed this novel represented something new in Verne's writing—a new "taste" that he felt confident would add some spice to Verne's corpus, saying: "My Dear Verne, everything that you have sent me from *Begum's Millions* seems to work very well and I believe that it will become a good book, as it has a particular little taste that will do no harm to your (literary) landscape as a whole" (303). What kind of "particular little taste" did Hetzel have in mind? Now with Stanford Luce's accurate twenty-first-century translation, a new generation of English-speaking readers will be able to judge for themselves how unique and riveting Verne's complete overhaul of Laurie's idea truly was. As the old saying goes, a genius can rewrite a lesser writer, but no one can rewrite a genius.

Verne's "Thanatopia"

"We are sick, that is absolutely certain, we are sick from too much progress," Emile Zola wrote in *Mes haines* (1866, *My Hatreds*). "This victory of nerves over blood has decided our mores, our literature, our whole era."[15] Can Zola's famous statement be applied to Jules Verne's vision of the nineteenth century as well? Although Verne's most famous works, such as *Le Tour du monde en quatre-vingts jours* (1874, *Around the World in Eighty Days*) or *Vingt mille lieues sous les mers* (1870, *Twenty Thousand Leagues under the Sea*), seem to endorse the virtues of technology and progress, the recently rediscovered manuscript of Verne's dystopian vision of Paris in the 1960s, *Paris in the Twentieth Century,* speaks out so unsparingly against the dehumanizing aspect of modernity that it also draws attention to his ambivalence toward his own century, which would resurface in *The Begum's Millions.* Indeed, the historical context of *The Begum's Millions* presents a dour nationalistic picture of two scientists, a benevolent Frenchman and an evil, despotic German, who each inherit millions from a long-lost relative. Whereas the Frenchman, Dr. Sarrasin, creates a utopia on the west coast of the United States called France-Ville, the German, Herr Schultze, builds Stahlstadt, a dystopian factory village bearing an uncanny resemblance to Verne's hegemonic 1960 Paris. Verne's descriptions of the "City of Steel" make it clear that "freedom and air were lacking in this narrow milieu" (chap. 7). Stahlstadt is essentially a slave camp similar to Fritz Lang's *Metropolis.*[16] While France-Ville is a peaceful socialist society appropriately situated along the Pacific Ocean, Stahlstadt is a warmongering hegemony, an environmental disaster of a city that manufactures cannons to sell to bellicose nations in general and to Germany in particular: "The general opinion, moreover, was that Herr Schultze was working on the construction of a dreadful engine of war, without precedent and destined to assure Germany worldwide domination" (chap. 7).

While *Paris in the Twentieth Century* was dismissed by Hetzel as an unpublishable "youthful error," *The Begum's Millions* responded to a general postwar, anti-German sentiment in France. But Verne's dystopian vision persists as a fulfillment of a general dread of global annihilation that he had to tone down after *Paris in the Twentieth Century*'s failure. As Arthur B. Evans has explained, the nationalistic, thanatos-driven microcosm depicted by Verne in works like *The Begum's Millions* mirrored a more general trend in post–Industrial Revolution France in which the "utopian focus of the French bourgeoisie of the Second Empire and the Troisième République began to shift with the times. The traditional utopian 'nowhere' was soon replaced by a potential 'anywhere'; the pastoral setting by the industrial; personal ethics by competitive expansionism."[17] As such, *The Begum's Millions* can be seen as more than a simple warning of what can happen when science and technology fall into the hands of an evil leader—a warning that would be repeated in *Face au drapeau* (1896, *For the Flag*), in which the French scientist Thomas Roch also invents an incredibly deadly weapon of mass destruction, which, after the inventor goes mad, falls into the hands of criminals who seek to use it for piracy rather than geopolitical conquest. In many ways, Verne's philosophical shift went hand in hand with France's as well, as Hetzel writes in his famous preface to the first edition of the *Voyages et aventures du capitaine Hatteras* (1866, *Voyages and Adventures of Captain Hatteras*): "When one sees the hurried public rushing to lectures that have spread out through a thousand points in France, and when one sees that, next to the art and theater critics, a spot has to be made in our newspapers for reports from the Academy of Sciences, it is time to admit that art for art's sake is no longer sufficient for our era, and that the time has come for Science to have its place in literature." Of course, although Hetzel's reference to science in this instance is meant to be an enthusiastic one, it is clear from a reading of *The Begum's Millions* that science can and should never replace the arts. Verne certainly tended to support Rabelais's maxim: "Science without conscience leads to the ruin of one's soul."

"Every time someone dies, it is Jules Verne's fault," Salvador Dali wrote in *Dali by Dali*. "He is responsible for the desire for interplanetary voyages, good only for boy scouts or for amateur underwater fishermen. If the fabulous sums wasted on these conquests were spent on biological research, nobody on our planet would die anymore. Therefore I repeat, each time someone dies it is Jules Verne's fault."[18] Ironically, Dali's mock accusation against Verne could have been written by Verne himself in the sense that a part of his happier and more hopeful writings may have died a little bit by the time he began to pen the nightmarish visions in *The Begum's Millions*. That Verne felt compelled to adjust the tone of his adventures is not surprising when one takes into consideration the shifts in paradigms from the early to the late nineteenth century. While the most optimistic of Verne's early novels endeavored to portray such characters as the young Axel in *Journey to the Center of the Earth* or the balloonists in *Five Weeks in a Balloon* as enthusiastic seekers of new geographies and discoveries for the sake of world edification, the realities of the mid- to late nineteenth century were hardly as sunny. More often than not, dreams of global social and political harmony resulted in their opposites, as general disillusionment and skepticism became the norm. Verne too was deeply affected by the changes in the European political landscape. The anxieties he tried to communicate through the aborted *Paris in the Twentieth Century* soon became realities as financial behemoths led by monopolistic banks and industrialists grew in strength and power. Growing imperialist ambitions led to escalating arms races, which in turn helped to fuel colonialist expansion and the wars needed to either find new colonies or defend newly acquired interests. Cynical treaties such as the Berlin Accords of 1885, which divided Africa among the European colonial empire builders, led to further power brokering rather than idealistic republics. Domestically, workers movements were repeatedly crushed while unpredictable attacks by anarchists and nihilists terrorized the home front. After France's bitter defeat at the hands of the Germans in the Franco-Prussian war, Verne could only wistfully shake his head as he wrote to a friend: "Yes, this is what the Empire has to show for itself after eighteen years in power: a billion to the bank, no more commerce, no more industry. Eighty stocks that are worth nothing, and that's without counting those that will collapse any minute. A military government that brings us back to the days of the Huns and the Visigoths. Stupid wars in hindsight."[19] As Jean Chesnaux has pointed out, the latter part of the nineteenth century was a period during which the wondrous dreams of the early part of the century had to be translated into social responsibility rather than carefree fantasy; shifts in world order created new social demands and needs: "Between about 1880 and 1890, the *Known and Unknown Worlds* alter their character. Man's efforts, his Promethean challenge to nature, are from then on expressed through well-defined social entities, clearly analyzed as such. Verne comes face to face with social realities. His scientific forecasts now give place to the problems of social organization, social conditions and the responsibility of scientists towards society; in each case, as we shall see, he reaches a pessimistic conclusion."[20]

As a "bridge" novel linking Verne's positivist and most popular works of the 1860s and 1870s and his more often pessimistic works of the 1880s and 1890s, it is quite appropriate that *The Begum's Millions* offers a two-fold vision of society. But the two visions are not polar opposites; even the utopian one has its dark underside. A gigantic inheritance leads to the creation of two states governed by excessively tight restrictions rather than a freedom from constraints and needs that a sudden windfall of cash might be expected to provide. While the peaceful Dr. Sarrasin, designer of France-Ville, benignly declares, "Do I need to tell you that I do not consider myself, in these circumstances, other than a trustee of science? [. . .] It is not to me that this capital lawfully belongs, it is to Humanity, it is to Progress!" (chap. 3), he—like Schultze—creates a centralized and strict state bent on controlling its citizens and destroying its enemies. For Schultze, the enemy is France, whom he sees (in what Chesneaux considers "proto-Hitlerean" terms) as a weak nation of *Untermenschen,* who must be conquered and then annexed into a greater German *Volk;* for Sarrasin, the enemy consists of germs, idleness, and uncleanliness, as he founds his city on the principles of Hygiene above all. One city will be driven by thanatos, the other by hypersanitization, or, rather, a *thanato*-sanitization. On hearing that Sarrasin's proposed utopia would be founded on "conditions of moral and physical hygiene that could successfully develop all the qualities of that race and educate generations that were strong and valiant," Schultze counters with a racially charged diatribe suggesting that France-Ville is opposed "to the law of progress which decreed the collapse of the Latin race, its subservience to the Saxon race, and, as a consequence, its total disappearance from the surface of the globe" (chap. 4). A chemist and the author of a treatise titled *Why Are All Frenchman Stricken in Different Degrees with Hereditary Degeneration?*, Schultze feels compelled to erect his military-industrial dystopia as a countermeasure to Sarrasin's racial inferiority and dangerously visionary aspirations:

> After all, what could not have been done with a man such as Dr. Sarrasin, a Celt, careless, flighty, and most certainly a visionary! [. . .] It was every Saxon's responsibility, in the interest of general order and obeying an ineluctable law, to annihilate if he could such a foolish enterprise. And in the present circumstances, it was clear to him, Schultze, M.D., *Privatdocent* of chemistry at the University of Iéna, known for his numerous comparative works about the different human races—works where it was proved that the Germanic race would absorb all the others—it was clear indeed that he was especially designated by the constantly creative and destructive force of Nature to wipe out the pygmies rebelling against it. (chap. 4)

Given that their respective inheritances were brought about by a union between their French mother and German father, they are doomed, almost like Cain and Abel, to violence and war that only the young hero, Marcel Bruckmann, an Alsatian orphan, whose name "bridge-man" implies a link between the two warring nations, can stop. Yet, while Schultze is obsessed with racial purity, Sarrasin is propelled by a fear of microbial contamination—or, rather, germs and science instead of *germ-ans* and empires. In each case, however, financial capital leads to a lack of freedom rather than an abundance of it. Whether it be Schultze's death-driven military-industrial complex or Sarrasin's hygienic but obsessive-compulsive one, Verne seems to suggest that the only choices available to each country would be either a mad and brutal dictatorship or a neurotic one. While seemingly at opposite poles, the fact that both men's names begin with "S" implies that their roots are fundamentally the same, and that they are nonetheless connected. Moreover, if that "S" could also stand for *serpent* (snake), as in the Garden of

Eden's biblical snake who leads Adam and Eve into temptation, Verne's modern "apple" might well be in the form of Capital that Schultze and Sarrasin eat from rather than Knowledge, which they both seem to abuse through Science. As Schultze understands it, finance capital is the most potent secret ingredient for the destruction he envisages:

> For all eternity, it had been ordained that Thérèse Langévol would marry Martin Schultze, that one day the two nationalities, represented by the person of the French doctor and the German professor, would clash and that the latter would crush the former. He had already half of the doctor's fortune in his hands. That was the instrument he needed. [. . .] Moreover, this project was for Herr Schultze quite secondary; it was to be added on to much larger ones he had had in mind for the destruction of all nations refusing to blend themselves with the German people and reunite with the Fatherland. (chap. 4)

If Schultze represents the cliché of a totalitarian Teuton bent on expanding his Reich, his portrayal is also a giant leap for Verne in a growing anti-Germanism that will culminate in *Le Secret de Wilhelm Storitz* (1910, *The Secret of Wilhelm Storitz*), one of his last books (published posthumously), in which an evil German satanically invents a chemical with which he can become invisible and with which he kidnaps the woman he loves unrequitedly. Although chunks of *Storitz* were rewritten by his son Michel (who placed it in the eighteenth century, instead of the nineteenth, and gave it a bit of a happier ending), Verne, throughout the novel, never ceases to equate Germans with brutality and evil, and the subjugation of the innocent and brave Hungarians. It is a far cry from the endearingly befuddled Dr. Lidenbrock, Axel's uncle in *Journey to the Center of the Earth,* who leads his nephew through an initiation to the center of the Earth with all its treasure trove of discoveries. With *The Begum's Millions,* childish yet innocent national rivalries, which had been mitigated by peaceful reconciliations and handshakes in Verne's previous adventure novels such as the *Voyages and Adven-*

tures of Captain Hatteras, give way to weapons of mass destruction, potential nuclear annihilation, and economic collapse when rumors of Schultze's disappearance and death at the end of the novel lead to a flight of capital, unemployment, and rapid decay in Stahlstadt. As Verne describes it, Stahlstadt's Wall Street–linked financial ruin prefigures the worldwide depression caused by the 1929 crash: "There were assemblies, meetings, discussions, and debate. But no set plans could be agreed to, for none were possible. Rising unemployment soon brought with it a host of ills: poverty, despair, and vice. The workshop empty, the bars filled up. For each chimney which ceased to smoke, a cabaret was born in the surrounding villages" (chap. 15). Once the capitalist strings that kept Schultze's war machine going are removed, there are no pretenses of production or conquest to keep the workers going, just human suffering, hopelessness, and destitution: "They stayed behind, selling their poor garments to that flock of prey with human faces that instinctively swoops down on great disasters. In a few days they were reduced to the most dire of circumstances. They were soon deprived of credit as they had been of salary, of hope as of work, and now saw stretched out before them, as dark as the coming winter, nothing but a future of despair!" (chap. 15).

Although he managed to suppress the glum and dystopian *Paris in the Twentieth Century* by not publishing it, and, most importantly, by exercising an almost tyrannical control over Verne's works in his role as well-meaning but intrusive mentor, Hetzel focused on keeping Verne's works cheerful enough to continue to attract throngs of young readers. But the city of Stahlstadt — ironically echoing Hetzel's own *nom de plume,* "Stahl" — allowed Verne the opportunity to recycle much of his dismal vision of Paris in 1960 that Hetzel had disapproved of. While Verne's future Paris is dystopian because monolithic banks are obsessed with financial control and perpetually expanding profits at the expense of "useless" romantic individualism, Stahlstadt is a pure industrial machine that exists exclusively for the sake of war and war production. *Paris in the Twentieth Century* opens with four concentric circles of a vast new commuter rail system that seems to snake around the city in a stranglehold, and the technological innovations that Verne describes in minute detail hold no enchantment for its citizens: "In this feverish century, where the multiplicity of businesses left no room for rest and allowed for no lateness whatsoever [. . .] the people in 1960 were hardly in admiration of these wonders; they quietly took advantage of them, without being any happier, because to see their rushed pace, their frenetic demeanor, their American fire, one could feel that the fortune demon was pushing them on unrelentingly, and without mercy."[21] Similarly, Schultze's Stahlstadt is also laid out in concentric circles consisting of a stranglehold of walls, gates, security checks, departments and doors:

> In this remote corner of North America, five hundred miles from the smallest neighboring town, surrounded by wilderness and isolated from the world by a rampart of mountains, one could search in vain for the smallest vestige of that liberty which formed the strength of the republic of the United States.
>
> When you arrive by the very walls of Stahlstadt, do not attempt to break through the massive gates which cut through the lines of trenches and fortifications. The most merciless of guards would deter you, and you would be required to return to the outskirts. You cannot enter the City of Steel unless you possess the magic formula, the password, or at least an authorization duly stamped, signed and initialed. (chap. 5)

In *The Begum's Millions,* the future Paris's light rail system is replaced by a subterranean railroad meant to transport workers and raw materials toward an industrialized Virgil-like trip to the underworld, a *nekya*, or descent into hell, for Marcel, the hero who will infiltrate Stahlstadt to save France-Ville:

> To his left, between the wide circular route and the jumble of buildings, the double rails of a circling train stood out first. Then a second wall rose up, paralleling the exterior wall, which indicated the overall configuration of Steel City.

It was in the shape of a circle whose sectors, divided into departments by a line of fortifications, were quite independent of each other, though wrapped by a common wall and trench. [. . .] The uproar of the machines was deafening. Pierced by thousands of windows, these gray buildings seemed more living than inert things. But the newcomer was no doubt used to the spectacle, for he paid not the slightest attention to it. (chap. 5)

As Chesneaux has observed, Stahlstadt, far from being the unreal vision of the future dismissed by Hetzel in *Paris in the Twentieth Century*, is extremely realistic for the late nineteenth century, when steel cities in England, France, and America were generating inhuman working conditions and industrial slums: "[T]he description of Stahlstadt is powerful and glaring with truth. This steel city of the future already foreshadows Le Creusot, the Ruhr, Pittsburgh."[22] As Verne understands it, Stahlstadt is an environmental disaster, hysterically driven by money, greed, and industrial might:

Black macadamized roads, surfaced with cinders and coke, wind along the mountains' flanks. [. . .] The air is heavy with smoke; it hangs like a somber cloak upon the earth. No birds fly through this area; even the insects appear to avoid it; and, within the memory of man, not a single butterfly has ever been seen. [. . .] Thanks to the power of an enormous capital, this immense establishment, this veritable city which is at the same time a model factory, has arisen from the earth as though from a stroke of a wand. (chap. 5)

Uniform rows of apartments house uniform workers all hired to serve an invisible Baal, whose presence is felt through the roaring of fuming volcano-like smoke stacks: "Here and there, an abandoned mine shaft, worn by the rains, overrun by briars, opens its gaping mouth, a bottomless abyss, like some crater of an extinct volcano" (chap. 5). As Marcel gradually moves up the ladder of the Stahlstadt hierarchy, even earning medals for his efficiency, he finally comes face to face with the nefarious Herr Schultze himself, (who considers him a "find" and "a pearl" [chap. 8]) in a chapter titled "The Dragon's Lair," which Simone Vierne views as a type of initiation ritual for the hero.[23] Yet it is truly a *nekya* rather than an initiation as Marcel performs an "Orphic" descent toward Hades, which Dr. Sarrasin describes to him in terms of Manichean peril: "the project would be not only difficult but also perhaps bristling with danger, [. . .] he was risking a sort of descent into hell where hidden abysses might be lurking under his every step" (chap. 16). Yet Marcel's (and the reader's) plunge is essentially an economic one during which Marcel, by making a bridge between France and Germany, or rather France-Ville and Stahlstadt, aims to create what might be considered a kind of ideal unified Europe rather than a jingoistic nation-state. Ross Chambers, for example, has pointed out that

> Marcel becomes not an individual hero but a figure of his
> society; and by virtue of his dual, Franco-German identity,
> the society he figures cannot be either France or Germany but
> must be something like Europe (a Europe reduced through
> the ideological limitation of Verne's vision, to its two major
> Continental powers). In this reading, the trauma of the French
> defeat in 1870 would combine with the inhuman conditions
> brought about by the Industrial Revolution, under the broad
> aegis of Germany as a figure of death, to form Europe's own
> initiatory ordeal—a descent into hell from which a new Europe
> is destined to emerge.[24]

It is during Marcel's tête-à-tête with Herr Schultze that the latter reveals his secret weapons, various crypto-"dirty bombs" that will break up into a myriad of deadly pieces once his gigantic cannon fires them off into France-Ville. Schultze boasts about his invention in terms that are chillingly modern. His claim that "with my system, there are no wounded, just the dead" is preceded by another one, "Every living being within a radius of thirty meters from the center of the explosion is both frozen and asphyxiated!," and, later, yet another one, "It's like a battery that I can throw into space and which can carry fire and death to a whole city by covering it with a shower of inextinguishable flames!" (chap. 8). By courageously facing his enemy, Marcel stands up to the rampant French wave of fear regarding Germany's threat to Europe, which had been propagated through literary and popular political pieces throughout the fin de siècle. With great prescience, Verne touched on a general collective anxiety that would progressively intensify as tensions between Germany and France eventually ballooned into World War I and, later, into World War II.

As Schultze brags about his weapon system, he is also delineating the modus operandi of Stahlstadt itself, which might be seen as more "thanatopia" than dystopia. It is a city pushed toward a kind of nuclear winter *avant la lettre* rather than world domination. Verne's worst fears about 1960 Paris are magnified into a diabolical empire firmly based in the realities of the day. Technology is no longer a toy for questing heroes to leap from adventure to adventure; it is rather a direct result of the death drive Freud so accurately pinpointed in *Civilization and Its Discontents*. As Schultze understands it, Stahlstadt represents the direct opposite of France-Ville's health mission in its sociopathic goals: "You see! [. . .] We're doing the opposite of what the founders of France-Ville do! We're finding the secret ways of shortening lives while they seek to lengthen them. But their work is doomed, for it is from death—sown by us—that life is to be born" (chap. 8). For Schultze, the death drive is a narcotic that fuels his quasi-Nietzchean outlook:

> Right, good, and evil are purely relative things, and all a matter of convention. There is no absolute except the great laws of nature. The law of living competitively is just as natural as the law of gravity. Resisting it is utter inanity; to accept it and act according to its precepts is both reasonable and wise—which is why I shall destroy Dr. Sarrasin's city. Thanks to my cannon,

my fifty thousand Germans will easily make an end of the hundred thousand dreamers over there who constitute a group condemned to perish! (102)

Yet, as Yves Chevrel has pointed out, despite all of Schultze's wickedness, Verne in fact gives him a uniquely grandiose death in which, "mummified like a pharaoh and wildly enlarged in the eyes of his observers, he remains a master of evil even in death. He is the only one of Verne's heroes—malevolent or benevolent—to survive in this manner."[25] When Verne first read the original version of *The Begum's Millions,* he remarked that "the Steel City, because it is described in detail and the hero walks around its streets and brings us with him, is more *interesting* than the Good City, a city that [. . .] we do not get to visit" (*Correspondance,* 294). Verne even suggests that Schultze should resemble Captain Nemo, who is also driven by a thanatosian desire in his hatred for civilization above ground, and for a love of the freedom found beneath the seas: "The head of the canon factory should have been a Nemo, and not this fellow who is ridiculous" (184). If Nemo could proclaim his aquatic battle cry: "Only here is there independence, here I do not recognize any master, here I am free!," there is little doubt that the monstrous Schultze, created ten years later, incarnated the lack of freedom to be found in many late-nineteenth-century industrialized cities.

When Marcel finds Schultze's frozen, magnified body in his laboratory after the latter's chemical explosion backfires on him, Verne seems to be warning us of the road to destruction that technology might be leading humanity toward. As Marcel looks upon the frozen Schultze in stunned silence, he notices that he was frozen in the act of writing. While the abandoned Stahlstadt resembles a "cemetery" where "Death alone seemed to float over the city, whose tall chimneys reared above the horizon like so many skeletons" (chap. 16), Schultze's last words once again irrationally call for the total destruction of France-Ville: "I want France-Ville to be a dead city within two weeks, that no inhabitant survive. A modern Pompeii is what I must have, and at the same time it must provoke the fear and astonishment of the whole world" (chap. 18). Although Schultze's nuclear-bomb-like missile is spun into space, and provokes a collective sigh of relief from the whole world as it is doomed to orbit the earth forever, Verne seems to warn us that, while the world was spared this time, we must be vigilant in the future, lest new evil scientists try to continue where Schultze left off.

If France-Ville appears more unrealistic in its utopian vision than Stahlstadt in its dystopian one, perhaps it is because Verne believed less in it, or even in its aspirations. Based on a medical fantasy titled *Hygeia, A City of Health* (1876) by a certain Dr. Richardson, a famous English doctor in his day who outlined a germ-free civilization,[26] France-Ville is a society filled with rules and restraints, where sanitation police are constantly watching over its worker-citizens, who live in rigidly uniform houses (with strict rules and measurements). Everything must be in order, as a brochure distributed to its newest citizens states emphatically: "Two dangerous elements of disease, veritable nests of miasma and laboratories of poison, are absolutely forbidden: carpets and wallpaper" declares rule number 8. According to rule number 9, "Eiderdown quilts and heavy bedcovers, powerful allies of epidemics, are naturally excluded" (chap. 10). While "all industries and commercial ventures are freely permitted," no one is allowed to be idle: "in order to obtain the right of residence, it is sufficient—provided that good references are supplied—to be able to perform a useful or liberal profession in industry, science, or the arts, and to pledge to obey all the laws of the city. Idle lives will not be tolerated" (chap. 10). Every inch of the citizens' lives is regulated, and the motto that each must subscribe to is a mantra that is exhibited in all of the village's rules and laws: "To clean, clean ceaselessly, to destroy as soon as they are formed, those miasmas which constantly emanate from a human collective, such is the primary job of the central government" (chap. 10). Parallel to Stahlstadt with its "Central Bloc" that watches over its beehive of productivity, France-Ville is also governed by a "Central Government" that passes down its own edicts for the good of its citizens. Although the government is well intentioned rather than militaristic, the tone of Verne's description is indelibly linked to that of *Paris in the Twentieth Century* rather than to the *Voyages extraordinaires*. Furthermore, while Schultze fantasizes about turning France-Ville into a new Pompeii through his weapons of mass destruction, Verne overdetermines Schultze's image by also thinking of it in terms of Pompeii, as if to confirm Schultze's vision: "As for the walls, clad in varnished bricks, they present to the eye the splendor and variety of the indoor apartments of Pompeii with a luxury of colors and longevity which wallpaper, loaded with its thousand subtle poisons, has never been able to rival" (chap. 10).

Although *The Begum's Millions* ends on a happy note, with France-Ville not only saved but taking over Stahlstadt and making it economically viable again, it is hard to see it as a "happy ending" in so much as even the victorious "ideal" society is somewhat frightful and industrial productivity remains the highlight of the utopian societies created by the Begum's fortune. Shockingly, Marcel refers to the defeated Stahlstadt as "the ruin of the admirable institution that [Schultze] had created" and declares that "we must not let his work perish" (chap. 18). Although Marcel and Sarrasin loftily plan on using Stahlstadt's industrial infrastructure primarily as a deterrent to war — "You will have all the capital you need, and thanks to you we will have in a resuscitated Stahlstadt an arsenal of instruments such that no one in the world will think of attacking us! And, while being the strongest, we'll also try to be the most just and bring the benefits of peace and justice to everyone around us" (chap. 18) — the novel ultimately proves that capital *does* fail us and can lead not only to aggression and exploitation, but also to depression, chaos, and potential global annihilation. In fact, the last line of the novel underscores the notion that the real utopian ideal put forth by the victors is essentially a capitalist-industrial one. Stahlstadt is merely converted into a more clement version of its old self: "We can thus be assured that the future will be in good hands thanks to the efforts of Dr. Sarrasin and of Marcel Bruckmann, and that the examples of France-Ville and Stahlstadt, as model city and factory, will not be lost on generations to come" (chap. 20). In this way, the "bridge" implicit in Marcel's name is one that marries the ethics of the French system with the industrial prowess of the German one in order to create more efficient factory towns rather than dreamy utopian states.

"We live in a time where everything happens—we almost have the right to say where everything has happened. [. . .] Moreover, no new legends are being created at the end of this practical and positive nineteenth century," Verne writes at the beginning of *Le Château des Carpathes* (1892, *The Carpathian Castle*).[27] If *The Begum's Millions* was not initially one of Verne's most popular works, and, despite its patriotic and timely anti-German vigor, was not as great a commercial success as his earlier, more Saint-Simonian works, perhaps it is because it ushers in a period of darker visions about government and nations only alluded to in prior novels. It is not surprising that the near apocalyptic struggle between the innocent France-Ville and the ruthless Stahlstadt takes place on American soil, which slowly becomes a land of failed social experimentation and a capitalist free-for-all in his later novels. In *Le Testament d'un excentrique* (1899, *The Will of an Eccentric*), for example, America becomes a giant *jeu de l'oie* game board for the billionaire William J. Hyperbone as his contestants race around the United States in order to win millions of dollars. In *L'Île à hélice* (1895, *Propeller Island*), two millionaires create a floating city, Standard Island, for their comfort, but their dollar-driven utopia soon crumbles under the weight of its citizens' conflicts. Even the charm of an America that can attempt to reach the moon, and where "nothing can astonish an American" in *From the Earth to the Moon*,[28] becomes dangerously absurd and destructive in *Sans dessus dessous* (1889, *Topsy-Turvy*), the cynical sequel to *Autour de la lune* (1870, *Around the Moon*), when Barbicane and J. T. Maston recklessly try to shift the axis of the globe in order to mine coal at the North Pole.

"It has often been asserted that the word 'impossible' is not a French one. People have evidently been deceived by the dictionary," Verne writes in *From the Earth to the Moon*. "In America, ev-

erything is easy, everything is simple; and as for mechanical difficulties, they are overcome before they arise. Between Barbicane's
proposition and its realization, no true Yankee would have allowed
even the semblance of a difficulty to be possible. What is said—
is done."[29] Sadly, what was said often *was* done—by malevolent
figures. As such, the early Verne's confidence in America may seem
naive in light of how he perceived the later part of the century's excesses and unscrupulous motivations. By the same token, in real
life, just as America would be transformed by robber barons and
industrial injustices, its image abroad also changed, becoming, little by little, the "*péril américain*," a land of exploitation rather than
innocent idealism. As Marie-Hélène Huet has noted, the whole
Verne-Hetzel literary project deflates in the face of the hard realities
of the fin de siècle. Indeed, Verne could no longer afford to merely
project cheerfully into the future for, as Huet remarks so succinctly,
"the present had invaded the works."[30]

When Verne and Hetzel discussed whether the crux of *The Begum's Millions* should be centered on Schultze's weapons and their
destructive capability or, rather, on the political-philosophical dif-
ferences between the two cities, Verne commented that "if we write
for 15,000 readers, they'll want [the former]. If we write for 1,500,
perhaps a philosophical thesis might do the trick, but, in any case,
it isn't in the novel as it is now" (*Correspondance*, 294). Although
the novel, in fact, sold around 17,000 copies—a big disappointment
at the time, as were many of his later novels with similarly tenebrific
undertones—Verne did manage to fuse the two approaches (cannons on the one hand, utopia/dystopia on the other), but his final
product remains fascinating for many other reasons as well. Just as
Marcel Bruckmann's name could serve as a metaphor for his being
a bridge between the two warring cities and nations, *The Begum's
Millions* can also be considered a bridge, not only between the "two
Vernes"—the early, successful positivist and the later, dour pessimist
—but between the two Frances as well. Just as France began the
nineteenth century with a "bang" so to speak—as it explored new
continents, created new inventions, and fostered a myriad of uto-

pian, socialist philosophers such as Prosper L'Enfantin and Saint-Simon—the weary fin de siècle France would yield a darker, sometimes decadent, but often nervous literature, as a reaction to the disillusionment and exhaustion caused by the failures of such idealistic models. The framework of the happy agrarian utopia of yore would soon give way to the industrial dystopia of the future when the century limped to a close. Verne's readers, perhaps put off by the negative images of science in the later novels, would also long for those initial "happy days" of Axel, the children of Captain Grant, and Phileas Fogg (the all-time Vernian champion who made *Around the World in Eighty Days* an international best seller). Although Stahlstadt was ultimately defeated by the forces of good, its somber vision would nonetheless grow more persistent in the latter half of Verne's *oeuvre* as the late nineteenth century gave way to a more serious and starker twentieth.

Peter Schulman
Old Dominion University

LES VOYAGES EXTRAORDINAIRES

LES

CINQ CENTS MILLIONS

DE

LA BÉGUM

SUIVI DE

LES RÉVOLTÉS DE LA « BOUNTY »

PAR

JULES VERNE

DESSINS PAR L BENETT

BIBLIOTHÈQUE
D'ÉDUCATION ET DE RÉCRÉATION
J. HETZEL ET Cⁱᵉ, 18, RUE JACOB
PARIS

—

1

Mr. Sharp Makes His Entrance

"These English newspapers are really quite well written!" the good doctor murmured to himself as he settled into a
large leather armchair.[1]

All his life Dr. Sarrasin had indulged in such soliloquies, no
doubt a sign of a certain absentmindedness.[2]

He was a man in his fifties with refined features, sparkling and clear eyes behind their steel-framed glasses, and a face which was both serious and friendly. He was one of those individuals who, at first glance, prompts people to say: "Now there's a fine fellow." Despite the early hour, the doctor had already shaved, and although his attire did not suggest excessive fussiness, he was sporting a white cravat.

Spread out over the rug and the furniture of his Brighton hotel room were the *Times,* the *Daily Telegraph,* and the *Daily News.* It was barely ten o'clock in the morning yet the doctor had already walked around the town, visited a hospital, returned to his hotel, and managed to read all the major London papers covering the detailed report he had presented the night before at the International Hygiene Association Conference on a "blood-cell counter," an instrument which he had invented.

He sat before a breakfast tray covered with a white napkin, on which were placed a cutlet, cooked medium rare, a steaming cup of tea, and a few buttered slices of toast that English cooks prepare so wonderfully, thanks to the special little rolls that bakers prepare for them.

"Yes," he repeated, "these British newspapers are really quite well done, there is no doubt about it! The vice president's speech, the reply of Dr. Cicogna of Naples, the full text of my own paper — everything was caught on the fly, captured just as it occurred, as though it were photographed."

"'Our honorable associate Dr. Sarrasin from Douai[3] took the floor. Speaking in French, he began by saying: 'My listeners will excuse me if I take this liberty, but they surely understand my language better than I could ever speak theirs . . .'"

"Five columns of small print followed! I don't know which is better, the article in the *Times* or the one in the *Telegraph* . . . Neither could be more exact, or more precise!"

Dr. Sarrasin had reached that point in his musings when the master of ceremonies himself—one would scarcely presume to give

Dr. Sarrasin

a lesser title to a person so formally attired in black—knocked on the door and asked if "monsiou" would accept a visitor.

"Monsiou" is the usual term that the English feel obliged to apply to all Frenchmen, without distinction, just as they would designate an Italian as "Signor" and a German as "Herr." Perhaps they are right to do so. This common custom at least has the advantage of immediately identifying a person's nationality.[4]

Dr. Sarrasin took the card that had been presented to him and was quite surprised to receive a visitor in a country where he knew no one. He was even more perplexed when he read on the minuscule calling card:

> "Mr. Sharp, solicitor,
> 93 Southampton Row,
> London."

He knew that a "solicitor" was the English term for a lawyer, or rather a hybrid attorney-at-law, intermediate between a notary, an attorney, and a lawyer—what used to be called a public prosecutor.

"What possible business could Mr. Sharp have with me?" he wondered. "Have I gotten into some kind of trouble without my being aware of it?"

"You're quite sure this is for me?" he asked.

"Oh! Yes, monsiou."

"Well! Please let him in."

The master of ceremonies let a youthful-looking man into the room, whom the doctor, at first sight, classified as being in the rather large family of "death-heads."[5] His thin, dried-up lips, his long white teeth, his hollow temples beneath skin like parchment, his mummy-like complexion, and his little gray eyes with their piercing stare fully qualified him for this classification. The remainder of his skeletal form, from his heels to his occiput, was hidden beneath a great, checkered "Ulster coat," and in his hand he clenched the handle of a polished leather briefcase.

This personage entered, quickly bowed, placed his briefcase

with his hat upon the floor, sat down without asking permission, and immediately said:

"William Henry Sharp, Jr., associate of the firm of Billows, Green, Sharp and Co. This is really Dr. Sarrasin that I have the honor . . . ?"

"Yes, sir."

"François Sarrasin?"

"That is indeed my name."

"From Douai?"

"Douai is my hometown."

"Your father was named Isidore Sarrasin?"

"Exactly."

"We can assume then that he was Isidore Sarrasin."

Mr. Sharp drew a notebook from his pocket, consulted it, and said:

"Isidore Sarrasin died in Paris in 1857, in the 6th arrondissement, 54 rue Taranne, Hôtel des Ecoles, since demolished."

"That is correct," said the doctor, more and more surprised. "But would you kindly explain to me . . . ?"

"The name of his mother was Julie Langévol," continued Mr. Sharp, unperturbed. "She was born in Bar-le-Duc,[6] a daughter of Benedict Langévol, the latter residing at Loriol cul-de-sac, and deceased in 1812,[7] as it appears on the register of the municipality of that city—those registers are a precious institution, sir, a very precious one indeed. Ahem! . . . ahem!—and also the sister of Jean-Jacques Langévol, drum major in the 36th light infantry . . ."

"I must confess," Dr. Sarrasin declared at this point, amazed by such a detailed knowledge of his family genealogy, "that you seem better informed than I am on certain points. It is true that the family name of my grandmother was Langévol, but that is all I know about her."

"She left the city of Bar-le-Duc around 1807 with your grandfather Jean Sarrasin, whom she had married in 1799. Both settled in Melun[8] as dealers in tin ware and remained there until 1811, date of the death of Julie Langévol, Sarrasin's wife. Their marriage gave but one child, Isidore Sarrasin, your father. From that moment on, the thread is lost, except for the date of the death of the latter, discovered in Paris . . ."

"I can pick up the thread," said the doctor, carried along despite himself by this quite mathematical precision. "My grandfather settled in Paris for the education of his son, who was destined for a career in medicine. He died in 1832, at Palaiseau, near Versailles, where my father exercised his profession and where I was born in 1822."

"You're my man," continued Mr. Sharp. "No brothers or sisters?"

"No. I was an only child, and my mother died two years after my birth. But now, sir, would you kindly tell me . . . ?"

Mr. Sharp rose.

"Sir Bryah Jowahir Mothooranath," he said, pronouncing these names with the respect that any Englishman professes for noble titles, "I am happy to have discovered you and to be the first to pay you my respects!"

"This man is insane," thought the doctor. "That's fairly common among 'death heads.'"

The solicitor read this diagnosis in his eyes.

"I am not the least bit crazy," he calmly replied. "You are, at the present time the only known heir to the title of baronet, presented in 1819 by the governor-general of Bengal to Jean-Jacques Langévol, a naturalized English subject and widower of the Begum Gokool, usufructuary of her wealth and deceased in 1841, leaving only one son, who died an imbecile, without posterity, incapable and intestate, in 1869. Thirty years ago, the estate was some five million pounds sterling. It remained impounded and under guardianship, and nearly all its interest went to increase its capital throughout the life of Jean-Jacques Langévol's imbecile son. In 1870, the total value of the estate was estimated, in round numbers, at twenty-one million pounds sterling, or five hundred twenty-five million francs. In accordance with an order signed by the Agra tribunal, countersigned by the Delhi court, recognized by the privy council, the property both real and personal was sold, and the total amount realized was placed in deposit at the Bank of England. At present, this amounts to some five hundred twenty-seven million francs, that you can withdraw with a simple check as soon as you have supplied genealogical proof of your identity to the Chancellery. Furthermore, as of today, I am authorized to offer you through the firm of Messrs. Trollop, Smith and Co., bankers, an advance of any amount on this account . . ."

Dr. Sarrasin was thunderstruck. For a moment, he remained entirely speechless. Then, feeling a bit guilty about his temporary lapse of critical reasoning and being unable to accept as proven fact this dream straight out of the *Thousand and One Nights,* he replied:

"But after all, sir, what proofs can you give me of this story, and what led you to find me here?"

"The proofs are all here," replied Mr. Sharp, tapping on his polished leather briefcase. "As for how I found you, it was quite natural. I've been trying to locate you for five years. Finding the next of kin for the numerous confiscated estates which are registered annually in the British colonies is a specialty of our firm. We have been working on the inheritance of the Begum Gokool for a full five years. We have carried out our investigations in all directions, reviewed hundreds of Sarrasin families, without finding the one descended from Isidore. I had even arrived at the conclusion that there was not one Sarrasin in France, when I was struck yesterday morning while reading in the *Daily News* the review of the International Hygiene Association that there was a doctor by this name with whom I was not familiar. Returning immediately to my notes and to the thousands of handwritten filing cards that we have accumulated about this inheritance, I noted with astonishment that the town of Douai had escaped our attention. Almost certain that I was now on the right track, I took the Brighton train and saw you leaving the meeting, and my conviction became stronger. You are the living portrait of your great-uncle Langévol as he appears in a photograph we have of him, from a painting of the Indian artist Saranoni."

Mr. Sharp drew a photograph from his notebook and passed it to Dr. Sarrasin. This photograph represented a man of great stature, with a splendid beard, a plumed turban, and a green robe of gold-laced brocade, in that posture so peculiar to historical portraits of a four-star general writing out an order to attack while attentively watching the spectator. In the background, one could vaguely make out the smoke of battle and a charge of cavalry.

"These papers will tell you more than I can," continued Mr. Sharp. "I'm going to leave them with you and I shall return in two hours, if you will permit, to take your orders."

With these words, Mr. Sharp withdrew from his polished briefcase seven or eight packets of documents, placed them on the table, and retreated out the door, murmuring:

"Sir Bryah Jowahir Mothooranath, I have the honor of wishing you a very good day."

Half believing and half skeptical, the doctor picked up the files and began to leaf through them.

A quick examination of them was enough to show him that the story was perfectly true and to dispel all his doubts. Indeed, how could one hesitate when reading a document with a title such as:

"Report to the Very Honorable Lords of the Queen's Privy Council, filed this fifth day of January 1870, concerning the vacant succession of the Begum Gokool of Ragginahra, Bengal province.

"Points of fact: at issue are the property rights to certain *mehals* and forty-three thousand *beegales* of arable land, along with diverse structures, palaces, buildings, villages, furniture, treasure, arms, etc., etc., accruing from the estate of the Begum Gokool of Ragginahra. From the accounts submitted to the civil court of Agra and to the higher court of Delhi there results that in 1819 the Begum Gokool, widow of the Rajah Luckmissur and heiress in her own right of considerable wealth, married a foreigner of French origin, named Jean-Jacques Langévol. This foreigner, after having served in the French army as drum major in the 36th Light Cavalry until 1815, embarked in Nantes,[9] at the time of the disbanding of the Loire army, as a cargo master on a commercial ship. He arrived in Calcutta, moved inland, and soon obtained the rank of captain as a military instructor in the small indigenous army that the Rajah Luckmissur was authorized to maintain. He eventually rose to the rank of commander-in-chief, and, shortly after the death of the Rajah, he obtained the hand of his widow. In consideration of various contributions to colonial policy and important services rendered during a perilous situation for Europeans in Agra by Jean-Jacques Langévol, who had become a naturalized British subject, the governor-general of Bengal requested and obtained the title of baronet for the husband of the Begum who also received the land of Bryah Jowahir Mothooranath as his kingdom. The Begum died in 1839, leaving her estate to Langévol, who followed her two years later to the grave. From their marriage there was but one son, who suffered in a state of imbecility since early childhood and whom it was necessary to place under guardians immediately. His estate was faithfully administered until his death in 1869. There are no known heirs to this enormous inheritance. The tribunal of Agra and the court of Delhi having ordered a sale by auction, at the request of the local government acting in the name of the State, we have the honor of requesting of the Lords of the Privy Council for the confirmation of these judgments, etc., etc." Signatures followed.

Certified copies of the legal judgments from Agra and from Delhi, certificates of sale, orders given for the deposit of capital in the Bank of England, a historical account of research carried out in France to find the Langévol heirs, and a veritable mass of documents of the same sort no longer permitted Dr. Sarrasin the slightest hesitation. He was the fitting and proper next of kin and successor to the Begum. The thickness of a birth certificate was the only thing between him and the five hundred twenty-seven million francs deposited in the bank's vault!

Such a stroke of fortune could well excite the calmest soul, and the good doctor could not entirely escape the emotion that such an unexpected event was sure to cause. However, his excitement was of short duration, and only manifested itself by a rapid pacing up and down his room for several minutes. He then quickly regained possession of himself, reproached himself for the weakness of yielding to such a feverish emotion, and settled himself into an armchair where he remained in deep reflection for some time.[10]

Then, jumping out of his chair, he suddenly started pacing up and down again. But this time his eyes burned with a pure flame, and one could tell that some generous and noble thought was evolving in his mind. He welcomed it, caressed it, held it close, and finally adopted it.

At that moment, there were knocks on the door. Mr. Sharp was returning.

"Please excuse my misgivings," the doctor told him cordially. "But I'm now quite convinced and infinitely obliged to you for the effort you have taken."

"Don't feel obliged . . . a simple matter . . . my job . . . ," responded Mr. Sharp. "May I hope that Sir Bryah will remain one of my clients?"

"That goes without saying, of course. I will place the whole business in your hands. I will only ask you to stop calling me by that absurd title."

"Absurd! A title that is worth twenty-one million pounds sterling?" Mr. Sharp thought to himself; but he was too gracious a courtier not to give in.

"As you wish; you are the master," he replied. "I am going to take the train back to London, and will await your orders."

"May I keep these documents?" asked the doctor.

"Of course, we have copies of them."

Dr. Sarrasin, alone again, sat down at his desk, took a sheet of writing paper and wrote the following:

"I'm going to take the train back to London."

"Brighton, October 28, 1871

"My dear son,

"We are the inheritors of an enormous, colossal, unbelievable fortune! Do not think I have been struck with some mental derangement, and do read the two or three printed pages that I enclose with my letter. You'll clearly see that I am heir to the title of English—or rather Indian—baronet, and to a capital fortune in excess of half a billion francs which are currently on deposit at the Bank of England. I can well imagine, dear Octave, the feelings you will undoubtedly have upon hearing this news. Like myself, you will understand the new responsibilities that such a fortune imposes upon us, as well as the many dangers it poses in using it wisely. I have come to learn of this hardly an hour ago, and already the awareness of such a responsibility almost stifles the joy it first brought me when thinking of you. Perhaps this event will change our destiny. Modest pioneers in science, we were happy in our obscurity. Will we continue to be? No, perhaps, unless—but I don't dare to tell you about an idea that has suddenly come to me!— unless this fortune itself becomes, in our hands, some new and powerful scientific instrument, a prodigious tool of civilization! We'll talk more about it later. Write me soon, tell me your reactions to this wonderful news, and be sure to pass the word on to your mother. I'm sure that, sensible woman that she is, she'll accept the news with perfect calmness. As for your sister, she is still too young to have her head turned by anything like this. Besides, her little head is quite sound, and were she able to understand all the possible ramifications of this news that I'm telling you, I'm sure that, of all of us, she would be the least disturbed. Give Marcel a good handshake for me. He is not absent from any of my future plans.

Your loving father,
François Sarrasin
Doctor of Medicine"

This letter, sealed in its envelope along with the most important papers, was addressed to "M. Octave Sarrasin, student at the Ecole

Centrale of Arts and Manufacture, 32 rue de Roi-de-Sicile, Paris." The doctor then took his hat, put his coat back on, and returned to the conference. A quarter of an hour later, the worthy fellow had completely ceased thinking about his millions.

2 Two Friends

The doctor's son, Octave Sarrasin, was not exactly what one would call lazy. He was neither stupid nor of superior intelligence, neither handsome nor ugly, neither tall nor short, neither brown- nor blond-haired. The latter was a kind of chestnut color, and Octave was in every way an average young man born into the middle class. In school he generally earned a second prize and two or three runners-up. At the *baccalauréat,* he was given a passing grade. Rejected the first time at the competitive exam for the Ecole Centrale, he was admitted on the second try with a rating of 127. His character was somewhat indecisive, one of those minds that is content with uncertainty, that seems to live perpetually in the "approximate," and that walks through life in semi-obscurity. The destiny of such people is often what a bottle cork is to the crest of a wave. Depending on whether the wind is blowing from the north or the south, they are carried off to either the equator or the pole. Chance alone decides the course of their lives. If Dr. Sarrasin had clearly understood his son's character, perhaps he would have hesitated in writing him the above letter. But even the most brilliant minds sometimes exhibit a little paternal blindness.[1]

During the early years of his education, Octave had the good fortune to come under the spell of an energetic individual whose somewhat exacting but benevolent influence had imposed itself by sheer strength upon him. In the Lycée Charlemagne where his father had sent him to do his studies,[2] Octave had become best friends with one of his classmates, an Alsatian named Marcel Bruckmann, who

Marcel and Octave

was younger than he by a year, but much his superior in terms of physical, intellectual, and moral vigor.

Orphaned at the age of twelve, Marcel Bruckmann had inherited a small income which was just enough to pay for his schooling.[3] Without Octave, who always brought him along to his parents' home during vacations, he would probably never have ventured outside the school walls.

As a consequence, the family of Dr. Sarrasin soon became the young Alsatian's family as well. Warm and sensitive beneath his apparently cold exterior, he understood that he owed his life to these worthy people who became both father and mother to him. So it is no surprise that he adored Dr. Sarrasin, his wife, and their kind and already serious-minded daughter Jeanne, who had all opened their hearts to him. But it was by facts, not words, that he proved his gratitude. Indeed, he had taken on the agreeable task of helping Jeanne, who loved learning, to become an upright young woman with a firm and judicious mind, and, at the same time, of making Octave a son worthy of his father. This latter task, one must say, proved to be a bit more difficult than in regard to the sister who was, for her age, already superior to her brother. But Marcel had promised himself to reach his double goal.

Marcel Bruckmann was one of those outstanding young champions, both spirited and discerning, that Alsace sends forth every year to fight in the great battlefield of Paris. As a child he had already distinguished himself by the toughness and flexibility of his muscles as well as by the sharpness of his mind. Strong on the outside, he was all purpose and courage on the inside.

Since his early school days, he felt a driving urge to excel in everything, on the horizontal bars as on the ball field, in the gymnasium as in the laboratory. If he missed a prize in his annual harvest, he felt the year was lost. At twenty he was tall in stature, robust, filled with zest and action, an organic machine at the peak of its performance.[4] His intellect had already attracted the attention of thoughtful minds. Having entered the Ecole Centrale the same year as Octave as the second-ranked student, he was determined to finish as number one.

Moreover, it was due to Marcel's persistent and overflowing energy—which was more than enough for two men—that Octave was eventually admitted to the university. For a whole year Marcel had mentored him, pushed him to work, and ultimately forced him to succeed. He felt a kind of friendly compassion for that vacillating and feeble character, like a lion might feel for a puppy. He enjoyed strengthening with his own energy that anemic plant and having it bear fruit before his eyes.[5]

The war of 1870 had broken out, surprising the two friends at a time when they were taking their exams. On the day after the last exam, Marcel, full of patriotic grief at the fate that was threatening Strasbourg and Alsace, had gone to enlist in the 31st Infantry Battalion. Octave had immediately followed his example.

Side by side as outposts, they had waged the difficult campaign of the siege of Paris. At Champigny, Marcel had received a bullet in his right arm; at Buzenval, a stripe on his left arm.[6] Octave had neither stripes nor wound. In truth, it was not his fault, for he had always followed his friend under fire. He had been scarcely six meters behind—but those six meters had made all the difference.

After peace was declared and normalcy returned, the two students decided to live together in two adjacent rooms of a modest hotel near the school. The misfortunes of France and the loss of Alsace and Lorraine had developed a certain maturity and manliness in Marcel.

"It is up to the French youth," he would say, "to repair the mistakes of their fathers, and this can only be achieved by hard work."

Rising at five o'clock, Marcel obliged Octave to do the same. He dragged him to his courses and, after class, kept a close eye on him. Returning home, they continued their studies, interrupting them periodically with a pipe and a cup of coffee. At ten o'clock, they went to bed, their hearts satisfied and their brains filled. A game of billiards from time to time, a carefully selected play, a concert at the National Conservatory every now and then, a horseback ride to Verrières, a walk in the woods, twice-a-week lessons in boxing or dueling, such were their diversions. Octave certainly showed an inclination to rebel sometimes, and he cast an envious eye on less praiseworthy distractions. He would talk about going to see Aristide Leroux, who was "reading for the bar" at the Saint-Michel tavern. But Marcel treated these fantasies with such contempt that they most often faded away.

On October 29, 1871, around seven o'clock in the evening, the two friends were seated as usual side by side at the same table under a common lamp they shared. Marcel had thrown himself body and soul into a fascinating problem of descriptive geometry as it applied to the cutting of precious stones. With similar zeal, Octave was devoting himself to an activity that, unfortunately, seemed just as important to him—the brewing of a liter of coffee. It was one of those rare skills in which he was proud to excel—perhaps because he found a daily chance to escape the dreadful necessity of balancing equations, in which, it seemed to him, Marcel spent altogether too much time. So he was pouring his boiling water drop by drop through a thick layer of powdered mocha, and this peaceful contentedness should have satisfied him. But Marcel's industriousness was weighing upon his conscience, and he felt the irresistible need of troubling him with some small talk.

"We'd do well to buy a percolator," he said all of a sudden. "This old, slow method of filtering is no longer in step with our modern civilization."

"Then buy a percolator! Maybe that'll keep you from wasting an hour every evening on your kitchen work," Marcel responded.

And he returned to his problem.

"An arch has an ellipsoid of three unequal axes for its intrados. Let ABDE be the ellipse at its base which encloses the maximum axis oA = a, and the central axis oB = b, whereas the minimal axis $(o, o'c')$ is vertical and equal to c, which makes the rise of the arch less than a half of its span . . ."

At that moment someone knocked at the door.

"A letter for Mr. Octave Sarrasin," said the hotel employee.

One can imagine how this fortunate diversion was welcomed by the young student.

"It's my father," said Octave. "I recognize the writing . . . This is what is called a real missive!" he added, weighing the sheaf of papers in his hand.

Marcel knew, as did his friend, that the doctor had been in England. Passing through Paris on his way there the week before, he had offered the two young men a lavish gourmet dinner in a restaurant in the Palais-Royal well known in days gone by, now out of fashion, but which Dr. Sarrasin continued to consider the last word in Parisian refinement.

"You'll let me know if your father mentions his Hygiene Conference to you," said Marcel. "It's a good idea he had to go there. French scientists are too inclined to isolate themselves."

And Marcel returned to his problem:

". . . The extrados will be formed by an ellipsoid similar to the first, having its center below o' on the vertical o. After having marked the foci F_1, F_2, F of the three principal ellipses, we trace the ellipse and the auxiliary hyperbola, whose common axes . . ."

A cry from Octave caused him to look up.

"What's the trouble?" he asked, a bit worried by seeing his friend so pale.

"Read this!" said the other, overwhelmed by the news he had just received.

Marcel took the letter, read it through, reread it a second time, cast a glance at the printed documents which accompanied it, and said:

"That's strange!"

Then he filled his pipe and lit it methodically. Octave waited anxiously for his opinion.

"Do you think it's true?" he asked him in a strangled voice.

"True?—obviously. Your father has too much good sense and scientific spirit to accept such a conviction blindly. Besides, the proofs are there, and basically it's quite simple."

The pipe was well and properly lit; Marcel went back to work.

Octave remained, his arms dangling, unable to even finish his coffee, let alone assemble any logical ideas. Yet he had to speak out, to be sure he was not dreaming.

"But . . . if that's true, it's absolutely mind-boggling! . . . You know, a half billion, that's an enormous fortune!"

Marcel raised his head and agreed.

"'Enormous' is the word. There is perhaps no equal in France, and only a few in the United States, scarcely a half-dozen in England, fifteen or twenty in the world."

"And a noble title to boot!" continued Octave, "A title of baronet! It's not that I've ever yearned to have one, but since it has happened, you can say anyway that it is more elegant than just calling yourself Sarrasin period."

Marcel blew a puff of smoke and said nothing. This puff said clearly: "Puff! . . . Puff!"

"It's certain," replied Octave, "that I never would've liked to do as so many people do, stick a 'de' onto their name, or invent a marquisate out of paper. But having an authentic title, duly listed in the peerage of Great Britain and Ireland, where no doubt or confusion is possible, as can too often be seen . . ."

The pipe kept saying: "Puff! . . . Puff!"

"My dear friend, you can say or do what you like," replied Octave with conviction, "but I can tell you that 'blood counts,' as the English say!"

He stopped short, seeing Marcel's mocking look, and returned to the subject of his millions instead.

"Do you remember," he continued, "that Mr. Binominal, our math teacher, rattled away every year in his first lesson on numeration that a half billion is too large a number for the strength of human intelligence to have a real concept of it if people did not have the resources of a graphic representation at their disposition? Imagine a man paying a franc a minute—it would take more than a thousand years to pay that sum! Ah! it is quite a . . . unique experience to consider oneself as heir to half a billion francs!"

"A half a billion francs!" exclaimed Marcel, shaken by the word more than he had been by the thing. "Do you know the best thing you could do with it? Give it to France to pay its ransom! Only it would take ten times as much! . . ."[7]

"Just don't take it into your head to suggest such an idea to my father!" cried Octave with the voice of a frightened man. "He would be quite capable of doing it! I've already noticed that he's ruminating some great project! It would be all right to make an investment in the State, but at least we should keep the revenue!"

"You were no doubt made to be a capitalist!" answered Marcel. "Something tells me, my dear Octave, that it would have been better for you, if not for your father who is an upright and sensible man, if this vast inheritance had been of more modest proportions. I would rather see you get a yearly income of twenty-five thousand pounds to share with your fine little sister than this great mountain of gold!"

And he went back to work again.

As for Octave, he was unable to do anything, and he fussed so much about the room that his friend, who was somewhat irritated, finally said to him:

"You'd better go out and get some fresh air! It's obvious you're not good for anything this evening."

"You're right," replied Octave, seizing with joy this quasi-permission to abandon any further work.

And, grabbing his hat, he rushed down the stairs and out on the street. He had scarcely taken ten steps before he stopped under a gaslight to reread the letter from his father. He needed to assure himself once more that he had not been dreaming.

"A half a billion! . . . A half a billion! . . ." he repeated. "That produces a yearly income of at least twenty-five million! . . . If my father gave me only one million a year as an allowance—or half a million, or even quarter of a million—I'd be very happy indeed! You can do a lot of things with money! I'm sure that I could use it well! I'm no imbecile, right? I got into the Ecole Centrale, didn't I? . . . And now I have a title as well! . . . And I'll know how to bear it properly!"

"A half a billion!"

He glanced at himself, while passing in front of the windows of a shop.

"I'll have a mansion, horses! There'll be one for Marcel. From the moment I get rich, it's quite clear, it'll be as though he were, too. It has all worked out perfectly! . . . A half a billion! . . . And a baronet too! . . . It's so strange; now that it's happened, it seems to me that I was almost expecting it! Something told me that I wouldn't always be grubbing along over books or drafting boards all my life! . . . Nevertheless, it's an amazing dream come true!"

As he ruminated upon these ideas, Octave walked along the arcades of the rue de Rivoli. He arrived at the Champs-Elysées, turned the corner onto the rue Royale, and came out at the Boulevards. Formerly he had regarded these elegant shops with indifference, like useless things with no place in his life. Now he stopped and thought with a thrill of pleasure that all those treasures could belong to him whenever he wished.

"It's for me," he said to himself, "that the spinners of Holland turn their spindles, that the factories of Elbeuf weave their softest cloth, that the watchmakers produce their timepieces, that the candelabra of the Opera shine their light, that violins play, that sopranos sing at the top of their voices! It's for me that thoroughbreds are raised in their stables and that the Café Anglais is all lit up! . . . Paris is mine! . . . Everything is mine! . . . I'll travel! . . . I'll visit my barony in India! . . . I could afford a pagoda someday, including the monks and ivory idols! . . . I'll have elephants! . . . I'll hunt tigers! . . . and have splendid arms! . . . and a handsome boat! . . . A boat? No! A fine steam-yacht rather, to take me wherever I want, to put into port or to sail off, whatever I chose! . . . Speaking of steam, I really must let my mother know about this news. Suppose I left for Douai! . . . There's school . . . Oh! school! I can get along without it! . . . But Marcel! He'll have to be told. I'll send him a message. He'll fully understand that I'm eager to see my mother and my sister under such a circumstance!"

Octave entered a telegraph bureau, informed his friend that he was leaving and would return in two days. Then, he hailed a carriage to take him to the Gare du Nord.

Once on the train he continued to savor his dream.

At two o'clock in the morning, Octave chimed the night bell so noisily at the door of his parents that he stirred up the peaceful neighborhood of the Aubettes.

"Who do you suppose is ill?" the gossips asked from one window to another.

"The doctor isn't in town!" shouted the old servant from the dormer window on the top floor.

"It's me, Octave! . . . Come down and let me in, Francine!"

After a ten-minute wait, Octave succeeded in entering the house. His mother and his sister Jeanne, having hurriedly come downstairs in their dressing-gowns, were awaiting an explanation of this unexpected visit.

Read out loud, the letter from the doctor soon gave them the key to the mystery.

For a moment Mme Sarrasin was astounded. She embraced her son and her daughter, weeping for joy. It seemed to her that the universe was theirs from now on, and that no misfortune could ever befall young people who possessed several hundred million francs. Yet, women tend to adjust more quickly than men to such wondrous changes in fate. Mme Sarrasin reread the letter from her husband, said to herself that it was her husband who was the one to decide on her destiny and that of their children, and calm was restored to her heart. As for Jeanne, she was happy at her mother and brother's joy, but her thirteen-year-old heart could not dream of any happiness exceeding that of the modest home where their life flowed by gently between the lessons of her teachers and the love of her parents. She did not quite see how a few bundles of banknotes could change her life very much, and this view did not trouble her for an instant.

Mme Sarrasin, married quite young to a man entirely absorbed by the quiet occupations of a devoted intellectual, respected the passion of her husband whom she loved tenderly, without, however, understanding him. Being unable to share the happiness that the doctor derived from his studies, she felt sometimes a bit lonely beside this relentless worker, and had as a result placed all her hope in her two children. She had always dreamed of a brilliant future for them, one that would make them happy. Octave, she was sure, was destined for great things. Since he had entered the Ecole Centrale, this unassuming and practical college for young engineers had been transformed in her mind into a breeding ground for illustrious men. Her sole concern had been that their modest fortune might eventually be an obstacle, a problem at least for the glorious career of her son, and might also harm the prospects of her daughter. Now, from what she had understood in her husband's letter, her fears were no longer justified. Her satisfaction was complete.

The mother and the son spent a great part of the night talking and making plans, whereas Jeanne, very happy with the present, without any concern for the future, had fallen asleep in an armchair.

Then, before finally retiring, Mme Sarrasin said to her son:

"You haven't talked to me about Marcel. Didn't you let him know about this letter from your father? What did he say about it?"

"Oh," replied Octave, "you know Marcel! He's more than an intellectual, he's a stoic! I think he was concerned by the enormity of this inheritance and its influence on us! I say 'us,' since his concern did not seem to extend to my father, whose good sense, he said, and scientific reasoning reassured him. But what else can I think? As far as you're concerned, mother, and Jeanne as well, and especially me, he did not hide the fact that he would have preferred our receiving a modest inheritance, say twenty-five thousand pounds of annual income . . ."

"Marcel might have been right," replied Mme Sarrasin, looking at her son. "Sudden wealth can pose a great danger for some people!"

Jeanne had just awoken. She had heard her mother's last words:

"You know, mother," she said to her, rubbing her eyes and head-

Octave's mother and sister Jeanne

ing for her little bedroom, "you know what you told me one day, that Marcel was always right! I, for one, always believe what our friend Marcel says!"

Then, kissing her mother, Jeanne retired for the night.

3 *A News Item*

Arriving at the fourth meeting of the Association of Hygiene Conference, Dr. Sarrasin could see that all his colleagues greeted him with utmost respect. Until then, Lord Glandover, Knight of the Garter, who held the office of president of the association, had scarcely deigned to notice the French doctor's existence.

This lord was an august personage,[1] whose role was limited to declaring the meeting open or closed and to mechanically grant the floor to the speakers listed on the paper placed before him. He kept his right hand habitually in the breast of his buttoned frock coat—not because he had fallen from his horse—but just because this uncomfortable posture was used by English sculptors in their bronzes of men of state.

His wan and beardless face, daubed with red spots, and topped with a brownish green wig raised pretentiously in a cowlick over a forehead that appeared hollow, seemed as comically aloof and ludicrously stiff as one could possibly imagine. Lord Glandover moved as one piece, as though he were made of wood or cardboard. Even his eyes did not seem to roll beneath their arched sockets, except by intermittent jerks, such as the eyes of a doll or a dummy.

During the initial presentations, the president of the Association of Hygiene had offered Dr. Sarrasin a greeting that was both protective and condescending and which could have been interpreted this way:

"Greetings, Mister Nobody! . . . You're the one who labors on these little insignificant machines to earn a meager life? . . . I must surely have sharp vision to perceive a creature so distant from me in the hierarchy of human beings! . . . You may remain in the shadow of My Lordship. You have my permission."

This time, Lord Glandover addressed him with the most gracious of smiles and pushed his courtesy so far as to point out an empty seat on his right. Moreover, all members of the association had risen when he approached.

Rather surprised by these tokens of such flattering attention, and saying to himself that no doubt the blood-cell counter had appeared to his colleagues a more worthy discovery than they had at first supposed, Dr. Sarrasin took the seat that was offered him.

But all his illusions as an inventor vanished when Lord Glandover leaned down toward his ear with such a contortion of cervical vertebrae as might result in a severe torticollis for His Lordship and whispered:

"I hear that you are a man of considerable property? They say that you are worth twenty-one million pounds sterling?"

Lord Glandover seemed very sorry at having treated so lightly the flesh-and-bone equivalent of such a large sum of money. His whole attitude seemed to reflect, "Why didn't you let us know? Frankly, that was not very nice! To expose people to such misunderstandings!"

Dr. Sarrasin, who did not feel "worth" one penny more than at the preceding sessions, wondered how the news had already been spread when his neighbor on the right, Dr. Ovidius from Berlin, told him with a false and lifeless smile:

"Why you're right up there with the Rothschilds! The *Daily Telegraph* carried the news! All my compliments!"

And he showed him a copy of the paper, dated the very same day. One could read in it the following "news item" whose editing plainly revealed the author:

"*A Monstrous Inheritance.* The famed estate in abeyance of the Begum Gokool has finally discovered its legitimate heir through the capable hands of Messrs. Billows, Green and Sharp, solicitors, 93 Southampton Row, London. The fortunate proprietor of the twenty-one million pounds sterling, deposited at present in the Bank of England, is the French Dr. Sarrasin, whose fine paper given at the Conference in Brighton was reported in our pages three days ago. Through great labor and despite impediments that would merit an entire novel in themselves, Mr. Sharp has managed to establish without any possible doubt that Dr. Sarrasin is the sole living descendant of Jean-Jacques Langévol, baronet, husband by second marriage to the Begum Gokool. This soldier of fortune was, it seems, born in the little French town of Bar-le-Duc. All that remains for him to do before taking possession of the estate are some simple formalities. The request has already been lodged with the Chancellor's Court. It has been a curious chain of circumstances that have come together to bestow on a French intellectual not only a British title but also the treasures amassed by a long list of Indian rajahs. Lady luck could not have made a more intelligent choice, and we must be thankful that such a large fortune should fall into hands that will know how to put it to good use."

In a rather singular reaction, Dr. Sarrasin was vexed to see the news publicized. It was not simply because of the many importunities which his experience with human nature led him to foresee, but he felt humbled by the importance people seemed to be attributing to this event. He seemed to have been diminished personally by the enormous size of his capital. He felt deeply that all his work, his personal merit, were being buried in this ocean of gold and silver, even in the eyes of his colleagues. They no longer saw in him the tireless researcher, the superior and subtle intelligence, the ingenious inventor—they saw the demi-billionaire. Had he been a goitrous inhabitant of the Alps, a besotted Hottentot,[2] any one of the most degraded specimens of humanity, instead of one of its superior representatives, his value would have been considered to be the same. Lord Glandover had used the word: he was "worth" henceforth twenty-one million pounds sterling, neither more nor less.

This concept sickened him, and the association, watching with a quite scientific curiosity about what made up a demi-billionaire, noted not without surprise that the doctor's face was veiled in a sort of sadness.

However, it was but a passing weakness. The grandeur of the goal to which he had resolved to dedicate this unexpected fortune suddenly came to the doctor's mind, and it reassured him. He awaited the end of the lecture which Dr. Stevenson from Glasgow was giving on the *Education of young idiots,* and requested the floor to make an announcement to the gathering.

Lord Glandover granted it to him immediately, by preference over Dr. Ovidius. He would have granted it to him even if all the intellectuals of Europe had protested as one against this favor! And here are the eloquent words that he addressed to the president and the members:

"Gentlemen," said Dr. Sarrasin, "I was planning to wait a few more days before informing you of the unusual good fortune that has befallen me, and the happy consequences that this event could have for science. But, the fact having now become public, it would be unseemly for me to not place it immediately in its proper light. Yes, gentlemen, it is true that a considerable sum of several hundred million, at present deposited in the Bank of England, seems to have become my legal property. Do I need to tell you that I do not consider myself, in these circumstances, other than a trustee of science? (*Profound reaction.*) It is not to me that this capital lawfully belongs, it is to Humanity, it is to Progress! (*Various movements. Exclamations. Unanimous applause. The whole association rises, electrified by that declaration.*) Please, don't applaud, gentlemen. I do not know a single man of science, truly worthy of the name, who would not have done in my place what I hope to do. There may be some who think that, as in many human actions, I do this more out of self-pride than devotion to the cause. (*No! No!*) It matters little! Let's just consider the results. I make this declaration, then, definitively and without reserve: the half-billion that chance has placed at my disposal, does not belong to me, but to Science! Do you wish to be the governing body who oversees its expenditure? I do not have sufficient confidence in my own wisdom to claim that I should dispose of it as an absolute master. You are my judges, and you are the ones who will decide on how we can best use this treasure!" (*Hurrahs. Great excitement. General delirium.*)

The association rises to its feet.[3] A few members, in their exultation, stand on tables. Professor Turnbull, from Glasgow, seems on the verge of apoplexy. Dr. Cicogna, from Naples, has lost his breath. Lord Glandover alone keeps the worthy and serene calm which is appropriate for his rank. He is perfectly convinced, moreover, that Dr. Sarrasin is joking, and has not the slightest intention of carrying out such an extravagant project.

"If I may, however," continued the speaker, when he had obtained a bit of silence, "if I may suggest a plan that would be easy to develop and to perfect, I propose the following."

Here, the assembly, having recovered its composure, listens with rapt attention.

"Gentlemen, among the many causes of sickness, suffering, and death which surround us, there is one in particular to which I believe it quite reasonable to attach a major importance: it is the deplorable hygienic conditions in which most humans are placed. They mass together in cities, in buildings often deprived of air and light, those two indispensable agents of life. Such human agglomerations become veritable centers of infection. Those who do not meet death here find that their health is seriously affected; their productive strength diminishes, and society thus loses great sources of labor which could be applied to the most useful ends. Why, gentlemen, shouldn't we try to remedy this situation with the most powerful means of persuasion . . . by example? Why shouldn't we gather together all the power of our imagination to design the plan of a model city along rigorously scientific principles? . . . (*Yes! yes! that's true!*) Why shouldn't we then devote the capital that we have to building that city and presenting it to the world as a practical illustration of what all cities ought to be?" (*Yes! yes!—thunderous applause.*)

The members of the association, in an ecstasy of contagious enthusiasm, shake each other's hands, crowd around Dr. Sarrasin, raise him up, carry him in triumph about the room.

"Gentlemen," continued the doctor when he had succeeded in returning to his place, "we will invite all the people of the world to this city which each of us can already visualize in our imagination, which may be a reality in a few months, this city of health and well-being; we will share its layout and the details of its design in all languages; we will invite to live there all honest families whom poverty and lack of employment might have driven from overpopulated lands. Also those—you will not be surprised at my thinking of them during these times—who have been forced into cruel exile due to foreign conquest will find a good use for their skills with us and an application for their intelligence, while bringing us a moral richness that would be a thousandfold more precious than gold and diamond mines. We will have large schools for our youth, who will be raised according to wise principles capable of developing all their faculties, moral, physical, and intellectual, thus preparing healthy generations for the future!"

It is impossible to describe the enthusiastic tumult which followed this talk. The applause, the hurrays, the "hip! hips!" continued for more than a quarter of an hour.

Dr. Sarrasin had barely managed to sit back down when Lord Glandover leaned over him again and murmured into his ear, with a wink.

"Sounds like a fine investment! You're no doubt counting on the revenue from the rents and town taxes, right? It's a sure thing provided it is well launched and sponsored by some well-known names! Why, all the convalescents and invalids will wish to live there at once! I hope you'll hold a nice lot in reserve for me, won't you?"

The poor doctor, annoyed by this stubborn insistence on giving a covetous motive to all his actions, was going to reply to His Lordship when he heard the vice president call for a vote of thanks by acclamation for the author of this philanthropic proposal which had just been submitted to the assembly.

"It would be," he said, "the eternal honor of the Brighton Conference that such a sublime idea had been born here—an idea that required no less to conceive it than the highest intelligence joined to the greatest heart and to an unprecedented generosity. And yet, now that the idea has been suggested, it seems astounding that it has never before been put into practice! How many billions have been spent on insane wars,[4] how much capital dissipated in ridiculous speculations that could have been consecrated to such an attempt!"

In conclusion, the speaker proposed that, in just homage to its founder, the city should be named "Sarrasina."

His motion was approved by acclamation, but a second vote was necessary at the request of Dr. Sarrasin himself.

"No," he said, "my name has no relevance here. Let us be careful not to deck out the future city with any of these appellations which, under pretext of deriving from Greek or Latin, bestow a pedantic effect to the thing or person who bears it. It shall be the City of Well-Being,[5] but I ask that its name be that of my country, and that we call it France-Ville!"

They could not refuse the doctor the satisfaction that he was due.

France-Ville was henceforth founded, at least in words; and soon—thanks to the minutes of the meeting which were to close the sessions—it would exist on paper as well. They passed immediately to a discussion of the project's general articles.

But we will now leave the association with this practical business, so different from the usual concerns reserved for these meetings, in order to follow, step by step, the fate of the aforementioned article published in the *Daily Telegraph* along one of its innumerable itineraries.

From the evening of the 29th of October, this notice, textually reproduced by the English journals, began to circulate through all the districts of the United Kingdom. It appeared especially in the *Hull Gazette,* at the top of page two in a copy of that modest journal that the *Queen Mary,* a three-masted ship loaded with coal, brought on November 1st to Rotterdam.

Immediately clipped out by the diligent scissors of the editor-in-chief and sole secretary of the *Netherlands' Echo* and translated into the language of Cuyp and Potter, the article arrived on November 2nd on the wings of steam to the *Bremen Chronicle.* There, with no change in content, it was given new garb, and it was not long before it was published in German. One must wonder why the Teutonic journalist, after having written at the top of the translation: *Eine übergrosse Erbschaft* (*A Colossal Inheritance*), had no qualms about resorting to a shabby subterfuge which took advantage of the credulity of his readers by adding in parentheses: "From our Special Correspondent in Brighton"?

Whatever the case, becoming thus Germanized by right of annexation, the anecdote reached the editor's desk of the imposing *North Gazette,* who gave it a place in the second column of page three but suppressed the title, which seemed too charlatan-like for such a serious person.

On the evening of November 3rd, after having passed through these successive transformations, it finally entered into the thick hands of a hefty Saxon manservant in the office–living room–dining room of Professor Schultze of the University of Iéna.[6]

As highly ranked as was such a fellow in the hierarchy of beings, he did not seem like very much at first glance. He was a fairly tall man of forty-five or forty-six years; his squared shoulders indicated a robust constitution; his forehead was bare, and the little hair he had kept on the back of his head and temples resembled light flax. His eyes were blue, that vague blue that never betrays one's thoughts. No gleam escaped from them, and yet they made you feel uncomfortable as soon as they fastened upon you. Professor Schultze's mouth was big, equipped with a double row of formidable teeth which never lose their prey, enclosed between thin lips whose principal purpose seemed to be counting the words that passed through them. His appearance was obviously disturbing and off-putting for others, a state of affairs which visibly satisfied the professor.

At the noise that his servant made, he raised his eyes to the fireplace, looked for the time of day on a lovely Barbedienne clock, singularly out of place in the midst of the common furnishings that surrounded it, and he said in a voice that was more stiff than stuffy:

"6:55! My mail arrives at 6:30, at the latest. Today you're twenty-five minutes late bringing it up. The next time that it is not on my table at 6:30, you will leave my service at 8:00."

"Does Monsieur wish to dine now?" asked the servant before withdrawing.

"It's 6:55, and I dine at 7:00. You've known that for the three weeks that you have been in my employment. Keep in mind that I do not change my schedule, and never repeat an order."[7]

The professor set his newspaper on the edge of the table and continued working on an article that was to appear two days later in the periodical *Annalen für Physiologie* (*Annals for Physiology*). There would be no indiscretion in revealing that this article had for its title:

Why Are All Frenchmen Stricken in Different Degrees
with Hereditary Degeneration?[8]

While the professor pursued his task, the dinner composed of a large plate of sausages and sauerkraut, flanked by a gigantic stein of beer, had been discreetly served on a round table by the corner of the fireplace. The professor set down his pen to eat his supper, which he savored more than one might expect of a man so serious.[9] Then he rang for his coffee, lit a great porcelain pipe, and returned to his work.

It was near midnight when the professor signed the last sheet, and immediately passed into his bedroom to take a well-deserved rest. It was not until he was in bed that he finally opened his newspaper and began to read it before going to sleep. At that very moment when sleep seemed near, the attention of the professor was attracted by a foreign name, that of Langévol, in the article relating to a colossal inheritance. He sought to recall what memory this name might evoke in him, but he failed. After a few minutes given over to this vain research, he tossed the newspaper aside, blew out his candle, and was soon producing a sonorous snoring.

By some physiological phenomenon that he himself had studied

"Today you're twenty-five minutes late bringing it up!"

and explained with great results, however, this name of Langévol pursued Professor Schultze well into his dreams. So much so that, waking up the next morning, he was surprised to find himself mechanically repeating it.

Then, just as he was about to consult his watch for the time, a flash of light suddenly crossed his mind. Grabbing the newspaper at the foot of his bed and brushing his hand over his forehead as if to concentrate his ideas, he read and reread several times the passage that he had almost let go by unnoticed. The light in his head was obviously growing, for without taking the time to pull on his flowered bathrobe, he ran to the fireplace, detached a little portrait in miniature that was hanging beside the mirror, and turning it over, rubbed his sleeve over the dusty cardboard that covered the back. The professor was not mistaken. On the back of the portrait could be read this name, traced with a yellowish ink, now almost erased by a half a century:

"*Thérèse Schultze eingeborene Langévol* [*Teresa Schultze, maiden name Langévol*]"

That very evening the professor caught the express train to London.

4 *Divided in Two*

On the 6th of November, at 7 o'clock in the morning, Herr Schultze arrived at the Charing Cross station.[1] At noon he presented himself at 93 Southampton Row, in a large room divided by a wooden barrier—the clerks on one side, the public on the other—furnished with six chairs, a black table, innumerable green boxes and a dictionary of addresses. On the clerks' side, two young people, seated before a table, were eating their traditional lunch of bread and cheese, which was customary among those in the legal profession.

"Messrs. Billows, Green, and Sharp?" said the professor with the same voice he used for ordering his dinner.

"Mr. Sharp is in his office. What's your name? Your business?"

"Professor Schultze, from Iéna. The Langévol affair!"

The young clerk murmured this information into the opening of an acoustic tube, and received a response in the opening of his own ear, a communication that he did not think best to make public. It ran roughly like this:

"The devil with that Langévol affair. One more fool who thinks he has a claim!"

The young clerk replied:

"He's a man that looks 'respectable.' He does not look friendly, but he's not like the first claimant."

A new mysterious exclamation:

"Does he come from Germany?"

"He claims so, at least."

A sigh passed through the tube:

"Send him up."

"Third floor, the door across the hall," said the clerk out loud, pointing to an inside hallway.

The professor strode into the hall, mounted the two flights and found himself facing a padded door, where the name Mr. Sharp stood out in black letters against a copper background.

This individual was seated in front of a large mahogany desk in a quite common room with a felt rug, leather chairs, and large, gaping filing cabinets. He scarcely rose from his chair, and, according to the courteous ways of office folk, he went back and flipped through his files for five minutes, just to give himself a busy look. Finally, turning toward Professor Schultze, who had walked over to him, he said:

"Sir, just tell me briefly what brings you here. My time is extraordinarily limited, and I can only give you a few minutes."

The professor had the semblance of a smile, letting him know that he cared very little about how he had been received.

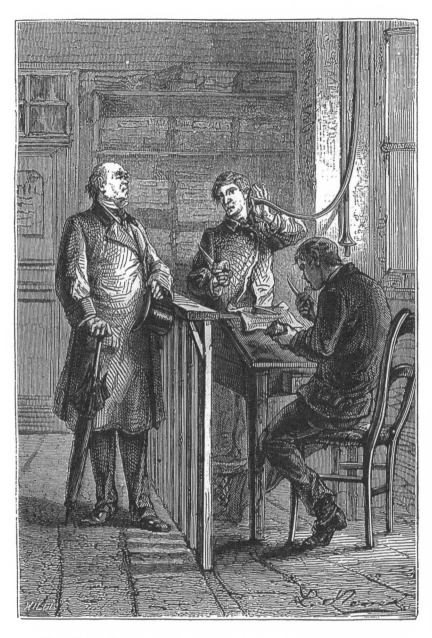

"Send him up."

"Perhaps you'll find it within you to grant me a few minutes extra," he said, "when you find out what brings me here."

"Then tell me, sir."

"It's a question of the succession of Jean-Jacques Langévol, from Bar-le-Duc, and I am the grandson of his elder sister, Thérèse Langévol, married in 1792 to my grandfather, a surgeon on the Brunswick army who died in 1814. I have in my possession three letters from my great-uncle, written to his sister, and numerous accounts of his returning home, after the battle of Iéna, without counting the items, duly legalized, which establish my kinship."

It is unnecessary to follow Professor Schultze in all the details he gave Mr. Sharp. He was, contrary to his nature, almost prolix. It is true, that was the only point where he was inexhaustible. Indeed, his aim was to show Mr. Sharp, an Englishman, the necessity of how the German race predominated over all others. His pursuit of the idea to reclaim his succession was especially to snatch it from French hands, since they could probably only put it to some inept use! What he detested in his adversary was especially his nationality! Had he been a German, he would not insist by any means, etc., etc. But that a self-proclaimed scientist, a Frenchman, should use that enormous capital for the benefit of French ideas . . . ! The very notion set him beside himself, and made him feel it a duty to stand up for his rights at all costs.

At first sight, the connection of ideas might not be obvious between this political digression and the opulent inheritance. But Mr. Sharp was a sufficiently keen businessman and could perceive the relationship that existed between the national aspirations of the Germanic race in general and the particular aspirations of Schultze as an individual toward the inheritance from the Begum.[2] They were, really, of the same order.

Besides, there was no possible doubt. As humiliating as it might be for a professor at the University of Iéna to have family relationships with people of an inferior race, it was clear that a French grandmother shared responsibility for bringing into the world this human product who had no equal. But this relationship, on a secondary level compared to that of Dr. Sarrasin, also gave him secondary rights to the aforementioned inheritance.

The solicitor saw, however, the possibility of supporting them with some appearances of legality, and that being possible, he foresaw another great advantage for Billows, Green, and Sharp: that of transforming the already lucrative Langévol affair into a magnificent business affair, on the order of Dickens's "Jarndyce versus Jarndyce."[3] A mass of stamped papers, deeds, documents of all sorts arose before the eyes of the lawyer. Or else, better yet, he imagined a compromise worked out by him, Sharp, in the interest of both clients and which would bring him, Sharp, almost as much honor as profit.

However, he made known to Herr Schultze the claims of Dr. Sarrasin, gave him the proofs to support them, and insinuated that if Billows, Green, and Sharp took it upon themselves to make an advantageous deal for the professor, with an appearance of legality —"appearance only, dear sir, and which I fear would not stand up in court"—which his relationship with the doctor conferred upon him, he hoped that the remarkable sense of justice, which all Germans possessed, would allow Billows, Green, and Sharp to also acquire, in that circumstance, rights of a different sort, but distinctly more commanding in recognition of the professor.

The latter was all too talented not to understand the logic of the businessman's reasoning. On this point he put the latter's mind at ease, without spelling out anything in detail however. Mr. Sharp politely asked for permission to examine this affair at his leisure and showed him out with much respectfulness. Now there was no longer any question of the strictly limited minutes which he had claimed to be so short of!

Herr Schultze withdrew. Although convinced that he had not a sufficient title to validate his claim on the inheritance of the Begum, he nevertheless believed that a struggle between the Saxon and the Latin races, beyond the fact that it was always meritorious, could only turn out to the advantage of the Saxon race if he fully knew how to go about it.

The important thing was to feel out Dr. Sarrasin's opinion. A telegram, sent immediately to Brighton, brought the French intellectual to the lawyer's office about 5:00 P.M.

Dr. Sarrasin learned about all that had occurred with a calmness that astonished Mr. Sharp. At Mr. Sharp's first words, the doctor declared that, in all honesty, he recalled having heard through family traditions of a great-aunt raised by a rich and titled woman, who emigrated along with her, and who presumably married in Germany. He did not know, however, either the name or the precise degree of relationship of this great-aunt.

Mr. Sharp had already referred to his documents, carefully catalogued in filing boxes that he willingly pointed out to the doctor. There was in all that—Mr. Sharp did not hide the fact—sufficient material for a trial, and trials of this sort could easily drag out for years. In truth, one was not obliged to make this admission to the opposing party about such a family tradition that Dr. Sarrasin had just made in all sincerity to his solicitor. But there were those letters from Jean-Jacques Langévol to his sister, which Herr Schultze had mentioned, and which constituted a presumption in his favor. Other proofs could no doubt be exhumed from the dust of municipal archives. Perhaps even the adverse party, lacking authentic documents, might well create some imaginary ones. One had to foresee everything! Who knows if new investigations might not even assign to this Thérèse Langévol, suddenly erupting out of the past, and to her present-day representatives, rights superior to those of Dr. Sarrasin? In any case, there could be long disputes, longer verifications, and an even more distant solution! The probabilities of gain were considerable on both sides, either could easily form a limited liability company to advance the expense of the procedure and exhaust all pleas of jurisdiction. One famous trial of this kind had been in the Chancellory Court for eighty-three consecutive years and had only ended for lack of funds: interest and capital, everything was gone! Inquests, commissions, transfer of funds, procedures would take an endless amount of time! In ten years the question could still be unresolved, and the half-billion still sleeping in the bank . . .

Dr. Sarrasin listened to all this verbiage and wondered when it would stop. Without accepting as gospel truth everything that was being said, a sort of weariness crept into his soul. Like some traveler who, leaning over the bow of a ship, sees the port that he thought he was about to enter slowly recede, become indistinct and finally disappear, he said to himself that it was impossible that this fortune, previously so close and with its purpose so established, might simply be evaporating away!

"Well, what should I do?" he asked the solicitor.

What to do? . . . Ahem! . . . Hard to say. Harder still to accomplish. But, anyway, everything could be arranged. He, Sharp, was convinced of it. English justice was a fine justice—a bit slow, perhaps, he agreed—yes, certainly a bit slow, *pede claudo* (it may be slow, but punishment always follows the crime) . . . ahem! . . . ahem! . . . but surer for all that! . . . assuredly Dr. Sarrasin could not fail to actually possess this inheritance in a few years, if of course . . . ahem! . . . ahem! . . . his titles were sufficiently strong . . . !

The doctor left the office at Southampton Row deeply shaken in his confidence and convinced that he was going either to have to undertake a series of interminable court trials or to give up his dream. So, as he thought about his beautiful philanthropic project, he could not help feeling a tinge of regret.

Mr. Sharp, however, sent for Professor Schultze, who had left him his address. He told him that Dr. Sarrasin had never heard of Thérèse Langévol, formally contested the existence of a German branch of the family, and refused all transaction. So the only thing the professor could do, if he believed his rights firmly established, was to "go to court." Mr. Sharp, who brought to this affair an absolute disinterest, only an amateur curiosity, certainly did not have the intention of dissuading him from it. What more could a solicitor ask for but a trial, ten trials, thirty years of trials, since the cause seemed to warrant it? Sharp, himself, was personally delighted with it. If he had not feared that Professor Schultze would think it a suspicious offer on his part, he would have pushed his disinterest so far as to suggest one of his colleagues, whom he could put in charge of his interests. And certainly such a choice was of great importance! The legal path had become a great highway! And unfortunately there were many adventurers and brigands along it! Although he was ashamed to do so, he had to state this sad truth . . . !

"If the French doctor was willing to arrange a deal, how much would it cost?" asked the professor.

As a wise man, words could not daze him! As a practical man, he was going straight to the mark without wasting any precious time on the way! Mr. Sharp was a bit disconcerted by this sort of action. He reminded Herr Schultze that things did not go quite that speedily; that one could not foresee the end when one was at the beginning; that to bring Mr. Sarrasin to terms, one had to drag things out a bit in order not to let him know that he, Schultze, was ready for a compromise.

"I beg you, sir," he concluded, "just let me go ahead, trust me, I'll take all responsibility."

"And so will I," replied Schultze, "but I'd like to know what to expect."

However, he could not, this time, ascertain from Mr. Sharp how much the solicitor valued Saxon gratitude, and he was obliged to give him *carte blanche* on the matter.

When Dr. Sarrasin, called back the next day by Mr. Sharp, asked him calmly if he had any serious news to give him, the solicitor, anxious about that very tranquility, informed him that a serious examination had convinced him that it would perhaps be best to go right to the heart of the matter and propose a settlement for this new claimant. Dr. Sarrasin would agree that that was an essentially disinterested piece of advice and which very few solicitors would have made in Mr. Sharp's place! But he personally felt quite a paternal interest in the affair, and, for no other reason than to satisfy his own self-esteem, he was intent on settling it rapidly.

Dr. Sarrasin listened to his advice and found it rather wise. In the last few days he had become so accustomed to the idea of realizing his scientific dream that he subordinated all to his project. To wait ten years or even one, before being able to carry it out, would now have been a cruel disappointment. Little accustomed moreover to legal and financial questions, and without being duped by the fine words of Master Sharp, he preferred to set aside his rights for a good sum in cash which would allow him to pass from theory to practice. He also gave Mr. Sharp *carte blanche* to work it out as best he could, and left.

The solicitor had obtained what he wanted. It was quite true that another in his place might have yielded to the temptation of instituting and prolonging the proceedings which might have become, over time, a large life annuity. But Mr. Sharp was not one to make long-term speculations. He could see within his reach an easy way to reap an abundant harvest, and he resolved to take it. The next day he wrote to the doctor letting him know that Herr Schultze might not be opposed to a possible compromise. In further visits, arranged by him, either with Dr. Sarrasin or Herr Schultze, he would say to one and then the other that the opposite party would hear none of it, and that in addition it was a question of some third party who had been attracted by the scent of so much money . . .

This game lasted a week. Everything was fine in the morning, and in the evening there suddenly rose an unforeseen objection which turned everything awry. There was nothing but schemes, hesitations, change. Mr. Sharp could not make up his mind to pull on the hook, he was so afraid that at the last moment the fish might struggle and break the line. But so much precaution was, in this instance, superfluous. From the first day as he had said, Dr. Sarrasin, who wanted above all to spare himself the trouble of a trial, had been ready for a settlement. When Mr. Sharp finally believed that the psychological moment, according to that well-known expression, had arrived, or that, in a somewhat less noble tongue, his client was "cooked to a T," he suddenly delayed no longer and proposed an immediate deal.

A kindly man appeared, the banker Stilbing, who offered to split the difference between the parties, to count out two hundred fifty million francs each and to claim as commission the remainder of the half-billion, or twenty-seven million francs.

Dr. Sarrasin would willingly have kissed Mr. Sharp, when he came to submit that offer, which, all in all, seemed superb to him. He was ready to sign, he was just asking to sign, he would also have approved gold statues for the banker Stilbing, for the solicitor Sharp, for all the high-ranking bankers and all the pettifoggers of the United Kingdom.

The contracts were drawn up, the witnesses solicited, and the stamping machines in Somerset House were ready to stamp. Herr Schultze had given in. Bristling but backed up against the wall by the aforesaid Sharp, the latter had made him understand that, with any adversary of lesser quality than Dr. Sarrasin, he probably would have gotten nothing for his trouble. It was quickly done. Against their formal writ and their acceptance of equal shares, the two heirs each received a check in the amount of a hundred thousand pounds sterling, payable on sight, with promises of definitive payment after the legal formalities.

Thus was settled this astounding affair, for the greater glory of Anglo-Saxon superiority.

We are told that, that very evening, while dining at the Cobden Club with his friend Stilbing, Mr. Sharp drank a glass of champagne to the health of Dr. Sarrasin, another to the health of Professor Schultze, and then, as he finished the bottle, permitted himself the following rather indiscreet exclamation:

"Hurrah! Rule Britannia! . . . There's no one like us! . . ."

The truth is that the banker Stilbing considered his host to be a pathetic man who, for a mere twenty-seven million, had let go of a deal that was potentially worth fifty million. In fact, the professor thought likewise from the moment when he, Herr Schultze, felt himself obliged to accept any arrangement at all! After all, what could not have been done with a man such as Dr. Sarrasin, a Celt, careless, flighty, and most certainly a visionary![4]

"Hurrah! Rule Britannia!"

The professor had heard about his rival's project of creating a French city founded on conditions of moral and physical hygiene that could successfully develop all the qualities of that race and to educate young generations that were strong and valiant. This enterprise seemed absurd to him and, to his way of thinking, was destined to fail since it stood in opposition to the law of progress which decreed the collapse of the Latin race, its subservience to the Saxon race, and, as a consequence, its total disappearance from the surface of the globe. This eventuality, however, might be delayed if the doctor started to carry out his project, or even more so if people began to believe in its success. It was every Saxon's responsibility, in the interest of general order and obeying an ineluctable law, to annihilate if he could such a foolish enterprise. And in the present circumstances, it was clear to him, Schultze, M.D., *Privatdocent* of chemistry at the University of Iéna, known for his numerous comparative works about the different human races—works where it was proved that the Germanic race would absorb all the others—it was clear indeed that he was especially designated by the constantly creative and destructive force of Nature to wipe out the pygmies rebelling against it. For all eternity it had been ordained that Thérèse Langévol would marry Martin Schultze, that one day the two nationalities, represented by the person of the French doctor and the German professor, would clash, and that the latter would crush the former. He had already half of the doctor's fortune in his hands. That was the instrument he needed.

Moreover, this project was for Herr Schultze quite secondary; it was to be added to the much larger ones he had had in mind for the destruction of all nations refusing to blend themselves with the German people and reunite with the Fatherland. However, wishing to get to the very bottom—if such things had a bottom—of his implacable enemy Dr. Sarrasin's plans, he became a member of the International Association of Hygiene and attended its meetings assiduously. While leaving one such meeting, several members, including Dr. Sarrasin himself, heard him declare that he himself would build, at the same time as France-Ville, a fortified city that would seek to eliminate such an absurd and abnormal anthill.[5]

"I hope," he added, "that the experiment we will conduct will serve as an example to the rest of the world!"

Good Dr. Sarrasin, as full of love for mankind as he was, realized that not all of his equals deserved to be called philanthropists. He carefully noted his rival's words, thinking, as any sensible man should, that no outside threat should be disregarded. A short time later, when he wrote to Marcel to invite him to help in this project, he told him about the incident and drew a portrait of Herr Schultze, which led the young Alsatian to believe the good doctor would have a tough adversary. And when the doctor added:

"We'll need strong and energetic men, active scientists, not only to erect, but to defend our structure," Marcel responded:

"If I cannot immediately bring you any support in founding your city, you may count on me anytime that I can be helpful. I will not lose sight of Herr Schultze, whom you describe so vividly. Being an Alsatian gives me the right to deal with his business. Whether near or far away, I shall always be at your service. If, for some reason, several months or even several years go by without your having any news from me, don't be concerned. Whether near or far away, I will have but one thought: working for you and, as a consequence, serving France."[6]

5 *The City of Steel*

The place and time have now changed.[1] For five years the Begum's inheritance has been in the hands of her two heirs. The scene has now shifted to the United States, in southern Oregon, ten leagues from the Pacific shore.[2] This region, which is still unmapped for the most part, forms a kind of American Switzerland.[3] Its northern border divides these two neighboring powers but remains poorly defined.

Switzerland, indeed, if one only considers its topography: the abrupt peaks that tower to the sky, the deep valleys which separate winding chains of mountains, and the grandiose and wild aspect of the entire territory as seen from a bird's-eye view.

But this false Switzerland is not, like the European Switzerland, given over to the peaceful work of the shepherd, the guide, or the hotel-keeper. It is only an alpine decor, a crust of rocks, earth, and ancient pines, sitting on a base of iron and oil.

If a tourist should stop in this wilderness and lend an ear to nature's sounds, he would not hear, as in the paths of Oberland, the harmonious murmur of life mixed with the grand silence of the mountains. Rather, he would perceive in the distance the dull blows of the pile driver, and under his feet the muffled detonations of gunpowder. It would seem to him that the ground had been mechanically hollowed out like the floor of a theater stage, that its gigantic rocks were empty and could sink into the mysterious depths at any moment.

Black macadamized roads, surfaced with cinders and coke, wind along the mountains' flanks. Under clumps of yellowish vegetation, one can see little piles of slag, dappled with all the colors of the prism, gleaming like the eyes of a basilisk. Here and there, an abandoned mine shaft, worn by the rains, overrun by briars, opens its gaping mouth, a bottomless abyss, like some crater of an extinct volcano.[4] The air is heavy with smoke; it hangs like a somber cloak upon the earth. No birds fly through this area; even the insects appear to avoid it; and, within the memory of man, not a single butterfly has ever been seen.

A false Switzerland! On its northernmost side, where the mountains melt into the plain, between two ranges of bleak hills, lies what was called until 1871 the "red desert," because of the color of the soil, which is impregnated with iron oxides. It is now called Stahlfeldt, "the field of steel."

Just imagine a plateau five to six leagues square, with a sandy soil scattered with stones. It was arid and desolate like the bed of some ancient inland sea. Nature had done nothing to enliven this land, nor to give it any life or movement; it was man who had done so, suddenly transforming it with unequaled energy and vigor.

Within five years on the bare and rocky plain, eighteen villages sprang up with little houses of uniform gray lumber, brought ready-made from Chicago to enclose a large population of rugged workmen.

In the center of these villages, at the very foot of those inexhaustible mountains of coal called Coal Buttes, a somber, monstrous, bizarre mass of look-alike buildings emerged, pierced with symmetrical windows, covered with red roofs, surmounted by a veritable forest of cylindrical chimneys vomiting into the air endless torrents of sooty vapors through their thousand mouths. The sky is veiled with a black curtain, through which flash intermittently rapid red flames. The wind brings the sound of a distant rumbling like thunder or the pounding swell of the sea, only more regular and solemn.

This mass of buildings is called Stahlstadt, the City of Steel, the German city, the personal property of Herr Schultze, the former professor of chemistry in Iéna. Thanks to the millions of the Begum, it has become the greatest steel-working plant, or more specifically, the greatest foundry of cannons in the world.

He indeed casts them in every shape and every caliber, smooth bore and rifled, movable breechblock and fixed, for Russia, for Turkey, for Rumania and for Japan, for Italy and China, but especially for Germany.

Thanks to the power of an enormous capital, this immense establishment, this veritable city which is at the same time a model factory, has arisen from the earth as though from a stroke of a wand. Thirty thousand workers, for the most part of German origin, have come to gather around it and form its outskirts. In only a few months, the overwhelming superiority of its products has earned them worldwide fame.

Professor Schultze extracts iron ore and coal from his own mines. On site he converts these into molten steel, and then he transforms the steel into cannons. What none of his rivals can produce, he succeeds in producing. In France they obtain ingots of steel weighing forty thousand kilos. In England they manufactured a cannon out of wrought iron weighing a hundred tons. In Essen Mr. Krupp managed to cast blocks of steel of five hundred thousand kilos.[5] But Herr Schultze knows no limits: ask him for a cannon of any weight or power, and he will deliver it, shiny as a new nickel and right on time.

He will, however, charge you dearly for it! It seems that the two hundred fifty million francs of 1871 only whetted his appetite!

In the cannon industry, as in everything, strength lies where one can do something that others cannot. And it must be acknowledged that not only do the cannons of Herr Schultze reach dimensions without precedent, but they also never blow up. The Stahlstadt steel seems to have very special properties. There have been many rumors about the use of mysterious alloys or secret chemicals. But what is certain is that no one knows what the answer is.

And what is also certain is that, in Stahlstadt, this secret is guarded with zealous care.

In this remote corner of North America, surrounded by wilderness, isolated from the world by a rampart of mountains, five hundred miles from the smallest neighboring town, one could search in vain for the smallest vestige of that liberty which formed the strength of the republic of the United States.

When you arrive by the very walls of Stahlstadt, do not attempt to break through the massive gates which cut through the lines of trenches and fortifications. The most merciless of guards would deter you, and you would be required to return to the outskirts. You cannot enter the City of Steel unless you possess the magic formula, the password, or at least an authorization duly stamped, signed and initialed.

No doubt, the young worker arriving at Stahlstadt one November morning had such an authorization; after leaving his small, quite worn leather valise at the inn, he walked toward the nearest gate of the village.

He was a tall fellow, strongly built, who was casually dressed

Stahlstadt, the City of Steel

like early American pioneers in a loose-fitting jacket, a wool collarless shirt, a pair of corduroy pants stuffed into great boots. He wore a broad felt hat pulled down to his face as though to better hide the layer of coal dust which impregnated his skin. He walked with a springing step, as he whistled through his brown beard.

Arriving at the gate, the young man showed the guard a printed authorization and was immediately admitted.

"Your order bears the address of foreman Seligmann, section K, Ninth Street, workshop 743," said the noncom. "You just have to follow this road on your right, to the marker K, and go to the doorkeeper. You know the rule? Expelled, if you enter a sector other than your own," he added just as the newcomer was heading away.

The young worker followed the directions he had been told and walked down the road. On his right was a trench, on the bank of which some guards were walking. To his left, between the wide circular route and the jumble of buildings, the double rails of a circling train stood out first. Then a second wall rose up, paralleling the exterior wall, which indicated the overall configuration of the Steel City.

It was in the shape of a circle[6] whose sectors, divided into departments by a line of fortifications, were quite independent of each other, though wrapped by a common wall and trench.

The young worker was soon at the K marker placed on the edge of the road across from a monumental doorway which was capped by the same letter, sculpted into the stone, and he presented himself to the doorkeeper.

This time, instead of dealing with a soldier, he found himself in the presence of an invalid with a wooden leg and a chest covered with medals.

The invalid examined the sheet, affixed a new stamp and said: "Straight ahead. Ninth street on the left."

The young man crossed this second entrenched line and found himself in sector K. The road leading from the doorway was the

The young man showed the guard a printed authorization.

axis. Rows of uniform constructions stretched out at right angles from each side.

The uproar of the machines was deafening. Pierced by thousands of windows, these gray buildings seemed more living than inert things. But the newcomer was no doubt used to the spectacle, for he paid not the slightest attention to it. In five minutes he had found Ninth street, workshop 743, reached a small office full of boxes and account books, and stood in the presence of foreman Seligmann.

The latter took the sheet covered with all its visas, examined it, and, casting his eyes on the young worker, asked:

"Hired on as a puddler, are you? You look quite young."

"Age makes no difference," replied the other. "I will soon be twenty-six, and I have already puddled for seven months. If you're interested I can show you the certificates which got me hired in New York by the head of personnel."

The young man spoke German fluently, but with a slight accent which seemed to arouse the suspicion of the foreman.

"Are you Alsatian?" he asked.

"No, I'm Swiss . . . from Schaffhausen. Here, my papers are all in order."

He drew out a leather purse and showed the foreman a passport, a scholastic record, and various certificates.

"That's fine. After all, you've already been hired; I only have to tell you what your position is," continued Seligmann, reassured by this display of official documents.

He wrote the name Johann Schwartz on a registry, which he copied onto the hired list, handed the young man a blue card with his name affixed and bearing the number 57,938, before adding:

"You must go to door K every morning at seven o'clock. Show this card which will have allowed you to pass through the outer wall. Take a token from the concierge's rack with your entry number and let me see it when you get here. When leaving the enclosure at seven in the evening, you will drop the token into a collection-box placed at the workshop door, and which will be open only at that moment."

"I know that system. Can I find lodging in the enclosure?" asked Schwartz.

"No. You must obtain lodging on the outside, but for a very modest price you will be able to have your meals in the canteen of the workshop. Your pay is a dollar a day at first. It grows 5 percent every four months. Expulsion is the only penalty for any infraction of the rules, decided by me on the first instance and by the engineer on appeal. Are you starting today?"

"Why not?"

"It will be only a half a day," observed the foreman, guiding Schwartz toward an interior corridor.

Both followed a wide hallway, crossed a courtyard, and entered a great area similar, in its dimensions and general layout, to the arrival platform of a first-class railroad station. Assessing it with a glance, Schwartz could not refrain from a gesture of professional admiration.

On each side of this great enclosure, two enormous rows of cylindrical columns, as broad in both diameter and height as those of Saint Peter's in Rome, rose from the ground to the glass vault that they transpierced through and through. They were the chimneys of as many puddler furnaces with brick bases. There were fifty in each row.

At one end of it, trains were constantly arriving loaded with cast iron ingots to feed the furnaces. At the other end, trains with empty cars took on and carried away this iron transformed into steel.

The operation of "puddling" has as its goal to carry out this metamorphosis. Teams of half naked giants, armed with long iron hooks, were working with great activity. Thrown into an oven lined with a covering of slag, the big iron ingots were first heated to a very high temperature. To obtain wrought iron, the workers would begin to puddle this iron as soon as it became pasty. To obtain steel, this carbide of iron, which was so close yet so distinct in its properties from its fellow metal, they waited for the pig iron to become fluid and were careful to maintain the heat in the furnaces. The puddler then, with the end of his hook, molded and rolled this metallic mass; he turned it over and over in the middle of the flame, then at the precise moment when the pig iron reached a certain degree of resistance by its mixture with the slag, he divided it into four balls or spongy lumps, which he turned over, one after the other, to the assistant hammer smiths. It is in the very axis of this vast area that the operation was carried out. Facing each furnace stood a corresponding giant power-hammer, which was set in motion by the steam from a vertical boiler installed within the chimney itself, and which kept a "shingler" busy. Armed from head to foot with boots and steel sleeves, protected by a thick leather apron, masked in metallic cloth, this cuirassier of industry seized the lump of iron with the end of his long pincers and held it under the hammer. Struck again and again under the weight of that enormous mass, it exuded like a sponge all the impure matter with which it was loaded, amidst a shower of sparks and spatter.

The shingler returned it to the helpers to put it back in the furnace, and, once reheated, it was hammered again.

In the immensity of this monstrous forge, there was a constant motion, torrents of endless belts, dull blows against the roar of a continuous throbbing, continuous fireworks of red sparks, and the glare of kilns raised to a white heat. Amidst the booming and raging of this raw matter in metamorphosis, man seemed almost like a child.

And yet they were tough fellows, these puddlers! Kneading at arm's length a metal paste of two hundred kilos in the torrid heat while staring at this blinding, incandescent steel is dreadful work which wears a man out in ten years.

Schwartz, as though to show the foreman that he could endure it, removed his jacket and his wool shirt and, exhibiting an athletic torso on which his muscles were finely etched, he picked up the hook which one of the puddlers was manning and began to manipulate it.

Noting that he seemed able to do the job quite well, the foreman soon left him to return to his office.

The young worker continued puddling the blocks of pig iron

Puddling

The giant power-hammer

until dinner time. But, either because he brought excessive ardor to his work, or because he had failed to eat that morning a substantial meal required by such a display of physical strength, he soon appeared worn and failing. The crew chief quickly noticed.

"You're not made to be a puddler, my lad," the latter said, "and you'd do better to ask for another sector right away, since they might be unwilling to grant it to you later."

Schwartz protested. It was but a passing fatigue! He could puddle as well as another!

The crew chief made his report nonetheless, and the young man was immediately summoned by the head engineer.

This man examined his papers, cocked his head, and asked him in an inquisitorial tone:

"You were a puddler in Brooklyn?"

Schwartz lowered his eyes, quite confused.

"I see that I must confess," he said. "I was employed in the casting section, and it was with hopes of bettering my pay that I had tried puddling."

"You are all alike!" replied the engineer shrugging his shoulders. "At age twenty-five you want to learn what few men can do at thirty-five! Are you a good caster, at least?"

"I was in the top class for at least a couple of months."

"You'd have done better to stay there, in that case! Here, you'll be starting in third class. You can just feel lucky that I'm having you change sector!"

The engineer wrote a few words on an authorization form, sent off a message, and said:

"Turn in your badge, leave this division and go directly to sector O, office of the engineer-in-chief. He's expecting you."

The same formalities occurred at sector O as when Schwartz had arrived at the gate of sector K. There, as in the morning, he was interrogated, accepted, and sent to a shop-head, who took him to a casting room. But here the work was quieter and more methodical.

"This is just a small gallery for casting pieces of forty-two millimeters," the foreman told him. "Only first class workers are admitted to the casting rooms of the heavy cannons."

The "little" gallery was nonetheless some hundred and fifty meters long by sixty-five wide. It must, by Schwartz's estimation, heat up at least six hundred crucibles, placed in fours, eights, or twelves, according to their size, in the lateral kilns.

The molds destined to receive the molten steel were stretched lengthwise along the axis of the gallery, at the base of a median trench. On each side of the trench, railroad tracks carried a mobile crane which, moving at will, could operate where necessary to move these enormous weights. As in the puddling hall, at one end the train emerged bringing blocks of melted steel, at the other, a train transporting the cannons after their molding.

Near each mold, a man armed with an iron rod watched the temperatures at state of fusion in the crucibles.

The procedures which Schwartz had seen in operation elsewhere were carried to a singular degree of perfection here.

When the moment came to operate a casting, a warning bell signaled all those attending the fusion. Immediately, with equal and rigorously measured stride, workers of like height, bearing a horizontal iron bar on their shoulders, came two by two, to place themselves before each kiln.

With a chronometer calibrated to the fraction of a second in his hand, an official carrying a whistle walked up to the mold, conveniently located in proximity to all the kilns in operation. On each side, channels of refractory earth covered with metal converged as they descended gentle slopes to a funnel-shaped basin placed directly above the mold. The chief gave a whistle blast. Immediately, a crucible drawn out of the fire with the help of pincers was hung on the iron bar of the two workers stopped in front of the kiln. The whistle then began a series of modulations, and both carefully approached to empty the contents of their crucible into the corresponding channel. Then they threw the empty but red-hot receptacle into a basin.

A mobile crane

At precise intervals and without interruption, so that the casting was absolutely regular and constant, the teams from the other kilns followed suit in succession.

The precision was so extraordinary that to the tenth of a second set by the last movement, the last crucible was empty and toppled into the basin. This perfect maneuver seemed more the result of a blind mechanism than that of the concourse of a hundred human wills. An inflexible discipline, the force of habit, and the power of a musical measure produced this miracle, however.

Schwartz seemed familiar with such a spectacle. He was soon paired with a worker of his size, tried out in a less-important casting, and was immediately recognized as an excellent caster. At the end of the day, his crew chief promised him a rapid advancement.

He had no sooner left at 7:00 in the evening from sector O and the outside area, than he went to pick up his suitcase at the inn. He then took one of the exterior paths and soon arrived at a group of houses he had noticed that morning. He readily found a bachelor lodging in the house of a fine woman who "took in boarders."

But no one saw this young worker go looking for a tavern after supper. He locked himself in his room, pulled a fragment of steel out of his pocket, picked up no doubt in the puddling room, and a fragment of earth from the crucible picked up in sector O. Then he examined them with great care, in the light of a smoky lamp.

He then took from his suitcase a large, wood-bound notebook, searched through the pages filled with notes, formulas, and calculations, and wrote the following in good French, but, to be cautious, converting it into a coded language which he alone could decipher.[7]

"November 10. Stahlstadt. There is nothing particular in the method of puddling except, of course, the choice of two different relatively low temperatures for the first heating and the second reheating, following the rules determined by Chernoff. As for the casting, it is carried out using the Krupp process but with a systematized movement that is quite remarkable. This precision of movement is the real German strength. It comes from a musical

The finished cannons

talent inborn in the Germanic race. Never could the English attain this perfection: they don't have the ear for it, or the discipline. The French can easily work it out, since they are the top dancers in the world. Up to now, there's nothing mysterious about such remarkable successes in this fabrication process. The mineral samples that I collected in the mountain are analogous to our good irons. The samples of coal are certainly quite handsome and of an eminently metallurgical quality, but there is nothing unusual about them. There is no doubt that the Schultze process takes special care to purge these raw materials of any foreign matter and only uses them in a state of perfect purity. But that also is a result which it is relatively easy to achieve. All that remains to do, then, in order to have all the elements of the problem, is to determine the composition of that fireproof earth from which the crucibles and the casting pipes are made. Once this is known and our casting crews are sufficiently trained, I see no reason why we could not make what is made here! Just the same, I have only seen two sectors, and there are at least twenty-four, without counting the central building, the department of plans and models, the secret office! What might they be plotting in that den? What might our friends have to fear after the threats expressed by Herr Schultze when he took possession of his inheritance?"

After these questions, Schwartz, rather worn out by his day, undressed, slipped into a little bed as uncomfortable as a German bed can be—which is saying quite a lot—lit up his pipe, and began smoking while he read an old book. But his thoughts seemed elsewhere. On his lips, the little puffs of odorous smoke followed in cadence and made a:

"Puff! . . . puff! . . . puff! . . . puff! . . ."

He finished, put his book down, and remained thoughtful for a long time, as though absorbed in the solution of a difficult problem.

"Ah!" he finally cried out, "even if the devil himself should take a hand in it, I'll somehow discover Herr Schultze's secret, and especially what he is contemplating against France-Ville!"

Schwartz fell asleep pronouncing the name of Dr. Sarrasin, but in his sleep it was the name of the girl Jeanne which returned to his lips. He remembered her as a child even though, since he left her, Jeanne had become a young lady. This phenomenon is easily explained by the ordinary laws of the association of ideas: the idea of the doctor led to that of his daughter, association by contiguity. So when Schwartz, or rather Marcel Bruckmann, woke up, still having the name of Jeanne on his mind, he was not surprised, and saw in this fact a new proof of the excellence of the psychological principles of John Stuart Mill.[8]

6   *The Albrecht Mine*

Mme Bauer, the good woman who had offered hospitality to Marcel Bruckmann, was Swiss by birth and the widow of a miner killed four years earlier in one of those cataclysms which makes the life of a coal miner a continual battle. The company gave her a small annual pension of thirty dollars, to which she added the meager income of one furnished room and the salary brought in weekly by her little son Carl.

Although hardly thirteen years old, Carl worked in the mine as a "trapper"; he opened and closed the air vents whenever the coal carts passed through. This was essential to maintain proper ventilation in the galleries, as it forced the air to flow in a predetermined direction. The house which his mother had leased was too far from the Albrecht mine for him to return home every evening, so he had been given an extra little night job at the very bottom of the mine. He kept and groomed six horses in their subterranean stable while the daytime stableman spent the night outside. As a result, Carl's life was almost entirely spent five hundred meters below ground. During the day he would be at his post next to his air vent; at night he would sleep on straw near his horses. Only on Sunday morning could he return briefly to the light of day and, for a few hours, share the common patrimony of all men: sun, blue sky, and a mother's smile.

As one might well imagine after such a week, when he emerged from the mine, he did not particularly look the part of a young dandy. He looked more like a fairy-tale gnome, a chimney sweep, or a Fiji Islander. So Mme Bauer would generally spend a good hour scraping off his coal dust with a copious supply of warm water and soap. Then she had him put on a good suit of heavy green cloth, sewed out of a paternal cast-off that she pulled out of the depths of her big, pine cupboard, and from that moment on until evening she never tired of admiring her son, finding him to be the handsomest son in the world.

With his sediment of dust removed, Carl was really no uglier than anyone else. His blond, silky hair, his gentle blue eyes matched his tint of an excessive pallor; but his body was too thin for his age. This sunless life had made him as anemic as a lettuce stalk, and it is likely that Dr. Sarrasin's blood-cell counter, applied to the blood of the young miner, would have revealed a totally inadequate supply of corpuscles.

Morally, he was a quiet child, phlegmatic, calm with a dash of that pride which the feeling of constant danger, the habit of regular work, and the satisfaction of difficulties overcome give to all miners without exception. His great happiness was to sit down beside his mother at the square table which occupied the center of the low-ceilinged room, and to arrange on a piece of cardboard all sorts of dreadful insects that he brought up from the entrails of the Earth. The tepid, unchanging atmosphere of the mines has its special fauna, little known to naturalists, like the moist walls of coal have their strange flora of greenish mosses, indescribable fungi, and amorphous lichen.[1] That's what the engineer Maulesmühle,[2] lover of entomology, had noticed, and he had promised Carl a penny for each new specimen that Carl could bring him. This golden opportunity had led the boy to explore the far corners of the coal mine with great care and, little by little, had turned him into a collector. So now it was for himself that he looked for the insects.

Besides, he did not limit his affection to spiders and lice. In his solitude, he maintained a close friendship with two bats and a large field mouse. According to him, these three animals were the most intelligent and the most amiable in the world; even smarter than his horses with their long silken hair and their gleaming rumps, which Carl always spoke of with the greatest admiration.

His favorite was Blair-Athol, the dean of the stable, an old philosopher, five hundred meters below water level for over six years and who had never again seen the light of day. He was now almost blind. But my, how he did know his subterranean labyrinth! How he could turn left or right without ever stumbling! How he could stop in exactly the right spot in front of the air vents, leaving just enough space for them to open up! How he whinnied affectionately, morning and evening, the exact moment when his feed was due! And so good, so gentle, so kind!

"I can assure you, mother, that he really does give me a kiss when he rubs his cheek against mine, when I stick my head out to him," Carl would say. "And it's so helpful, you know, that Blair-Athol has a sort of clock in his head. Without him we wouldn't know, all week long, when it was night or day, evening or morning!"[3]

The child rattled on this way, and Mme Bauer listened to him with rapt attention. She loved Blair-Athol, too, with all the affection that her son bore him, and never failed to send him a bit of sugar. What would she not have given to go see this old servant that her husband had known and also visit that sinister place where the body of poor Bauer, black as ink, charred by the firedamp, had been found after the explosion? But women are not allowed in the mine, and she had to be content with the endless descriptions that her son supplied her.

Ah! she knew it well, that coal pit, that great black hole from which her husband had not returned! Many were the times she had waited, beside that gaping maw eighteen feet across, running her eyes along the enclosure wall of hewn stone, the double cage of oak in which the basket slid along, hooked to their cables and suspended from steel pulleys, examining the high exterior frame, the building that housed the steam boiler, the marking shed, and all the rest! How many times had she warmed herself at the great oven of glowing coals where the miners emerged from the abyss to dry their clothes, where impatient smokers lit their pipes! How familiar she was with the noise and activity of this infernal gate! The receivers who unhooked the wagons loaded with coal; the hitchers, the washers, mechanics, boiler crew, she had seen them all, over and over again, on the job!

What she had not been able to see, yet saw so clearly, through the eyes of her feelings, was what happened when the basket descended into the abyss, filled with its cluster of human laborers, among them her late husband, and now her only child![4]

She heard their voices, their laughter, fade into the depths, become softer, then cease. She followed that cage in her thoughts, sinking into that narrow, vertical gut to the level five or six hundred meters below—four times the height of the great pyramid! She saw it finally arrive at the end of its course, the cables coming to a stop, and the men hastily stepping out onto the solid ground.

Then off they would go, spreading themselves through the underground city, one to the left and the next to the right; the rollers to their wagon; the pick-men, armed with the iron pick they are named after, heading for the mass of coal they must attack; the shorers, banking up those areas where the treasures of coal had been removed; the framers, reinforcing the walls and galleries with wooden beams, struts, and buttresses; the roadmen repairing the tracks, laying the rails; the masons assembling the vaults . . .

A central gallery leads from the entrance shaft to become a wide boulevard at another mine shaft two or three kilometers away. From there, secondary galleries stretch out at right angles, and from these, parallel lines of a third order. Between the passages stand walls, columns formed by the coal itself or by the rock. Everything orderly, squared off, solid, black!

And all along this labyrinth of roads, equal in breadth and length, a whole army of half-dressed miners moving about, talking, and working in the light of their safety lamps!

That is what Mme Bauer often imagined, when she was alone and thoughtful, beside her fireplace. In these many interlacing galleries, she could visualize one in particular, one that she knew better than the others, the one whose gate little Carl opened and shut.

When evening came, the day crew came back to the surface to be replaced by the night crew. But her little boy did not take his place in the basket. He was off to the stables, returning to his dear Blair-Athol, to whom he served a supper of oats and hay; then he ate in his turn the little cold supper sent down from above, played for a bit with his pet rat who sat unmoving at his feet, with his two bats thumping their wings around him, finally falling asleep on his bed of straw.

How well Mme Bauer knew all that, and how well she understood all those half-expressed details which Carl offered to her!

"Mother, you know what Mr. Maulesmühle, the engineer, told me yesterday? He said that if I found the right answers to arithmetic problems he gave me, someday he would take me to hold the surveying line when he draws up the plans in the mine with his compass. I guess they're going to pierce a gallery through to join the Weber shaft, and he'll have a tough time making it come out right!"

"Really!" exclaimed Mme Bauer, enthusiastically. " Mr. Maulesmühle the engineer said that!"

And she already imagined her boy holding the line the whole length of the galleries, while the engineer, notebook in hand, jotted down the figures, his eye glued to the compass, determining the direction of the shaft-to-be.

"But I'm sad," continued Carl, "that I don't have anyone to teach me arithmetic, and I'm so scared I'll make a mistake."

At this point, Marcel, who was quietly smoking by the fireplace since his role as boarder gave him that right, joined the conversation to say to the boy:

"If you can tell me what's causing you trouble, maybe I could explain it to you."

"You could?" asked Mme Bauer incredulously.

"Probably," answered Marcel. "Do you think I don't learn any-

That is what Mme Bauer often imagined . . .

"You could?" asked Mme Bauer incredulously.

thing in my evening courses, where I regularly go after supper? The teacher is very happy with me and says that I might help him as a monitor!"

Having said this, Marcel then went to get a notebook of white paper from his room, sat down beside the young boy, asked him what was giving him trouble in his problem, and explained it to him so clearly that Carl, delighted, no longer found it difficult at all.

From that day on, Mme Bauer had more consideration for her boarder, and Marcel felt a growing affection for his little comrade.

Marcel had shown himself to be an exemplary worker, and had taken little time in being promoted to second, then to first class. Every morning at seven o'clock he was at gate O. Every evening, after supper, he went to the course taught by the engineer Trubner. Geometry, algebra, blueprints, and machinery, he studied everything with equal ardor, and his progress was so rapid that his teacher was deeply impressed. Two months after entering the Schultze factory, the young worker had already been recognized as having one of the keenest minds, not only in section O, but in the entire City of Steel. A report of his immediate foreman, sent off at the end of the trimester, bore this formal mention:

"Schwartz (Johann) age twenty-six, first class in casting. I must point out this person to the central administration, as being without peer in the three areas of theoretical knowledge, practical ability, and a markedly inventive mind."

Nonetheless, it took an extraordinary event for Marcel to draw the attention of his superiors. This circumstance was not long in coming, as always happens sooner or later: unfortunately, this time, it was under the most tragic conditions.

One Sunday morning, Marcel, quite surprised to hear ten o'clock ring without his little friend Carl appearing, went down to ask Mme Bauer if she knew the cause of his delay. He found her very upset. Carl should have been home two hours ago at least. Seeing her anxiety, Marcel offered to search for news of him and left in the direction of the Albrecht shaft.

En route, he met several miners and made a point of asking if they had seen the young lad; then after receiving a negative reply and exchanging with them the usual "Glück auf!" (Happy exit!), which is the greeting of German coal miners, Marcel continued his walk.

He arrived about eleven o'clock at the Albrecht shaft. It did not look as bustling or turbulent as during the week. At most there was a young "modiste"—that's the name that the miners jokingly—and ironically—bestow upon the women "coal sorters"—who was chatting with the checker, whose job required that he be on duty, even on the holy day, at the mouth of the shaft.

"Have you seen the young Carl Bauer, no. 41,902?" asked Marcel of the functionary.

The man consulted his list and shook his head.

"Is there any other way out of the mine?"

"No, that's the only one," replied the checker. "The other shaft, soon to crop out to the north, is not yet finished."

"So the lad is still down there?"

"Must be, which is quite extraordinary since, on Sunday, only the five special guards are supposed to be down there."

"Can I go down to find out?"

"Not without permission."

"There could have been an accident," said the modiste.

"No accidents possible, on a Sunday!"

"But anyway," continued Marcel, "I've got to find out what happened to that child!"

"Go see the machine foreman, in that office, if he's still there . . ."

The foreman, in his fine Sunday suit, with a shirt collar stiff as tin, had fortunately stopped to linger over his figures. As an intelligent human being, he immediately shared Marcel's concern.

"We'll go see what the problem is," he said.

And, giving the order to the mechanic on duty to be ready to let out the cable, he got ready to descend into the mine with the young workman.

74

"Don't you have that Galibert equipment?" asked the latter. "It might come in handy . . ."

"You're right. You never know what you'll find at the bottom of the pit."

From a cabinet the foreman took two zinc tanks, like the coconut peddlers in Paris carry on their backs. They are compressed air tanks, connecting to one's mouth via two rubber tubes, and whose mouthpiece is held between one's teeth. They are filled with the help of special bellows, constructed in such a way as to completely empty themselves. With one's nose held by wooden pincers, it is possible with this supply of air to walk without danger through the most unbreathable atmosphere.

Once equipped, the foreman and Marcel took their places in the basket, the cable unwound through pulleys, and the descent began. In the glow of two small electric lights, they talked as they sank into the depths of the Earth.[5]

"For one who isn't used to this, you're a plucky fellow," said the foreman. "I've seen others unable to make up their mind to go down, or huddle in the basket like some rabbit!"

"Really?" replied Marcel. "It doesn't bother me at all. In fact, I've gone down several times into the mines."

Soon they reached the bottom of the shaft. A guard who was stationed at the arrival point said he had not seen little Carl.

They went off toward the stable. The horses were there by themselves and seemed very bored. Such at least was the conclusion one could draw from the welcoming whinny by which Blair-Athol greeted the three human figures. Carl's cloth sack was hanging on a nail, and in a corner beside a currycomb, his arithmetic book.

Marcel called pointed out to the others that Carl's lantern was missing, an extra proof that the child was probably somewhere in the mine.

"He might have been caught in some cave-in," said the foreman, "but it's unlikely! Why would he have been in the mining galleries, on a Sunday?"

"Maybe he was looking for some insects before leaving," replied the guard. "It's a real passion of his!"

The alternate stable hand, who arrived in the midst of this discussion, confirmed this supposition. He had seen Carl leave about seven o'clock with his lantern.

The only thing left to do was to begin a systematic search. They called the other guards in with a whistle, divided up the task on a big map of the mine, and, each of them, carrying his own lamp, began to explore the second- and third-level galleries which he had been assigned.

In two hours, all areas of the coal mine had been examined, and the seven men met again at the foot of the shaft. Nowhere was there the slightest evidence of a cave in, but there was no trace of Carl. The foreman, perhaps urged on by a growing appetite, was of the opinion that the boy could have gone up unnoticed, and just would be at his home now; but Marcel, convinced of the contrary, insisted on a new search.

"What's all that?" he said, pointing out a dotted area on the map which resembled, in the middle of otherwise very precise drawings, those *terrae incognitae* that geographers mark on the borders of the Arctic continents.

"That's the zone that has been temporarily abandoned because of the scarcity of the ore there," responded the foreman.

"That's an abandoned zone? Well, that's where we must look," continued Marcel with an authority the other men submitted to.

They were not long in reaching the opening to the galleries which indeed, judging from the gummy, musty look of the walls, had been abandoned for several years. They had already followed them for quite a while without seeing anything suspicious, when Marcel, stopping them, said: "Don't you feel a bit weighted down, and with a headache?"

"Why! that's right," replied his two companions.

"Myself," said Marcel, "for a moment I felt somewhat giddy. There must be some carbon dioxide here. Would you allow me to light a cigarette?" he asked the foreman.

"Light up, my lad, go right ahead."

Marcel drew from his pocket a little smoking kit, struck a match and bending over he brought the small flame toward the earth. It immediately went out.

"I was sure . . ." he said. "The gas, heavier than air, remains close to the ground. We mustn't stay here — I'm talking about those men who do not have a Galibert apparatus. If you like, sir, we can continue the search together."

This plan being agreed upon, Marcel and the foreman each took their air tank hoses between their teeth, pinched their noses with a clamp, and plunged down a succession of old galleries.

A quarter of an hour later they withdrew to renew their air supply; then, once this was accomplished, they started down again.

On the third attempt their efforts were finally crowned with success. A little bluish light, an electric lamp, appeared far off in the darkness. They ran toward it.

At the foot of the dampened wall lay poor little Carl, motionless and already cold. His lips were blue, his face congested, his pulse silent, everything, along with his posture, explained what had happened.

He had wanted to pick something up from the ground, had bent over and literally drowned in the carbon dioxide.

All efforts to summon him back to life were useless. He had died no doubt some four or five hours earlier. The next evening there was one more small grave in the new cemetery of Stahlstadt. And poor Mme Bauer was now the widow of her child as she had been of her husband.[6]

At the foot of the dampened wall lay poor little Carl.

7 The Central Block

A detailed report from Dr. Echternach, head physician of the Albrecht shaft area, established that the death of Carl Bauer, no. 41,902, age thirteen, "trapper" in gallery 228, was due to asphyxia resulting from the absorption through the respiratory organs of a strong dose of carbon dioxide.[1]

Another report no less detailed from engineer Maulesmühle had shown the need to include a ventilation system in zone B of Plan XIV, as its galleries were producing this deleterious gas by a kind of slow and unnoticeable distillation.

Finally, a note from the same official brought to the attention of the authorities the devotion of foreman Rayer and of the first-class caster Johann Schwartz.

A week or ten days later, the young worker, arriving to pick up his identity card in the concierge's box, found on a hook an order addressed to him, which said:

"The worker named Schwartz will present himself today at ten o'clock at the office of the director general, Central Block, gate and route A. Outdoor attire required."

"Finally! . . ." thought Marcel. "They took their time, but we're getting there!"

Through his conversations with friends and from his Sunday walks around the City of Steel, he had acquired enough general knowledge about the organization of the city to know that authorization to penetrate into the Central Block was not commonly given. In fact, legends were widespread about it. It was said that some indiscreet individuals, who had tried to sneak their way into this private precinct, had not been seen again. There were rumors that workers and employees who were admitted entry were first submitted to all sorts of Masonic ceremonies, obliged to avow under the most solemn of oaths to reveal nothing of what they saw, and were mercilessly executed by a secret tribunal if they violated their vow. An underground train connected this sanctuary with the outer line. Night trains brought in unknown visitors. Sometimes supreme counsels were held there with mysterious personages who came to sit in on and to participate in the discussions.

Without putting too much faith in these tales, Marcel knew that they were in general the popular expression of a perfectly real fact: the extreme difficulty of penetrating into the central sector. Of all the workers he knew—and he had friends among the miners as well those as in the coal field, among the metal refiners and among the employees in blast furnaces, among the sergeants and carpenters as well as among the ironsmiths—not a single one had ever crossed the threshold of Gate A.

So it was with great curiosity and a secret pleasure that he appeared at the indicated hour. He could soon see that the precautions and penalties were extremely strict.

First of all, Marcel was expected. Two men dressed in gray uniforms, saber at the side and revolver in the belt, were standing in the concierge's office. This office, like that of the extern sister of a cloistered convent, had two doorways, one on the outside, the other on the inside, which were never both opened at the same time.

The pass was examined and stamped, and Marcel, without evincing any surprise, was then given a white handkerchief which the two acolytes in uniform used to carefully blindfold him.[2]

Then, taking him by the arms, they marched him away without saying a word.

After two or three thousand steps, they went up a flight of stairs, a door opened and closed, and Marcel was authorized to remove his blindfold.

He found himself in a very simple room, furnished with a few chairs, a blackboard and a drafting board equipped with all the necessary instruments for linear designs. Light came in through tall windows with frosted glass panes.

Almost immediately, two people who looked as if they were from a university entered the room. "You have been singled out as a distinguished subject," said one of them. "We are going to examine you to see if there is sufficient reason to admit you to the models division. Are you ready to answer our questions?"

Marcel modestly declared himself ready for the test.

The two examiners then asked a series of questions on chemistry, geometry, and algebra. The young worker satisfied them in all areas by the clarity and precision of his answers. The figures he traced with chalk on the board were neat, distinct, elegant. His equations lined up crisp, compact, in uniform rows like the ranks of an elite regiment. One of his demonstrations even was so remarkable and so original to his judges that they expressed their astonishment about it, asking him where he had learned it.

"In Schaffhouse, where I come from, in primary school."

"You seem to be a good draftsman."

"That was my strongest point."

"Education given in Switzerland is definitely quite extraordinary!" one of the examiners said to the other . "We are going to give you two hours to execute this plan," he continued, giving the candidate a cross-section of a fairly complex steam-driven machine. "If you acquit yourself well, you'll pass with the honorable mention: *Perfectly satisfactory and beyond expectation.*"

Left alone, Marcel set to work with great vigor.

When his judges returned at the end of the examination period, they were so stunned by his design that they added to the promised mention: *We have no other designer of equal talent.*

The young worker was then taken in hand again by the gray-clad assistants, and with the same ritual—that is to say, blindfolded—he was led to the office of the director general.

"You are hereby offered admission to one of the design studios, in the division of models," said the director. "Are you now ready to submit to its conditions and regulations?"

"I do not know what they are," said Marcel, "but I presume they are acceptable."

"They are as follows: 1. During the entire time of your employment, you are bound to reside in the division itself. You may only leave on special and quite exceptional authorization. 2. You are subject to military discipline and you owe absolute obedience, under military penalty, to your superiors. On the other hand, you will be like the noncommissioned officers of an active army and may, through regular advancement, rise to higher ranks. 3. You are obligated under oath never to reveal to anyone what you see in this part of the division to which you have access. 4. Your correspondence will be opened by higher-ranking personnel, outgoing as well as incoming, and must be limited to your family."[3]

"In short, I'm in prison," thought Marcel.

Then he replied very simply:

"Those conditions sound fair and I am ready to follow them."

"Fine. Raise your hand. Take the oath. You are assigned as draftsman in studio no. 4. Lodging will be assigned you, and, for meals, you have here a first-class canteen. You don't have your luggage with you?"

"No, sir. Not knowing what you wanted of me, I left my things at my landlady's."

"We'll get them for you, for you must no longer leave the division."

"I did well," thought Marcel, "writing my notes in code! All they'd have to do is find them . . . !"

Before day's end, Marcel was set up in a smart little room on the fourth floor of a building overlooking a vast courtyard, and he was beginning to get a better idea of his new life.

It did not seem as grim as he had thought at first. His comrades —whom he met in the restaurant—were in general quiet and gentle, like all hard-working men. In an attempt to brighten things up, for gaiety was lacking in this machine-like existence, several of them had formed an orchestra and each evening produced music of quite good quality. A library and reading room offered the mind valuable resources from the scientific point of view, but only during the rare leisure hours. Some special courses, given by top-quality professors, were required for all employees, who were also obliged to undergo frequent exams and competitions. But freedom and air were lacking in this narrow milieu. It was college with many severe add-ons and for the use of men already matured. The atmosphere could not help but weigh down on their spirits no matter how accustomed they became to the iron discipline.

Winter passed by in these occupations to which Marcel had devoted himself, body and soul. His assiduousness, the perfection of his layouts, the extraordinary progress of his instruction, acknowledged unanimously by all the teachers and all the examiners, had raised him in short order to a relative celebrity among those dedicated men. By common consent, he was the most capable draftsman, the most ingenious, the richest in resources. Whenever there was a problem, they came running to him. Even the head men took advantage of his expertise with the respect that merit always elicits from the most jealous.

But if the young man had counted on penetrating the intimate secrets of Stahlstadt by arriving at the heart of the model division, he was far from the goal. His life was enclosed in an iron grillwork three hundred meters in diameter, which surrounded the segment of the Central Block to which he was attached. Intellectually, his activity could and should have extended to the furthermost branches of the metallurgical industry. In practice it was limited to plans for steam-operated machines. He constructed them in all dimensions and powers, for all sorts of industries and usages, warships and printing presses; but he did not leave his specialty. The division of work pushed to its extreme limit was squeezing him in its vice.

After four months in section A, Marcel knew no more about the overall work going on in Steel City than before entering it. At most he had collected some general information about the organization of which he was—despite his merits—but a lowly cog. He knew that the center of this spider web of Stahlstadt was the Tower of the Bull, a sort of cyclopean construction which dominated all the neighboring buildings.[4] He had also learned, always through rumors circulated at the canteen, that the personal residence of Herr Schultze was located in the base of that tower and that the well-known secret room occupied its center. It was said that the vaulted room, protected against fire and armored on the inside like a Monitor is on the outside, was closed by a system of steel doors with machine-gun locks, worthy of the most suspicious of banks. The general opinion, moreover, was that Herr Schultze was working on the construction of a dreadful engine of war, without precedent and destined to assure Germany worldwide domination.

In order to solve this mystery, Marcel had pondered the most audacious plans of entry and disguise. But he had had to admit to himself that they contained nothing feasible. These rows of somber, massive walls, lit by night with floodlights, guarded by experienced sentries, would forever constitute an impassable obstacle to his efforts. Even if he succeeded in getting through at one point, what would he see? Details, nothing but details; never the whole!

No matter. He had sworn to himself not to give up; he would not give up. If it took ten years of preparation, he would wait ten years. But the day would eventually come when the secret would become his! It had to be so. France-Ville was prospering then, a city of happiness whose charitable institutions favored each and all by showing new horizons of hope to disheartened people. Marcel did not doubt that, faced with such a triumph of the Latin race, Schultze would be all the more determined to make good on his threats. Steel City and its manufacturing goals were themselves proof of that.

Several more months passed by.

One day in March, Marcel had just repeated to himself for the thousandth time that vow of Hannibal,[5] when one of the gray-clad assistants informed him that the director general wanted to speak to him.

"I have received from Herr Schultze," this high functionary told him, "the order to send him our best draftsman. That is you. Kindly pack up your things and come with me into the inner circle. You are promoted to the rank of lieutenant."

So, at the very moment when he almost despaired of success, the logical and natural effect of his heroic labor granted him this admittance he so desired! Marcel was so filled with joy that he could not hide the expression of his feelings on his face.

"I am happy to announce such a fine piece of news to you," continued the official, "and I can only urge you to continue the path which you have been following so courageously. A most brilliant future lies before you. Go to it, sir."

Finally, Marcel, after such a long period of trial and tribulation, now glimpsed the goal he had sworn to reach!

Cramming his things into his valise, following the men in gray, crossing this last wall, the only entrance open onto route A and so long forbidden to him, now took but a few moments for Marcel to accomplish.

He was at the foot of that inaccessible Tower of the Bull of which he had only seen the haughty head, lost in the distant clouds.

The scene which stretched out before him was surely among the most unexpected.

Just imagine a man suddenly transported, without any transition whatever, from a noisy, commonplace European workshop to the depths of a virgin forest of the tropics. This was the surprise that awaited Marcel at the heart of Stahlstadt.

Moreover, as a virgin forest gains in beauty when viewed through the descriptions of great writers,[6] so too was Herr Schultze's park more beautiful than the most exotic of pleasure gardens.[7] Towering palms, bushy banana trees, the stoutest of cactuses, all growing in massive clumps. Vines wound elegantly around the thin eucalyptus, draped themselves in green festoons, or fell as opulent tendrils. The most unusual thick-growing plants bloomed on open ground. Pineapples and guavas ripened beside the oranges. Hummingbirds and birds of paradise spread the richness of their plumage into the open air. And the temperature itself was as tropical as the vegetation.

Marcel looked around for the large windows and the furnaces which produced this miracle and was surprised to see nothing but the sky.

Herr Schultze's park

Then he recalled that not far away there was a coal mine in a state of permanent combustion, and he understood that Herr Schultze had ingeniously put this subterranean heat to good use, maintaining the constant temperature of a greenhouse.

But this explanation, supplied by the young Alsatian's mind, did not stop his eyes from being astonished and charmed by the green of the lawns, nor his nostrils from breathing in with delight the aromas filling the atmosphere. After six months of deprivation, without seeing even a blade of grass, it was truly delightful. A sandy walkway led him along a slight slope to the foot of a marble staircase, overshadowed by a majestic colonnade. Behind it reared the enormous mass of a great square building which was like the pedestal for the Tower of the Bull. Under the peristyle, Marcel noticed seven or eight valets in red livery, a Swiss with halberd and tricorne. He saw between the columns some rich candelabra of bronze, and as he mounted the steps, heard a slight rumbling which revealed the underground train passing beneath his feet.

Marcel gave his name and was immediately admitted into a vestibule, which was a veritable museum of sculpture. Without taking the time to stop, he crossed a red-and-gold reception room, then a black-and-gold reception room, to arrive finally at a yellow-and-gold reception room where the valet left him alone for five minutes. Finally he was introduced into a splendid green-and-gold office.

Herr Schultze in person, smoking a long clay pipe beside a tankard of beer called to mind, in the midst of all this luxury, a splotch of mud on a polished boot.

Without getting up or even turning his head, the King of Steel said coldly and simply:

"You're the draftsman?"

"Yes, sir."

"I've seen some of your drawings. They're very good. But you don't know how to make anything but steam engines?"

"They've never asked me for anything else."

"Have you ever studied ballistics?"

"I've studied it in idle moments and for my pleasure."

"So, will you undertake to design a cannon with me?"

This went straight to Herr Schultze's heart. He deigned to look at his employee.

"So, will you undertake to design a cannon with me? We'll see how you get along . . . Ah! you'll have trouble replacing that idiot Sohne,[8] who killed himself this morning handling a stick of dynamite! The half-wit might have blown us all up!"

One must admit that this lack of sympathy did not seem too unusual coming from the mouth of Herr Schultze!

8 *The Dragon's Lair*

The reader who has followed the progress of the young Alsatian's fortune will probably not be surprised to find him, at the end of a few weeks, working closely and becoming very familiar with Herr Schultze.[1] The two had become inseparable. Work, meals, promenades in the park, leisurely smoking over draughts of beer—they did everything in common. Never had the former professor from Iéna met a collaborator who seemed so much after his own heart, who understood his every notion, so to speak, who knew how to put into practice so quickly his theoretical ideas.

Marcel was not only of transcendent value in all branches of his trade; he was also the most charming companion, the most assiduous of workers, the most modestly fertile inventor.

Herr Schultze was delighted with him. Ten times a day he would say to himself *in petto:*

"What a find! What a pearl is this young lad!"[2]

The truth is that Marcel, from the first glance, had seen through the character of his formidable employer. He had understood that the latter's most dominant trait was an immense and insatiable egotism, manifested on the outside by an extreme vanity, and Marcel had decided to regulate his own conduct on it at every instant.

In a matter of days, the young Alsatian had learned the finger-positions of this human keyboard so well that he soon succeeded in "playing" Schultze like a piano. His tactic consisted simply in demonstrating his personal worth as much as possible, but in such a way as to always leave Schultze an opportunity to reestablish his superiority over him. For example, in completing a design, he did it perfectly—except for one easy-to-see and easily correctable defect, which the former professor never failed to point out with great satisfaction.

Were he to develop some theoretical concept, he sought to have it come out in conversation in such a way that Herr Schultze could believe *he* had discovered it. Sometimes he went even further, saying, for example:

"I've laid out this plan for a ship with a detachable ram at the bow, which you asked me for."

"Me?" replied Herr Schultze, who had never imagined such a thing.

"Why, yes! Perhaps you have forgotten? A detachable ram, leaving in the enemy's flank a cone-shaped torpedo which explodes within three minutes."

"Ah! I just had no recollection. So many ideas jostling about in my head!"

And Herr Schultze conscientiously pocketed the credit for the new invention.

Perhaps, after all, he was but a partial dupe to this maneuvering. Deep down, it is probable that he felt Marcel to be the stronger. But like one of those mysterious fermentations which operate in human minds, he was content to "appear" superior, and especially to maintain this illusion before his subordinate.

"Is he ever stupid for all his intelligence, this fellow!" he said to himself on occasion, silently baring in a mute smile the thirty-two "ivories" in his mouth.

Besides, his vanity had soon found a scale of compensation. He alone in the world could bring about these kinds of industrial dreams! These dreams only had value through him and by him!

Marcel, after all, was just one of the cogs of the organization that only he, Schultze, had been able to create! etc., etc. . . . .

Nevertheless, he never divested himself, one might say. After five months within the Tower of the Bull, Marcel knew little more than at the outset about the mysteries of the Central Block. In truth, his suspicions had become virtual certitudes. He was more and more convinced that Stahlstadt was hiding a secret, and that Herr Schultze had yet another goal than that of commercial gain. The nature of the latter's obsessions—and even his industry—made infinitely more reasonable the hypothesis that he had invented some new engine of war.

But the answer to this enigma still remained obscure.

Marcel at last concluded that he would not obtain this knowledge without a crisis of some sort. Not seeing one come along on its own, he decided to provoke one.

It was evening, the 5th of September, at the end of dinner. One year before to the day, he had found the body of his little friend Carl in the Albrecht mine. Outside, the long severe winter of this American Switzerland still covered the countryside with its white cloak. But in the park of Stahlstadt the temperature was as warm as in June, and the snow, melted before it struck the ground, settled as dew rather than falling in flakes.

"Those sausages and sauerkraut were delicious, weren't they?" remarked Herr Schultze, who had not lost his taste for his favorite dish despite the Begum's millions.

"Delicious," responded Marcel, who ate some heroically every evening, though he had ended up by hating the sight of this dish.

His stomach's revolt led him to try an experiment he had been considering.

"I even wonder how people who have neither sauerkraut nor sausages nor beer, can tolerate existence!" continued Herr Schultze with a sigh.

"Life for them must be one long torture," replied Marcel. "It would truly be a charity to reunite them in the Fatherland."

"Well! Well! . . . That day will come! . . . It'll come!" exclaimed the Steel King. "We're already set up here in the heart of America. Let us take an island or two near Japan, and you'll see what strides we can take around the globe!"

The footman had brought in their pipes. Herr Schultze stuffed his and lit it. Marcel had chosen this daily moment of complete bliss with premeditation.

"I must say," he added after a moment of silence, "I don't much believe in this conquest!"

"What conquest?" asked Herr Schultze, who had already lost track of this conversation.

"The conquest of the world by the Germans."

The former professor thought he had misunderstood.

"You don't believe in the German conquest of the world?"

"No."

"Well! Indeed! That's a good one! And I'd be curious to know the reasons for this doubt!"

"Just because the French artillery will end up surpassing you, and then crushing you! My countrymen the Swiss, who know them well, are firmly convinced that one Frenchman forewarned is worth two Germans. The lesson of 1870 will turn against those who gave it.[3] No one in my little country has any doubt about it, sir, and if I must tell you, that's the opinion of the smartest men in England."

Marcel had proffered these words in a cold, dry, and cutting tone—which doubled the effect that this blasphemy, shot point-blank at him, produced on the King of Steel.

Herr Schultze seemed to choke, turned pale, and appeared momentarily overwhelmed. Blood rose to his face with such violence that the young man was afraid that he had gone too far. However, seeing that his victim, after having nearly suffocated with rage, would apparently not die of it right away, he continued:

"Yes, it's perhaps annoying to say this, but that's the way it is. Although our rivals aren't making any noise about it, they're doing their work. Do you think they haven't learned anything since the war? While we go blindly increasing the weight of our cannons, you can be sure they're preparing something new, and that we'll notice it when the time comes around!"

"Something new! Something new!" stammered Herr Schultze. "We're making something new as well, sir!"

"Well, sure, but let's be honest! We're remaking in steel what our predecessors made out of bronze, that's all! We're doubling the size and the range of our cannons!"

"Doubling! . . . ," retorted Herr Schultze in a tone of voice that meant: "Really! we can do better than doubling!"

"But basically," went on Marcel, "we're just plagiarists. Look. You want me to tell you the truth? We lack inventive genius. We don't discover anything, and the French do, you can be sure of it!"

Herr Schultze, at least outwardly, seemed to have refound a bit of calm. Yet, the trembling of his lips, the pallor which had followed the apoplectic red of his face showed the feelings that were agitating him well enough.

Must he endure such a degree of humiliation? To carry the name of Schultze, to be absolute master of the largest factory and the top foundry of cannons in the entire world, to see at his feet both kings and parliaments, and to hear himself told by a little Swiss draftsman that we lack innovative power, that we're less than a French artilleryman! And all that when you have nearby, the thickness of an armor-plated wall away, enough to confound a thousand times over this impudent clown, to shut his mouth, to destroy his stupid arguments? No, it was not possible to endure such torture!

Herr Schultze rose up so brusquely he broke his pipe. Then, looking at Marcel with an eye filled with irony, and clenching his teeth, he said to him, or rather he hissed these words:

"Follow me, sir, I'm going to show you if I, Herr Schultze, am lacking in inventiveness."

Marcel was playing big stakes, but he had won thanks to the surprise produced by his so audacious and so unexpected words and to the violence of the scorn he had provoked. The vanity of the former professor was stronger than his prudence, and Schultze was now eager to unveil his secret. Almost despite himself, he led the way into his study—whose door he reclosed with care—walked straight to his bookcase and touched one of its panels. Immediately an opening, hidden by the rows of books, appeared in the wall.[4] It was the entrance to a narrow passageway, which led down a stone staircase, to the very base of the Tower of the Bull.

There, an oak door was opened with the help of a small key which never left the German's possession. A second door appeared, closed by a syllabic padlock of the sort used on strongboxes. Herr Schultze formed the code word and opened the heavy iron door, which was armed on the inside by a complicated apparatus of explosive weapons that Marcel, no doubt out of professional curiosity, would have liked to examine. But his guide did not give him the time to do so.

Both were now facing a third door, with no apparent keyhole, which opened by a single push given in precisely the right place.

This third barrier crossed, Herr Schultze and his companion had to climb the two hundred steps of an iron staircase, and they arrived at the peak of the Tower of the Bull, which dominated the entire city of Stahlstadt.

On this tower of solid granite, there was a rounded sort of casemate, pierced with several embrasures. In the center of the casemate stood a steel cannon.

"There!" said the professor, who had not uttered a word during the trip.

It was the most gigantic piece of ordnance that Marcel had ever seen. It must have weighed at least three hundred thousand kilos. A breech-loader, the diameter of its mouth measured a meter and a half. Mounted on a steel carriage and rolling on tracks of the same metal, it might have been maneuvered by a child, the movements were made so easy by a system of cogged wheels. A compensating spring set up at the rear of the steel carriage canceled the recoil, or at least produced a rigorously equal reaction, and automatically restored the piece to its original position after each firing.

"And what is its power of penetration?" asked Marcel, who could not help but admire such a work.

Herr Schultze's giant cannon

"At twenty thousand meters, with a full projectile, we pierce a plank of wood forty inches thick as though it were a slice of bread and butter!"

"What is its range?"

"Its range!" cried Schultze, who was really warming up. "Ha! You were saying a moment ago that our genius in imitating others could do more than double the range of existing cannons! Well, with this cannon I can send a projectile, with reasonable accuracy, a distance of ten leagues!"

"Ten leagues!" cried Marcel. "What new powder do you use then?"

"Oh! I can explain it all to you now," answered Herr Schultze in a peculiar tone. "I see no problem in revealing my secrets! Coarse-grained powder is a thing of the past. What I use is gun-cotton whose explosive power is four times greater than ordinary powder, a power that I can quintuple by mixing in eight-tenths of potassium nitrate!"

"But," observed Marcel, "no piece, even made of the best steel, can resist the blast of this pyroxylin! Your cannon after three, four, five shots would have become deteriorated beyond use!"

"If it fired once, just once, that'd be enough!"

"It would be very expensive!"

"One million, since that's the cost of production."

"One firing for a million!"

"What's the difference, if it can destroy a billion's worth!"

"A billion!" exclaimed Marcel.

Yet he restrained himself, not showing the horror mixed with admiration that this prodigious object of destruction inspired within him. Then he added:

"It is truly an astounding and prodigious piece of artillery, but which, despite all its merits, absolutely justifies my thesis: perfecting, imitating, not inventing!"

"Not inventing!" responded Herr Schultze, shrugging his shoulders. "I repeat that I shall keep no more secrets from you! Come then!"

The King of Steel and his companion left the casemate behind and descended to the lower floor by means of a hydraulic elevator. There, one could see a large quantity of long objects, cylindrical in shape, which might at a distance have been mistaken for other un-mounted cannons.

"These are our shells," said Herr Schultze.

This time, Marcel was obliged to recognize that these weapons did not resemble anything that he recognized. They were enormous tubes, two meters long and one meter ten centimeters in diameter, clad on the outside with a lead casing made to fit the riflings of the gun, closed off at the rear by a steel plaque bolted on, and at the front having an ogival steel point, equipped with a percussion cap.

What was the special nature of these shells? Nothing in their appearance gave it away. Marcel felt that they must contain within their flanks some dreadful explosive, exceeding anything that had been made of this sort.

"You can't guess?" asked Herr Schultze, seeing that his companion remained silent.

"Indeed, no, sir! Why would a shell be so long and so heavy — at least in appearance?"

"The appearance is misleading," replied Herr Schultze, "and the weight is not significantly more than an ordinary shell of that caliber. Well, I'll have to tell you! A flare-shell of glass clad in oak, charged with over seventy atmospheres of interior pressure — of liquid carbon dioxide. When falling to the ground, the casing explodes and the liquid returns to a gaseous state! Consequence: a sudden cold of a hundred degrees below zero centigrade in all the surrounding area, at the same time an enormous volume of carbon dioxide in the encompassing air! Every living being within a radius of thirty meters from the center of the explosion is both frozen and asphyxiated! I say thirty meters as a basic calculation, but the effect may really extend much further, up to perhaps one or two hundred meters in radius. An even more advantageous circumstance, the carbon dioxide remaining a long time within the lower levels of the atmosphere, since its weight exceeds that of the surrounding air,

"These are our shells," said Herr Schultze.

the danger zone maintains its lethal properties after the explosion, and any human attempting to penetrate it is sure to die. The effect of that cannon shot will be both instantaneous and long lasting! Thus, with my system, there are no wounded, just the dead!"[5]

Herr Schultze felt such a manifest pleasure in outlining the merits of his invention. His good humor returned, he was flushed with pride and was beaming with all his teeth!

"You can just imagine," he added, "a sufficient number of my cannon aimed at a besieged city! Just suppose we had one piece for each hectare of surface, for a city of a thousand hectares, a hundred batteries of ten pieces each, properly spaced. Let us suppose as well that all our pieces are in place, each with its line of fire drawn, a calm and favorable atmosphere, and then a common signal given through an electric wire. In a minute, there will not be a single living being over a surface of a thousand hectares! A veritable tide of carbon dioxide will have submerged the city! This idea came to my mind last year upon reading the medical report on the accidental death of a young miner in the Albrecht pits! I had my first inspiration about it in Naples when I visited the Grotto of the Dog.* But it took this last fact to give my thought its full scope. You understand the principle, right? An artificial ocean of pure carbon dioxide! A proportion of just a fifth of this gas is enough to make the air unbreathable."

Marcel said not a word. He was truly reduced to silence. Herr Schultze felt his triumph so vividly that he did not wish to take advantage of it.

"There's just one detail that bothers me," he said.

"What's that?" asked Marcel.

"It's that I have not succeeded in suppressing the noise of the

---

*The Grotto of the Dog, near Naples, borrows its name from the curious property that its atmosphere possesses of asphyxiating a dog, or any quadruped with short legs, without injuring a man standing up—due to a layer of carbon dioxide of about ten centimeters thick whose specific weight holds it down to ground level. (*Author's note.*)

explosion. There is too much similarity between the sound of my cannon going off and that of a common cannon. Just try to imagine what it would be like if I succeeded in making it silent! That sudden death arriving noiselessly to a hundred thousand people all at once, on a calm and serene evening!"

This enchanting prospect made Herr Schultze suddenly become dreamy-eyed, and perhaps his reverie, which was no more than a deep immersion into the wellspring of self-love, would have continued for a long time if Marcel had not interrupted it with this observation:

"That's fine, sir, well and good! But, a thousand cannons of this sort, that's a lot of time and money."

"Money? We're loaded with it! Time? . . . Time belongs to us!"

And indeed, this German—the last of his school—believed what he said!

"Fine," responded Marcel. "Your shell, charged with carbon dioxide, is not absolutely new since it derives from asphyxiating projectiles, known for any number of years; but it can be eminently destructive, no question. Only . . ."

"Only?"

"It is relatively light for its volume, and if that thing ever goes ten leagues . . . !"

"It is made to go only two leagues," replied Herr Schultze, smiling. "But," he added, pointing to another shell, "there's a cast projectile. It's loaded, that one, and contains thirty little cannons arranged symmetrically, cast one inside the other like the tubes in a telescope, and which, after being shot off like projectiles, become cannons in their turn, to spit out, one after another, little shells loaded with incendiary materials.[6] It's like a battery that I can throw into space and which can carry fire and death to a whole city by covering it with a shower of inextinguishable flames! It has the desired weight I talked about for crossing ten leagues. And soon, such an experiment will be made with it that any disbeliever will be able to touch with his finger a hundred thousand bodies which will have been laid to rest!"

The ivories gleamed at that moment with such an intolerable burst in the mouth of Herr Schultze that Marcel had the most violent desire to knock out a dozen of them. Yet he had the strength to restrain himself once more. He had not reached the end of what he was to hear.

Indeed, Herr Schultze continued: "As I've told you, before long, a decisive experiment will be conducted!"

"How? . . . Where?" cried Marcel.

"How? With one of those shells, which will cross the chain of the Cascade Mountains, shot by my cannon on the platform! . . . Where? On one of the cities from which we are separated by at most ten leagues, which can't be expecting such a thunderbolt from above and, even if they were expecting it, would be just as powerless to ward off its slaughterous results! It's the 5th of September now! . . . Well, on the 13th, at eleven forty-five in the evening, France-Ville will disappear from the American soil! The incineration of Sodom will have had its equal! Professor Schultze will have unleashed all the flames of heaven in his turn!"

This time, at that unexpected declaration, all Marcel's blood surged upward! Fortunately, Herr Schultze saw nothing of what the lad was experiencing.

"You see!" he continued with the most casual tone. "We're doing the opposite of what the founders of France-Ville do! We're finding the secret ways of shortening lives, while they seek to lengthen them. But their work is doomed, for it is from death — sown by us — that life is to be born.[7] However, everything has its role in nature, and Dr. Sarrasin's founding of that isolated city has, without his knowing it, placed within my range the most magnificent proving ground!"[8]

Marcel could not believe what he had just heard.

"But," he said in a voice whose involuntary tremor seemed for an instant to attract the attention of the King of Steel, "the residents of France-Ville have done you no harm, sir! As far as I know, you have no reason to seek a quarrel with them."

"Oh, my dear lad," replied Herr Schultze, "there are in your mind, well organized from other points of view, a welter of Celtic ideas which would injure you deeply were you to live long enough! Right, good, and evil are purely relative things, and all a matter of convention. There is no absolute except the great laws of nature. The law of living competitively is just as natural as the law of gravity. Resisting it is utter inanity; to accept it and act according to its precepts is both reasonable and wise—which is why I shall destroy Dr. Sarrasin's city. Thanks to my cannon, my fifty thousand Germans will easily make an end of the hundred thousand dreamers over there who constitute a group condemned to perish!"

Marcel, understanding the futility of trying to reason with Herr Schultze, no longer sought to bring him around.

They both left the shell room, whose secret doorways were again locked, and they returned to the dining room.

With the most natural air, Herr Schultze raised his foaming stein of beer to his mouth, rang a bell, had another pipe brought in to replace the one he had broken, and addressing the valet, he asked:

"Are Sigimer and Arminius still there?"

"Yes, sir."

"Tell them to remain within the range of my voice."

When the servant had left the dining room, the King of Steel, turning toward Marcel, looked him in the face. The latter did not bat an eye before his look, which had taken on a metallic hardness.

"Really," Marcel said, "you're going to execute this project?"

"Really. I know to a tenth of a second, in longitude and in latitude, the location of France-Ville, and on September 13th, at eleven forty-five in the evening, it will cease to be."

"Perhaps you should have kept this plan absolutely secret!"

"My dear fellow," replied Herr Schultze, "decidedly you will never be logical. That makes me regret less that you are going to have to die young."

Marcel, upon these words, had stood up.

"How is it that you've never understood," added Herr Schultze coldly, "that I do not speak about my projects except to those who will no longer be able to talk about them?"

Arminius and Sigimer

The bell rang. Arminius and Sigimer, two giants, appeared at the door of the room.[9]

"You tried to discover my secret," said Herr Schultze. "Now you have! All that remains is for you to die."

Marcel gave no answer.

"You're too intelligent," continued Herr Schultze, "to suppose that I can allow you to live, now that you know all my plans. It would be an unpardonable slight; it would be illogical. The greatness of my purpose forbids me to compromise its success for a consideration of relative value as minimal as the life of one man—even a man such as you, my dear fellow, whose particularly fine cerebral organization I esteem. Also, I do regret that a little impulse of vanity dragged me a bit too far, and simply forces me to do away with you. But you must understand, faced with the interests to which I have devoted myself, there's no question of sentiment. I can tell you this now: it's for having penetrated my secret that your predecessor, Sohne, is dead, and not by the explosion of a stick of dynamite! The rule is absolute. It must be inflexible! I cannot change it!"

Marcel looked at Herr Schultze. He understood, from the sound of his voice, by the bestial stubbornness of that bald head, that he was doomed. So he did not take the trouble of protesting.

"When will I die and of what sort of death?" he asked.

"Don't worry about that detail," calmly replied Herr Schultze. "You'll die, but you'll be spared suffering. One morning, you just won't wake up. That's all."

With a gesture of the King of Steel, Marcel saw himself led off and consigned to his bedroom, the door of which was guarded by the two giants.

But, when he found himself alone, he thought, trembling with anguish and rage, about the doctor, about his family, about all his fellow compatriots, about all those whom he loved!

"The death that awaits me is of little importance," he mused. "But how can I avert the danger that threatens them?"

9 Absent without Leave

The situation was, indeed, extremely grave. What could Marcel do, he whose remaining hours were now numbered and perhaps whose last night would arrive with the setting of the sun?

He did not sleep an instant—not for fear of never waking up again, as Herr Schultze had said, but because his thoughts never left France-Ville, threatened by impending catastrophe!

"What can I do?" he kept repeating to himself. "Destroy the cannon? Blow up the tower it's in? How could I manage that? Flee? When my room is guarded by those two giants? And then, even if I succeeded in leaving Stahlstadt before September 13th, how could I prevent this tragedy? Of course, if I can't save our dear city, I might at least save its inhabitants! I must go to them, cry out to them: 'Flee the city! Flee! Now! You are threatened with death by fire, by steel! Flee! All of you!'"

Then Marcel's ideas took a different course.

"That wretched Schultze!" he thought. "Even admitting that he exaggerated the destructive effects of his shell, and that he cannot set fire to the entire city, it is certain that he can, with one blow, incinerate a considerable part of it! It's a dreadful machine that he has created—despite the considerable distance separating the two cities, that formidable cannon can surely reach it with its shells! And at an initial speed twenty times over any speed obtained today! Something like ten thousand meters, two and a half leagues per second! Why, that's about a third of the orbiting speed of the earth. Is that really possible? . . . Yes, yes! . . . if his cannon doesn't blow up on the first shot! But it won't blow up, for it's made of a metal whose resistance to explosion is practically infinite! And the wretch knows the exact location of France-Ville! Without leaving his den he'll point the cannon with mathematical precision, and as he said, the shell will land in the very heart of the city! How can those poor residents be warned?"

Marcel had not closed his eyes when the new day dawned. He left the bed on which he had been tossing all night with feverish insomnia.

"Well," he said to himself, "it'll be for another night! Perhaps this executioner who wants to spare me any suffering is just waiting until sleep, chasing away all these worries, finally takes possession of me. And then! But what death is he saving for me? Is he thinking of killing me by some inhalation of prussic acid while I slumber? Will he give me a dose of that carbon dioxide he has at his disposal? Might he not rather use that gas in a liquid state, the way he inserts it into his glass shells and whose sudden return to a gaseous state will create a cold of 100° below zero! And the following day, instead of 'me,' this strong and vigorous body, full of life, they will just find a mummy, dried up, frozen, shriveled! Oh! that wretch! Well, let my heart dry out, if necessary, let my life freeze in this unbearable temperature, but let my friends, Dr. Sarrasin, his family, Jeanne, my little Jeanne, be saved! But if that is to be, then I must escape. So escape I will!"

Pronouncing this last word, Marcel had by instinct placed his hand on the door lock, although he believed himself locked in his room.

To his extreme surprise, the door opened. He could descend, as usual, into the garden where he used to take walks.

"Aha!" he said, "I'm a prisoner in the Central Block but I'm not locked in my room! That's something at least!"

Only, no sooner was Marcel outside than he saw clearly that, although seemingly free, he would not be able to take a step without being escorted by the two giants who answered to the two historic names of Arminius and Sigimer.[1]

He had already wondered more than once, when seeing them in passing, what could be the true function of those two colossal men in gray cassocks, with bull necks and herculean biceps, with red faces bristling with thick moustaches and bushy sideburns!

Now he knew their role. They were the executors of the high commands of Herr Schultze, and for the time being his own personal bodyguards.

Those two giants kept an eye on him, slept at his doorway, followed him around the park. Hanging from their uniforms was a formidable array of revolvers and knives, emphasizing even more the deadly seriousness of their surveillance.

Moreover, they were as mute as fish. Marcel had tried in a diplomatic way to start up a conversation with them, but he received nothing but ferocious looks in reply. Even the offer of a beer, which he believed to be irresistible, had remained unanswered. After fifteen hours of observation, he saw in them only one vice—a single one—the pipe that they took the liberty of smoking when following him. Could Marcel exploit this sole vice of theirs to his advantage? He did not know how, he could not imagine how, but he had vowed to escape and nothing should be neglected that might aid him in this effort.

Now, time was running out. How to go about it?

At the slightest sign of revolt or flight, Marcel was sure of getting two bullets in his head. Even supposing that they might miss, he was still in the middle of this triple line of fortifications, along with its triple row of sentries.

According to his custom, the former student at the Ecole Centrale had framed the question as a mathematical problem.

"Given, a man guarded in plain view by two strapping fellows, unscrupulous, each stronger than he and also armed to the teeth. This man's first move must be to escape the vigilance of his warders. Once this is accomplished, he must escape from a fortified area whose every access is rigorously guarded . . ."

He pondered that double question a hundred times over, and a hundred times over he found the solution impossible.

Did the extreme gravity of the situation finally drive his inventive faculties to the limit? Would it all just depend on chance? It would be hard to say.

It happened that the next day, while Marcel was walking along

His eyes fell upon a shrub by the edge of the garden.

in the park, his eyes fell upon a small shrub by the edge of the garden, and its appearance struck him.

It was a sad looking plant, herbaceous, with alternate leaves, oval, pointed and geminate, with large bell-shaped, single-petaled red flowers supported by an axillary peduncle.

Marcel, who had never studied botany except as an amateur, thought nonetheless that he recognized in that shrub the physical characteristics of the Solanaceae. Just on a hunch, he picked one leaf and chewed it slowly as he walked on.

He had not been wrong. A heaviness in his limbs accompanied by an onset of nausea soon warned him that he held in his hand a natural version of belladonna, which is to say one of the most active of narcotics.

He strolled idly on until he reached a little artificial lake, which stretched out toward the south of the park and which fed a waterfall, quite slavishly copied from the one in the Bois de Boulogne.

"Where do you suppose the water goes from that cascade?" he wondered.

First it flowed into the bed of a small river, which after a dozen or so twists and turns disappeared on the far edge of the park. There had to be some outlet there and, according to all probability, the river had to then flow through it and into one of the subterranean canals which watered the plains outside Stahlstadt.

In this waterway, Marcel saw a way out. It was obviously not a carriage-size entrance, but it was a door to the outside.

"But suppose the canal is barred with iron grillwork!" immediately objected a prudent inner voice.

"Nothing risked, nothing gained! Files weren't invented for cutting through corks, and there are some excellent ones in the laboratory!" replied another, ironic voice, used to dictating bold resolutions.

In two minutes Marcel made his decision. One idea—quite some idea!—had occurred to him, an unrealizable one perhaps, but one that he would try out if death did not overtake him before.

He then calmly returned to the red-flowered shrub, detached

two or three leaves, in such a way that his guards could not help seeing him.

Then, once back in his room, he dried the leaves before the fireplace and mixed them with his tobacco. During the following six days, Marcel, to his extreme surprise, woke up each morning. Had Herr Schultze, whom he no longer saw and no longer met during his walks, changed his mind about getting rid of him? No, this was not very likely, any more than his not following through on his plan to destroy Dr. Sarrasin's town.

So Marcel took full advantage of the permission he had been given to live, and each day he repeated his little maneuver. He was careful, of course, not to smoke the belladonna; to be sure, he had two packets of tobacco, one for his personal use, the other for his daily manipulation. His goal was simply to arouse the curiosity of Arminius and Sigimer. As hardened smokers, those two brutes could not fail to notice the shrub from which he picked his leaves, and copy his operation, trying out the taste of this tobacco mixture.

His calculation was a logical one, and the foreseeable result came about, you might say, mechanically. On the sixth day—the day before the fatal 13th of September—Marcel, looking behind him out of the corner of his eye without appearing to be concerned about it, had the satisfaction of seeing his guardians pick their little provision of green leaves.

An hour later, he noticed they were drying them out in the warmth of the fireplace, rolling them with their large calloused hands, mixing them into their tobacco. They even seemed to be licking their lips in anticipation!

Was Marcel just intending to put Arminius and Sigimer to sleep? No. It was not enough just to escape their surveillance. He still had to test the possibility of getting out through the canal, through the mass of water pouring out, even if that canal measured several kilometers in length. Now this had to be the way out that Marcel imagined. It is true that his chances of perishing were nine out of ten, but the sacrifice of his life, already condemned, had already been decided for a long time.

Evening arrived, and with it his dinner hour, then the moment for his last walk about the park. The inseparable trio started off.

Without hesitation, without losing a minute, Marcel deliberately went toward a building that stood in a clump of trees and that was none other than the workshop for the models. He picked an out-of-the-way bench, stuffed his pipe and began to smoke it.

Immediately, Arminius and Sigimer, who were holding their pipes in readiness, installed themselves on a nearby bench and began to inhale enormous puffs.

The effect of the narcotic was not long in coming.

Not five minutes had passed when the two heavy Teutons were yawning and stretching like bears in a cage. A cloud obscured their eyes, their ears were buzzing; their faces went from pink to dark red, their arms fell inert, their heads rolled back against the bench rail.

Their pipes fell to the ground.

Soon, two sonorous snores arose to join the warbling of the birds, which a perpetual summer retained in the Stahlstadt park.

Marcel was just waiting for this moment. With what impatience, one can imagine, since the evening of the next day at eleven forty-five, France-Ville, condemned by Herr Schultze, would cease to exist.

Marcel rushed into the model workshop. This vast room contained an entire mechanical museum. Models of hydraulic machines, locomotives, steam engines, locomobiles, exhaust pumps, turbines, drills, marine machinery, ship hulls—there were several million masterpieces. There were wooden models of everything that the Schultze factory had manufactured since its founding: miniatures of cannons, torpedoes, and shells were everywhere.

The night was dark, and thus propitious for the bold plan that the young Alsatian had in mind. At the same time that he was implementing his escape plan, he wanted to destroy the model museum of Stahlstadt. Oh! if he were only able to also destroy, along with the casemate and cannon that it sheltered, that enormous, indestructible Tower of the Bull! But he could not even think of it.

Marcel's primary concern was to take a little steel saw that could cut iron and which was hanging from one of the tool racks, which he slipped into his pocket. Then, without hesitation, he struck a match that he drew out of his box, and brought the flame to a corner of the room where boxes of working drawings were heaped up, as well as lightweight models fashioned out of pine.

Then, he left.

A moment later, the fire's intense flames, fed by all these combustible materials, were roaring through all the windows of the room. Immediately the alarm sounded, an electric current set off the bells in the various quarters of Stahlstadt, and the firemen, dragging their steam engines, rushed to the blaze from all directions.

At the same time Herr Schultze, whose presence readily motivated all the workers, appeared.

A few moments later, the steam furnaces had developed sufficient pressure and the powerful pumps began to turn at high speed. A deluge of water was emptied against the walls and even the roof of the model museum. But the fire was stronger than the water, the latter having vaporized on contact with the building, which it was unable to save. In five minutes the inferno had acquired such an intensity that everyone had to give up any hope of mastering it. The spectacle of this blaze was grandiose and awesome.[2]

Marcel, crouched in a corner, did not lose sight of Herr Schultze. The latter was urging the men onward as if they were assaulting a city. Marcel did not need to give a helping hand to the fire. The model museum was isolated in the park, and it was now certain that it would be completely consumed.

At that moment, Herr Schultze, seeing that the building was doomed, roared out the following words: "Ten thousand dollars for the man who saves model no. 3175, enclosed under the central glass case!"

This model was the exact miniature of the enormous cannon

Firemen rushed to the blaze.

perfected by Schultze, and more precious in his eyes than any of the other objects on display in the museum.

But in order to save this model, it would be necessary to plunge into a sheet of fire and go through an atmosphere of unbreathable black smoke. Nine chances out of ten you would never make it back! So, despite the reward of ten thousand dollars, no one answered Herr Schultze's appeal.

Then one man came forward.

It was Marcel.

"I'll go," he said.

"You?" exclaimed Herr Schultze.

"Yes, me!"

"That will not save you, you can be sure, from the sentence of death already pronounced against you!"

"I am not trying to change that; I just want to save that precious model from destruction!"

"Go ahead," replied Herr Schultze, "and I swear that, if you succeed, your next of kin will receive the ten thousand dollars."

"I'll count on that," replied Marcel.

They had brought several of those Galibert apparatuses, ever ready in case of fire, and which permit breathing in areas filled with toxic fumes. Marcel had already used them when he had tried to save the life of little Carl, Madame Bauer's boy, in the mine.

One of those apparatuses, with a tank loaded with air under pressure of several atmospheres, was placed on his back. The pincher was set on his nose, the tube opening was placed in his mouth, and he plunged into the smoke. "Finally," he said to himself, "I've got a fifteen-minute supply of air in the tank! May God now be with me!"

One can easily imagine that the furthest thing from Marcel's mind was to save the model of Herr Schultze's cannon. With his life in peril, he made his way across the smoke-filled room amid showers of sparks and fiery debris, walked among charred beams, which miraculously did not burn him, and at the very moment when the roof began to fall in a great crash of fireworks which the wind swirled high into the clouds, he escaped through a door opening on the opposite side and ran out into the park.

Racing toward the little river, running along its bank to the unknown outlet which would lead him outside Stahlstadt, then plunging in without hesitation, was for Marcel a matter of but a few seconds.

A rapid current swept him into a flood of water seven or eight feet deep. He did not need to find his way, the current bore him straight and true as though he were holding Ariadne's thread. He perceived almost immediately that he was in a narrow canal, a sort of pipe that the overflow of the river had filled almost to the top.

"How long is this pipe?" wondered Marcel. "Everything depends on that! If I have not cleared it in a quarter of an hour, the air will run out, and I'm done for!"

Marcel remained calm. For ten minutes the current pushed him along when suddenly he struck an obstacle.

It was an iron grillwork, mounted on hinges, which blocked the canal.

"I could have expected it!" Marcel simply said to himself.

And, without losing a moment, he pulled out the saw from his pocket and began sawing away on the tongue of the latch.

Five minutes later, and the latch had still not been cut through. The grating remained obstinately shut. Already Marcel could breathe only with extreme difficulty. The air in the tank was almost depleted. Buzzing in his ears, blood in his eyes, congestion in his brain—everything indicated that asphyxia was imminent! He resisted, however, and held his breath in order to consume the least oxygen possible from what remained! . . . And still the latch did not yield!

At that moment, the saw slipped from his grasp.

"Surely God cannot be against me!" he thought.

And, grasping the grillwork with both hands, he began to shake it with the desperate strength that the instinct of self-preservation often triggers.

The grate opened! The latch was finally broken, and the current

The current bore away poor Marcel.

bore away poor Marcel, now almost entirely suffocated, but who was struggling nonetheless to breathe in the very last molecules of air from his tank!

The next day, when Herr Schultze's men ventured into the building entirely consumed by the fire, they found no remains of a human body among the debris or smoldering cinders. It was certain that this courageous young worker had become the victim of his devotion. And that did not surprise those who had known him in the workshops of the factory.

The precious model had not been saved, but the man who possessed all the secrets of the King of Steel had died.

"Heaven is my witness that I wished to spare him any suffering," Herr Schultze said to himself in a matter-of-fact voice. "But, at least that saves me ten thousand dollars!"

And such was the only funeral oration offered for the lost young Alsatian!

10 *An Article from* Unsere Centurie, *a German Journal*

One month prior to the time in which the above events took place, a journal in a salmon-colored jacket entitled Unsere Centurie (Our Century) *published the following article about France-Ville.[1] This article was especially appreciated by those discerning people of the German Empire, perhaps because it claimed to study that city from an exclusively materialist point of view.*

"We have already reported to our readers about the extraordinary phenomenon which has developed on the west coast of the United States. The great American republic, thanks to the large proportion of immigrants which its population contains, has for many years accustomed the world to many surprises. But the latest and most singular is that of a city named France-Ville; the basic concept for it did not even exist five years ago, yet it is today a flourishing city that has rapidly arrived at the pinnacle of prosperity.

"This marvelous city has risen as if by magic on the balmy Pacific coast. We will not check to see, as we have been assured it is the case, whether the original plan and the first concept of this enterprise belong to a Frenchman, a certain Dr. Sarrasin. It is quite possible, given that this doctor can boast of a distant kinship with our illustrious King of Steel. We might also add in passing, it is rumored that the solicitation of a sizable inheritance which was legitimately due Herr Schultze, certainly played more than a small role in the foundation of France-Ville. Everywhere that some good is done in the world, one can be sure of its Germanic origin; it is a truism we are proud to state whenever the occasion presents itself. But, be that as it may, we owe our readers some precise and authentic details about the sudden, spontaneous growth of this model city.

"Do not attempt to look up the name on a map. Even the great 378 volumes in folio of our eminent Tuchtigmann, where you can find every shrub and clump of trees of the Old and New Worlds recorded with rigorous exactitude, even this generous monument of geographic science so useful for snipers does not yet bear the slightest trace of France-Ville. Five years ago, at the place where this new city now sits, there was total wilderness. Its exact location is at the 43rd degree 11'3" north latitude and the 124th degree 41'17" of west longitude from Greenwich.[2] As one can see, this is along the edge of the Pacific Ocean and at the foot of the secondary chain of the Rocky Mountains, the Cascade Mountains, which lie twenty leagues to the north of Cape Bianco, State of Oregon, North America.

"This most attractive spot had been researched and chosen among a great number of other favorable sites. Among the reasons contributing to its adoption are especially the temperate latitude of the northern hemisphere, always the source of earth's top civilizations; its position within a federal republic and in a brand-new state which allowed it to provisionally claim its independence and its rights analogous to those in Europe (which the principality of Monaco possesses), on condition of entering into the Union a certain number of years later; its situation on the ocean, which is becoming more and more the great global trade route; the hilly countryside, fertile and eminently healthy soil; the proximity of a mountain chain which simultaneously blocks winds from the north, from the south and from the east, leaving to the Pacific breeze the care of refreshing the atmosphere of the city; its little river, whose fresh water, sweet, clear, oxygenated by repeated waterfalls and by the rapidity of its course, flows to the sea and remains perfectly pure throughout its course; and, lastly, a natural port formed by a long promontory shaped like a hook and very easy to develop with jetties.

"We will also point out a few secondary advantages: the proximity of fine quarries of marble and stone, deposits of kaolin, and even some traces of gold-bearing nuggets. Indeed, this detail almost made them abandon the territory; the founders of the city feared that gold fever might compromise their plans. But, fortunately, the nuggets were small and rare.

"The choice of the territory, although decided upon only by serious and profound study, had not taken more than a few days and did not call for a special expedition. The knowledge of our world is now far enough advanced for us to be able to obtain information both exact and precise about most regions without even leaving our office.

"This point settled, two commissioners of the organizational committee took the first steamship out of Liverpool, arrived in eleven days in New York, and seven days later in San Francisco, where they hired a steamer to drop them off at the designated site ten hours later.

"Making contact with the Oregon legislature, obtaining a grant of land stretching from the coastal waters to the peak of the Cascade Mountains, over a width of four leagues, and buying off, with a few thousand dollars or so, a half dozen planters who had real or supposed rights to this land, all of this took less than a month.

"By January 1872, the territory was already reconnoitered, measured, staked out, sounded, and an army of twenty thousand Chinese coolies, under the direction of five hundred European foremen and engineers, were on the job. Signs posted throughout the State of California, a special publicity car attached to the express train departing every morning from San Francisco to cross the American continent, and a daily announcement in the twenty-three newspapers of that city had been sufficient to assure the recruitment of workers. It was not even necessary to resort to mass media advertising by means of gigantic letters sculpted into the peaks of the Rocky Mountains that one company had offered to them at reduced rates. We must also say that the influx of Chinese coolies into western America at that time caused a serious disturbance in the wage and salary market.[3] Several states had resorted to mass expulsions of these unfortunates in order to protect the livelihoods of their own residents and to avoid bloody encounters. The founding of France-Ville came just in time to prevent their perishing. Their wages were uniformly fixed at a dollar a day, which was not to be paid them until completion of the project, plus living expenses in kind, distributed by the municipal administration. They thus avoided the disorder and shameful speculation which all too often dishonors these large displacements of population. The fruit of their work was deposited every week in the presence of the delegates, at the great Bank of San Francisco, and each coolie in cashing it had to promise not to return. This was an indispensable precaution to get rid of the yellow population, which, if allowed to remain, would have most certainly lowered the standard and character of the new city. Since the founders had moreover reserved the right to grant or refuse residency in the city, the application of this measure was relatively easy.

"The first great enterprise was the establishment of a branch railroad, linking the new city territory to the trunk line of the Pacific Railroad and connecting it with the city of Sacramento.[4]

During construction, they carefully avoided all landslides or deep trenches, which might have had an unfortunate effect on the health of the workers. These projects, along with those of the harbor, were pushed forward with extraordinary rapidity. In the month of April, the first direct train from New York brought into the France-Ville station the members of the committee, who had remained in Europe until then.

"In the meanwhile, the working plans of the city, the detail of houses and public monuments had been halted.

"It was not that materials were lacking: from the first news about this project, American industry had rushed ahead to flood the wharves with all imaginable construction materials. The founders were only faced with the difficulty of choice. They decided that cut stone would be reserved for national edifices and for general ornamentation, whereas the houses would be of brick. Not, of course, the sloppily molded bricks with a lump of earth more or less baked, but light bricks, perfectly regular in shape, weight, and density, transpierced lengthwise with a series of cylindrical and parallel holes. Assembled end to end, these holes were to form conduits that were open at both ends, and thus permit the air to circulate freely through the exterior envelope of the houses, as in the interior partitions.* This arrangement had, at the same time, the excellent advantage of deadening sounds and providing a complete independence for each apartment.

"The committee did not claim to impose any standard design of a house on the builders—on the contrary, they were opposed to all insipid and boring uniformity. But they did set a certain number of fixed rules, which architects were supposed to follow:

"1. Every house will be separate on a lot planted with trees, lawn, and flowers. It will be the property of a single family.

---

*These designs, as well as the general idea of Well-Being, are borrowed from the scientist Benjamin Ward Richardson, member of the London Royal Society.[5] (*Author's note*)

The establishment of a branch railroad

"2. No house shall have more than three stories; air and light may not be monopolized by some to the detriment of others.

"3. The front of all houses shall be set back thirty meters from the street from which they will be separated by a fence, chest high. The distance between fence and façade is to be arranged as a flower garden.

"4. The walls will be made of certified tubular bricks, in conformity with the model. Every liberty is left to the architects as to ornamentation.

"5. The roofs shall be slightly inclined in four directions, covered with asphalt, edged with a cornice, high enough to make accidents impossible, and carefully guttered for the immediate drainage of rain water.

"6. Houses will be built over an open basement, with openings on all sides and thus providing under the ground-floor a subsoil of aeration as well as a kind of hall. The water pipes and drains will be exposed, installed against a central pillar in such a way that their state can be easily verified, and in case of fire to have easy access to water. The floor of this level, rising five or six centimeters above the street level, will be covered with clean sand. A door and special stairway will put it in direct communication with the kitchen and related rooms, and all household operations can be conducted without offending one's eyes or nose.

"7. Kitchens and related rooms, contrary to custom, are situated on the upper floor and connected with the terrace which will thus become a large open-aired annex. An elevator, moved by mechanical power, will permit the transport of all loads to this floor, and artificial light and water will be provided at reduced prices.

"8. The layout of the interior rooms is left to the individual's desires. But those two dangerous sources of disease — veritable hotbeds of miasma and poison — are absolutely forbidden: carpets and wallpaper. The floors, artistically constructed of precious woods assembled as mosaics by gifted cabinetmakers, would be a total waste if they were to be buried under wool fabrics of dubious cleanliness. As for the walls, clad in varnished bricks, they present to the eye the splendor and variety of the indoor apartments of Pompeii with a luxury of colors and longevity which wallpaper, loaded with its thousand subtle poisons, has never been able to rival. They are washable, like mirrors and windows, and can be scrubbed like floors and ceilings. Thus not one single unhealthy germ can reside there.

"9. Every bedroom is apart from the bathroom. We cannot recommend too highly making this room, where a third of one's life is spent, the largest, most aerated, and at the same time the simplest. It should serve only for sleeping: four chairs, an iron bed, supplied with a spring mattress and a wool mattress, which should be beaten often, are the only pieces of furniture needed. Eiderdown quilts and heavy bedcovers, powerful allies of epidemics, are naturally excluded. Good wool blankets, light and warm, easy to wash, can replace them. Curtains and drapes are not forbidden, but they should be made of material capable of being washed frequently.

"10. Each room has its fireplace, heated according to one's tastes by either wood or coal, but each fireplace has a corresponding air vent from outdoors. As for the smoke, instead of rising into the air from the rooftops, it is carried through subterranean conduits which suck it into special burners, supplied at the city's expense to the rear of the houses, at the rate of one burner for each two hundred inhabitants. There, the smoke is stripped of its carbon particles and is then discharged in a colorless state into the atmosphere at a height of thirty-five meters above ground.

"Such are the ten general rules, imposed for the construction of each private dwelling.

"The overall design of the city is itself no less well thought out:

"First, the city plan is essentially simple and regular, in such a way as to adapt itself to all situations. The streets, crossing at right angles, occur at regular intervals, are of standard width, bordered with trees, and designated by numbers in ascending order.

"From half-kilometer to half-kilometer, streets increasing in width by a third take the name of boulevard or avenue, and have along one side an open space for tramways and metropolitan trains.

At every crossroad, a public park has been set aside and adorned with beautiful copies of masterpieces of sculpture, until the time when the artists of France-Ville have produced original pieces worthy of replacing them.[6]

"All industries and commercial ventures are freely permitted.

"In order to obtain the right of residence, it is sufficient—provided that good references are supplied—to be able to perform a useful or liberal profession in industry, science, or the arts, and to pledge to obey the laws of the city. Idle lives will not be tolerated.

"Public buildings are already in great number. The most important are the cathedral, a certain number of chapels, museums, libraries, schools and gymnasiums, all of which are equipped with the comforts and an understanding of hygienic appropriateness that are truly worthy of a great city.

"Needless to say that children are required, from the age of four, to perform the intellectual and physical exercises which alone can develop their cerebral and muscular strength. They must be brought up with such a rigorous sense of cleanliness that they consider a spot on their simple clothes as a dishonor.

"This question of individual and collective cleanliness is, moreover, the major preoccupation of the founders of France-Ville. To clean, clean ceaselessly, to destroy as soon as they are formed those miasmas which constantly emanate from a human collective, such is the primary job of the central government. To this effect, the products of the sewers are centralized outside the city, treated by procedures which permit their condensation and daily transportation into the countryside.

"Water flows everywhere in great abundance. Streets are paved with tarred wood, and the stone sidewalks are as gleaming as a flagstone in a Dutch courtyard. Food markets are subject to ongoing surveillance, and severe penalties are applied to wholesalers who dare to jeopardize the public health. A merchant who sells a spoiled egg, a tainted chunk of meat, a liter of adulterated milk is simply treated as the poisoner that he is. This necessary and scrupulous task is confided to the sanitary police force, composed of men of experience in these matters, true specialists, trained at the most prestigious universities.

"Their jurisdiction extends also to large, centralized laundries that contain steam-driven machinery, artificial dryers, and special disinfectant chambers. No body linens are returned to their owners without having been truly bleached to the core, and special care is taken never to process two different families' wash in the same batch. This simple precaution is especially effective.

"Hospitals are not numerous because a system of home medical assistance is standard, and they are reserved for the homeless and a few exceptional cases. It goes without saying that the idea of making a hospital an edifice larger than any other and of thus creating an enormous center of infection by congregating there seven or eight hundred patients would never have entered the minds of founders of this model city. Instead of seeking systematically to unite all patients, they only seek to isolate them. It is in the patients' best interest as well as the general public's. Even in private homes, isolating the patient as much as possible in a separate wing is recommended. The hospitals are nothing more than limited and exceptional structures for the temporary accommodation of a few urgent cases. Twenty, thirty patients at most can be found there—each having a private room—centralized in lightweight houses constructed of pine lumber, which are burnt annually and replaced. The units are all designed from the same model and have the advantage of being able to be transported easily to any place in the city, according to need, and reproduced as often as necessary.

"An ingenious innovation linked to this health care system is that of a corps of experienced home-care nurses specially trained for this profession, and offered by the central administration to the public at large. These women, chosen with care, are a most precious and devoted complement to doctors. They bring to the bosom of the families the practical knowledge so needed and so often missing in a moment of danger, and it is their mission to prevent the propagation of disease as well as to minister to the sick.

"There would be no end to it if one wished to enumerate fully

France-Ville

all the hygienic improvements that the founders of this new city have inaugurated. Upon his arrival, each citizen receives a little brochure in which the most important principles of a life regulated by science are explained in a simple, clear language.

"He sees there that the perfect balance of all his activities is one of the basic necessities of health; that work and repose are equally indispensable to his organs; that fatigue of the mind is as necessary as of the muscles; that nine-tenths of all disease are due to contagion transmitted through the air or in food. Accordingly, it is impossible to surround one's house and person with too many sanitary safeguards. Avoid the use of poisonous stimulants; get plenty of physical exercise; conscientiously, every day, do some functional task; drink good pure water; eat meats and healthy vegetables simply prepared; sleep regularly seven to eight hours at night. These are the ABCs of good health.

"Starting with these basic principles set forth by the founders, we have spoken of this unique city as if it were already established. This is because, in truth, once the first houses were built, others have subsequently risen from the earth as though by magic. You need to have visited the Far West in order to understand this sudden springing up of cities. Still a wilderness until January 1872, the site counted six thousand houses in 1873 and nine thousand by 1874, with all city buildings fully occupied.

"It must be said that speculation played its role in this unheard-of success. Constructed for the most part on immense properties, and valueless at the outset, the houses were sold at very moderate prices, and rented under very modest conditions. The absence of any city tax, the political independence of this small territory, the attraction of its novelty, and the mildness of its climate all contributed to encouraging emigration. At present, France-Ville counts nearly a hundred thousand inhabitants.

"Moreover, another interesting fact is that the results of this sanitary experiment have been quite conclusive. While the annual mortality rate in the most favored cities of old Europe or the New World has never noticeably gone below three percent, in France-Ville the average over these five years is only one and a half percent. And that figure includes a small bout of malaria which marked their first year. Last year's percentage, by itself, was but one and a quarter. An even more important consideration is that, almost without exception, all the deaths registered were due to specific maladies, most of which were hereditary. At the same time, accidental illnesses have been a great deal rarer, more limited, and less dangerous than in any other environment. As for outright epidemics, none has been reported.

"It will be interesting to follow the continuing developments of this endeavor, and especially curious to find out if the influence of such a scientific regime over a generation—and even more so over several generations—might not help to weaken the hereditary predisposition for disease.

"'It is assuredly not too much to hope for,' wrote one of the founders of this astounding city, 'and, if so, what a grand result it would be! People living up to ninety or a hundred years old and dying only from old age, like most animals and plants!'

"Such a tantalizing dream!

"Nevertheless, if we may be permitted to express our sincere opinion, we have only moderate faith in the definitive success of this experiment. We see therein an inherent—and likely fatal—flaw since it is in the hands of a committee where the Latin element dominates and the Germanic element is systematically excluded. That is a distressing symptom. Since the beginning of the world, nothing durable has been created except by Germany, and nothing definitive can be produced without her. The founding fathers of France-Ville will have been able to clear the land, to elucidate a few specific points; but it is not in this corner of America, but rather on the borders of Syria, that we will someday see arise the true model city."[7]

11
Dinner at Dr. Sarrasin's

On the 13th of September—only a few hours before the time designated by Herr Schultze for the destruction of France-Ville—neither the governor nor any of the residents had any notion of the frightful danger threatening them.

It was seven o'clock in the evening.

Nestled in thick beds of laurel roses and tamarinds, the city stretched graciously to the foot of the Cascade Mountains and presented its marble docks to the soft, caressing waves of the Pacific. Watered with care and refreshed by the breeze, the streets of France-Ville offered to the eye a cheerful and animated sight. The shade trees rustled gently. The lawns grew green. The flowers in their beds, spreading their colorful petals all at the same time, exhaled sweet fragrances. The very houses seemed to smile, quiet and coquettish in their whiteness. The air was warm, and the sky as blue as the sea that one could see glistening at the end of the long avenues.

A traveler arriving in the city would have been struck by the healthy appearance of the residents, by the bustling activity in the streets. They were just closing the doors of the Academies of painting, music, sculpture and the library, which were all in the same neighborhood. There, excellent public courses were offered in small classes, which permitted each student to get the very most out of each lesson. The crowd leaving these establishments caused a certain congestion, but no exclamation of impatience, no outcry could be heard. The general aspect was of calm and satisfaction.

It was not in the center of the city but on the Pacific shore that the Sarrasin family had built its home. Their house was among the first constructed in France-Ville, and the doctor had come to settle there definitively with his wife and his daughter Jeanne.

Octave, the impromptu millionaire, had wanted to remain in Paris, but he no longer had Marcel to serve as his mentor.

The two friends had almost lost sight of each other since the days when they lived together on the rue du Roi de Sicile. When the doctor had emigrated with his wife and daughter to the Oregon coast, Octave had remained behind on his own. He was soon spending less and less time at school, where his father had wanted him to continue his studies, and he failed his last exam, whereas his friend had left at the top of his class.

Until then, Marcel had been Octave's compass; now he was incapable of leading himself. When the young Alsatian had left, his childhood friend ended up living what is often called the "high life." In this case the word was all the more appropriate since he spent a large part of his life atop the seat of an enormous coach with four horses, constantly traveling between Avenue Marigny, where he had an apartment, and the various racetracks of the suburb. Octave Sarrasin, who three months earlier scarcely knew how to stay in the saddle in the riding school where he rented a horse by the hour, had suddenly become one of the men in France most deeply versed in the mysteries of hippology. His erudition was borrowed from an English groom whom he had attached to his service and who completely dominated him by the extent of his special knowledge.

Tailors, saddle-makers, and bootmakers took up his mornings. His evenings belonged to the small theaters and the salon of a new club, which had just opened at the corner of rue Tronchet, and which Octave had chosen because the people that he found there rendered to his wealth homage that his personal merits alone had not received elsewhere. These society people seemed to him the ideal of distinction. Of particular attention was a sumptuously framed list, which stood out in the waiting room and scarcely held any but foreign names. Titles abounded, and, in counting them, one might have believed that one was in the antechamber of some heraldic university. But if you were to penetrate deeper, you would think you were in a living exposition of ethnology. All the big noses and all the bilious complexions of the two worlds seemed to have arranged to meet each other there. Supremely well dressed, moreover, were these cosmopolitan personages, although a marked taste for whitish clothes revealed the eternal aspiration of yellow or black races toward the color of the "pale faces."

Octave Sarrasin seemed a young god among these people. They quoted him, copied his ties, accepted his judgments as articles of faith. And he, intoxicated by this sweet flattery, seemed unaware that he was regularly losing money at baccarat or the races. Perhaps some club members, in their quality as Orientals, thought they had rights to the Begum's inheritance. In any case, they knew how to attract it into their pockets through a slow but continuous process.

In this new life, the bonds between Octave and Marcel Bruckmann had quickly grown loose. The two comrades scarcely exchanged a letter at long intervals. What could there be in common between this keen worker, solely occupied in bringing his intelligence to a superior degree in culture and in strength, and the pretty boy, all swollen with his opulence, his mind stuffed with stories from the club and the stable?

We know under what circumstances Marcel had left Paris, at first to observe the activities of Herr Schultze, who had just founded Stahlstadt, the rival of France-Ville, on the same independent land of the United States, and then to enter the service of the King of Steel.

For two years Octave led his useless and dissipated existence. Finally, the ennui of these hollow pleasures overcame him. And, one fine day, after having allowed several millions to be devoured, he rejoined his father—which saved him from impending ruin, one more moral than physical. He now lived in France-Ville in the doctor's house.

His sister Jeanne, judging from her appearance at least, was at that time a delightful young girl nineteen years of age. Her stay of four years in her new country had bestowed upon her all the American qualities, added to all her French graces. Her mother sometimes said that having Jeanne as a constant companion made her realize that she had never before known the charm of such absolute closeness.

As for Mme Sarrasin, since the return of her prodigal son, her prince, the eldest son of her hopes, she was as completely happy as one can be on this earth, for she participated in all the good that her husband could do and was doing, thanks to his immense fortune.

That evening, Dr. Sarrasin had received at his table two of his most intimate friends, Colonel Hendon—a piece of worn debris from the Civil War, who had left an arm in Pittsburg and an ear in Seven Oaks, but who was still as good on a chess board as anyone —and Mr. Lentz, superintendent of schools in the new city.

The conversation turned to the plans of city administration and the results already obtained in the various public sectors: institutions, hospitals, mutual assistance funds.

Mr. Lentz, following the doctor's proposal that the teaching of religion not be forgotten, had founded several primary schools where the concerns of the teacher tended to develop the child's spirit by submitting him to an intellectual gymnastics, calculated in such a way as to follow the natural evolution of his faculties. They taught him to love a science before stuffing himself with it, avoiding that knowledge which Montaigne claims "floats on the surface of the brain" but does not penetrate the student's understanding, making him neither wiser nor better. Later on, a well-prepared intelligence would be able, by itself, to choose its route and follow it with profit.

Hygiene was of utmost importance in such an orderly education. For man, both body and soul must be equally served: if either is defective, he suffers from it, and the soul will soon succumb.[1]

At this stage, France-Ville had attained the highest degree of prosperity, not only material but intellectual as well. There, in its public meetings, were assembled the greatest thinkers of the two worlds. Artists, painters, sculptors, and musicians, attracted by the reputation of this city, flocked to it. Young Francevillagers studied under the masters of the arts and showed promise of some day bringing fame to this corner of America. It was predicted that this

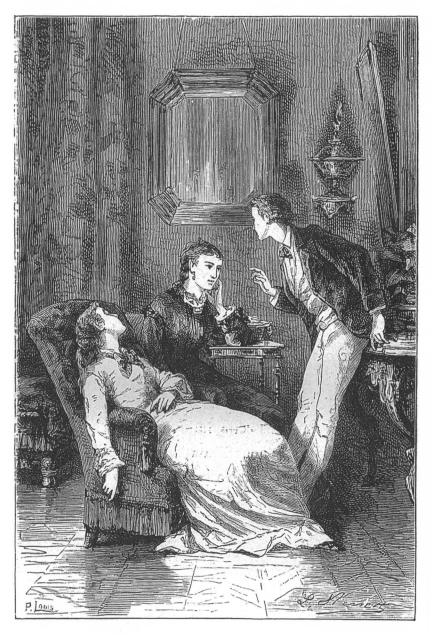

Octave, the prodigal son, returned home.

new Athens, French in origin, would soon take its place among the great cities of the world.

It should be added that students in the high schools were provided with a military education along with their civil education. Upon leaving school, the young men were quite proficient not only in manipulating arms but also in the basic elements of strategy and tactics.

When discussing this topic of conversation, Colonel Hendon declared that he was delighted by all his recruits.

"They are," said he, "already accustomed to forced marches, to fatigue, to all physical exercises. Our army is composed of all its citizens, and when needed, they will prove to be both seasoned and disciplined."

France-Ville had the best of relationships with all the neighboring states, for it had taken every occasion to assist them whenever it could. But in matters of self-interest, ingratitude sometimes speaks so loudly that the doctor and his friends had not lost sight of the maxim that Heaven helps those who help themselves.

They were at the end of dinner; the dessert had just been removed, and according to the Anglo-Saxon custom which they chose to follow, the ladies had just left the table.

Dr. Sarrasin, Octave, Colonel Hendon, and Mr. Lentz continued their conversation and began to discuss the highest questions of economic policy, when a servant entered and handed the doctor his newspaper.

It was the *New York Herald*. This honorable paper had always shown itself to be extremely favorable toward the foundation, then the development of France-Ville. And the notables of the city were in the habit of seeking within its columns the possible variations of public opinion in the United States concerning them. This community of contented people, free and independent, on this small neutral territory, had prompted many envious citizens to attack them. In any case, the *New York Herald* continued to support them, and did not fail to show its expression of admiration and esteem.

While talking, Dr. Sarrasin had pulled off the wrapper from the paper and cast a glance mechanically on the lead article.

To his stupefaction, he read the following few lines, to himself at first, and then aloud, to the surprise and deepest indignation of his friends:

"New York, September 8th. A violent attack against the rights of man will shortly be carried out. We have learned from a reliable source that formidable instruments of war are being manufactured in Stahlstadt with the aim of attacking and destroying France-Ville, the city of French origin. We do not know whether the United States will be able or should intervene in this struggle,[2] which will renew tensions between the Latin and Saxon races; but we denounce this odious abuse of power. May France-Ville not waste an instant in preparing its defenses . . . etc."

12 *The Council*

The King of Steel's hatred for Dr. Sarrasin's work was no secret. Everyone knew that he had come to set up his own city against theirs. But no one believed that he would go so far as to attack this peaceful city and to attempt to destroy it in one fatal blow. Yet, the article in the *New York Herald* was quite clear. The correspondents of this powerful paper had somehow uncovered the plans of Herr Schultze, and—as they said—there was not a moment to lose!

The worthy doctor remained a moment in confusion. Like all honest souls, he refused as long as possible to believe in such evil. It seemed impossible to him that one could push perversity to the point of wishing to destroy, for no reason and out of pure malice, a city which was in many ways the common property of mankind. "Just think that our death rate this year will be under one and a quarter percent!" he exclaimed naively, "that we do not have anyone over ten years of age who does not know how to read, that neither murder nor theft has been committed here since the foundation of France-Ville! And to think that barbarians[1] would come destroy such a successful experiment in its early stages! No! I cannot believe that a chemist, that a scientist, were he German a hundred times over, could be capable of such a thing!"

It was necessary, however, to trust in the evidence of a paper that was thoroughly devoted to the doctor's work and take counsel without delay. The first moment of despondency now past, Dr. Sarrasin collected himself and addressed his friends:

"Gentlemen," he said to them, "you are members of the Civic Council, and it is your responsibility as well as mine to take all necessary measures for the safety of the city. What is our first move to be?"

"Is there any possibility of conciliation?" asked Mr. Lentz. "Can we honorably avoid this war?"

"That's impossible," replied Octave. "It is obvious that Herr Schultze wants it, come what may. His hatred will accept no compromise!"

"So be it!" exclaimed the doctor. "We must come to an agreement in order to be in a position to answer him. Do you believe, Colonel, that there is a way to defend ourselves against the cannons of Stahlstadt?"

"Any human force can be effectively countered by another human force," replied Colonel Hendon, "but it is not our duty to think up a defense with the same arms that Herr Schultze will use to attack us. The construction of war machines capable of resisting his would require much time, and I do not believe that we could manufacture them, since we do not have such workshops. We have but one chance of safety: keep the enemy from arriving at our doors and making a blockade impossible."

"I am going to call a Council meeting immediately," said Dr. Sarrasin.

He preceded his guests into his office.

It was a modestly furnished room, three sides of which were covered by shelves of books, while the fourth, under some pictures and

"Do you believe, Colonel, that there is a way to defend ourselves?"

art objects, contained a row of numbered telephone mouthpieces, like so many ear-trumpets.

"Thanks to the telephone," he said, "we can hold council in France-Ville and remain each in his own home."

The doctor touched an alarm bell which immediately communicated his call to the home of all the Council members. In less than three minutes, the word "present!" was carried in succession along each communicating wire, announcing that the Council members were ready. The doctor placed himself in front of the mouthpiece of his sending apparatus, shook a little bell, and said:

"The session is now open. My honorable friend, Colonel Hendon, has the floor to make a communication of the highest gravity to the Civic Council."

The colonel placed himself before the telephone and, after having read the article from the *New York Herald,* requested that the first measures be taken immediately.

Scarcely had he concluded when number 6 asked him a question:

"Did the colonel believe defense possible, if the means on which he was counting to halt the enemy did not succeed?"

Colonel Hendon replied affirmatively. The question and the response had arrived instantaneously to each invisible member of the Council, just like the explanations that had preceded.

Number 7 asked how much time, in his estimation, the citizens of France-Ville had to ready themselves.

The colonel did not know, but it was essential to act as if they were to be attacked within two weeks.

Number 2: "Must we await the attack or would it be better to prevent it?"

"We must do everything possible to prevent it," replied the Colonel, "and if we are threatened by an invasion from the sea, we must blow up Herr Schultze's ships with our torpedoes."

On this proposition, Dr. Sarrasin offered to call for advice the most distinguished chemists, as well as the most experienced artillery officers, and to give them the responsibility of examining the plans which Colonel Hendon could supply them with.

Question from Number 1:

"What is the needed sum to begin immediately the defense efforts?"

"It would take some fifteen to twenty million dollars."

Number 4: "I propose the immediate convocation of the plenary assembly of citizens."

President Sarrasin: "I place this proposition up for vote."

Two rings on each phone announced that it was adopted unanimously.

It was eight-thirty. The Civic Council had not lasted eighteen minutes and had not inconvenienced anyone.

The people's assembly was convoked in an equally simple way and nearly as expeditiously. No sooner had Dr. Sarrasin transmitted the vote of the Council at the town hall, again via the intermediary of the telephone, than an electric carillon was set into motion at the top of every column placed at the 280 crossroads in the city. These columns were mounted by luminous dials whose hands, moved by electricity, had immediately stopped at eight-thirty, the hour of the convocation.

All the residents, alerted at the same time by this unsettling call, which continued for more than fifteen minutes, promptly raised their eyes to look at the nearest dial and, understanding that a national duty was calling them to the city hall, hurried off to the meeting.

At the appointed hour, that is to say in less than forty-five minutes, the assembly was complete and full. Dr. Sarrasin was there already at the place of honor, surrounded by the entire Council. At the foot of the rostrum, Colonel Hendon was waiting for his turn to speak.

Most of the citizens had already been apprised of the reason for the meeting. Indeed, the discussion of the Civic Council, automatically transcribed by the telephone at the town hall, had been immediately sent to the newspapers, which had put out a special edition, posted in the form of notices all over the city.

The city hall was an immense nave with a glass roof, where air circulated freely, and was abundantly lighted by a row of gas jets hanging from the arches of the vaulted ceiling.

The crowd was standing, calm, almost silent. Their faces were cheerful. Good health, a full and regular life, and awareness of their own moral strength placed them above any emotional alarm or anger.

As soon as the president touched the hand bell, a profound silence fell.

The colonel mounted the rostrum.

There, in a language both sober and strong, with neither useless ornamentation nor pretentious oratory—the language of men who, knowing what they are saying, spell things out clearly because they understand them—Colonel Hendon spoke of the inveterate hatred that Herr Schultze bore against France, Dr. Sarrasin, and his work, as well as the formidable preparations announced by the *New York Herald*, which were intended to destroy France-Ville and its inhabitants.

He explained that it was up to them to choose the best course to follow, and that many people without courage and without patriotism would perhaps prefer giving away their land and allow aggressors to take over their new country. But the colonel was sure in advance that such pusillanimous notions would find no echo among his fellow citizens. Men who had understood the grandeur of the goal pursued by the founders of this model city, men who had known how to accept its laws, were of necessity men of courage and intelligence. Sincere representatives and soldiers of progress, they would prefer doing all they could to save this incomparable city, this glorious monument raised to the art of bettering man's fate! Their duty was to give their lives for the cause that they represented!

An immense round of applause greeted this peroration.

Several orators came to second the motion of Colonel Hendon.

Dr. Sarrasin moved to set up without delay a Defense Council, which would be charged with taking all necessary measures in the secrecy required of military operations. The proposal was adopted.

In the same session, a member of the Civic Council suggested the appropriateness of voting a provisory credit of five million dollars, destined for the first stage. All hands rose to ratify the measure.

At twenty-five minutes past ten, the meeting was over, and the residents of France-Ville, having appointed their leaders, were about to retire when an unexpected incident occurred.

At the rostrum, which had been empty for a moment, there now stood someone with the strangest demeanor. This man had appeared as if by magic. His energetic face showed that he was in a state of fearful excitement, but his attitude was calm and resolute. His clothes half-stuck to his body and still caked with mud and his bloodied forehead suggested that he had just passed through some terrible ordeal.

At the sight of him, everyone paused. With a gesture of command, the unknown man had created immobility and silence.

Who was he? Where did he come from? No one, not even Dr. Sarrasin, attempted to ask him.

Besides, they were soon informed as to his identity.

"I have just escaped from Stahlstadt," he said. "Herr Schultze had condemned me to death. God permitted me to come before you just in time to attempt to save you. I am not unknown to all of you here. My respected master, Dr. Sarrasin, will be able to affirm, I hope, that despite my present appearance which makes me unrecognizable even to him, you may have confidence in Marcel Bruckmann!"

"Marcel!" cried out at the same moment the doctor and Octave.

Both were about to rush toward him, but a new gesture from him stopped them.

It was indeed Marcel, miraculously saved. After he had forced

At the rostrum, there now stood someone with the strangest demeanor.

open the grillwork of the canal, nearly asphyxiated, the current had carried him on like a lifeless body. But, fortunately, that grill closed off the outermost perimeter of Stahlstadt, and two minutes later Marcel was cast upon the shore, free at last, but only barely alive!

During long hours, the courageous young man had remained lying there unmoving, in the middle of that somber night, in that deserted country, far from all help.

When he returned to his senses, it was daylight. Then he remembered! . . . Thanks to God, he was finally outside that cursed Stahlstadt! He was no longer a prisoner. All his thinking was then concentrated on Dr. Sarrasin, his friends, his fellow citizens!

"I must reach them!" he cried out from the shore of the river.

By a supreme effort, Marcel managed to get to his feet.

Ten leagues separated him from France-Ville, ten leagues to cover, with no train, no vehicle, no horse, across this entirely deserted countryside surrounding the terrible City of Steel. Those ten leagues, he crossed without taking an instant to rest, and at a quarter past ten that night he arrived at the first houses of the city of Dr. Sarrasin.

The notices posted on the walls told him everything. He understood that the residents had been forewarned of the danger threatening them; but he also understood that they did not realize how imminent the danger was, or how strange its nature.

The catastrophe, planned by Herr Schultze, was to occur that very evening at eleven forty-five. It was already ten-fifteen!

Making one last effort, Marcel crossed the city with great speed, and, at ten twenty-five, at the very moment when the assembly was going to break up, he climbed up to the rostrum.

"It is not in a month, my friends," he cried out, "nor even a week, that the first danger may befall you! In less than an hour, a disaster without precedent, a rain of fire and steel is going to fall upon your city! At this very moment I am speaking to you, a weapon worthy of Hell and able to shoot over a distance of ten leagues, is being aimed at France-Ville. I have seen it. All women and children must immediately seek shelter in cellars which present some guarantee of solidity, or else flee the city now to find some refuge in the mountains! All healthy men must prepare to fight fire by every means possible! Fire, for the moment, is your only enemy! Neither army nor soldiers are on the march. Your adversary has disdained ordinary means of attack. If the plans and calculations of one man, whose power for evil is known to you, are finally materialized—if Herr Schultze has not made the first mistake of his life—fires will break out suddenly in a hundred different locations in France-Ville! It is on these hundred different fronts that we'll have to face his flames! Whatever may happen, it is the population that must be saved; if your houses or monuments cannot be saved, should the whole city even be destroyed, money and time will be able to restore them!"

In Europe, they would have taken Marcel for a madman. But in America, people would never take it into their heads to deny the miracles of science, even the most unexpected ones. They listened to the young engineer, and, on the advice of Dr. Sarrasin, they believed him.

The crowd, convinced as much by the tone of the orator as by his words, obeyed him without even dreaming of disputing him. The doctor vouched for Marcel Bruckmann. That was enough.

Orders were immediately given, and messengers left in all directions to spread them.

As for the inhabitants of the city, some returned to their homes, resigned to undergo the horrors of a bombardment; others, on foot, on horseback, or by carriage fled to the countryside and took refuge beyond the first slopes of the Cascade Mountains. During this time, all able-bodied men rushed to meet on the central square and at a few other special locations indicated by the doctor. They gathered together there all materials that could serve to fight the fires, that is to say, water, earth and sand.

Meanwhile, back in the hall, discussion and deliberation continued.

It seemed as though Marcel was obsessed by an idea that left no room for anything else in his mind. He spoke no more, but his lips murmured these few words:

145

"At eleven forty-five! Is it possible that this cursed Schultze will get the better of us with his diabolical invention?"

Suddenly, Marcel pulled a notebook from his pocket. He made a gesture to request silence, and, pencil in hand, he scribbled feverishly a few figures on one of the pages of his pad. And then, little by little, his brow cleared and his face suddenly became radiant:

"Ah! my friends!" he cried out, "either these figures here are lying, or everything we fear is going to disappear like a nightmare when confronted by the evidence of a ballistic problem whose solution I sought in vain until this very moment! Herr Schultze has made a mistake! The danger he threatened us with is but a dream! For once, his science is faulty![2] Nothing he announced can happen! His dreadful shell will pass over France-Ville without touching us, and if there remains something else to fear from him, it will only be in the future!"

What did Marcel mean? They could not understand him!

But then the young Alsatian showed them the result of the calculations he had just made. His clear, vibrant voice explained his figures in such a way as to render it luminous even for the ignorant. It was clarity following obscurity, calm following anguish. Not only would the projectile not touch the doctor's city; it would not touch "anything at all." It was destined to be swallowed up in space!

Dr. Sarrasin gave a gesture indicating approval of Marcel's calculations and then, suddenly pointing a finger toward the room's luminous clock, said: "In three minutes, we'll find out which one of the two, Schultze or Marcel Bruckmann, is right! Be that as it may, my friends, let us not regret any of the precautions taken, or neglect anything that might foil the inventions of our enemy. His strike, if it should fail, as Marcel has just given us hope, will not be the last! Schultze's hatred will not recognize defeat and be stopped by one failure."

"Come!" exclaimed Marcel.

And all followed him outside onto the great square.

The three minutes passed. Eleven forty-five rang from the bell tower. Four seconds later, very high in the sky, a dark mass flew

Very high in the sky, a dark mass flew over them.

over them and, as rapid as a heartbeat, soon passed from view beyond the city with a sinister whistling sound.

"Bon voyage!" shouted Marcel, breaking into a laugh. "With that initial speed, Herr Schultze's cannon shell has already exceeded the limits of the atmosphere and can never again fall upon terrestrial soil!"

Two minutes later, a detonation was heard, a sort of dull rumble, that one might have thought emerged from the entrails of the earth!

It was the noise of the cannon arriving from the Tower of the Bull. This sound was arriving one hundred and thirteen seconds behind the projectile itself, which was moving with a speed of one hundred and fifty leagues per hour.[3]

13

Letter from Marcel Bruckmann to Professor Schultze, Stahlstadt

"France-Ville, September 14

"It seems appropriate for me to inform the King of Steel that I most fortunately passed over the border of his possessions the evening before yesterday, preferring my own health to that of the model for the Schultze cannon.

"In presenting my farewell, I should be completely lacking in my duties if I failed to let you know, in turn, my own secrets; but you can rest easy, for you will not pay for this knowledge with your life.

"My name is not Schwartz, and I am not Swiss. I am Alsatian. My name is Marcel Bruckmann. I am a passably competent engineer, according to your own judgment, but above all I am French. You have shown yourself to be the implacable enemy of my country, my friends, my family. You devised odious plans to destroy all that I love. I risked everything, I did all I could to learn of them. I shall do anything now to foil them.

"I hasten to inform you that your first shot has failed and, thank heaven, did not hit its mark. Nor could it have! Your cannon is no less a wondrous piece of armament, but the projectiles that it discharges—and may yet discharge—with such enormous charges of powder will never hurt anyone! In fact, they will never fall anywhere! I suspected that this was the case, and now it is, to your greater glory, an established fact that Herr Schultze has invented a terrifying cannon that is . . . entirely harmless.

"So it is with great pleasure that we tell you that we saw your all-too-perfect shell pass above our city last night at eleven forty-five and four seconds. It was heading west, circling in a vacuum, and it will continue on its route around the earth until the end of time. A projectile, raised to an initial speed twenty times faster than its primary speed, that is to say ten thousand meters per second, can never 'fall'! Its forward motion, combined with the attraction of the earth, destines it to continue circling our globe forever.

"You should have known that.

"I hope, moreover, that the cannon in Tower of the Bull has been completely ruined by this first trial. After all, two hundred thousand dollars is not too much to pay for the pleasure of having endowed the planetary system with a new star and the world with its second satellite!

"Marcel Bruckmann."

An express mail left France-Ville immediately for Stahlstadt. One must forgive Marcel for not having been able to resist the jeering satisfaction of immediately sending this letter to Herr Schultze.

Indeed, Marcel was right when he said the infamous projectile, at that speed and circling above the atmosphere, would no longer fall to the earth's surface. He was also right when he hoped that, due to its enormous charge of pyroxylin, the cannon in the Tower of the Bull had most likely been damaged beyond use.

The receipt of this letter was a harsh discovery for Herr Schultze, a dreadful shock to his vanity. Reading it turned him livid, and after reading it his head fell to his chest as though he had been bludgeoned. He did not recover from that state of prostration until a quarter of an hour later, but with such a raging fury! Arminius and Sigimer alone could have described those tantrums of rage.

However, Herr Schultze was not a man to admit defeat. The fight between Marcel and himself would be to the death. Did he not still have those projectiles loaded with liquid carbon dioxide that less powerful but more practical cannons could shoot for a short distance?

Calming himself with great effort, the King of Steel returned to his office and returned once more to his work.

It was clear that France-Ville, more threatened than ever, could not afford to neglect anything in preparing its defenses.

14 *Preparing for Combat*

If the danger was no longer imminent, it was still serious. Marcel informed Dr. Sarrasin and his friends of all that he knew about the preparations of Herr Schultze and his engines of destruction. And the next day the Defense Council, of which he was a member, began to discuss a plan of resistance and to prepare for its execution.

Marcel was seconded in all this by Octave, whom he found morally changed and quite eager to help. What resolutions were taken by the Defense Council? No one knew the details. Only the general principles were systematically communicated to the press and made known to the public. It was not difficult to recognize in this the practical hand of Marcel.

"In all defense," he explained to the citizens of the city, "the major thing is to know the enemy's strength and to adapt your system of resistance to these same forces. No doubt, Herr Schultze's cannons are formidable. Yet it is better to have those cannons facing you—whose number, caliber, range, and effects are known—than to have to fight against unknown weapons."

Everything came down to preventing their city from being surrounded, either by land or by water.

That was the question which the Defense Council was actively studying, and the day when an announcement stated that the problem was resolved, no one doubted it. Citizens volunteered in droves to help carry out the necessary work. No job was disdained which could contribute to the work of defense. Men of all ages and of all positions became just simple workers in that circumstance. And the work was carried out quickly and cheerfully. Food for two years was stored in the city. Large quantities of coal and iron were brought in: the iron as the raw material for making armaments, and the coal for heat and fuel—both indispensable for the upcoming battle.

But while iron and coal were being heaped up in the squares, one could also see that gigantic piles of sacks of flour, quarters of smoked meat, rounds of cheese, mountains of edible preserves, and dried vegetables were transforming the meeting halls into food warehouses. Numerous herds of animals were also kept in the public parks, turning France-Ville into a vast pasture.

Finally, when the decree appeared for mobilizing all men capable of bearing arms, the enthusiasm that greeted it gave witness once again to the fine character of these soldier-citizens. Equipped simply with wool jackets, khaki pants, and half boots, topped with a rawhide hat, and armed with Werder rifles, they marched up and down the avenues.

Swarms of coolies worked the earth, built trenches, set up retrenchments and redoubts at all favorable points. The casting of artillery pieces had begun and was proceeding with great rapidity. One very favorable circumstance in these labors was the use of a great number of smoke-consuming furnaces which the city possessed and which could be readily transformed into casting ovens.

Amid this incessant movement, Marcel showed himself to be tireless. He seemed to be everywhere, and always equal to the task at hand. If some theoretical or practical difficulty presented itself, he immediately knew how to resolve it. When the need arose, he

The Defense Council of France-Ville

Swarms of coolies worked the earth.

rolled up his sleeves and proceeded to give a practical demonstration. As a result, his authority was accepted without question, and his orders were punctually executed.

At his side, Octave also did his best. If at first he had considered trimming his uniform with gold braid, he gave up on that idea, realizing that he should be no more than a simple soldier at the outset.

So he joined the ranks of the battalion he was assigned to, and conducted himself as a model soldier. To those who began to feel sorry for him:

"To each according to his merits!" he replied. "I might never have learned how to command! . . . The least I can do is to obey!"

A news report was received—a false one, it was later discovered—which spurred on the defense efforts with an even stronger impulse. Herr Schultze, it said, was trying to negotiate with various maritime companies for the transport of his cannons. From that moment, it seemed that hoaxes of this sort circulated throughout the city almost every day. One day it was the Schultzian navy that had set sail for France-Ville, or the train line from Sacramento which had been cut by the "uhlans," or cavalry, who had apparently fallen from the heavens.

But these rumors, which were soon contradicted, had been dreamed up by newspaper reporters who were hoping to pique the curiosity of their readers. In truth, Stahlstadt gave no sign of life at all.

This absolute silence, while giving Marcel the time to complete his defense projects, nevertheless worried him in his rare moments of leisure.

"Could that rascal have changed his tactics and is now preparing some new trick of his own invention?" he sometimes wondered.

But the plan, either to stop enemy ships or to prevent blockades, promised to answer all problems, and Marcel simply redoubled his activity during such moments of worry.

His only pleasure and his only rest after a laborious day was the brief hour that he spent every evening in Mme Sarrasin's living room.

From the first day, the doctor had required that he come to dinner every evening, unless prevented by some other engagement; but by some singular chance, no other engagement enticing enough to make Marcel give up this privilege had as yet presented itself. The never-ending chess game between the doctor and Colonel Hendon did not, however, offer sufficient interest to explain this assiduity. It seems that some other charm was acting upon Marcel. Perhaps one might be able to guess its nature, although he certainly did not yet suspect it himself. One need only observe the interest which his evening chats with Mme Sarrasin and Mlle Jeanne seemed to have for him, when the three of them were seated near the dining table on which the noble ladies were preparing needed ambulance supplies in case of future need.

"Will these new steel bolts be better than the ones you showed us the sketch of?" asked Jeanne, who took an interest in all the defense projects.

"No doubt about it, mademoiselle," replied Marcel.

"Oh! I'm glad! But the slightest industrial detail represents so much research and effort! You told me that five hundred new meters of trenches were dug yesterday. That's a lot, isn't it?"

"Well, no, it's not near enough! At that pace we won't have finished the enclosure by the end of the month."

"I'd so like to see it finished, and then let those dreadful Schultzians arrive! Men are so fortunate to be able to do something, to make themselves useful. The waiting is not so tedious for them as it is for us, who can't do much to help."[1]

"Not much help!" exclaimed Marcel, usually more calm, "not much help indeed! And who do you think these worthy men, who have given up everything to become soldiers, what do you think they're working for, if not to assure the safety and happiness of their mothers, wives, and fiancées? The fervor shown by each one of them, where does it come from if not from you? And who is responsible for their willing sense of sacrifice, if not . . ."

With these last words, Marcel, suddenly a little embarrassed, stopped speaking. Mlle Jeanne did not insist, and it was the good

Mme Sarrasin who was obliged to finish the discussion, saying to the young man that the love of duty was enough, no doubt, to explain the zeal of the majority of them.

And when Marcel, called back again to his unrelenting work to complete some project or calculation, regretfully tore himself away from this gentle conversation, he bore with him an unshakable resolution to save France-Ville and all of its inhabitants.

He could not have suspected what was about to happen, and yet it was the natural and ineluctable consequence of this unnatural state of things—this concentration of all power in one person—that was the fundamental law of the City of Steel.[2]

15 *The San Francisco Stock Exchange*

The San Francisco Stock Exchange, a condensed and rather algebraic expression of an immense industrial and commercial system, is one of the busiest and strangest in the world. As a natural consequence of being located in California's capital, it has a distinctive cosmopolitan character, which is one of its most outstanding traits. Under its porticoes of beautiful red granite, the Saxon with blond hair and tall stature stands elbow to elbow with the Celt with his dull complexion, darker hair, more supple and slender limbs. Here, the Negro meets the Finn and the Hindu. The Polynesian, with surprise, meets the Greenlander. The Chinaman with his oblique eyes and his carefully braided pigtail tries to outdo the Japanese, his historic trading enemy. All languages, all dialects, all jargons can be heard here, as if it were a modern Babel.[1]

The opening on October 12th of that unique stock exchange presented nothing extraordinary. As eleven o'clock approached, one could see the major brokers and business agents approach each other, cheerfully or gravely according to their individual temperaments, exchange handshakes, go to the bar, and precede the day's business with propitiatory libations. They went, one by one, to open the little copper door with numbered boxes which receive, in the vestibule, the correspondence of subscribers; they pulled out enormous packets of letters and ran through them with a distracted eye.

Soon the day's first market prices were posted, at the same time that the busy crowd slowly grew larger. A slight hubbub arose from the increasingly numerous groups.

The telegraphic dispatches then proceeded to pour in from all points of the globe. Not a minute would go by without another fresh strip of blue paper, read aloud at the top of a man's voice amid a tumult of other voices, being added to the north wall to the collection of telegrams posted by the Stock Exchange guardians.

The intensity of movement grew minute by minute. Messengers raced in, left, rushed toward the telegraph office, brought in answers. All the notebooks were opened, annotated, scratched out, torn up. A sort of wild contagion seemed to have taken possession of the crowd, when, toward one o'clock, something mysterious passed like a shiver through these agitated groups.

An astounding, unexpected, and unbelievable bit of news had just been brought by one of the associates of the "Bank of the Far West" and circulated with lightning speed.

Some said:

"What a joke! It must be a ploy! How can we deal with a blunder like that?"

"Hey! Hey!" said the others, "there's no smoke without fire!"

"How can a man fail in a situation like his?"

"People can fail in any situation!"

"But sir, his real estate and equipment alone are worth more than eighty million dollars!" exclaimed another.

"Without counting the pig-iron and steel, provisions, and manufactured goods," came the reply.

"You bet! That's what I was saying! Schultze is good for ninety million dollars, and I'll take charge of selling it all off whenever he wants, to his credit."

"Well, how do you explain this suspension of payments?"

"I don't understand it at all! I just don't believe it!"

"As if things like that didn't happen every day, and in the most reputable businesses!"

"Stahlstadt is not a business—it's a whole city!"

"After all, it can't be over. A holding company will no doubt be quickly organized to resume this business!"

"But why the devil didn't Schultze arrange for that, before being declared insolvent?"

"That's just it, sir, it's just so absurd that it doesn't make sense! It's pure and simple a false piece of news, probably tossed out by Nash, who has a desperate need for a rise in the price of steel!"

"But it's not a false piece of news! Not only is Schultze bankrupt, he has fled!"

"Come on, now!"

"He has fled, sir. The telegram announcing it has just been posted!"

An enormous human wave surged toward the telegraph board. The last strip of blue paper was worded in these terms:

"New York, 12:10.—Central Bank. Stahlstadt factory. Payments suspended. Known liabilities: forty-seven million dollars. Schultze disappeared."

This time there was no longer any doubt, however surprising the news, and various rumors and theories immediately began to fly about.

At two o'clock, the listings of secondary bankruptcies brought on by that of Herr Schultze began to flood the exchange. It was the Mining Bank of New York which was losing most heavily; next, Westerly and Son from Chicago, which was involved for seven million dollars; Milwaukee House, from Buffalo, for five million; the Industrial Bank of San Francisco for a million and a half; then the small change of third-class firms.

Moreover, and even without awaiting this news, the natural after-effects of the event unfurled with a fury.

The San Francisco market, which was so sluggish in the morn-

An enormous human wave surged toward the telegraph board.

ing according to the experts, certainly was not at two o'clock in the afternoon! What plunges! What rises! What a wild flurry of speculative investing!

Steel stocks, going up minute after minute. A similar rise in all the foundries in the United States! Rise in all types of products manufactured by the steel industry! Rise also in the value of real estate in France-Ville. Fallen to zero, having disappeared from the board as of the declaration of war, they were now suddenly quoted at one hundred and eighty dollars an acre!

That very evening, the news media were besieged by the curious. But the *Herald,* like the *Tribune,* the *Alta,* like the *Guardian,* the *Echo,* like the *Globe,* in vain began printing in large type since the meager information that they had been able to collect was, in truth, next to nothing.

All they knew is that on September 25th a draft of eight million dollars was accepted by Herr Schultze and drawn by Jackson, Elder and Company of Buffalo, but then when it was presented to Schring, Strauss and Company, bankers of the King of Steel, in New York, those gentlemen had observed that the balance of their client's account was insufficient to cover this enormous payment, and had immediately advised him of the fact by telegram, and had received no response. They had then consulted their books and discovered with stupefaction that, for thirteen days, no letter and no draft had reached them from Stahlstadt—that from that date forward, all drafts and checks withdrawn by Herr Schultze on this account had arrived daily and each had suffered the same fate: they were returned to their place of origin with the notice "insufficient funds."

For four days, requests for information, concerned telegrams, and angry questions had rained down upon the bank and upon Stahlstadt.

Finally, a decisive response from the latter arrived:

"Herr Schultze not seen since September 17," read the telegram. "No one able to shed light on this mystery. He has left no orders and his cash boxes are empty."

From that moment, it had been impossible to hide the truth. The principal creditors grew frightened and sent their bills receivable to the commercial court. Bankruptcies among them began to multiply with lightning rapidity, setting off a series of secondary collapses. At noon on October 13th, the total of known deficits amounted to forty-seven million dollars. Everything seemed to indicate that, with the additional debts coming in, the liability would approach sixty million.

That is what they knew and all that the papers, with a few exaggerations along the way, were printing. It goes without saying that, the next day, they were all announcing "exclusive" special coverage of the latest news in the matter.

And, in fact, each had immediately sent its correspondents on the road to Stahlstadt.

From the evening of October 14th, the City of Steel had been surrounded by a veritable army of reporters, their notebooks aflap and their pencils afly. But this army came to crash like waves against the exterior ramparts of Stahlstadt. The guards had been maintained, and the reporters had tried in vain every ploy imaginable, every possible bribe. But it was impossible for them to find anyone who would allow them inside.

They did discover, however, that workers knew nothing, and that nothing was changed in their daily routine. The foremen had simply announced the day before, by orders from higher up, that there were no funds in individual cashboxes, nor instructions from the Central Block, and as a consequence work would be suspended the following Saturday, barring contrary instruction.

All that, instead of clearing up the situation, only complicated it. That Herr Schultze had disappeared nearly a month before no one really doubted. But what was the cause and the effect of this disappearance, that is what no one knew. A vague impression still prevailed that this mysterious personage might reappear from one moment to the next, and this lessened their uneasiness to some extent.

In the factory, during the early days, work had continued as usual by simple momentum. Everyone had pursued his partial task within the limited horizon of his section. The individual cashier desks had paid salaries every Saturday. The principal treasurer had been responsible so far for local needs. But centralization in Stahlstadt had been pushed to a high degree of perfection; the master had reserved for himself an absolute supervision of all business matters, so much so that his absence would have brought, in short order, a serious breakdown of the entire machine. Thus, from September 17th, the day when for the last time the King of Steel had signed his orders, until October 13th, when the news of the suspension of payments had burst like a thunderclap, thousands of letters—a great number probably containing large sums of money—passed through the Stahlstadt post office, had been deposited in the box of the Central Block, and no doubt had arrived in Herr Schultze's office. But he reserved the right to open them himself, to annotate them with a red pencil, and then transmit the contents to the main cashier. The highest official in the factory would never have dreamed of exceeding his regular responsibility in these matters. In relation to their subordinates, each official had a near absolute power, but in relation to Herr Schultze—and even in relation to his memory—they were like so many instruments without authority, without initiative. Ensconcing themselves within their narrowly defined jobs, they waited, deferred action, and watched to see what would happen next.

What happened next was that this remarkable situation continued until the moment when all those major companies involved had suddenly been stricken with panic and had telegraphed, solicited a reply, demanded, protested, and finally took their legal precautions. It had taken some time for this to occur. They could not easily bring themselves to suspect that such a famous fortune could have feet of clay. But the fact was now evident: Herr Schultze had slipped away from his creditors.

That is all that the reporters could gather. Even the illustrious Meiklejohn himself, famed for having succeeded in squeezing out of President Grant—the most taciturn figure of his century—certain political statements, and even the indefatigable Blunderbuss, simple correspondent of the *World,* famed for having announced to the Czar the great news of the capitulation of Pleven, even these great reporters had not, this time, been any more fortunate than their colleagues.[2] They were obliged to admit to themselves that the *Tribune* and the *World* might not be able to have the last word on the Schultze affair.

What turned this industrial disaster into a quite unique event was the unusual situation of Stahlstadt itself, an independent and isolated city which permitted no regular or legal inquiry. The signature of Herr Schultze was, of course, now worthless in New York, and his creditors had every reason to believe that the assets represented by the factory could help indemnify them. But to what court do you go to obtain seizure or sequestration? Stahlstadt had remained a special territory that was not yet politically defined and where everything belonged to Herr Schultze. If only he had left a representative, an administrative board, a substitute! But there was nothing—not a council, not even a legal advisor. He was everything simultaneously: king, judge, four-star general, lawyer, notary, and the only commercial tribunal of the city. He had realized in his own person the ideal of centralization. So, once he was gone, absolutely nothing held the system together, and his entire formidable edifice crumpled like a house of cards.

In any other situation, the creditors would have been able to form an association, replace Herr Schultze, take over his assets, and manage his business. Seemingly, all that was lacking to keep the business running was a little money, perhaps, and a regulating authority.

But none of that was possible. There was no legal instrument that would allow them to take over Herr Schultze's enterprise. They found themselves blocked by a moral barrier, more insurmountable, if possible, than the circumvallations raised around the City of Steel itself. These unfortunate creditors saw before them the collateral for their debt but they could not seize it.

All they could do was to meet in general assembly, work together, and send a request to Congress to ask the government to take up their cause, to espouse the interests of the American citizens, to pronounce the annexation of Stahlstadt to the American territory, and to bring that monstrous creation under the common law of the United States. Several members of Congress were personally interested in the affair; the request, in more than one way, attracted the American temperament, and there was reason to believe that such a political solution would be successful. Unfortunately, Congress was not in session, and long delays were to be feared before the affair could be submitted to it.

While awaiting that moment, nothing stirred in Stahlstadt, and the furnaces were extinguished, one by one.

So the consternation was profound among the population of some ten thousand families who made a living at the factory. But what was to be done? Continue the work, trusting in a salary that might materialize in six months, or might never materialize? No one seemed to find this option acceptable. Besides, what work would there be? The source of arms orders had dried up. All Herr Schultze's customers were awaiting a legal solution before doing any further business with him. And the section chiefs, engineers, and foremen, all of whom were deprived of orders, could not act.

There were assemblies, meetings, discussions, and debates. But no set plans could be agreed to, for none were possible. Rising unemployment soon brought with it a host of ills: poverty, despair, and vice. With the workshop empty, the bars filled up. For each chimney which ceased to smoke, a cabaret was born in the surrounding villages.

The wisest of the workers, the most cautious, were those who had foreseen hard times ahead and had saved for the future. They hastened to flee with bag and baggage—taking with them tools, the household bedding, and their chubby-cheeked children who were delighted by the spectacle of the world revealed to them through their wagon door. These are the ones who left, scattered across the four corners of the continent, and they soon found, one in the east, this one to the south, that one to the north, another factory, another forge, another home . . .

But for the one or even the ten that could manage to realize that dream, how many there were whose poverty nailed them to their homes! There they had to remain, their eyes hollow, their hearts broken!

They stayed behind, selling their poor garments to that flock of birds of prey with human faces that instinctively swoops down on great disasters. In a few days they were reduced to the direst of circumstances. They were soon deprived of credit as they had been of salary, of hope as of work, and now saw stretched out before them, as dark as the coming winter, nothing but a future of despair!

16   *Two Frenchmen against a City*

When the news of Schultze's disappearance reached France-Ville, Marcel's first words had been:

"Suppose it's just a ruse of war?"

No doubt, upon reflection, he would have realized that the results of such a tactic would have been so grievous for Stahlstadt that the hypothesis was not logically admissible. But it is often said that hatred is not rational, and the exasperated rage of a man like Herr Schultze might well have made him capable at any moment of sacrificing everything to his passion. Whatever the case, it was necessary to remain alert.

At Marcel's request, the Defense Council immediately issued a proclamation to exhort the residents to remain on guard against false news sown by the enemy for the purpose of undermining the vigilance of France-Ville residents.

In general, France-Ville's response to what could be a maneuver of Herr Schultze was more vigorous work and training. But the details, true or false, published in the newspapers of San Francisco, Chicago, and New York about the financial and commercial consequences of the Stahlstadt catastrophe constituted a network of circumstantial evidence that, even if each piece was individually weak, seemed so powerful when considered together as not to permit further doubt.

One fine morning the doctor's city awoke definitely saved, like a sleeper who escapes a bad dream by the simple fact of his awakening. Yes! France-Ville was evidently out of danger, without having had to strike a blow. Marcel, now firmly convinced of this, spread the news by all the means of publicity he had at his disposal.

Then there came a universal movement of relaxation and joy, a festive air, an immense sigh of relief. People were shaking hands, congratulating each other, inviting others in for dinner. Women dressed up, men took momentary leave of their training, maneuvers, and labors. All were reassured, satisfied, joyous. It was almost like a city of convalescents.

But, without doubt the happiest of all was Dr. Sarrasin. The worthy man felt responsible for the fate of all those who had come with confidence to settle in his territory and had placed themselves under his protection. For a month, the fear of having lured them to their ruin had not left him—he who had only their happiness in mind—a moment's rest. Finally, he was relieved of such a dreadful concern and was breathing easily.

Meanwhile, the common danger had served to further unite all the citizens. The classes had grown closer, and they recognized each other as brothers, animated by the same feelings, touched by the same interests. Everyone felt a new awakening in their hearts. Henceforth, the inhabitants of France-Ville felt a sense of "homeland." They had been afraid, they had suffered for their city, and now they were fully aware of how much they loved it.

The material results of their city having been put on the defensive were also to their common advantage. They had learned to know its strengths. They would no longer have to improvise. They were surer of themselves. In the future, whatever the event, they would be ready.

Finally, the prospects of Dr. Sarrasin's work had never seemed so bright. And, surprisingly, the citizens were also grateful to Marcel. While the safety of the population had not been his work, public thanks were voted for the young engineer as the organizer of the defense, to whose devotion the city would have owed its survival, if Herr Schultze's projects had succeeded.

Marcel, however, did not feel his task was done. The mystery surrounding Stahlstadt could still hide some danger to France-Ville, he thought. He would not feel satisfied until he had shone a bright light into the midst of that gloom which still enveloped Steel City.

So he resolved to return there and to stop at nothing until he had uncovered its final secrets.

Dr. Sarrasin attempted to explain to him how the project would be not only difficult but also perhaps bristling with danger, that he was risking a sort of descent into hell where hidden abysses might be lurking under his every step.[1] Herr Schultze, such as he had been depicted, was not the kind of person to disappear without harming others, to be buried alone under the ruins of all his hopes. They had every reason to fear the last desperate actions of such a man as they would the terrifying death throes of a shark!

"It's precisely because, dear Doctor, everything you imagine is possible," Marcel replied, "that I believe it's my duty to go to Stahlstadt. It is a bomb whose fuse I must snatch out before it explodes, and I'll even ask permission to take Octave with me."

"Octave!" exclaimed the doctor.

"Yes! He is now a fine lad who can be counted on; and I assure you that this excursion will do him good!"

"May God protect you, and be with you both!" answered the doctor, embracing him with emotion.

The next morning, a carriage crossed through the abandoned villages and dropped Marcel and Octave at the gate of Stahlstadt. Both were equipped, well armed, and very determined not to return without having cleared up this dark mystery.

They walked side by side on the outer road which circled the fortifications, and the truth, which Marcel had stubbornly doubted until that very moment, was now clearly laid out before him.

The factory was at a total standstill; that was evident. He walked with Octave along the road, under the black and starless sky. Previously, one could have seen the glow of gas lamps, the light glinting from the bayonet of a sentinel, a thousand signs of life that were now absent. The illuminated windows of the various sectors would have shone like so many glittering stained-glass windows. Now everything was dark and silent. Death alone seemed to float over the city, whose tall chimneys reared above the horizon like so many skeletons. Marcel and Octave's footsteps echoed into nothingness. The expression of solitude and desolation was so strong that Octave could not help remarking:

"It's strange, I've never encountered a silence quite like this! You'd think we were in a cemetery!"

It was seven o'clock when Marcel and Octave arrived at the edge of the moat, facing the main entryway to Stahlstadt. Not a single living being appeared at the top of the wall; of the sentinels who formerly stood from post to post, like so many human poles, there was no longer the slightest trace. The drawbridge was raised, leaving before the doorway a gulf that was five or six meters wide.

It took more than an hour to secure a cable and to throw it with all their strength over one of the beams. After a number of tries, Marcel succeeded, and Octave pulled himself up the rope hand over hand to the roof above the entry. Marcel passed along to him their arms and munitions and then climbed up in turn.

They then hauled up the rope, moved to the other side of the wall, lowered down their impedimenta, and finally began to slide down themselves.

The two young men were then on the parapet walk that Marcel remembered following the first day of his entry into Stahlstadt. Around them, nothing but silence and solitude. Facing them, there rose, black and mute, the imposing mass of buildings, which, from their thousand glass windows, seemed to be glaring at the intruders as though to say:

"Go away! You have no business trying to penetrate our secrets!"

Marcel and Octave discussed what to do next.

Marcel and Octave slid down the rope.

"It's best to enter by gate O, where I know my way around," said Marcel.

They headed west and soon arrived in front of the monumental doorway arch which bore on its front the letter O. But both doors, made of solid oak and reinforced with heavy steel nails, were locked. Marcel approached them and knocked several times with a paving stone that he picked up on the street.

Only an echo answered.

"Well, let's go to work!" cried Octave.

They had to recommence the tedious job of throwing the rope above the doorway in order to hook to an obstacle where it could get solidly attached—a difficult task. But, eventually, Marcel and Octave succeeded in clearing the wall, and found themselves at the crossroads of sector O.

"Fine!" exclaimed Octave, "so where'd all this trouble get us? We haven't made very much progress. We manage to climb one wall and there's another facing us!"

"Silence in the ranks!" replied Marcel. "There's my old workshop. I'm not unhappy to see it again since we can take from it certain tools that we'll surely be able to use, including a few sticks of dynamite."

It was the great hall of casting where the young Alsatian had been admitted when he first arrived at the factory. How dismal it seemed with its furnaces cold, its rails rusting, its cranes covered with dust and their great sad arms raised in the air, like so many gallows. All that gave one's heart a chill, and Marcel felt the need of a diversion.

"Here's a workroom that will interest you more," he said to Octave, leading him toward the canteen.

Octave nodded in agreement, which became a sign of satisfaction when he saw, lined up in battle formation on a wooden shelf, a virtual regiment of red, yellow, and green bottles. Some canned goods also showed their metal jackets, stamped with the best brands. There was enough on hand to make a good lunch, a need, moreover, which was making itself felt. They spread the tablecloth over the tin counter, and the two young men replenished their strength to continue their expedition.

Marcel, while eating, thought about what he had to do. Climbing the wall of the Central Block was out of the question. The wall was prodigiously high, isolated from other buildings, with no projection to hook a rope on. To find the door—probably the only one —they would have to go through all the sectors, which was no easy task. There remained the use of dynamite, which was always risky, for it seemed impossible that Herr Schultze had disappeared without placing traps on the property he was leaving, or countermining the mines that those who tried to take over Stahlstadt would not fail to set. But in the face of these dangers Marcel was not intimidated.

Seeing Octave back in shape and rested, Marcel walked with him toward the end of the street that formed the crossroads of the sector, up to the foot of the huge wall of cut stone.

"What would you say about creating a little crawl space through there?" he asked.

"It would be hard, but we're up to it!" replied Octave, ready for anything.

The work began. They had to loosen the base of the wall, introduce a lever into the joint between two stones, detach one of them, and finally, with the help of a drill, open up several little parallel trenches. At ten o'clock everything was done, the sticks of dynamite were in place, and the fuse was lit.

Marcel knew it would burn for five minutes, and since he had noticed that the canteen located in the sub-basement was built like a real stone-vaulted cellar, he and Octave went down there to protect themselves from the blast.

Suddenly, the edifice and the basement itself shuddered as though from an earthquake. A formidable detonation, like that of three or four batteries of cannons, triggered at the same moment, tore through the air, following on the heels of the explosion itself. Then, after two or three seconds, an avalanche of debris began to fall back to earth. For a few moments, they could hear a continuous

A formidable detonation . . .

roar of roofs caving in, beams cracking, walls collapsing, and shattered windowpanes cascading to the ground.

Finally, that dreadful din came to a close, and Octave and Marcel left their retreat.

As used as he was to the prodigious effects of explosives, Marcel marveled at the results he saw. Half of the sector had blown up, and the dismantled walls of the workshop near the Central Block looked like those of a bombed city. There were heaps of debris everywhere, shards of glass and plaster covered the ground, and clouds of dust, drifting down from the sky where the explosion had thrown them, were settling like snow on the ruins.

Marcel and Octave ran to the inside wall. It had a large hole in it eight to ten meters wide, and on the other side of the breach, the former designer from the Central Block could make out the familiar courtyard, where he had spent so many monotonous hours.

Since the courtyard was no longer under guard, the iron fence surrounding it was not impassable. They were soon over it.

Everywhere the same silence.

Marcel saw the workshops where formerly his comrades admired his designs. In a corner he rediscovered, half sketched out on his table, the plans for a steam engine he had started, when an order from Herr Schultze had called him to the park. In the reading room, he saw again the familiar journals and books.

Everything had the look of work suddenly suspended, of a life rudely interrupted.

The two young men reached the inside limits of the Central Block and soon found themselves at the foot of the wall which probably, Marcel believed, separated them from the park.

"Are we going to have to make those quarry stones dance again?" asked Octave.

"Perhaps . . . but to get in we could first look for a door that a small charge would blow out."

Both started around the park, following its wall. From time to time they had to take a detour, to cross around a group of buildings which jutted out like a buttress, or to climb a fence. But they never lost it from view, and they were soon repaid for their troubles. A small door, low in the wall, appeared to their eyes.

In two minutes, Octave had drilled a hole through the oak planks. Marcel, applying his eye immediately to the hole, recognized to his great satisfaction that on the other side the tropical park spread out with its eternal green and its spring-like temperature.

"Just one door to blow, and we'll be in the park!" he said to his companion.

"A powder charge for that little square of wood?" replied Octave, "That would be giving it more credit than it deserves!"

And he started attacking the postern with great blows of his pickax.

He had barely started to shake it, when they heard a key turn in a lock, and two bolts sliding back.

The door opened part way, held on the inside by a heavy chain.

"*Wer da?*" [Who goes there?], said a hoarse voice in German.

17 *Explanations at Gunpoint*

The two young men were hardly expecting such a question. They were more surprised by this than if they had been met by gunfire.

Of all the speculations that Marcel had imagined about this dormant city, the only one that had not crossed his mind was this one: a living person quietly asking him for the reason for his visit. His attempt to enter Stahlstadt, which he had supposed was completely deserted, seemed a fairly legitimate mission; but it took on an entirely different aspect if the city still had residents. What was, in the first case, only a kind of archaeological exploration became, in the second, an armed attack and break-in.

These ideas came to Marcel's mind so forcibly that he just stood for a moment as if dumbfounded.

"*Wer da?*" repeated the voice, with a hint of impatience.

Such impatience was evidently well justified. For intruders to have reached this door after overcoming so many varied obstacles, climbing walls, and blowing up sections of the city—to have done all that and yet still not have anything to say when simply asked, "Who goes there?" was understandably a bit astonishing. Half a minute was enough for Marcel to recognize the awkwardness of his position and to then reply in German:

"Friend or foe as you please! I wish to speak with Herr Schultze."

He had no sooner articulated those words than an exclamation of surprise was heard through the half-open door:

"Ach!"

And, through the opening, Marcel caught a glimpse of reddish whiskers, a bristling moustache, a vacant stare which he recognized immediately. They all belonged to Sigimer, his former bodyguard.

"Johann Schwartz!" cried the giant with stupefaction mingled with joy. "Johann Schwartz!"

The unforeseen return of his prisoner seemed to astound him almost as much as his mysterious disappearance must have.

"Can I speak to Herr Schultze?" repeated Marcel, seeing that he received no other response than that exclamation.

Sigimer shook his head.

"No order!" he said. "No entering here without order!"

"Can you at least tell Herr Schultze that I am here and desire to speak to him?"

"Herr Schultze not here. Herr Schultze gone!" replied the giant with a shade of sadness.

"But where is he? When will he be back?"

"Not know. Orders no change! Nobody enter without order!"

These bits of phrases were all that Marcel could draw from Sigimer, who resisted all questions with animal-like stubbornness.

Octave finally grew impatient.

"What's the point of asking permission to enter?" he said. "It's a lot easier to just enter!"

And he threw himself against the door in an attempt to force it open. But the chain held, and a push from the opposite side, much stronger than his, had soon closed it back up and locked the two bolts.

"There must be several people behind that door," exclaimed Octave, somewhat humiliated by this result.

He put his eye up to the drilled hole, and almost immediately gave a cry of surprise:

"There's a second giant!"

"Arminius?" replied Marcel.

And he looked in turn through the hole.

"Yes! It's Arminius, the companion of Sigimer!"

Suddenly, another voice, which seemed to come from above, caused Marcel to raise his head.

"*Wer da?*" the voice said.

This time, it was the voice of Arminius.

The guardian's head rose above the top of the wall that he must have reached from the end of a ladder.

"Come on, you know full well who I am, Arminius," replied Marcel. "Will you open up, yes or no?"

No sooner had he spoken than the barrel of a gun poked over the top of the wall. A detonation rang out, and a bullet brushed the edge of Octave's hat.

"Well, and here's my answer to you!" replied Marcel, who placed a stick of dynamite under the door and shattered it to bits.

As soon as they had they broken through, Marcel and Octave, carbines in hand and knives held tightly between their teeth, leaped forward into the park.

Against the wall, cracked by the explosion they had just set off, a ladder was still standing, and at its foot were traces of blood. But neither Sigimer nor Arminius was there to defend the passage.

The gardens appeared before the two assailants in all the luxuriant splendor of their vegetation. Octave was astounded.

"It's beautiful! But watch out! We had better spread out and advance like infantrymen! Those sauerkraut-eaters might well be hiding behind the shrubs!"

Octave and Marcel separated, each taking a side of the broad

Marcel and Octave advanced carefully.

pathway before them. They advanced carefully, from tree to tree, obstacle to obstacle, according to the most fundamental lessons of strategy.[1]

The precaution was wise. They had not advanced a hundred paces when a second shot was fired. A bullet nipped some bark from a tree that Marcel had just left.

"Let's not take any chances! Down on all fours!" said Octave in a low voice.

And, setting an example to the warning, he started crawling on elbows and knees up to a thorny bush bordering the central garden where the Tower of the Bull rose up. Marcel, who had not followed this advice, promptly felt a third bullet brush by and hardly had the time to leap behind a palm tree to avoid a fourth.

"A good thing those fellows shoot like raw recruits!" shouted Octave to his companion, some thirty paces away.

"Shh!" replied Marcel, with his eyes as much as his lips. "Do you see the smoke that's coming out of that window, on the ground floor? That's where they're hiding, the rascals! Now I'm going to show them a thing or two!"

In the wink of an eye Marcel had cut down a stick of reasonable length. He then removed his jacket, tossed it onto the pole with his hat on top, and in that way created a presentable dummy. He stuck it into the ground where he had been standing, so as to leave the hat and both sleeves in sight, and, crawling toward Octave, whispered in his ear:

"Keep them busy by firing at the window, sometimes from my station, sometimes from yours! And I'll go around and take them from behind!"

And Marcel, as Octave continued shooting at the building, silently crept through the bushes around the central garden.

A quarter of an hour passed. A score of bullets were exchanged without result.

Marcel's jacket and hat were literally riddled, but he suffered no ill. As for the first-floor window blinds, Octave's carbine had reduced them to shreds.

Suddenly, their firing stopped, and Octave distinctly heard this stifled cry:

"Help! I've got him!"

Leaving his shelter, racing out of cover into the central garden, and springing through the window took Octave but a moment. An instant later he was standing in the reception hall.

On the rug, entwined like two serpents, Marcel and Sigimer were struggling desperately. Surprised by the sudden attack of his adversary, who had forced an interior door, the giant had been unable to use his weapons. But his herculean strength made him a formidable adversary. Although thrown to the ground, he had not lost hope of regaining the upper hand. Marcel, for his part, displayed a remarkable strength and suppleness.

The struggle, of necessity, would have ended with the death of one of the combatants if the intervention of Octave had not occurred just in time to bring about a less tragic end. Sigimer, seized by both arms and his rifle wrested from him, was tied up in a way to prevent further movement.

"What about the other?" asked Octave.

Marcel pointed out a sofa at the end of the room where Arminius lay bleeding.

"Did he take a bullet?" asked Octave.

"Yes," replied Marcel.

Then he approached Arminius.

"Dead," he observed.

"Too bad," cried Octave, "but the wretch deserved it."

"So now we're masters of the place!" replied Marcel. "We'll have to give it a good once-over. Starting with Herr Schultze's office!"

From the reception room where this final act of resistance had taken place, the two young men followed the suite of rooms which led to the sanctuary of the King of Steel.

Octave felt a growing admiration at the sight of such splendor.

Marcel smiled while watching him and opened one at a time the doors before him until they reached the green-and-gold salon.

He was expecting to find something new, but nothing quite as

Surprised by the sudden attack of his adversary . . .

strange as the spectacle which now stood before his eyes. It was as if all the mail contained in the Post Office of New York or Paris, suddenly robbed, had been thrown pell-mell into this salon. There was nothing on all sides but letters and sealed cartons, on the desk, on the furniture, on the carpet. They waded knee-deep through this flood of mail. All the financial, industrial, and personal correspondence of Herr Schultze, accumulated day after day from the mailbox outside the park and faithfully brought in by Arminius and Sigimer, was heaped there in the master's office.

How many questions, sufferings, anxieties, miseries, tears were contained in those mute folds of paper addressed to Herr Schultze! How many millions were there also, no doubt in paper, in checks, in money orders, in banknotes of all kinds! They were all lying dormant here, immobilized by the absence of the sole hand that had the right to tear open these fragile but inviolable envelopes.

"Now, it's a question," said Marcel, "of refinding the secret door to the laboratory!"

So he began by removing all the books from the library shelves. But this was in vain; he could not discover the hidden passageway that he had gone through with Herr Schultze. He then rattled, one by one, all the bookcase panels, to no avail. Then, arming himself with a poker from the fireplace, he tapped on the wall, hoping to find a hollow sound! It was soon clear that Herr Schultze, probably worried about no longer being the sole possessor of the secret to his laboratory door, had decided to remove it.

But he must necessarily have had another entrance made.

"Where?" wondered Marcel. "It can only be here, since it is here that Arminius and Sigimer brought the letters! So it is in this room that Herr Schultze continued to remain after my departure! I know his habits well enough to realize that, after having the old passage walled up, he would have needed to make another, within his reach, and yet hidden from indiscreet eyes! Might there be a trapdoor beneath the carpet?"

The carpet showed no sign of being cut. It was nonetheless taken

It was like an invitation to climb.

up. The flooring underneath was examined, board by board, and showed nothing suspicious.

"But are you certain that the opening must be in this room?" asked Octave.

"I'm sure!" replied Marcel.

"Well, all that's left to explore is the ceiling," said Octave, climbing up on a chair.

His intent was to climb along as far as the chandelier and knock on the ceiling around the central design. But Octave had no sooner grasped the gilded candelabra than, to his extreme surprise, he felt it move lower in his hand. A portion of the ceiling then slid back, revealing a large opening, from which a light steel ladder automatically descended to floor level.

It was like an invitation to climb.

"Well, what do you know! There we are!" said Marcel quietly, and he started right up the ladder, followed closely by his companion.

18 *The Kernel of the Mystery*

The top of the steel ladder led to a vast circular room with no communication to the outside. This room would have been in total darkness if a dazzling white light had not filtered upward through the thick glass of a round window embedded in the center of its oak floor. It resembled the disk of the moon when, facing the sun, it appears in its full brilliance and purity.

The silence was absolute within these deaf and eyeless walls. The two young men imagined they were in the antechamber of a tomb.

Marcel had a moment of hesitation before going to lean over the glistening pane of glass. He had attained his goal! From here, he could no longer doubt, he would finally discover the impenetrable secret that he had come to find in Stahlstadt!

This feeling passed in an instant. Octave and he went to kneel down near the disk and peered down through it, exploring the entirety of the room beneath them.[1]

A horrible and unexpected sight met their eyes!

This glass disk, convex on both faces, lens-shaped, magnified the objects seen through it enormously.

Beneath them was the secret laboratory of Herr Schultze. The intense light which came through the disk, like that from the dioptric apparatus of a lighthouse, came from a double electric lamp still burning in its airless chamber, powered by the electric current from a powerful battery. In the middle of the room and bathed in this radiance, an enormous human form, enhanced by the refraction from the lens and appearing as large as one of the sphinxes from the Libyan desert, was seated in an immobility of marble.

Around this specter, shell fragments were strewn on the floor.

There was no doubt! It was Herr Schultze! He was recognizable by the horrible smile on his face and by his gleaming teeth.[2] But it was also a gigantic Herr Schultze who, due to the accidental explosion of one of his dreadful armaments, had been asphyxiated and instantly frozen by an arctic cold beyond description!

The King of Steel was seated at his desk, holding a gigantic pen, as big as a lance, and he appeared to be still writing! Had it not been for the glassy stare of his dilated pupils and the immobility of his mouth, one would have believed him to be alive. Like those mammoths discovered inside the glaciers of polar regions, his body had been there for a month, hidden from view. Around him everything was still frozen, the reagents in their jars, the water in its containers, even the mercury in its thermometer.

Marcel, in spite of the horror of this spectacle, had an impulse of satisfaction, thinking to himself how happy he was to have been able to see this laboratory, for very certainly Octave and he would have been stricken with sudden death upon entering there.

How had this horrible accident come about? Marcel figured it out without difficulty, when he saw the shell fragments spread across the floor which were nothing but slivers of glass. He knew

Herr Schultze had been instantly frozen.

that the inner case, which contained the liquid carbon dioxide in Herr Schultze's asphyxiating projectiles, given the enormous pressure that it had to support, was made of tempered glass—glass which had ten to twelve times the resistance of ordinary glass. But one of the defects of this product, which was brand-new, was that, through some mysterious molecular action, it sometimes shattered for no apparent reason. That is what must have happened. Perhaps the interior pressure had caused even more inevitably the explosion of the shell which had been deposited in the laboratory. Then the carbon dioxide, suddenly decompressed and returning to a gaseous state, had produced a fearful drop in the ambient temperature of the room.

In any case, the effect must have been lightning-fast. Herr Schultze, surprised in death in the position he had at the moment of the explosion, had been instantaneously mummified at a temperature of a hundred degrees below zero Celsius.

One circumstance that especially struck Marcel was that the King of Steel had been caught in the act of writing.

Now, what words was he inscribing on that sheet of paper, with the pen still held frozen in his hand? It might be of interest to read his last thoughts, to know the last words of such a man.

But how would he obtain that paper? He could not consider even for an instant breaking the luminous disk and descending into the laboratory below. The carbon dioxide, no doubt under a frightful pressure, would have spilled forth and asphyxiated every living being with its smothering vapor. It would have been risking certain death, and obviously, the risks were out of proportion with the advantages that could be gained from the possession of this paper.

If it was impossible to obtain from the late Herr Schultze the last lines written with his own hand, it was nevertheless probable that they could decipher them, enlarged as they must be by the refraction of the lens. Was not the disk there with its powerful rays that it caused to magnify all objects in the laboratory, so brightly illuminated by the double electric lamp?

Marcel knew Herr Schultze's handwriting and, through trial and error, he finally succeeded in reading the following ten lines.

Like everything Herr Schultze wrote, it was more a command than an instruction.

"Order to B. K. R. Z. to advance by two weeks the planned expedition against France-Ville. On reception of this order, carry out the measures I have devised. This time it must be overwhelming and complete. Do not change one iota in the plans I have decided upon. I want France-Ville to be a dead city within two weeks, that no inhabitant survive. A modern Pompeii is what I must have,[3] and at the same time it must provoke the fear and astonishment of the whole world. My orders, if they are well executed, will make this result inevitable.

"You will send me the bodies of Dr. Sarrasin and Marcel Bruckmann. I wish to see them, and to have them for myself.

"Schultz . . ."

His signature was incomplete; the final "e" and the usual flourish at the end were missing.[4]

Marcel and Octave gazed silently and motionless before this strange spectacle, before this evocation of an evil genius which seemed to border on the supernatural.

But they had to tear themselves away from this lugubrious scene. The two friends, deeply moved, left the room above the laboratory.

There, in that tomb where complete darkness would reign, when the lamp would eventually be extinguished for lack of electric current, the corpse of the King of Steel was to remain alone, desiccated like one of those Pharaoh mummies whom twenty centuries had not reduced to dust!

One hour later, after having untied Sigimer, who seemed not to know what to do with the freedom that was returned to him, Octave and Marcel left Stahlstadt to follow the route back to France-Ville, which they reached that very evening.

Dr. Sarrasin was working in his office when the return of the two young men was announced.

"Show them in!" he exclaimed, "show them in quickly!"

His first word upon seeing them both was:

"Well?"

"Doctor," replied Marcel, "the news that we bring from Stahlstadt will put your mind at rest for a long time. Herr Schultze is no more. Herr Schultze is dead!"

"Dead!" exclaimed Doctor Sarrasin.

The good doctor remained thoughtful for a while, facing Marcel, and did not add another word.

"My poor lad," he then said to him, "do you understand that this news which should make me rejoice since it removes from us what I most hate, war, the most unjust war, the least motivated! do you understand how it has, contrary to logic, broken my heart! Oh! why did that man with such powerful faculties set himself up as our enemy? Why could he not have devoted his rare intellectual qualities to the service of good? What a terrible waste of aptitude, which would have been so valuable if only he could have joined it to ours in a common goal! That's what struck me at first, when you said: 'Herr Schultze is dead.' But now tell me what you know about his unexpected end."

"Herr Schultze," continued Marcel, "met his death in the mysterious laboratory which, with diabolical genius, he had rendered totally inaccessible during his lifetime. No one but he himself knew of its existence, and therefore no one would have been able to penetrate into it, even to bring help. He was thus a victim of that incredible concentration of forces that he had brought together by his own hand—forces that he had erroneously counted on controlling all alone. As the result of a dreadful accident taking place at a precise moment decided by God, these forces suddenly turned against him and his goal!"

"It could not have been otherwise!" replied Dr. Sarrasin. "Herr Schultze started off with a belief that was fundamentally wrong. Indeed, is not the best government the one whose leader, after his death, can be most readily replaced, and the one which continues to function precisely because its machinery has no secrets?"

"You will see, Doctor," replied Marcel, "that everything that has happened in Stahlstadt is the demonstration, *ipso facto*, of what you've just said. I found Herr Schultze seated at his desk—that central point from which came all the orders the City of Steel had to follow, without a single one ever questioned. Death had left him so life-like that I thought for an instant this specter would speak to me! But the inventor was the victim of his own invention! He was killed by one of those shells which were to destroy our city! His weapon broke in his hand, at the very moment when he was tracing the last letter of his order of extermination! Listen:"

And Marcel read out loud the terrible lines, written by the hand of Herr Schultze, of which he had made a copy.

Then he added:

"Even if I had never seen him, what would've constituted for me the best proof that Herr Schultze was dead was that everything around him had ceased to live! Everything in Stahlstadt had ceased to breathe! Like the palace of Sleeping Beauty, sleep had suspended all life, arrested all movement! The paralysis of the master had with the same blow paralyzed the servants as well as the machines!"

"Yes," replied Dr. Sarrasin, "here we see God's justice! It was in trying to push beyond all reason his attack against us, in forcing the scope of his plans, that Herr Schultze succumbed!"

"Indeed," answered Marcel, "but now, Doctor, let's not think any more about the past and live in the present. Herr Schultze's death not only brings us peace, but it also represents the ruin of the admirable institution that he had created, and for the time being, its failure. His imprudence, colossal like everything that the King of Steel imagined, hollowed out ten abysses. Blinded, on the one hand by his success, on the other by his passion against France and against you, he furnished powerful armaments, without taking due precautions, to all who would be our enemy. Despite that, and although payment for most of his debts might be delayed a long time, I think that a firm hand could perhaps reestablish Stahlstadt on a solid footing and have the forces it had accumulated for evil turn to the good. Herr Schultze has only one possible heir, Doctor, and that heir is you. We must not let his work perish. We believe too much in this world that we can only profit from a rival's destruction. That's a great mistake, and you will agree with me, I hope, that on the contrary we must save out of this immense disaster everything that can serve the good of mankind. Now, for that task I am ready to devote myself entirely."

"Marcel is right," said Octave, shaking his friend's hand, "so here I am, ready to work under his orders, if my father consents to it."

"I certainly approve, my dear young men," said Dr. Sarrasin. "Yes, Marcel, you will have all the capital you need, and, thanks to you, we will soon have from a resuscitated Stahlstadt such an arsenal that no one in the world will think of attacking us! And, while being the strongest, we'll also try to be the most just and bring the benefits of peace and justice to everyone around us. Oh, Marcel, such beautiful dreams! And when I sense that by you and with you, I will be able to see a good part of this accomplished, I wonder why . . . yes! why I don't have two sons! Why are you not the brother of Octave! For the three of us, nothing would have seemed impossible!"

19 *A Family Affair*

Perhaps, in the course of this narrative, the personal lives of those who play the heroes have not been discussed enough. That is just one more reason for us to return to them now and provide more details about them.

The good doctor, it must be said, was not so taken with humanity as a collective being that the concept of the individual disappeared in his eyes, even when he was completely immersed in his idealism. He was thus struck by the sudden pallor which had come to cover Marcel's face when he spoke these last words. His eyes sought to read in those of the young man the hidden meaning of this sudden emotion. The silence of the old practitioner questioned the silence of the young engineer and waited, perhaps for the latter to break it; but Marcel, regaining mastery of himself by a strong effort of will, had not been long to recover his composure. His complexion had returned to its natural color, and his attitude was only that of a man awaiting the remainder of an interrupted conversation.

Dr. Sarrasin, perhaps a bit put off by Marcel's prompt return to his cool-headed self, approached his young friend then, and with a familiar gesture of the medical profession, he took his arm and held it as he would have done with that of a patient whose pulse he wanted to take, discreetly or distractedly.

Marcel had gone along, but without quite recognizing the doctor's intention, and said nothing.

"My good Marcel," his old friend said to him, "later on we'll pick up our conversation about the future destiny of Stahlstadt. But now it is not forbidden, just when we are vowing to better the fate of all, to also take care of the fate of those whom we love, of those who touch us most deeply. I think the moment has come to tell you what a young woman—whose name I will give you shortly—replied to her father and mother when, at least twenty times this past year, her hand was asked for in marriage. The requests were generally from those whom the most demanding would have had no reason to refuse, and yet the young lady consistently replied no, always no!"

At that moment, Marcel, with a rather brusque movement, removed his wrist from the doctor's grasp. But whether the latter felt sufficiently edified about the health of his patient or he had not noticed that the young man had withdrawn both hand and confidence at the same moment, he continued his story without seeming to have noticed the incident.

"But finally the mother said to the young person I'm speaking about, 'Tell us at least the reasons for these multiple refusals. Education, wealth, honorable situation, physical advantages, everything is there! Why these "nays" so firm, so resolute, so prompt, to requests in marriage that you don't even take the trouble to examine? You're not usually so peremptory!'

"Faced with her mother's reproach, the young woman at last decided to break her silence, and then, with a clear mind and an honest heart, she said:

"'I say "no" with as much sincerity as I would use in answering "yes" to you, dear mother, if "yes" were indeed ready to come from my heart. I agree with you that a good number of choices that you offer me are—to different degrees—acceptable. But aside from my imagining that all those requests are addressed much more to what is considered the handsomest—that is to say, the wealthiest—match in the city, than to my person, and that that idea would not be apt to solicit a "yes" from me, I will tell you now that not one of those requests is the one I was waiting for, the one I am still waiting for, and that unfortunately I might have to await a long time for, if it ever comes along!'

"'What's this, my dear?' said the mother, totally astonished, 'you . . .'

"She didn't finish her sentence because she didn't know how to end it, and in her distress she cast toward her husband some looks that plainly implored for help and assistance.

"But whether he did not wish to enter such a quarrel, or whether he found it necessary for a bit more light to come between the mother and the daughter before intervening, the husband did not seem to understand. So the poor child, blushing from embarrassment and a bit of anger as well perhaps, suddenly decided to follow through to the very end.

"'I told you, dear mother,' she said, 'that the request I was hoping for might keep me waiting for a long time, and that it was even possible that it would never come. I might add that this delay, even if it were indefinite, would neither surprise me nor hurt me. I have the misfortune to be, so they say, very rich; the man who should make this request is very poor, and for this very reason he doesn't make it. It's up to him to wait . . .'

"'Why can't we speak . . .' said the mother, hoping perhaps to keep her daughter from saying the words that she was afraid to hear.

"It was then that the husband intervened.

"'My dear,' he said, affectionately taking both of his wife's hands in his own, 'it is not with impunity that a mother as attentively listened to by her daughter as you celebrates in front of her, practically since her birth, the praise of a handsome and worthy lad who is almost one of the family, that she calls to everyone's attention the solidity of his character, and that she applauds when her husband has occasion to boast about his extraordinary intelligence, when he speaks with tenderness of the thousand proofs of devotion that he has received from him! If she who saw this young man, singled out among all others by her father and mother, had not admired him in her turn, she would have failed in her filial duty!'

"'Oh! father!' cried the young girl, throwing herself into her mother's arms to hide her confusion, 'if you had seen through me so well, why did you force me to speak?'

"'Why, indeed?' the father continued. 'Why just to have the joy of hearing you, my darling, to be more assured that I was not mistaken, and finally to be able to tell you and to have your mother tell you that we approve the path your heart has taken, that your choice fills all our wishes, and that to spare that poor and proud fellow we're talking about from making a request which his sensitivity is loath to do, then I will make it—yes! I will make it because I have read his heart as I have read yours! So put your mind at ease! At the first propitious moment, I will take the liberty of asking Marcel if, by any chance, he would enjoy becoming my son-in-law!'"

Taken by surprise by this sudden peroration, Marcel jumped to his feet as though propelled by some spring. Octave grasped his hand while the doctor opened his arms. The young Alsatian was as pale as death.[1] But is that not the appearance that happiness sometimes takes when it enters without warning into a strong heart?

Marcel, Jeanne, and baby

20 *Conclusion*

France-Ville, rid of all worry, at peace with all its neighbors, well governed, happy thanks to the wisdom of its residents, is now in full prosperity. Its success is so justly deserved that it does not elicit envy, and its strength imposes the respect of even the most bellicose.

The City of Steel had been a formidable arms factory and a fearful engine of destruction under the iron hand of Herr Schultze. But thanks to Marcel Bruckmann, the liquidation of its debts was carried out without loss to anyone, and Stahlstadt soon became an incomparable center of production of useful industries.

For a year now, Marcel has been the very happy spouse of Jeanne, and the birth of a baby has just added to their happiness.[1]

As for Octave, he works gallantly under the orders of his brother-in-law, and supports him with all his efforts. His sister is now in the act of marrying him off to one of her friends, a charming young woman, whose qualities of good sense and reason will protect her husband against all relapses.

The wishes of the doctor and his wife have thus been fulfilled, and they are at the very zenith of happiness and even glory—if glory had ever figured in any way in the plan of their honest ambitions.

We can thus be assured that the future will be in good hands thanks to the efforts of Dr. Sarrasin and of Marcel Bruckmann, and that the examples of France-Ville and Stahlstadt, as model city and factory, will not be lost on generations to come.

THE END

NOTES

INTRODUCTION

I would like to gratefully acknowledge the help of the following people for their assistance with this project (and their enthusiasm for the work of Jules Verne): Jean-Michel Margot, Arthur B. Evans, Terry Harpold, the entire staff of the Inter-Library Loan office at Old Dominion University, and the Rosdeitcher family.

1. René Barjavel, "Sans lui notre siècle serait stupide," *Nouvelles Littéraires*, Mar. 24, 1966: 1, 7. All translations from the French, unless otherwise attributed, are my own.

2. See http://www.unesco.org/xtrans/stat/xTransStat.a?VL1=A&top=50&lg=o.

3. I. O. Evans, introduction to Jules Verne's *The Begum's Fortune* (New York: Arco, 1958), 5-7.

4. For more on the influence of *Paris in the Twentieth Century*, see Peter Schulman, "*Paris au XXème siècle*'s Legacy: Eccentricity as Defiance in Jules Verne's Uneasy Relationship with his Era." *Romance Quarterly* 48 (Fall 2001): 257-66.

5. Quoted by Marguerite Allotte de la Fuÿe, *Jules Verne, sa vie, son oeuvre* (Paris: Simon Kra, 1928), 188.

6. Gaston Leroux, *Rouletabille chez Krupp* (Paris: Editions Pierre Laffite, 1933), 16.

7. Daniel Compère and Jean-Michel Margot, *Entretiens avec Jules Verne* (Geneva: Slatkine, 1998), 224.

8. "I have no regrets about *The Begum*, I am very flattered that Mr. Jules Verne has adapted it, and the modifications that he has undertaken have taught more about the art of success than ten months of personal effort. That's how I see things," Laurie wrote to Hetzel in a letter dated December 31, 1879 (quoted by Francis Lacassin in his "Le Communard qui écrivit trois romans de Jules Verne," *Europe* 595-96 [1978]: 96).

9. Although Verne refers to Schultze's secret weapon as a "torpedo," it is really a sort of missile. For Verne, Laurie's depictions of Schultze's weapons (notably the large super-cannon and the torpedo-missile launched against France-Ville) were at the heart of the novel's narrative rather than the questions of ideology that Hetzel found the most interesting.

10. Verne always referred to Grousset/Laurie as *l'abbé* (the abbot) to protect his anonymity.

11. Olivier Dumas, Piero Gondolo della Riva, and Volker Dehs, *Correspondance inédite de Jules Verne et de Pierre-Jules Hetzel (1863–1886)*, 3 vols. (Geneva: Slatkine, 1999–2002), 3:289. All subsequent references to this edition of the correspondence between Hetzel and Verne will be identified in the text of the introduction as *Correspondance*.

12. Verne is referring to his earlier novel *From the Earth to the Moon* (1865).

13. See Volker Dehs, "Le Premier Dénouement des *Cinq Cents Millions de la Bégum*," *Bulletin de la Société Jules Verne* 123 (1997) : 37–41.

14. Charles-Noël Martin, *La Vie et l'oeuvre de Jules Verne* (Paris: Michel de L'Ormeraie, 1978), 280–81.

15. Emile Zola, *Mes haines* (Paris: Charpentier-Fasquelle, 1913), 57–58.

16. Yves Gilli and Florent Montaclair have also seen similarities between *The Begum's Millions* and Fritz Lang's work. They compare Schultze to Dr. Mabuse: "The illustration that is found in *The Begum's Millions* featuring Professor Schultze, invites a comparison to Harry Killer and Mabuse." Gilli and Montaclair, *Jules Verne et l'utopie* (Besançon: Presses du Centre Unesco de Besançon, 1999), 50.

17. Arthur B. Evans, "The Vehicular Utopias of Jules Verne," in *Transformations of Utopia: Changing Views of the Perfect Society*, ed. George Slusser et al. (New York: AMS, 1999), 99.

18. Salvador Dali, *Dali par Dali* (Montrouge: Draeger, 1970), 136. I am grateful to Jean-Michel Margot for providing me this reference.

19. Quoted by Allotte de la Fuÿe, *Jules Verne, sa vie, son œuvre*, 141.

20. Jean Chesneaux, *The Political and Social Ideas of Jules Verne* trans. Thomas Wikeley (London: Thames and Hudson, 1972), 181.

21. Jules Verne, *Paris au XXème siècle* (Paris: Hachette, 1994), 43.

22. Chesneaux, *The Political and Social Ideas of Jules Verne*, 182.

23. Vierne goes into great detail in explaining the initiation symbols associated with Marcel's journey: "Finally, always because of his superior qualities, he is judged worthy to enter into direct contact with the master of the evil city. However, the 'Dragon's Lair' itself contains circles, and doors that must be opened in order to gain the great secret." Simone Vierne, *Jules Verne et le roman initiatique: Contribution à l'étude de l'imaginaire* (Paris: Editions du Sirac, 1973), 133. In fact, as Vierne points out, there

are many details in *The Begum's Millions* that are associated with magic words, secret passageways, and heroic quest-type challenges.

24. Ross Chambers, "Cultural and Ideological Determinations in Narrative: A Note on Jules Verne's *Les Cinq cents Millions de la Bégum*," *L'Esprit Créateur* 21.3 (Fall 1981): 69–78.

25. Yves Chevrel, "Questions de méthodes et d'idéologies chez Verne et Zola: *Les Cinq cents millions de la Bégum* et *Travail*," *La Revue des Lettres Modernes* 523–29 (1978): 69–96.

26. See Piero Gondolo della Riva, "De qui est 'France-Ville'?" *Revue Jules Verne*, no. 7, (1er semestre 1999): 43–47, for an in-depth discussion of this manuscript.

27. Jules Verne, *Le Château des Carpathes* (1892; rpt., Paris: Livre de poche, 1966), 2.

28. Jules Verne, *De la terre à la lune* (1865; rpt., Paris: Hachette, 1994), 30.

29. Ibid., 32.

30. Marie-Hélène Huet, *Histoire des voyages extraordinaires: Essai sur l'oeuvre de Jules Verne* (Paris: Minard, 1973), 72.

The Begum's Millions

CHAPTER 1

1. The role of newspapers, telegrams, and telegraphs in Verne's work is very important. These are among his favored means of highlighting an important event, as when Phileas Fogg makes his bet to go around the world in eighty days in *Around the World in Eighty Days* or when the balloonists fly over Africa in *Five Weeks in a Balloon*. For more on this subject, see the chapter "Le message écrit, générateur de l'aventure" in Laurence Sudret, *Nature et artifice dans les Voyages extraordinaires de Jules Verne* (Villeneuve d'Asq: Presses Universitaires du Septentrion, 2002), 253–78.

2. For more on the symbolic importance of soliloquies in *The Begum's Millions*, see Nicolas Wagner, "Le Soliloque utopiste des *Cinq cents millions de la Bégum*," *Europe* 595–96 (1978): 117–26. Wagner argues that in *The Begum's Millions* none of the characters communicate and that the two monolithic utopian structures, France-Ville and Stahlstadt, are too ideologically set in their ways to allow for any form of dialogue.

3. Douai is a small French town in the Department of Nord on the River

Scarpe and approximately twenty miles south of Lille. It is a historic town that flourished in the Middle Ages and is known for its ramparts. In the late nineteenth century it became a coal town, known also for its chemical products and metallurgy. This seems ironically significant in the context of *The Begum's Millions,* in which Dr. Sarrasin's mortal enemy will be one who constructs a murderous coal-metallurgical town and invents strange chemical mixes to create the perfect weapon. The romantic poet Marceline Desbordes-Valmore (1786–1859) was also born there. Perhaps another factor in Verne's decision to make Douai Sarrasin's hometown is that Verne was greatly concerned about the Franco-Prussian War and lamented the Prussian rout of the French at Wissembourg under the command of Abel Douai. It was in fact a crushing defeat for the French. Verne to Hetzel, Aug. 6, 1870, in Olivier Dumas, Piero Gondolo della Riva, and Volker Dehs, *Correspondance inédite de Jules Verne et de Pierre-Jules Hetzel (1863–1886),* 3 vols. (Geneva: Slatkine, 2001), 1:147.

4. It is interesting to note that this seemingly innocuous sentence, appearing early in the novel's plot, will in fact prove to be an important foreshadowing of the *Begum's* major themes revolving around notions of nationality, as in Herr Schultze's ferocious anti-French obsession and his pan-German nationalism.

5. That Sharp resembles a "death-head" is highly suggestive in this context as he is the one to reveal the news of the inheritance to Dr. Sarrasin, which will, in turn, lead to the creation of Schultze's death-oriented dystopia and weapons factory. For a detailed analysis of the death drives in *The Begum's Millions,* see Jean-Pierre Picot, "Jules Verne et la constellation Thanatos," in *Fins de siècle: Terme, évolution, révolution?* ed. Gwenhaël Ponnau (Toulouse: Presses Universitaires du Mirail, 1989), 465–74. Indeed, in the paragraph describing Sharp, death imagery abounds: he has "dried-up lips," a "mummy-like complexion," a "skeletal form, from his heels to his occiput," etc.

6. Bar-le-Duc is an ancient town in Lorraine. It was occupied by the Prussians in 1887–71 and used as a garrison town during the Third Republic. During World War I, it was used as a supply route for the deadly battlefields in the east and was once again occupied by the Germans during World War II. The town is also famous for the funerary statue of Ligier Richier, who has a particularly horrifying "death head" (see http://caoa55. free.fr/chap5/SqueletteBlD/actualite_squeletteBlD.htm for photos and a

description of the recent restoration of the statue). There are also several other, equally sepulchral monuments by Richier in the city.

7. It is fitting that Julie Langévol dies in 1811, as this date in Napoleonic history signals the beginning of the end of Napoleon's empire. Just as Verne criticizes Schultze's obsessive desire for world conquest, he praises the peaceful nature of Sarrasin's utopian dreams.

8. Melun is a small town in the Seine-et-Marne department of France, not far from Paris. Its motto since its earliest days has been "Fidèle à ses murs jusqu'à manger des rats" ("Loyal to its walls to the point of eating rats"). Recalling, perhaps, life during the siege of the Paris Commune, this image might also foreshadow France-Ville's defenses when it is under attack from Schultze.

9. Nantes is, of course, Jules Verne's hometown!

10. Sarrasin reacts to the legal documents he has just read in a manner that is reminiscent of Axel's response to reading Saknussemm's decrypted message in *Journey to the Center of the Earth*. Both pace around the room and then sink into a chair in order to best prepare for the new future each will have to embark upon after learning of his life-altering news. These reactions highlight the thoughtfulness of these two characters in contrast to the blustery, savage Schultze, whose thoughts become immediately aggressive.

CHAPTER 2

1. Verne's opening description of the prodigal Octave recalls Verne's troubled relationship with his own son, Michel.

2. The Lycée Charlemagne, dating back to the Middle Ages, is one of the most prestigious secondary schools in France. It is a preparatory school for France's elite universities. In the context of *The Begum's Millions*, the Charlemagne allusion fits into the general theme of French pride and nationalism.

3. Verne is fascinated with orphan heroes such as Axel of *Journey to the Center of the Earth*, Dick Sand of *Un Capitaine de quinze ans* (1878, *A Captain of Fifteen*), Miss Campbell in *Le Rayon vert* (1882, *The Green Ray*), and the child in *P'tit-bonhomme* (1893, *Foundling Mick*), or protagonists in search of their fathers, as in *Le Superbe Orénoque* (1898, *The Mighty Orinoco*) or *Les Enfants du capitaine Grant* (1867, *The Children of Captain Grant*).

4. Just as Marcel's surname, Bruckmann ("Bridge Man"), foreshadows his future role as a bridge between France-Ville and Stahlstadt, which he will infiltrate, the fact that he is described early on as an "organic machine" further overdetermines how much, as an Alsatian, he can belong to both worlds, or, rather, the caricatures of worlds: France and Germany. As the spiritual heir to Sarrasin, whose name denotes a healing plant, Marcel is organic, natural, and sensitive. Yet his German side is also mechanical, fastidious, disciplined, and hardworking (in contrast to the purely Gallic Octave). This is why he not only will be successful in penetrating Stahlstadt clandestinely, but also will actually excel in that environment, earning promotions as well as the respect of Schultze himself, who will never have met "a collaborator who seemed so much after his own heart, who understood his every notion [. . .] who knew how to put into practice so quickly his theoretical ideas" (chap. 8). Indeed, once Marcel penetrates the "Dragon Lair," the "organic machine" imagery reaches its peak, as he is described as "the most assiduous of workers, the most modestly fertile inventor" (chap. 8).

5. Plant imagery abounds in the novel. Although Dr. Sarrasin's surname is botanical, in that it comes from an Asian healing plant, Octave, as his heir, is not strong enough to stand on his own. That is why Marcel will be the strong one and will be Sarrasin's "second son." While Sarrasin will be associated with healing and health, Schultze will also have a very lush garden, but it will be illusory and contain poisonous plants, such as belladonna.

6. Champigny was the site of a particularly bloody battle between the French and the Prussians during the siege of Paris (Nov. 30 and Dec. 2, 1870); Buzenval, a castle near Paris, was the site of a costly and deadly battle won by the Germans on January 19, 1871, one in which the French Academic painter Henri Reignault was killed.

7. According to conditions of Treaty of Frankfurt (May 10, 1871), France was obliged to pay a war indemnity of some 5 billion gold francs in five years. German troops remained in parts of France until the last installment of the indemnity was paid off, early, in 1873. See http://www.wordiq.com/definition/War_reparations.

CHAPTER 3

1. Once again Verne endows one of his characters with mechanical imagery. Yet, in this case, unlike Phileas Fogg, for example, who is at first described entirely in mechanical terms only to break out of his shell and go around the world in eighty days, much of the mechanical imagery in *Begum's Millions* is rather dour, as Verne seems to be commenting on the alienating nature of an overly mechanized industrial society.

2. The Hottentots, a pastoral people of Namibia and South Africa, also show up in *Five Weeks in a Balloon:* "They have put themselves at the head of a numerous and well-equipped expedition; their mission is to ascend the lake and return to Gondokoro; they have received a subsidy of more than five thousand pounds, and the Governor of the Cape of Good Hope has placed Hottentot soldiers at their disposal . . ." (*Cinq semaines en ballon* [Paris: Hachette, 1998], 34).

3. Verne often uses the present tense in his characters' accounts in order to give them a journalistic sensation of urgency and immediacy. In *Journey to the Center of the Earth,* for example, Axel uses the present tense for his journal entries during the storm on the Lidenbrock Sea. Similarly, Kazallon's narrative is entirely in the present tense in the nautical tale *The Chancellor.* For more on this subject, see William Butcher, "Le Verbe et la chair, ou l'emploi du temps," in *Jules Verne 4: Texte, image, spectacle,* ed. François Raymond (Paris: Minard, 1983), 125–48.

4. Verne himself had written with great melancholy about the human costs of wars, and notably the Franco-Prussian War. At the start of the conflict, for example, Verne wrote to his brother: "What a debacle of public funds and stocks! [. . .] What a great year 1870 turned out to be, the plague, the war and famine. God protect France" (Jules Verne to Pierre Verne, July 28, 1870, in *Bulletin de la Societé Jules Verne* 144 [2002]: 10). When the war started, Verne was rather humanistic toward the Germans: "Let us not be foolish or boastful and let us agree that the Prussians are as good as the French" (ibid., 10). Later, however, when a German reader approached Verne to suggest that he write an adventure in Germany in order to create better links between Germany and France, Verne wrote back, unhappily: "I don't think I'm up to the task of reestablishing an intimacy between the two people. [. . .] If they are enemies, it is not because they do not know each other well enough; quite the contrary, and the novel which seems to haunt you would have no success. Only an act of reparation

can modify French feelings toward the Germans. I can't tell you what that act might be; but anything that would be done outside that act would be in vain, illusory, unexecutable" (May 9, 1890, *Bulletin de la Société Jules Verne* 144 [2002]: 17).

5. In Grousset's original manuscript, the City of Well Being was simply called "Goodcity" (Villebonne), presumably in contrast to Schultze's evil one.

6. That Schultze is from the University of Iéna is significant in terms of Napoleonic history, a theme that appears throughout the novel. The battle of Iéna (Jena) was one of Napoleon's biggest victories over the Prussians in 1806. Hetzel, however, viewed Schultze as a German Napoleon: "It's about the concentration of all the material powers in the hands of one individual, in one individual's head. He's a type of German Napoleon the first. It leads to the explosion of both machine and man." Hetzel to Verne, Sept. 2, 1878, in Olivier Dumas, Piero Gondolo della Riva, and Volker Dehs, *Correspondance inédite de Jules Verne et de Pierre-Jules Hetzel (1863–1886)*, 3 vols. (Geneva: Slatkine, 2001), 2:292.

7. Although Schultze seems to resemble Phileas Fogg in his precision and strict adherence to a rigid schedule, he is, of course, his diabolical opposite. Just as Fogg personified a type of "impassive Byron" and a fine example of a perfect British gentleman, Schultze is the cliché of the punctual but overbearing German.

8. This confrontational title is, of course, a forerunner of future pamphlets during the Nazi regime declaring the "Latin race" (and non-Aryan ones) degenerate and weak. Fascist French writers during World War II, such as Céline in his infamous pamphlet *Bagatelles pour un massacre* (1937, *Bagatelles for a Massacre*), would also accuse the French of being feeble and powerless.

9. Schultze's Rabelaisian appetite seems disjunctive in relationship to the military-industrial dystopia he creates. While he is often described as a destruction-bent sociopath, his lusty attachment to food endows him with a bit of humanity as well. Yet this image is one that is also in keeping with the clichés associated with stein-clinking and sausage- devouring Germans who threaten the more "refined and civilized French." He is more animal than human and, as such, scarier to the French public, who might be fearful of being "swallowed" by their coarser, barbaric neighbors.

CHAPTER 4

1. The chapter's title, "Divided in Two," alludes to a biblical type of ruling, similar to a Cain and Abel arrangement or a Solomon-like decision.

2. As with many other characters in the novel, Sharp's name is also indicative of his persona, as he is indeed a very "sharp" individual.

3. Verne was a great reader of Dickens and had read his complete works many times. In an interview with the journalist R. H. Sherard, he remarked: "My favorite author, however, is, and always has been, Dickens. [. . .] I love him immensely and, in my forthcoming novel, *P'tit Bonhomme* [*Foundling Mick*], the proof of this is given and acknowledgment of my debt is made" ("Jules Verne at Home: His Own Account of His Life and Work Reported by R. H. Sherard," *McClure's Magazine*, January 1894, 115–24. Edited to HTML by Zvi Har'El, http://jv.gilead.org.il/sherard.html). A few years later, Verne told Gordon Jones, another journalist: "For me, the works of Charles Dickens stand alone, dwarfing all others by their amazing power and facility of expression. What humour and what exquisite pathos are to be found contrasted in his pages! [. . .] I have read and re-read his masterpieces again and again, and so has my wife. *David Copperfield, Martin Chuzzlewit, Nicholas Nickleby, The Old Curiosity Shop*—we have read them all . . ." ("Jules Verne at Home by Gordon Jones," *Temple Bar* 129 [June 1904]: 664–71. Edited to HTML by Zvi Har'El from an Etext by Arthur B. Evans. Available at http://jv.gilead.org.il/evans/Gordon_Jones_interview_of_JV.html).

4. If indeed *The Begum's Millions* marks a shift in Verne's attitude toward life, from sunny optimist in his writings to moderate pessimist, Schultze's depiction of Sarrasin as a "flighty [. . .] visionary" would correspond to Verne's somewhat defeatist position—a position held by Michel in the doomed and aborted *Paris in the Twentieth Century*. One of his own characters, Robur, for example, starts off as a poetic visionary in *Robur-le-conquérant* (1886, *Clipper of the Clouds*) but ends up as a psychotic megalomaniac in *Maître du monde* (1904, *Master of the World*), written at the end of Verne's career.

5. Schultze's use of such terms as "anthills" and "pygmies" to describe his enemies goes hand in hand with his distorted vision of the universe, in which the reader, like Gulliver, must witness a series of anamorphoses that culminate in the hallucinatory vision of Schultze at the end of the novel.

6. The chapter ends on a strikingly patriotic note, which must have

been especially rousing to young French readers in need of a boost so shortly after France's defeat at the hands of the Prussians. It is particularly significant in light of the fact that Marcel is from Alsace, a region France lost to the Germans in the Franco-Prussian War, but regained after World War I.

CHAPTER 5

1. Although France and Germany both had equivalents of the City of Steel, since the story takes place in the United States, one might also think of Pittsburgh, America's Steel City, which at the beginning of the Industrial Revolution was already a polluted factory town. The Ruhr factory town of Essen is the real model for Stahlstadt, however. The inspiration for many of Verne's descriptions of Stahlstadt, including the descriptions of puddling, the secret meetings, the encircling train, come from a tendentious anti-German book by Victor Tissot, *Les Prussiens en Allemagne* (*The Prussians in Germany*) published by Dentu in Paris in 1876.

2. The Pacific Ocean also serves as a metaphor for Dr. Sarrasin's peaceful intentions and his desire for peace and harmony despite the bellicose nature of his neighbor.

3. When Verne compares Oregon to an "American Switzerland," one thinks of a type of neutral, rather nondescript country where, among other linguistic groups, French and German communities live side by side within one nation. The notion of Switzerland appears under a different light in Verne's *Seconde patrie* (1900, *Second Homeland*), a sequel to Rudolf Wyss's *Swiss Family Robinson* in which he intertwines two stories: that of the colonists who stay on their island, New Switzerland, and that of the travelers who leave for England at the end of Wyss's novel.

4. References to extinct or inactive volcanoes abound in the *Voyages extraordinaires* (notably Snaeffels in *Journey to the Center of the Earth* and Lincoln Island in *Mysterious Island*). As with many natural cataclysms — such as storms, fires, or avalanches — the volcanoes often erupt at critical moments in the narrative. For more on the importance of volcanoes in Verne's work, see Jean-Pierre Picot, "Le Volcan chez Jules Verne: Du géologique au poétique," *Bulletin de la Société Jules Verne,* n.s., 28.111 (1994): 20–30.

5. Indeed, Krupp was the model for Schultze. In a letter to Hetzel, Verne writes: "What shall we say about the Krupp factory now, as it's really

Krupp who is in play here, and his factory that is so forbidden to indiscreet eyes?" Verne to Hetzel, Sept. 1, 1878, in Olivier Dumas, Piero Gondolo della Riva, and Volker Dehs, *Correspondance inédite de Jules Verne et de Pierre-Jules Hetzel (1863–1886)*, 3 vols. (Geneva: Slatkine, 2001), 2:289.

6. The notion of circles—and circulation—is an important Vernian theme. Most often, circles are associated with great travel, such as in *Around the World in Eighty Days*, *Around the Moon*, or Miss Campbell's quest for the green ray around Scotland in *The Green Ray*. Here, as in *Paris in the Twentieth Century*, circles are shackles that imprison the city's inhabitants within them. In *Paris in the Twentieth Century*, Verne describes society in terms of round jail cells. As Quinsonnas sees it: "American Philanthropists had already imagined locking their prisoners up in round cells so that they might not even enjoy being distracted by angles. Well, my son, today's society is round like those prisons" (*Paris au XXème siècle* [Paris: Hachette, 1994], 72). Furthermore, Marcel's workstation in Stahlstadt is in the O section, another encircling prison.

The trope of the circle as *enclosure* is another aspect of this formal principle. The architecture of Stahlstadt recalls the *bolgias* of Dante's *Inferno*. The notion of hellish prisons is reiterated throughout the novel, such as the ban on all departures in the Central Block and Sarrasin's observation to Marcel that he will be "risking a sort of descent into hell" (chap. 16). Consider too Schultze's ghoulish frozen body in chapter 18.

7. Codes are ubiquitous in the *Voyages extraordinaires* and appear in many of Verne's novels such as *Journey to the Center of the Earth*, *La Jangada* (1881, *The Jangada*), and *Mathias Sandorf* (1885). Following in the footsteps of Poe, Verne often uses ingenious cryptograms or other types of encrypted messages to propel the various quests and missions of his stories. In this instance, rather than serving as a key to discovery, the code is used by the main protagonist for the purpose of self-defense, as he is descending into an evil counter-universe.

8. Verne invokes the English philosopher John Stuart Mill (1806–73) in order to whimsically bring up his utilitarian theories, such as that articulated in Mill's famous apothegm "Actions are right in proportion as they tend to promote happiness, wrong as they tend to produce the reverse of happiness." Since thinking of Jeanne clearly makes Marcel happy, it is the right thing. Verne could also be referring to Mill's *System of Logic*, his analysis of inductive proof. In terms of the novel as a whole, however,

it would be hard to ignore Mill's *On Liberty* in the context of the two contrasting cities, Stahlstadt and France-Ville. In the former, Schultze has no confidence in humans and only wishes to subjugate his citizens for his own personal gain, whereas France-Ville purports to have great trust in human nature, giving people the right amount of liberty to thrive and seek happiness (Verne refers to it in his letters to Hetzel as "La Cité du Bien-être," the feel-good city, or the city of happiness, which is compatible with Mill's notion of a utilitarian society). In *On Liberty,* however, Mill also demonstrates his fears of American society, which he, like Alexis de Tocqueville before him, considered to be a rather conformist, middle-class one that, despite its prosperity, cared little about individual liberty.

CHAPTER 6

1. Carl Bauer, the innocent boy whose surname means "farmer" in German, seeks out nature in the alienating, unnatural metropolis Schultze has created, one that is centered on death and destruction. He is "farming" the last vestiges of life in the deadly environment that eventually kills him. As in the case of Nemo in *Twenty Thousand Leagues under the Sea* or Axel and Lidenbrock in *Journey to the Center of the Earth,* one can make important scientific discoveries beneath the Earth's surface, rather than on top of it, where war and injustice run wild.

2. Maulesmühle means the "Mill of the [animal's] Mouth." Here "mouth" has a derogatory connotation in both German and French ("ta gueule" in French is used to say "shut up!"). In the name of Maulesmühle, who is an engineer for Schultze, one can interpret the mine that Bauer explores as the animal mouth that spews up the minerals Schultze uses to create his weapons of war, and at the bottom of which is only poison.

3. Unlike Schultze who, in a manner reminiscent of Master Zacharius, needs to control time through precise clocks and watches, the workers who toil in Stahlstadt's mines are so removed from natural society that they lose all sense of normal rhythm. They are similar to the workers in Fritz Lang's *Metropolis,* who know no sunlight or moonlight and must rely on a work schedule that is dictated to them from money-hungry, wealthy rulers who live above them.

4. Through the eyes and imagination of Mme Bauer, Verne is also showing us what we, the readers, cannot see. Forbidden to actually descend to its depths, she constructs a whole vision of the mine based on what she

has been told by others. One can perhaps read in her ability to see without being able to see a reference to the blind poet Homer, for example, whom Victor Hugo so admired for being able to see more clearly into things than those with perfect eyesight. In the dark world of Stahlstadt, Verne seems to highlight the very human notion of using imagination and dreams to escape the harsh realities of unrelenting fear and despair.

5. Once again, a Vernian hero descends into the Earth, a mythical journey into Hell (a *nekya*), in this case not for scientific discovery but on a rescue mission reminiscent of Jack Ryan's saving Starr and Ford in *Les Indes noires* (1877, *The Black Indies*).

6. The chapter ends in tragedy as Mme Bauer outlives her child as well as her husband. This ending is similar to other great mining epics, such as Zola's *Germinal* or G. W. Pabst's classic film *Kameradschaft*. Verne, in fact, heavily researched mining conditions for *The Black Indies* and discussed similar technical issues with Hetzel for *The Begum's Millions*, such as whether or not to use a Galibert device. The scenes in the mine were sections of Grousset's manuscript that Verne originally did not like because he felt he had already written about them in *The Black Indies*: "As for the episode with little Carl, and his death in the mine which has nothing to do with the story's subject; besides which, I've already done all that in the *Black Indies*." Verne to Hetzel, Sept. 1, 1878, in Olivier Dumas, Piero Gondolo della Riva, and Volker Dehs, *Correspondance inédite de Jules Verne et de Pierre-Jules Hetzel (1863–1886),* 3 vols. (Geneva: Slatkine, 2001), 2:289.

CHAPTER 7

1. Carl Bauer's death by carbon dioxide in the depths of the mine while Stahlstadt's leader enjoys the luxuries of life in the clouds in his Tower of the Bull, is echoed in a famous *Star Trek* episode titled "The Cloud Minders." In it, the mineworkers are called Troglytes and live in a steel city similar to Stahlstadt. They are enslaved by capitalist exploiters who live high above the mines in a cloud village called Stratos and who use a carbon dioxide–like substance to maintain the workers in a state of submissiveness. See "The Cloud Minders" (teleplay: Margaret Armen, David Gerrold, and Oliver Crawford), in James Blish, *Star Trek 6,* (New York: Bantam Books, 1972), 94–118.

2. Verne's blindfold imagery is of course suggestive of a Masonic ritual,

as Simone Vierne has richly analyzed in her classic work *Jules Verne et le roman initiatique* (Paris: Editions du Sirac, 1973). That Marcel must go through an examination session, and then work in relation to a mine, is a cruel distortion of the famous Masonic credo: "Visita interioria terrae recticando invenies occultum lapidum" ("Visit the interior of the earth and by rectification you will find the hidden rock"). Although Marcel must be subjected to a warped initiation into the Stahlstadt elite, his mission is essentially bent on finding Schultze's secret weapon, located deep within Schultze's secret labyrinth, in order to "rectify" the imbalance between the warmongering dystopia and the ever-peaceful utopia.

3. Not only was Verne prescient in anticipating submarine and air travel in his earlier novels, but, in this instance, he was painfully accurate in his description of the kind of repressive totalitarian state that would later be developed by regimes such as Hitler's Germany and Stalin's Soviet Union.

4. In this sentence, Verne touches on two key myths relating to the *The Begum's Millions:* Theseus and the Minotaur and the myth of the Cyclopes in *The Odyssey.* As in the Minotaur myth, Marcel must grasp the thread from the spider web/maze of the Tower of the Bull, where the Minotaur, Herr Schultze, awaits. Significantly, the labyrinth in Greek mythology is built by the inventor Daedalus; in this case the inventor, Herr Schultze, functions also as the Minotaur. The second myth, that of the Cyclopes, is also extremely relevant as they were metalworkers; Schultze mixes different magical metals into a single overpowering cannon—a variant of the thunder and lightening that the Cyclopes created. Moreover, just as the Cyclopes only had one eye, Schultze is monomaniacal in his single vision of dominating the world for Germany and destroying France-Ville.

Of equal interest, in terms of the rest of Verne's works, is the Cyclopes episode of *The Odyssey,* in which Odysseus saves his life by saying "*nemo*" or "nobody" when the Cyclopes ask him his name. As we know, it is from this episode that Verne took the name for Captain Nemo, who is cloaked in his invisible submarine in order to remain incognito from the warships above him. Verne had originally thought Schultze was much more interesting than Dr. Sarrasin in Grousset's original story and wanted to make him more like Nemo, as he explains in a letter to Hetzel: "The head of the canon factory should have been Nemo, and not such a fellow who is ridiculous." Verne to Hetzel, June 2, 1877, in Olivier Dumas, Piero Gondolo della

Riva, and Volker Dehs, *Correspondance inédite de Jules Verne et de Pierre-Jules Hetzel (1863–1886)*, 3 vols. (Geneva: Slatkine, 2001), 2:184.

In terms of the narrative, Marcel, like Odysseus, is trapped in the Cyclopes cave and must renounce his identity, becoming another "nobody," Johann Schwartz. Just as Odysseus tricks the Cyclopes into drinking too much wine and passing out, Marcel will attempt to trick the secret weapon out of Schultze through "too much wine," which in this case is Schultze's vanity.

5. The reference is to the vow Hannibal made to his father when he was nine years old, promising that he would maintain a hatred for the Romans until Carthage was avenged and Rome was in ruins. This fits into the many military images and allusions that continually pepper Verne's narrative.

6. One wonders whether Verne is poking fun at Hetzel here when he says "a virgin forest gains in beauty when viewed through the descriptions of great writers," as Stahlstadt is in fact named after Hetzel's *nom de plume* Stahl.

7. Schultze's luxurious garden is another example of his sybaritic excesses, which, in this instance, seem disturbingly decadent. It is fitting that Marcel, who has been described as an "organic machine," is able to exploit the garden in order to engineer his escape. Once again, his ability to fit into both worlds—the natural and the mechanical—ensures his survival. The image of the garden is particularly frightening inasmuch as it represents the opposite of the innocence and purity a normal garden might suggest. It is a patch of freedom and nature that is entirely appropriated by the cruel and tyrannical Schultze for his selfish pleasures alone while his workers are forced to toil in a polluted, dark, and mechanical factory hell.

8. Sohne's name alludes to the word for "son" (*Sohn*) in German. Just as the villagers were forced to sacrifice their daughters and sons to the Minotaur to be devoured by him, Sohne is gratuitously sacrificed to Schultze. Stahlstadt continues to be the polar opposite of France-Ville in this way. If in France-Ville the father-son dynamic between Dr. Sarrasin and Marcel is a loving one, the Sohne-Schultze and then the Marcel/Schwartz-Schultze relationships are twisted, murderous ones.

CHAPTER 8

1. Yves Chevrel notes that Verne could well have gotten the title of this chapter from Victor Tissot's *Les Prussiens en Allemagne*, in which

he describes getting lost in an opulent German house that he refers to as "the dragon's lair" ("l'antre d'un dragon"). Yves Chevrel, "Questions de méthodes et d'idéologies chez Verne et Zola," in *L'Ecriture vernienne 2*, ed. François Raymond (Paris: Lettres Modernes, 1978), 77.

2. Marcel and Schultze's relationship is curious in the sense that it is initially a kind of father-and-son rapport. This is why Marcel Bruckmann is the one to go infiltrate Stahlstadt and not Octave. As his name Bruckmann ("bridge man") implies, he has the moral qualities of a Frenchman in Verne's typology and the practicality and assiduity of a German.

3. Verne's invocation of the "lesson of 1870" is of course meant to stir the passions of his French readers; it certainly provoked the Nazis to take the book out of German libraries during World War II.

4. The hidden staircase behind the bookcase is a touch worthy of the Fantômas cycle or Gaston Leroux. For a study of the fantastic elements in Verne's work, see Volker Dehs, "Inspiration du fantastique? Jules Verne et l'oeuvre de E. T. A. Hoffmann," *La Revue des Lettres Modernes: Histoire des Idées et des Littératures* 812–17 (1987): 163–90; and Oliver Dumas, "Le Fantastique chez Jules Verne," *Bulletin de la Société Jules Verne,* (Oct.– Dec. 1984): 162–63. See also François Raymond, ed., *Jules Verne 5: Emergences du fantastique* (Paris: Minard, 1987).

5. With Schultze's bomb, which freezes and kills people but leaves buildings standing, Verne predicts the neutron bomb that was created during the Cold War. Moreover, he also foresees the weapons of mass destruction that were perfected in the last part of the twentieth century, as well as the chemical weapons that began to be used during World War I, a war that once again pitted the Germans against the French.

6. Schultze's description of projectiles containing, in turn, several other smaller projectiles "like tubes in a telescope" are precursors to the twentieth-century MIRVs (multiple independently targeted reentry vehicles), which, like Schultze's invention, are also ballistic missiles, only deadlier, as they contain various nuclear warheads that can destroy a wide range of targets despite being launched from a single location.

7. Schultze's statement "But their work is doomed, for it is from death — sown by us — that life is to be born" is echoed in Francis Thompson's (1859–1907) famous poem, "Ode to the Setting Sun": "But death hath in itself the germ of birth. [. . .] For there is nothing lives but something dies

/ And there is nothing dies but something lives / For they are twain yet one, and Death is Birth."

8. This could sum up Verne's later vision of America as a "proving ground" for lunatics and ideologues for whom anything is permissible with enough money, as exemplified by the millionaires who create *Propeller Island* or the protagonists of *Topsy-Turvy* who want to shift the axis of the earth in order to melt the North Pole's glaciers and exploit the North Pole for its mineral riches.

9. In *Tintin chez Jules Verne* (Brussels: Editions Lefrancq, 1998), Jean-Paul Tomasi and Michel Deligne suggest that Hergé's beloved characters Dupond-Dupont were inspired by Sigimer and Arminius. They also point out that a version of Verne's Schultze is reproduced in Hergé's *Mysterious Star* in the form of "Herr Doctor Otto Schulze of the University of Iéna" (129–31).

CHAPTER 9

1. Arminius and Sigimer are ancient Germanic names. Arminius was the war-chieftain of the Cherusci in year 1 C.E., and Sigimer was his father. Arminius is famous for winning the decisive battle at Varus and stopping the Roman expansion into Germany. As Arminius was only twenty-seven years old when he won this victory, one can think of Marcel now stopping the German expansion into France-Ville. Once again, Verne uses ancient military imagery to maintain the impression of larger-than-life adversaries over which the young hero must prevail.

2. Verne use of cataclysmic fire as a denouement is frequent in his works. One thinks of the endings to *Master of the World,* for example, when Robur's airship, *L'Epouvante* (The Terror), blows up in flames, or the volcanic eruption that puts an end to Axel and Lidenbrock's journey to the center of the Earth; the one that terminates the gold hunt in *Le Volcan d'or* (1906, *The Golden Volcano*); the fiery end of Lincoln Island in *The Mysterious Island;* and the burning of the *Forward* at the end of Book I of *The Voyages and Adventures of Captain Hatteras.*

CHAPTER 10

1. Verne decried the fact that Grousset seemed to insert the article on France-Ville, which he thought was boring, almost randomly. He also

thought the city seemed more American than French, as the French would have more artistry in their city: "I also don't see any delineated contrast between the city of steel and the city of well-being. The latter, which is not described at all, except within a newspaper clipping, which is very boring, doesn't strike me as a French city but an American one. That Dr. Sarrazin [*sic*] is really just a Yankee. A Frenchman, in opposition to a German, must function more as an artist than he does here." Verne to Hetzel, Sept. 1, 1878, in Olivier Dumas, Piero Gondolo della Riva, and Volker Dehs, *Correspondance inédite de Jules Verne et de Pierre-Jules Hetzel (1863–1886)*, 3 vols. (Geneva: Slatkine, 2001), 2:289.

2. Verne's coordinates would seem to be slightly off, as they would put France-Ville about twenty miles out to the sea.

3. Verne inserts an interesting bit of American history by referring to the Chinese coolies. Although they were instrumental in building the Central Pacific Railroad, they did not bask in the glory of its completion (pictures celebrating it always omitted the Chinese workers). When the gold rush ended, local workers turned on the Chinese and sacked their business establishments, and laws were passed to encourage them to leave the United States. In Los Angeles in 1873, for example, "19 Chinese laborers were hanged and shot in one evening. The massacre was accompanied by the theft of over $40,000," according to Henry K. Norton in *The Story of California from the Earliest Days to the Present* (Chicago: McClurg, 1924), 283–96. Norton goes on to evoke racial stereotypes that fit into the obsession with work and productivity exhibited both by Stahlstadt and France-Ville: "Probably the most conspicuous characteristic of the Chinese is their passion for work. [They] seemingly must work. [. . .] With proper instruction their industrial adaptability is very great. They learn what they are shown with almost incredible facility and soon become adept" (284).

4. Verne was fascinated with railroads, as in Fogg's trip across the United States. For more on the use of rail travel in Verne's work, see Pierre Terrasse, "Jules Verne et les chemins de fer," *Bulletin de la Société Jules Verne* 14 (Apr.–June 1970): 116–21, rpt. in *Grand Album Jules Verne* (Paris: Hachette, 1982), 30–43.

5. According to Piero Gondolo della Riva, Dr. Benjamin Ward Richardson was born in Somersby, England, in the same year as Verne, 1828. He was a famous doctor known for his studies of tuberculosis, alcoholism, and nicotine addiction. In addition to his scientific treatise, he wrote

a few plays, a historical novel, and a utopia titled *Hygeia, a City of Health* (1876), which was the object of his session at the Social Science Association conference in Brighton in 1875. This is the text that inspired both Grousset and Verne. Gondolo della Riva asserts that the description of the city found in *The Begum's Millions,* along with its rules and its credos, is extracted almost word for word from Richardson's piece. For a detailed account of the origins of France-Ville, see Gondolo della Riva, "De qui est 'France-Ville'?" *Revue Jules Verne,* no. 7, (1er semestre 1999), 43–47.

6. It is interesting to note the parallel between Schultze's bought sculpture garden, which is completely private and for his own exclusive enjoyment, and France-Ville's, which can only afford copies but which is completely public and built for the public good.

7. Verne is probably referring here to New Jerusalem, to be rebuilt after the Apocalypse (Revelation 21:1–6).

CHAPTER 11

1. France-Ville takes the old saying *mens sana in corpore sano* (a sound mind in a sound body) as its motto.

2. Verne touches on an issue that would continue to be relevant throughout the twentieth century: should America intervene in foreign wars? In World Wars I and II, Americans indeed came to the aid of the French against the Germans. Ironically in *The Begum's Millions,* however, the war is fought not in a far-off Europe but on American soil in the Northwest, where—according to the novel—anyone can buy a piece of land if the price is right.

CHAPTER 12

1. The threat of "barbarians" destroying Sarrasin's advanced city has been foreshadowed throughout the text with an abundance of Roman and medieval war images: While Sarrasin's name mainly comes from an Asian healing plant (also known as "black wheat"), it is also a name given during the Middle Ages by Europeans to Muslims, notably in *The Song of Roland,* when Charlemagne's troops stop the invading Saracens, and in the battle of Poitiers, where the Saracens were defeated. Similarly, there are references to Hannibal, Arminius, Napoleon, and, obliquely, to the Crusaders in Verne's reference to Jerusalem, the "model city" on the borders of Syria.

2. That Schultze has made a mistake and therefore accidentally saves France-Ville is common to Verne's novels, where mistakes often lead to happy results, such as Paganel's miscalculations in *The Children of Captain Grant*, Fogg's winning his bet because of his forgetting about the International Dateline, or Maston's error in *Topsy-Turvy* by which the disastrous rotation of the Earth's axis is averted by the misplacing of a decimal point. For more on the importance of errors in Verne's work, see Peter Schulman, "Eccentricity as Clinamen: Jules Verne's Error-Driven Geniuses," *Excavatio* 16, nos. 1–2 (2002): 274–84.

3. Verne meant to say "per minute." It was going 150 leagues per *minute,* for it covered the ten leagues from Stahlstadt to France-Ville in four seconds. Some modern French editions of *Les Cinq cents millions de la Bégum* (e.g., the Livre de poche edition) have corrected this error in the text.

CHAPTER 14

1. Indeed, the role of women seems to be shortchanged in this novel and relegated to that of mother or love-object, as the men, engaged in war or work, are the focus of the narrative. For more on the role of women in Jules Verne's work, see "*Jules Verne au féminin*" in the special issue of *Revue Jules Verne* 9 (1er semestre 2000). Not surprisingly, there seem to be no women working in Stahlstadt. The City of Steel appears to an entirely male metropolis with the exception of Carl Bauer's mother, whereas France-Ville, while also male-driven (Sarrasin remarks: "We'll need strong and energetic men, active scientists, not only to erect, but defend our structure" [chap. 4]) is also based on familiar "family values."

Although the relegation of female characters to a supporting role is common in Verne's work, it may bring attention to a thematic element of this novel: Schultze, unlike Sarrasin, is not only a bachelor but has no romantic attachments at all. In fact he is interested in his garden rather than in women. Since he is completely sterile in this way, his only focus is on machines and instruments of death, and thus the destruction of families rather than their preservation. Since his Steel City is driven purely by thanatos, eros has no place in the slave state he controls. As a result, the novel's ending with an image of marriage and family represents Schultze's true ideological defeat.

2. For more on Verne's political-philosophical vision of the ideal politi-

cal state, see Jean Chesneaux's classic text, *The Political and Social Ideas of Jules Verne,* trans. Thomas Wikeley (London: Thames and Hudson, 1971). Yves Chevrel also has an interesting discussion of France-Ville, which he believes owes much to the philosopher Etienne Cabet's (1788–1856) socialist theories. Cabet's ideal state, Icaria—which, interestingly, was originally going to be called Sarrasina—stresses the power of the public over the centralized power in the hands of a dictator. Cabet himself could have been a model for the pioneering Sarrasin as he actually established a communist-like society in Nauvoo, Illinois, in the 1850s with a group of mostly middle-class French idealists. According to the *Illinois Alive!* project, "The group settled at the site, located on the Mississippi River, after the Mormons departed. Cabet and his followers tried to set up a brotherhood based upon the principles of peace and justice expounded in Cabet's book *Voyage in Icaria,* inspired by Sir Thomas More's *Utopia.* At its peak, the colony numbered over 500 members, but dissension over legal matters and the death of Cabet caused some members to leave this parent colony and move to other Icarian locations in East St. Louis, Iowa, and California" (http://history.alliancelibrarysystem.com/IllinoisAlive/files/wi/htm4/wi000182.cfm).

CHAPTER 15

1. Once again, Verne makes a biblical reference. Rather than the Tower of the Bull, laden with Greek mythology and terror, the Tower of Babel focuses on American cultural hybridity outside the utopia-dystopia and French-German dialectic of France-Ville and Stahlstadt. If, in Genesis, the Tower of Babel is a symbol for humanity's rebellion against God in its attempt to reach the heavens, the San Francisco Stock Exchange's Babel might be seen as similarly hubristic in that its participants are trying to reach a financial heaven through the accumulation of stocks and bonds. Verne's portrayal of the nefarious role of money in American society will continue to be a theme of some of his later works, such as *Propeller Island* and *Topsy-Turvy.* Interestingly, in his earlier novels, such as *From the Earth to the Moon*—where Verne also uses the metaphor of a Tower of Babel when describing the international crowd assembled at the launch site at Stone's Hill in Florida—this theme of hyperbolic Yankee capitalism is treated with humor and gentle satire.

2. The reporters Meiklejohn and Blunderbuss are no doubt Verne's

humorous inventions. Blunderbuss in particular fits into the theme of the blusterous Schultze, who is also a "blunderbuss," the term stemming from a type of pistol used by pirates, known for making a thunderous noise ("blunder" meaning *thunder* in Dutch). It fits in with the continuous war imagery in the novel as well.

CHAPTER 16

1. Marcel descends into yet another Virgil-like *nekya* into the underworld, this time accompanied by his friend Octave, whom he will try to "initiate" into manhood through the experience.

CHAPTER 17

1. Note how, in contrast to the way Octave was first portrayed in the novel—as having followed Marcel into battle but "six meters behind"—in this instance he and Marcel are attacking their enemy side by side. As mentioned in the note to chapter 16, for Octave, this expedition into Stahlstadt constitutes a kind of heroic quest and initiation rite by which he finally proves himself and becomes a man.

CHAPTER 18

1. It is interesting that Marcel and Octave make this discovery by peering through a window into Schultze's laboratory. Windows play an important role in Verne's *Voyages extraordinaires,* especially in the marvelous vehicles in which his characters are frequently transported, such as the Nautilus in *Twenty Thousand Leagues under the Sea* or the space capsule in *Around the Moon.* In these adventures, such "windows on the world" allow the heroes to make dangerous and extraordinary discoveries from the comfort and safety of the vehicle, almost as though they were watching a film. In *The Begum's Millions,* however, the object of the spectacle is frozen and immobile. Moreover, rather than looking out on a new world, the protagonists are now looking inward, and rather than observing the natural phenomena of new, virginal worlds, they now see the horrors of what too much man-made industry can unleash. For a more in-depth analysis on the role of windows and other "strategic" narrative devices in Verne's work, see Arthur B. Evans, *Jules Verne Rediscovered: Didacticism and the Scientific Novel* (Westport, Conn.: Greenwood Press, 1988), 109–58.

2. Verne may be alluding to Dante's *Inferno* XXXIV, where Satan is dis-

covered by Dante locked in the ice at the center of Dis, the lowest circle of Hell, eternally chewing at the bodies of Brutus, Cassius, and Judas Iscariot from his three mouths.

3. Pompeii is a reoccurring image in Verne's works, most notably in *Twenty Thousand Leagues under the Sea* when he describes the lost continent of Atlantis: "Rapid currents carried away all these gases in diffusion, and torrents of lava slid rapidly to the bottom of the mountain like an eruption of Vesuvius on another Torre del Greco. [. . .] There indeed, under my eyes, in ruins, laid low, was a city destroyed, its roofs open to the sky, its temples fallen, its arches dislocated, its columns lying on the ground from which one could still recognize the solid proportions of Tuscan architecture [. . .] a perfect Pompeii buried beneath the waters which Captain Nemo resurrected before my eyes." *The Complete 20,000 Leagues under the Sea,* translated with introduction and notes by Emanuel J. Midal (Bloomington: Indiana University Press, 1984), 371.

4. Although both Verne and Grousset spelled Schultze's name with an "e," in his correspondence with Hetzel about Grousset's manuscript, Verne consistently refers to this character as "Schultz." Since Verne maintained the "e" in this name for his final version of *The Begum's Millions,* one wonders if perhaps he was thinking of the famous German biologist Max Schultze (1825–74), a successor to Hermann von Helmholtz at the University of Bonn and one of the founding fathers of cell biology. It is not inconceivable that Verne came across Schultze's work in one of the science magazines he routinely read.

Ironically, in his early English translation of this work, W. H. G. Kingston changed "Schultze" to "Schultz"—as per the more common British spelling of this German name. But this small name change would have unforeseen textual repercussions, as Kingston would now find himself required to rewrite Verne's text as follows: "'Schult. . . . ' This signature was unfinished, the final 'z' and the usual flourish being wanting." *The Begum's Fortune,* trans. W. H. G. Kingston (London: Sampson Low, 1879), 228. Incidentally, without the "e" and "z," *Schult-heiß* in German means a "sheriff or mayor of a village."

CHAPTER 19

1. Just as the novel begins with death imagery surrounding Sharp as he announces that Sarrasin has just inherited his millions (and foreshadows

the death and misery that will also sprout as a result of Schultze's inheriting a fortune as well), it closes with a reference to death, even though Marcel has just emerged victorious from Schultze's Hades.

CHAPTER 20

1. The novel ends with a marriage and consequently on a happy note
—the traditional ending for nontragic novels of the nineteenth century.
Yet the ending appears slightly contrived in the context of the rest of the
novel, focused as it is on the epic and violent struggle between two societies. According to his correspondence with Hetzel, Verne originally wished
to end the novel abruptly with Schultze's death; but Hetzel protested, saying, "Conclude with the death of Schultze? So be it. But marry off Marcel
all the same; otherwise, what is to become of him? He is too important and
too well developed to be allowed to just fizzle out at the end. It's he who is
Schultze's real antagonist." Hetzel to Verne, Oct. 17, 1878, in Olivier Dumas, Piero Gondolo della Riva, and Volker Dehs, *Correspondance inédite
de Jules Verne et de Pierre-Jules Hetzel (1863–1886),* 3 vols. (Geneva: Slatkine, 2001), 2:302.

Like *The Odyssey,* most of Verne's narratives are essentially circular: the
hero returns home once the foes have been defeated, the adventures completed, or the secrets discovered, and life returns to normal. The science-
fictional "novum" (submarine, flying machine, artificial island, etc.) generally disappears, along with the speculative quality of the text itself, which
now reassumes a wholly mimetic character. Despite ending with a victory
for good and the hero happily married, *The Begum's Millions* nevertheless
lacks a certain degree of closure. Although it will be under more peaceful
control, Stahlstadt will eventually be rebuilt and reused as a factory village
—and will continue to manufacture weapons of mass destruction (osten-
sibly only for self-defense). This fact alone leaves the reader with a somewhat unsettled feeling despite the "felicity" of family values implied by
Marcel and Jeanne's domesticity.

BIBLIOGRAPHY

WORKS OF JULES VERNE

All works were published in Paris by J. Hetzel unless otherwise indicated. Most novels by Verne were first published in serial format in Hetzel's *Magasin d'Education et de Récréation,* then as octodecimo books (normally unillustrated), and finally as octavo illustrated "luxury" editions in red and gold. The date given is that of the first book publication. Many entries have been gleaned from the excellent bibliographical studies of Volker Dehs and Jean-Michel Margot, François Raymond, Olivier Dumas, Edward Gallagher, Judith A. Mistichelli, and John A. Van Eerde, and especially those of Piero Gondolo della Riva and Brian Taves and Stephen Michaluk Jr.

Works in the Series
Voyages extraordinaires (Extraordinary Voyages)

Novels marked by an asterisk were published after Jules Verne's death in 1905. It is important to understand that most of these post-1905 works were either substantially revamped or, in some cases, almost totally written by Jules Verne's son, Michel. For each novel listed, information about its first English-language edition is provided (date of publication, publisher, and translator) as well as the alternate English titles sometimes used. Also included are recommendations about the translation quality of certain English-language editions.

Cinq semaines en ballon (1863, illus. Edouard Riou and Henri de Montaut). *Five Weeks in a Balloon* (1869, New York: Appleton, trans. William Lackland). Recommended: translation by William Lackland. Not recommended: Chapman and Hall edition (rpt. 1995, Sutton "Pocket Classics"), the Routledge edition (rpt. 1911, Parke), and translations by Arthur Chambers (1926, Dutton; rpt. 1996, Wordsworth Classics) and by I. O. Evans (1958, Hanison, "Fitzroy Edition").

Voyage au centre de la terre (1864, illus. Edouard Riou). *A Journey to the Centre of the Earth* (1871, Griffith and Farran, translator unknown). Alternate titles: *A Journey to the Interior of the Earth, Journey to the Cen-*

ter of the Earth. Recommended: translations by Robert Baldick (1965, Penguin, *Journey to the Center of the Earth*) and by William Butcher (1992, Oxford, *Journey to the Centre of the Earth*). Not recommended: all reprints of the Griffith and Farran ("Hardwigg") edition, which begin "Looking back to all that has occurred to me since that eventful day . . ." (1965, Airmont; 1986, Signet Classics; 1992, Tor; among many others).

De la terre à la lune (1865, illus. Henri de Montaut). *From the Earth to the Moon* (1867, Gage, translator unknown). Alternate titles: *From the Earth to the Moon Direct, in Ninety-seven Hours Twenty Minutes, The Baltimore Gun Club, The American Gun Club, The Moon Voyage*. Recommended: translations by Harold Salemson (1970, Heritage, *From the Earth to the Moon*) and by Walter James Miller (1978, Crowell, *The Annotated Jules Verne: From the Earth to the Moon*). Not recommended: translations by Louis Mercier and Eleanor King (1873, Sampson Low, *From the Earth to the Moon Direct, in Ninety-seven Hours Twenty Minutes;* rpt. 1967, Airmont; 1983, Avenel; among many others), by Edward Roth (1874, King and Baird, *The Baltimore Gun Club;* rpt. 1962, Dover), and by Lowell Bair (1967, Bantam, *From the Earth to the Moon*).

Voyages et aventures du capitaine Hatteras (1866, illus. Edouard Riou and Henri de Montaut). *At the North Pole: The Voyages and Adventures of Captain Hatteras* and *The Desert of Ice: The Voyages and Adventures of Captain Hatteras* (1874–75, Osgood, translator unknown). Alternate titles: *The English at the North Pole* and *The Field of Ice, The Adventures of Captain Hatteras*. Recommended: Osgood edition (rpt. 1976, Aeonian). Not recommended: I. O. Evans "Fitzroy Edition" translation (1961, *The Adventures of Captain Hatteras: At the North Pole* and *The Adventures of Captain Hatteras: The Wilderness of Ice*).

Les Enfants du capitaine Grant (1867–68, illus. Edouard Riou). *In Search of the Castaways* (1873, Lippincott, translator unknown). Alternate titles: *The Mysterious Document/On the Track/Among the Cannibals, The Castaways, or A Voyage around the World, Captain Grant's Children*. Recommended: Routledge edition (1876, translator unknown, *Voyage Round the World: South America/Australia/New Zealand*). Not recommended: the Lippincott edition or the I. O. Evans "Fitzroy Edition" translation (1964, Arco, *The Children of Captain Grant: The Mysterious Document* and *The Children of Captain Grant: Among the Cannibals*).

Vingt mille lieues sous les mers (1869–70, illus. Edouard Riou and Alphonse-Marie de Neuville). *Twenty Thousand Leagues under the Seas* (1872, Sampson Low, trans. Louis Mercier). Alternate titles: *Twenty Thousand Leagues under the Sea, 20,000 Leagues under the Sea, At the Bottom of the Deep, Deep Sea*. Recommended: translations by Walter James Miller and Frederick Paul Walter (1993, Naval Institute Press, *Jules Verne's Twenty Thousand Leagues under the Sea*) and by William Butcher (1998, Oxford, *Twenty Thousand Leagues under the Seas*). Not recommended: translation by Louis Mercier cited above (rpt. 1963, Airmont; 1981, Castle; 1995, Tor; among many others).

Autour de la Lune (1870, illus. Emile-Antoine Bayard and Alphonse-Marie de Neuville). *Round the Moon* (1873, Sampson Low, trans. Louis Mercier and Eleanor King). Alternate titles: *All Around the Moon, Around the Moon, A Moon Voyage*. Recommended: translations by Jacqueline and Robert Baldick (1970, Dent, *Around the Moon*) and by Harold Salemson (1970, Heritage, *Around the Moon*). Not recommended: translations by Louis Mercier and Eleanor King (cited above) and by Edward Roth (1874, Catholic, *All Around the Moon;* rpt. 1962, Dover).

Une Ville flottante (1871, illus. Jules-Descartes Férat). *A Floating City* (1874, Sampson Low, translator unknown). Alternate title: *The Floating City*. Recommended: translation by Henry Frith (1876, Routledge, *The Floating City*). Not recommended: I. O. Evans "Fitzroy Edition" translation (1958, Hanison, *A Floating City*).

Aventures de trois Russes et de trois Anglais (1872, illus. Jules-Descartes Férat). *Meridiana: The Adventures of Three Englishmen and Three Russians in South Africa* (1872, Sampson Low, trans. Ellen E. Frewer). Alternate titles: *Adventures of Three Englishmen and Three Russians in Southern Africa, Adventures in the Land of the Behemoth, Measuring a Meridian*. Recommended: translation by Henry Frith (1877, Routledge, *Adventures of Three Englishmen and Three Russians in Southern Africa*). Not recommended: Shepard edition (1874, translator unknown, *Adventures in the Land of the Behemoth*) and I. O. Evans "Fitzroy Edition" translation (1964, Arco, *Measuring a Meridian*).

Le Pays des fourrures (1873, illus. Jules-Descartes Férat and Alfred Quesnay de Beaurepaire). *The Fur Country* (1873, Sampson Low, trans. N. D'Anvers). Alternate title: *Sun in Eclipse/Through the Behring Strait*. Recommended: translation by Edward Baxter (1987, NC Press, *The*

Fur Country). Not recommended: I. O. Evans "Fitzroy Edition" (1966, Arco, *The Fur Country: Sun in Eclipse* and *The Fur Country: Through the Behring Strait*).

Le Tour du monde en quatre-vingts jours (1873, illus. Alphonse-Marie de Neuville and Léon Benett). *A Tour of the World in Eighty Days* (1873, Osgood, trans. George M. Towle). Alternate titles: *The Tour of the World in Eighty Days, Around the World in Eighty Days, Around the World in 80 Days, Round the World in Eighty Days*. Recommended: translation by William Butcher (1995, Oxford, *Around the World in Eighty Days*). Not recommended: translations by Lewis Mercier (1962, Collier/Doubleday) and by K. E. Lichtenecker (1965, Hamlyn).

Le Docteur Ox (1874, illus. Lorenz Froelich, Théophile Schuler, Emile-Antoine Bayard, Adrien Marie, Edmond Yon, and Antoine Bertrand). *Doctor Ox* (1874, Osgood, trans. George M. Towle). Short story collection. Alternate titles: *From the Clouds to the Mountains, A Fancy of Doctor Ox, Dr. Ox and Other Stories, Dr. Ox's Experiment and Other Stories, A Winter amid the Ice and Other Stories, A Winter amid the Ice and Other Thrilling Tales*. Collection contains the following short stories and nonfiction: "Une Fantaisie du docteur Ox" (Doctor Ox), "Maître Zacharius" (Master Zacharius), "Un Hivernage dans les glaces" (A Winter amid the Ice), "Un Drame dans les airs" (A Drama in the Air), and "Quarantième ascension du Mont-Blanc" (Fortieth French Ascent of Mont Blanc, written by Verne's brother, Paul). Recommended: translation by Towle cited above. Not recommended: translation by Abby L. Alger (1874, Gill, *From the Clouds to the Mountains*) and I. O. Evans "Fitzroy Edition" translation (1964, Arco, *Dr. Ox and Other Stories*).

L'Ile mystérieuse (1874–75, illus. Jules-Descartes Férat). *The Mysterious Island: Dropped from the Clouds/The Abandoned/The Secret of the Island* (1875, Sampson Low, trans. W. H. G. Kingston). Alternate titles: *The Mysterious Island: Dropped from the Clouds/Marooned/Secret of the Island, Mysterious Island*. Recommended: translations by Sidney Kravitz (2001, Wesleyan University Press) and by Jordon Stump (2001, Modern Library).

Le Chancellor (1875, illus. Edouard Riou and Jules-Descartes Férat). *The Wreck of the Chancellor* (1875, Osgood, trans. George M. Towle). Alternate titles: *The Survivors of the Chancellor, The Chancellor*. Recommended: translation by Towle cited above. Not recommended: I. O. Evans "Fitzroy Edition" translation (1965, Arco, *The Chancellor*).

Michel Strogoff (1876, illus. Jules-Descartes Férat). *Michael Strogoff* (1876, Leslie, trans. E. G. Walraven). Alternate titles: *Michael Strogoff: From Moscow to Irkoutsk; Michael Strogoff, or the Russian Courier; Michael Strogoff, or the Courier of the Czar*. Recommended: translation by Kingston as "revised" by Julius Chambers (1876, Sampson Low).

Hector Servadac (1877, illus. Paul Philippoteaux). *Hector Servadac* (1877, Sampson Low, trans. Ellen E. Frewer). Alternate titles: *To the Sun?* and *Off on a Comet!*, *Hector Servadac: Travels and Adventures Through the Solar System, Anomalous Phenomena/Homeward Bound, Astounding Adventures among the Comets*. Recommended: Frewer translation cited above. Not recommended: translations by Edward Roth (1877–78, Claxton et al., *To the Sun?* and *Off on a Comet!*; rpt. 1960, Dover) and by I. O. Evans (1965, Arco, *Hector Servadac: Anomalous Phenomena* and *Hector Servadac: Homeward Bound*).

Les Indes noires (1877, illus. Jules-Descartes Férat). *The Black Indies* (1877, Munro, translator unknown). Alternate titles: *The Child of the Cavern, The Underground City, Black Diamonds*. Recommended: translation by W. H. G. Kingston (1877, Sampson Low, *The Child of the Cavern*). Not recommended: I. O. Evans "Fitzroy Edition" translation (1961, Arco, *Black Diamonds*).

Un Capitaine de quinze ans (1878, illus. Henri Meyer). *Dick Sand; or a Captain at Fifteen* (1878, Munro, translator unknown). Alternate titles: *Dick Sands, The Boy Captain, A Fifteen Year Old Captain, Captain at Fifteen*. Recommended: Munro edition cited above. Not recommended: translation by Forlag (1976, Abelard-Schuman, *Captain at Fifteen*).

Les Cinq cents millions de la Bégum (1879, illus. Léon Benett). *The 500 Millions of the Begum* (1879, Munro, translator unknown). Alternate titles: *The Begum's Fortune, The Begum's Millions, The Five Hundred Millions of the Begum*. Recommended: Stanford Luce translation (2005, Wesleyan University Press, *The Begum's Millions*). Not recommended: Munro edition cited above, W. H. G. Kingston translation (1879, Sampson Low, *The Begum's Fortune*), and I. O. Evans "Fitzroy Edition" translation (1958, Hanison/Arco, *The Begum's Fortune*).

Les Tribulations d'un Chinois en Chine (1879, illus. Léon Benett). *The Tribulations of a Chinaman in China* (1879, Lee and Shepard, trans. Virginia Champlin [Grace Virginia Lord]). Alternate titles: *The Tribulations of a Chinese Gentleman, The Tribulations of a Chinaman*. Recommended: translation by Champlin cited above. Not recommended: I. O. Evans "Fitzroy Edition" translation (1963, Arco, *The Tribulations of a Chinese Gentleman*).

La Maison à vapeur (1880, illus. Léon Benett). *The Steam House, or A Trip across Northern India* (1880, Munro, trans. James Cotterell). Alternate titles: *The Steam House, The Demon of Cawnpore/Tigers and Traitors*. Recommended: translation by Agnes D. Kingston (1880, Sampson Low, *The Steam House*). Not recommended: I. O. Evans "Fitzroy Edition" translation (1959, Hanison, *The Steam House: The Demon of Cawnpore* and *The Steam House: Tigers and Traitors*.

La Jangada (1881, illus. Léon Benett and Edouard Riou). *The Jangada, or 800 Leagues over the Amazon* (1881, Munro, trans. James Cotterell). Alternate titles: *The Giant Raft, The Jangada, The Giant Raft: Down the Amazon/The Cryptogram*. Recommended: translation by W.J. Gordon (1881–82, Sampson Low, *The Giant Raft*). Not recommended: I. O. Evans "Fitzroy Edition" translation (1967, Arco, *The Giant Raft: Down the Amazon* and *The Giant Raft: The Cryptogram*).

Le Rayon vert (1882, illus. Léon Benett). *The Green Ray* (1883, Munro, trans. James Cotterell). Recommended: translation by Mary de Hautville (1883, Sampson Low, *The Green Ray*).

L'Ecole des Robinsons (1882, illus. Léon Benett). *Robinson's School* (1883, Munro, trans. James Cotterell). Alternate titles: *Godfrey Morgan: A California Mystery, An American Robinson Crusoe, The School for Crusoes*. Recommended: translation by J. C. Curtin (1883, Redpath's Weekly, *An American Robinson Crusoe*). Not recommended: I. O. Evans "Fitzroy Edition" translation (1966, Arco, *The School for Crusoes*).

Kéraban-le-têtu (1883, illus. Léon Benett). *The Headstrong Turk* (1883–84, Munro, trans. James Cotterell). Alternate titles: *Kéraban the Inflexible: The Captain of the Guidara* and *Kéraban the Inflexible: Scarpante, the Spy*. Recommended: translation by J. C. Curtin (1883, Redpath's Weekly, *The Headstrong Turk*).

L'Archipel en feu (1884, illus. Léon Benett). *Archipelago on Fire* (1885,

Munro, translator unknown). Alternate title: *The Archipelago on Fire*. Recommended: Sampson Low edition (1885, trans. anon.).

L'Etoile du sud (1884, illus. Léon Benett). *The Southern Star* (1885, Munro, translator unknown). Alternate titles: The *Vanished Diamond: A Tale of South Africa, The Southern Star Mystery, The Star of the South*. Recommended: translation by Stephen Gray (2003, Pretoria: Protea Book House, *The Star of the South*). Not recommended: I. O. Evans "Fitzroy Edition" translation (1966, Arco, *The Southern Star Mystery*).

Mathias Sandorf (1885, illus. Léon Benett). *Mathias Sandorf* (1885, Munro, trans. G. W. Hanna).

L'Epave du Cynthia (1885, illus. George Roux). *Waif of the "Cynthia"* (1885, Munro, translator unknown). Alternate title: *Salvage from the Cynthia*. Recommended: Munro edition cited above. Not recommended: I. O. Evans "Fitzroy Edition" translation (1964, Arco, *Salvage from the Cynthia*).

Robur-le-conquérant (1886, illus. Léon Benett). *Robur the Conqueror* (1887, Munro, translator unknown). Alternate titles: *The Clipper of the Clouds, A Trip Round the World in a Flying Machine*. Recommended: the Sampson Low edition (1887, trans. anon., *The Clipper of the Clouds*). Not recommended: the Munro edition cited above and the I. O. Evans "Fitzroy Edition" translation (1962, Arco, *The Clipper of the Clouds*).

Un Billet de loterie (1886, illus. George Roux). *Ticket No. "9672"* (1886, Munro, trans. Laura E. Kendall). Alternate title: *The Lottery Ticket*. Recommended: translation by Kendall.

Le Chemin de France (1887, illus. George Roux). *The Flight to France, or The Memoirs of a Dragoon* (1888, Sampson Low, translator unknown).

Nord contre Sud (1887, illus. Léon Benett). *Texar's Vengeance, or North versus South* (1887, Munro, translator unknown). Alternate titles: *Texar's Revenge, or North against South, North against South: A Tale of the American Civil War, North against South: Burbank the Northerner/ Texar the Southerner*. Recommended: Sampson Low edition (1887, trans. anon., *Texar's Revenge, or North against South*). Not recommended: I. O. Evans "Fitzroy Edition" translation (1965, Arco, *North against South: Burbank the Northerner* and *North against South: Texar the Southerner*).

Deux Ans de vacances (1888, illus. Léon Benett). *A Two Years' Vacation*

(1889, Munro, translator unknown). Alternate titles: *Adrift in the Pacific; Adrift in the Pacific/Second Year Ashore; Two Years' Holiday; A Long Vacation.* Recommended: Munro edition cited above. Not recommended: I. O. Evans "Fitzroy Edition" translation (1965, Arco, *Two Years' Holiday: Adrift in the Pacific* and *Two Years' Holiday: Second Year Ashore*) and translation by Olga Marx (1967, Holt, Rinehart and Winston, *A Long Vacation*).

Sans dessus dessous (1889, illus. George Roux). *The Purchase of the North Pole* (1890, Sampson Low, translator unknown). Alternate title: *Topsy-Turvy.* Recommended: Sampson Low edition cited above. Not recommended: Ogilvie edition (1890, trans. anon., *Topsy-Turvy*) and I. O. Evans "Fitzroy Edition" translation (1966, Arco, *The Purchase of the North Pole*).

Famille-sans-nom (1889, illus. Georges Tiret-Bognet). *A Family without a Name* (1889, Munro, Lovell, translator unknown). Alternate titles: *A Family without a Name: Leader of the Resistance/Into the Abyss; Family without a Name.* Recommended: translation by Edward Baxter (1982, NC Press, *Family without a Name*). Not recommended: I. O. Evans "Fitzroy Edition" translation (1963, Arco, *Family without a Name: Leader of the Resistance* and *Family without a Name: Into the Abyss*).

César Cascabel (1890, illus. George Roux). *Caesar Cascabel* (1890, Cassell, trans. A. Estoclet). Alternate title: *The Travelling Circus/The Show on Ice.* Recommended: translation by Estoclet cited above. Not recommended: I. O. Evans "Fitzroy Edition" translation (1970, Arco, *César Cascabel: The Travelling Circus* and *César Cascabel: The Show on Ice*).

Mistress Branican (1891, illus. Léon Benett). *Mistress Branican* (1891, Cassell, trans. A. Estoclet). Alternate titles: *Mystery of the Franklin, The Wreck of the Franklin.* Recommended: translation by Estoclet cited above.

Le Château des Carpathes (1892, illus. Léon Benett). *The Castle of the Carpathians* (1893, Sampson Low, translator unknown). Alternate title: *Carpathian Castle.* Recommended: Sampson Low edition cited above. Not recommended: I. O. Evans "Fitzroy Edition" translation (1963, Arco, *Carpathian Castle*).

Claudius Bombarnac (1893, illus. Léon Benett). *The Special Correspon-*

dent, or the Adventures of Claudius Bombarnac (1894, Lovell, translator unknown). Alternate title: *Claudius Bombarnac* (same translation).

P'tit-Bonhomme (1893, illus. Léon Benett). *Foundling Mick* (1895, Sampson Low, translator unknown).

Mirifiques aventures de Maître Antifer (1894, illus. George Roux). *Captain Antifer* (1895, Sampson Low, translator unknown).

L'Ile à hélice (1895, illus. Léon Benett). *The Floating Island* (1896, Sampson Low, trans. W. J. Gordon; rpt. 1990, Kegan Paul). Alternate title: *Propeller Island*. Recommended: none.

Face au drapeau (1896, illus. Léon Benett). *Facing the Flag* (1897, Neely, translator unknown). Alternate titles: *For the Flag, Simon Hart: A Strange Story of Science and the Sea*. Recommended: Cashel Hoey translation (1897, Sampson Low, *For the Flag*). Not recommended: I. O. Evans "Fitzroy Edition" translation (1961, Arco, *For the Flag*).

Clovis Dardentor (1896, illus. Léon Benett). *Clovis Dardentor* (1897, Sampson Low, translator unknown).

Le Sphinx des glaces (1897, illus. George Roux). *An Antarctic Mystery* (1898, Sampson Low, trans. Mrs. Cashel Hoey). Alternate titles: *The Sphinx of the Ice, An Antarctic Mystery*. Recommended: Hoey translation cited above. Not recommended: Basil Ashmore "Fitzroy Edition" translation (1961, Arco, *The Mystery of Arthur Gordon Pym by Edgar Allan Poe and Jules Verne*).

Le Superbe Orénoque (1898, illus. George Roux). *The Mighty Orinoco* (2002, Wesleyan University Press, trans. Stanford Luce).

Le Testament d'un excentrique (1899, illus. George Roux). *The Will of an Eccentric* (1900, Sampson Low, translator unknown).

Seconde patrie (1900, illus. George Roux). *Their Island Home* and *The Castaways of the Flag* (1923, Sampson Low, trans. Cranstoun Metcalfe).

Le Village aérien (1901, illus. George Roux). *The Village in the Treetops* (1964, "Fitzroy Edition," Arco, trans. I. O. Evans).

Les Histoires de Jean-Marie Cabidoulin (1901, illus. George Roux). *The Sea Serpent: The Yarns of Jean-Marie Cabidoulin* (1967, "Fitzroy Edition," Arco, trans. I. O. Evans).

Les Frères Kip (1902, illus. George Roux). *The Kip Brothers*. No published English translation yet available.

Bourses de voyage (1903, illus. Léon Benett). *Travel Scholarships*. No published English translation yet available.

Un Drame en Livonie (1904, illus. Léon Benett). *A Drama in Livonia* (1967, "Fitzroy Edition," Arco, trans. I. O. Evans).

Maître du monde (1904, illus. George Roux). *The Master of the World* (1911, Parke, translator unknown). Recommended: translation by Cranstoun Metcalfe (1914, Sampson Low). Not recommended: Parke edition cited above and I. O. Evans "Fitzroy Edition" translation (1962, Arco).

L'Invasion de la mer (1905, illus. Léon Benett). *Invasion of the Sea* (2001, Wesleyan University Press, trans. Edward Baxter).

*Le Phare du bout du monde (1905, illus. George Roux). *The Lighthouse at the Edge of the World* (1923, Sampson Low, trans. Cranstoun Metcalfe).

*Le Volcan d'or (1906, illus. George Roux). *The Golden Volcano: The Claim on the Forty Mile* and *The Golden Volcano: Creek Flood and Famine* (1962, "Fitzroy Edition," Arco, trans. I. O. Evans).

*L'Agence Thompson and Co. (1907, illus. Léon Benett). *The Thompson Travel Agency: Package Holiday* and *The Thompson Travel Agency: End of the Journey* (1965, "Fitzroy Edition," Arco, trans. I. O. Evans).

*La Chasse au météore (1908, illus. George Roux). *The Chase of the Golden Meteor* (1909, Grant Richards, trans. Frederick Lawton). Alternate title: *The Hunt for the Meteor*.

*Le Pilote du Danube (1908, illus. George Roux). *The Danube Pilote* (1967, "Fitzroy Edition," Arco, trans. I. O. Evans).

*Les Naufragés du Jonathan (1909, illus. George Roux). *The Survivors of the Jonathan: The Masterless Man* and *The Survivors of the Jonathan: The Unwilling Dictator* (1962, "Fitzroy Edition," Arco, trans. I. O. Evans). A translation of the original manuscript of this novel was published as *Magellania* (2002, Welcome Rain, trans. Benjamin Ivry).

*Le Secret de Wilhelm Storitz (1910, illus. George Roux). *The Secret of Wilhelm Storitz* (1963, "Fitzroy Edition," Arco, trans. I. O. Evans).

*Hier et demain (1910, illus. Léon Benett, George Roux, and Félicien Myrbach-Rheinfeld). *Yesterday and Tomorrow* (1965, "Fitzroy Edition," Arco, trans. I. O. Evans). Short story collection. Original French collection contains the following short stories: "La Famille Raton" (The Rat Family), "M. Ré-Dièze et Mlle Mi-Bémol" (Mr. Ray Sharp and Miss Me Flat), "La Destinée de Jean Morénas" (The Fate of Jean Moré-

nas), "Le Humbug" (The Humbug), "Au XXIXème siècle: La Journée d'un journaliste américain en 2889" (In the Twenty-ninth Century: The Diary of an American Journalist in 2889), and "L'Eternel Adam" (The Eternal Adam). The 1965 Arco English translation does not contain the same stories as the original French edition: "La Famille Raton" (The Rat Family) and "Le Humbug" (The Humbug) were deleted and replaced with "Une Ville idéale" ("An Ideal City"), "Dix heures de chasse" ("Ten Hours Hunting"), "Frritt-Flacc" ("Frritt-Flacc"), and "Gil Braltar" ("Gil Braltar").

*L'Etonnante aventure de la mission Barsac (Hachette, 1919, illus. George Roux). The Barsac Mission: Into the Niger Bend and The Barsac Mission: The City in the Sahara (1960, "Fitzroy Edition," Arco, trans. I. O. Evans).

Novellas and Short Stories

In the octavo illustrated editions of Verne's *Voyages extraordinaires,* some novels were supplemented with a novella or a short story that had often been previously published in a periodical journal (e.g., *Musée des familles*) or a newspaper (e.g., *Le Figaro*). Only two short story collections were published as part of the *Voyages extraordinaires*—*Le Docteur Ox* (Doctor Ox) and *Hier et demain* (Yesterday and Tomorrow)—and most of the stories contained therein also had appeared earlier. The latter collection was published only after Verne's death in 1905, and many of the short stories in it were either significantly revamped or entirely written by Jules Verne's son, Michel.

"Un Drame au Mexique. Les premiers navires de la marine mexicaine" (1876, illus. Jules-Descartes Férat) with *Michel Strogoff.* First published as "L'Amérique du Sud. Etudes historiques. Les premiers navires de la marine mexicaine" in the *Musée des familles* (July 1851, illus. Eugène Forest and Alexandre de Bar): 304–12. "The Mutineers: A Romance of Mexico" with *Michel Strogoff, the Courier of the Czar* (1877, Sampson Low, trans. W. G. Kingston). Alternate titles: "A Drama in Mexico," "The Mutineers, or A Tragedy in Mexico," "The Mutineers."

"Un Drame dans les airs" (1874, illus. Emile-Antoine Bayard) in *Le Docteur Ox.* First published as "La science en famille. Un voyage en ballon" in the *Musée de familles* (Aug. 1851, illus. Alexandre de Bar): 329–36. "A Voyage in a Balloon" in *Sartain's Union Magazine of Literature and Art* (May 1852, trans. Anne T. Wilbur): 389–95. Alternate titles: "A Drama in the Air," "Balloon Journey," "A Drama in Mid-Air." This was the first Verne story to be translated into English.

"Martin Paz" (1875, illus. Jules-Descartes Férat) with *Le Chancellor*. First published as "L'Amérique du Sud. Moeurs péruviennes. Martin Paz, nouvelle historique" in the *Musée des familles* (July–Aug.1852, illus. Eugène Forest, Emile Berton): 301–13, 321–35. "Martin Paz" in *The Survivors of the Chancellor; and Martin Paz* (1876, Sampson Low, trans. Ellen E. Frewer). Alternate title: "The Pearl of Lima."

"Maître Zacharius" (1874, illus. Théophile Schuler) in *Le Docteur Ox*. First published as "Maître Zacharius, ou l'horloger qui avait perdu son âme. Tradition génèvoise" in the *Musée des familles* (Apr.–May 1854, illus. Alexandre de Bar and Gustave Janet): 193–200, 225–31. "Master Zacharius" in *Dr. Ox and Other Stories* (1874, Osgood, trans. George M. Towle). Alternate titles: "Master Zachary," "The Watch's Soul."

"Un Hivernage dans les glaces" (1874, illus. Adrien Marie) in *Le Docteur Ox*. First published in the *Musée des familles* (Apr.–May 1855, illus. Jean-Antoine de Beauce): 161–72, 209–20. "Winter in the Ice" in *Dr. Ox and Other Stories* (1874, Osgood, trans. George M. Towle). Alternate titles: "A Winter amid the Ice," "A Winter among the Ice-Fields," "Winter on Ice."

"Le Comte de Chanteleine." Published as "Le Comte de Chanteleine. Épisode de la révolution" in the *Musée des familles* (Oct.–Nov. 1864, illus. Edmond Morin, Alexandre de Bar, Jean-Valentin Foulquier): 1–15, 37–51. No English translation available.

"Les Forceurs de blocus" (1871, illus. Jules-Descartes Férat) with *Une Ville flottante*. First published in the *Musée des familles* (Oct.–Nov. 1865, illus. Léon Morel-Fatio, Evrémond Bérard, Fréderic Lixe, and Jean-Valentin Foulquier): 17–21, 35–47. "The Blockade Runners" in *The Floating City, and the Blockade Runners* (1874, Sampson Low, translator unknown).

"Le Docteur Ox" (1874, illus. Lorenz Froelich) in *Le Docteur Ox*. First published in the *Musée des familles* (Mar.-May 1872, illus. Ulysse Parent and Alexandre de Bar): 65–74, 99–107, 133–41. "Doctor Ox's Experiment" in *Dr. Ox and Other Stories* (1874, Osgood, trans. George M. Towle). Alternate titles: "A Fancy of Doctor Ox," "Dr. Ox," "Dr. Ox's Hobby."

"Les Révoltés de la Bounty" (1879, illus. S. Drée) with *Les Cinq cents millions de la Bégum*. First published in the *Magasin d'Education et de Récréation* (Oct.–Dec. 1879, illus. S. Drée): 193–98, 225–30, 257–63. "The Mutineers of the Bounty" in *The Begum's Fortune, with an account of The Mutineers of the Bounty* (1880, Sampson Low, trans. W. H. G. Kingston).

"Dix heures en chasse" (1882, illus. Gédéon Baril) with *Le Rayon vert*. First published in the *Journal d'Amiens, Moniteur de la Somme* (Dec. 19–20, 1881): 2–3. "Ten Hours Hunting" in *Yesterday and Tomorrow* (1965, "Fitzroy Edition," Arco, trans. I. O. Evans).

"Frritt-Flacc" (1886, illus. George Roux) with *Un Billet de loterie*. First published in *Le Figaro illustré* (1884–85): 6–7. "Dr. Trifulgas: A Fantastic Tale" in *Strand Magazine* 4 (July–Dec. 1892, translator unknown): 53–57. Alternate titles: "Fritt-Flacc," "The Ordeal of Dr. Trifulgas," "Fweeee—Spash!"

"Gil Braltar" (1887, illus. George Roux) with *Le Chemin de France*. "Gilbraltar" (1938, Hurd and Walling, trans. Ernest H. De Gay).

"Un Express de l'avenir." Written by Verne's son, Michel, and first published in *Le Figaro* (Sept. 1, 1888). Translated and published (under his father's name) as "An Express of the Future" in *Strand Magazine* 10 (July–Dec. 1895): 638–40.

"La Journée d'un journaliste américain en 2889" (1910, illus. George Roux) in *Hier et demain*. Written by Verne's son, Michel, and first published in English (under his father's name) as "In the Year 2889" in *The Forum* 6 (Sept. 1888–Feb. 1889, illus. George Roux): 662–77. Later modified by Jules Verne and published as "La Journée d'un journaliste américain en 2890" in *Mémoires de l'Académie d'Amiens* 37 (1890): 348–70. The latter version was then published as "Au XXIXème siècle: La Journée d'un journaliste américain en 2889" in *Hier et demain* (Paris: Hetzel, 1910). It was then translated and reprinted as "In the Twenty-ninth Century: The Diary of an American Journalist in 2889" in *Yesterday and Tomorrow* (1965, "Fitzroy Edition," Arco, trans. I. O. Evans).

"La Famille Raton" (1910, illus. Félicien Myrbach-Rheinfeld) in *Hier et demain.* First published as "Aventures de la famille Raton. Conte de fées" in *Le Figaro illustré* (Jan. 1891): 1–12. *Adventures of the Rat Family,* trans. Evelyn Copeland (1993, Oxford).

"La Destinée de Jean Morénas" (1910, illus. Léon Benett) in *Hier et demain.* Written by Verne's son, Michel, from his father's unpublished short story "Pierre-Jean" (see under "Rediscovered Works"). "The Fate of Jean Morénas" in *Yesterday and Tomorrow* (1965, "Fitzroy Edition," Arco, trans. I. O. Evans).

"Le Humbug" (1910, illus. George Roux) in *Hier et demain.* "Humbug, The American Way of Life" (1991, Acadian, trans. William Butcher) and "The Humbug" in *The Jules Verne Encyclopedia,* ed. Brian Taves and Stephen Michaluk Jr. (1996, Scarecrow, trans. Edward Baxter).

"Monsieur Ré-Dièze et Mademoiselle Mi-Bémol" (1910, illus. George Roux) in *Hier et demain.* First published in *Le Figaro illustré* (Dec. 25, 1893): 221–28. "Mr. Ray Sharp and Miss Me Flat" in *Yesterday and Tomorrow* (1965, "Fitzroy Edition," Arco, trans. I. O. Evans).

"L'Eternel Adam" (1910, illus. Léon Benett) in *Hier et demain.* Written by Verne's son, Michel, from his father's unfinished short story "Edom" (see under "Rediscovered Works") and first published in *La Revue de Paris* (Oct. 1, 1910): 449–84. Translated as "Eternal Adam" in *Saturn* 1.1 (Mar. 1957, trans. Willis T. Bradley): 76–112.

Rediscovered Works: Unpublished Early Novels, Short Stories, and Original Manuscripts

Un Prêtre en 1835 (A Priest in 1835, written 1846–47). Published as *Un Prêtre en 1839* (1992, Cherche Midi, illus. Jacques Tardi).

"Jédédias Jamet" (Jedediah Jamet, written 1847). Published as "Jédédias Jamet" in *San Carlos et autres récits inédits,* 177–206 (1993, Cherche Midi, illus. Jacques Tardi).

"Pierre-Jean" (written ca. 1852). Published as "Pierre-Jean" in Olivier Dumas, *Jules Verne,* 205–34 (1988, La Manufacture). Original manuscript of "La Destinée de Jean Morénas."

"Le Siège de Rome" (The Siege of Rome, written ca. 1853). Published as "Le Siège de Rome" in *San Carlos et autres récits inédits,* 81–146 (1993, Cherche Midi, illus. Jacques Tardi).

"Le Mariage de Monsieur Anselme des Tilleuls" (The Marriage of M. Anselme des Tilleuls, written ca. 1855). Published as "Le Mariage de M. Anselme des Tilleuls. Souvenirs d'un élève de huitième" (1991, Olifant, illus. Gérard Bregnat) and as "Le Mariage de M. Anselme des Tilleuls. Souvenirs d'un élève de huitième" in *San Carlos et autres récits inédits*, 47-80 (1993, Cherche Midi, illus. Jacques Tardi).

"San Carlos" (San Carlos, written ca. 1856). Published as "San Carlos" in *San Carlos et autres récits inédits*, 147-76 (1993, Cherche Midi, illus. Jacques Tardi).

Voyage en Angleterre et en Ecosse — Voyage à reculons (written 1859-60). Published as *Voyage à reculons en Angleterre et en Ecosse* (1989, Cherche Midi). Translated by William Butcher as *Backwards to Britain* (1992, Chamber).

Paris au XXème siècle (written 1863). Published as *Paris au XXème siècle* (1994, Hachette, illus. François Schuiten). Translated by Richard Howard as *Paris in the Twentieth Century* (1996, Random House, illus. Anders Wenngren).

L'Oncle Robinson (Uncle Robinson, written 1870-71). Published as *L'Oncle Robinson* (1991, Cherche Midi). Original manuscript of *L'Ile mystérieuse*.

Le Beau Danube jaune (The Beautiful Yellow Danube, written 1896-97). Published as *Le Beau Danube jaune* (1988, Société Jules Verne). Original manuscript of *Le Pilote du Danube*.

En Magellanie — Au bout du monde (In the Magellanes — At the End of the World, written 1896-99). Published as *En Magellanie* (1987, Société Jules Verne). Original manuscript of *Les Naufragés du Jonathan*, published in English as *Magellania* (2002, Welcome Rain, trans. Benjamin Ivry).

Le Volcan d'or — Le Klondyke (The Golden Volcano — The Klondyke, written 1899-1900). Published as *Le Volcan d'or. Version originale* (1989, Société Jules Verne). Original manuscript of *Le Volcan d'or*.

Le Secret de Wilhelm Storitz — L'Invisible, L'Invisible fiancée, Le Secret de Storitz (The Secret of Wilhelm Storitz, written 1901). Published as *Le Secret de Wilhelm Storitz* (1985, Société Jules Verne). Original manuscript of *Le Secret de Wilhelm Storitz*.

La Chasse au météore — Le Bolide (The Hunt for the Meteor — The Bolide, written 1901). Published as *La Chasse au météore. Version originale* (1986) and as *La Chasse au météore (Version originale) suivi de Edom*

(1994, Société Jules Verne, illus. George Roux). Original manuscript of *La Chasse au météore.*

"Voyage d'études" (Study Trip, written 1903–4). Unfinished manuscript, completed and published by Michel Verne as *L'Etonnante aventure de la mission Barsac* (1919). Original version published in *San Carlos et autres récits inédits,* 207–60 (1993, Cherche Midi, illus. Jacques Tardi).

"Edom." (Edom, written 1903–5). Unfinished manuscript, rewritten and published in *Hier et demain* by Michel Verne as "L'Eternel Adam." Original version published in the *Bulletin de la Société Jules Verne* 100 (1991): 21–48.

Theater Plays and Operettas (Performed or Published)

Les Pailles rompues (Broken Straws, 1849). First performed at the Théâtre Historique on June 12, 1850. Published by Beck (Paris) in 1850.

Monna Lisa (Mona Lisa, 1852). Published posthumously in *Jules Verne,* ed. Pierre-André Touttain, 1974.

Les Châteaux en Californie (Castles in California, 1852). Published in the *Musée des familles,* June 1852.

Le Colin-Maillard (Blind Man's Bluff, 1852). First performed at the Théâtre Lyrique on April 28, 1853. Published by Michel Lévy (Paris) in 1853.

Les Compagnons de la Marjolaine (The Companions of the Marjolaine, 1853). First performed at the Théâtre Lyrique on June 6, 1855. Published by Michel Lévy (Paris) in 1855.

Monsieur de Chimpanzé (Mister Chimpanzee, 1857). First performed at the Bouffes-Parisiennes on February 17, 1858. Published in the *Bulletin de la Société Jules Verne* 57 (1981).

L'Auberge des Ardennes (The Ardennes Inn, 1859). First performed at the Théâtre Lyrique on September 1, 1860. Published by Michel Lévy (Paris) in 1860.

Onze jours de siège (Eleven Days of Siege, 1854–60). First performed at the Théâtre du Vaudeville on June 1, 1861. Published by Michel Lévy (Paris) in 1861.

Un Neveu d'Amérique, ou Les Deux Frontignac (A Nephew from America, or the Two Frontignacs, 1872). First performed at the Théâtre Cluny on April 17, 1873. Published by Hetzel (Paris) in 1873.

Le Tour du monde en 80 jours (Around the World in Eighty Days, 1874). First performed at the Théâtre de la Porte Saint-Martin, November 7, 1874. Published in *Les Voyages au théâtre* by Jules Verne and Adolphe d'Ennery (Paris, J. Hetzel, 1881).

Les Enfants du capitaine Grant (The Children of Captain Grant, 1878). First performed at the Théâtre de la Porte Saint-Martin on December 26, 1878. Published in *Les Voyages au théâtre* by Jules Verne and Adolphe d'Ennery (Paris, J. Hetzel, 1881).

Michel Strogoff (Michael Strogoff, 1880). First performed at the Théâtre de Châtelet on November 17, 1880. Published in *Les Voyages au théâtre* by Jules Verne and Adolphe d'Ennery (Paris, J. Hetzel, 1881).

Voyage à travers l'impossible (Journey through the Impossible, 1882). First performed at the Théâtre de la Porte Saint-Martin on November 25, 1882. Published by Jean-Jacques Pauvert (Paris) in 1981. Published in English as *Journey through the Impossible,* trans. Edward Baxter, ed. Jean-Michel Margot (Amherst, NY: Prometheus, 2003).

Kéraban-le-têtu (Keraban the Stubborn, 1883). First performed at La Gaîté-Lyrique on September 3, 1883. Published in the *Bulletin de la Société Jules Verne* 85–86 (1988).

Mathias Sandorf (Mathias Sandorf, 1887). First performed at the Théâtre de l'Ambigu on November 26, 1887.

Poetry and Song Lyrics

Collected in *Poésies inédites,* ed. Christian Robin (1989, Cherche Midi) and in *Textes oubliés,* ed. Francis Lacassin (1979, "10/18").

Literary Criticism, Nonfiction, Speeches, and Other Prose

"A propos du 'Géant'" (Concerning the "Giant"). *Musée des familles* (Dec. 1863): 92–93. Rpt. in *Textes oubliés,* ed. Francis Lacassin (1979, "10/18").

"Edgard Poë [*sic*] et ses oeuvres" (Edgar Poe and His Works). *Musée des familles* (Apr. 1864): 193–208. Rpt. in *Textes oubliés,* ed. Francis Lacassin (1979, "10/18"). Translated by I. O. Evans as "The Leader of the Cult of the Unusual" in *The Edgar Allan Poe Scrapbook,* ed. Peter Haining (1978, Schocken).

Géographie illustrée de la France et de ses colonies (Illustrated Geography of France and Its Colonies, 1866, illus. Edouard Riou, Hubert Clerget), coauthored with Théophile Lavallée.

"Une Ville idéale" (An Ideal City). *Mémoires de l'Académie des sciences, belles-lettres, et arts d'Amiens* 22 (1874–75): 347–78. Rpt. in *Textes oubliés,* ed. Francis Lacassin (1979, "10/18"). Translated by I. O. Evans as "An Ideal City" and included in *Yesterday and Tomorrow* (1965, Arco).

Histoire des grands voyages et des grands voyageurs: Découverte de la terre (1878), *Les Grands navigateurs du XVIIIème siècle* (1879, illus. Léon Benett, Paul Philippoteaux), and *Les Voyageurs du XIXème siècle* (1880). Translated by Dora Leigh as *The Exploration of the World: Famous Travels and Travellers, The Great Navigators of the Eighteenth Century, The Exploration of the World* (1879, Scribners).

"The Story of My Boyhood." *The Youth's Companion* (Apr. 9, 1891): 221. Verne's original autobiographical essay, "Souvenirs d'enfance et de jeunesse" (Memories of Childhood and Youth), was published in French for the first time in *Jules Verne,* ed. Pierre-André Touttain (1974, Cahiers de l'Herne).

"Discours de distribution des prix au Lycée de Jeunes Filles d'Amiens" (July 29, 1893). Rpt. in *Textes oubliés,* ed. Francis Lacassin (1979, "10/18"). Translated by I. O. Evans as "The Future for Women: An Address by Jules Verne," in *The Jules Verne Companion,* ed. Peter Haining (1978, Souvenir).

"Future of the Submarine." *Popular Mechanics* 6 (June 1904): 629–31.

"Solution of Mind Problems by the Imagination." *Hearst's International Cosmopolitan* (Oct. 1928): 95, 132. Written in 1903.

Interviews

Belloc, Marie A. "Jules Verne at Home." *Strand Magazine* (Feb. 1895): 207–13.

Compère, Daniel, and Jean-Michel Margot. *Entretiens avec Jules Verne 1873–1905.* Geneva: Slatkine, 1998.

De Amicis, Edmondo. "A Visit to Jules Verne and Victorien Sardou." *Chautauquan* (Mar. 1897): 702–7.

Jones, Gordon. "Jules Verne at Home." *Temple Bar* 129 (1904): 664–70.

Sherard, Robert H. "Jules Verne at Home." *McClure's Magazine* (Jan. 1894): 115–24.

———. "Jules Verne Revisited." *T.P.'s Weekly* (Oct. 9, 1903): 589.

Correspondence and Other Autobiographical Writings

Bottin, André. "Lettres inédites de Jules Verne au lieutenant colonel Hennebert." *Bulletin de la Société Jules Verne* 18 (1971): 36–44.

Dumas, Olivier, Piero Gondolo della Riva, and Volker Dehs. *Correspondance inédite de Jules et Michel Verne avec l'éditeur Louis-Jules Hetzel (1886–1914)*. Vol. 1: (1886–1896). Geneva: Slatkine, 2002.

———. *Correspondance inédite de Jules Verne et de Pierre-Jules Hetzel (1863–1886)*. Vol. I (1863–1874). Geneva: Slatkine, 1999.

———. *Correspondance inédite de Jules Verne et de Pierre-Jules Hetzel (1863–1886)*. Vol. 2 (1875–1878). Geneva: Slatkine, 2001.

———. *Correspondance inédite de Jules Verne et de Pierre-Jules Hetzel (1863–1886)*. Vol. 3 (1879–1886). Geneva: Slatkine, 2002.

Martin, Charles-Noël. *La Vie et l'oeuvre de Jules Verne*. Paris: Michel de l'Ormeraie, 1978.

Parménie, A. "Huit lettres de Jules Verne à son éditeur P.-J. Hetzel." *Arts et Lettres* 15 (1949): 102–7.

Parménie, A., and C. Bonnier de la Chapelle. *Histoire d'un éditeur et de ses auteurs, P.-J. Hetzel (Stahl)*. Paris: Albin Michel, 1953.

Turiello, Mario. "Lettre de Jules Verne à un jeune Italien." *Bulletin de la Société Jules Verne* 1 (1936): 158–61.

Verne, Jules. "Correspondance." *Bulletin de la Société Jules Verne* 49 (1979): 31–34.

———. "Correspondance avec Fernando Ricci," *Europe* 613 (1980): 137–38.

———. "Correspondance avec Mario Turiello." *Europe* 613 (1980): 108–35.

———. "Deux lettres à Louis-Jules Hetzel." In *Jules Verne*, ed. Pierre-André Touttain, 73–74. Paris: Cahiers de l'Herne, 1974.

———. "Deux lettres inédites." *Bulletin de la Société Jules Verne* 48 (1978): 253–54.

———. "Jules Verne: 63 lettres." *Bulletin de la Société Jules Verne* 11–13 (1938): 47–129.

———. "Lettre à Nadar." *L'Arc* 29 (1966): 83.

———. "Lettre à Paul, à propos de Turpin." In *Jules Verne,* ed. Pierre-André Touttain, 81–82. Paris: Cahiers de l'Herne, 1974.

———. "Lettres à Nadar." In *Jules Verne,* ed. Pierre-André Touttain, 76–80. Paris: Cahiers de l'Herne, 1974.

———. "Lettres diverses." *Europe* 613 (1980): 143–51.

———. "Quelques lettres." *Livres de France* 6 (May–June, 1955): 13–15.

———. "Sept lettres à sa famille et à divers correspondants." In *Jules Verne,* ed. Pierre-André Touttain, 63–70. Paris: Cahiers de l'Herne, 1974.

———. "Souvenirs d'enfance et de jeunesse." In *Jules Verne,* ed. Pierre-André Touttain, 57–62. Paris: Cahiers de l'Herne, 1974.

———. "Spécial Lettres No. 1." *Bulletin de la Société Jules Verne* 65–66 (1983): 4–50.

———. "Spécial Lettres No. 2." *Bulletin de la Société Jules Verne* 69 (1984): 3–25.

———. "Spécial Lettres No. 3." *Bulletin de la Société Jules Verne* 78 (1986): 3–52.

———. "Spécial Lettres No. 4." *Bulletin de la Société Jules Verne* 83 (1987): 4–27.

———. "Spécial Lettres No. 5." *Bulletin de la Société Jules Verne* 88 (1988): 8–18.

———. "Spécial Lettres No. 6." *Bulletin de la Société Jules Verne* 94 (1990): 10–33.

———. "Trente-six lettres inédites." *Bulletin de la Société Jules Verne* 68 (1983): 4–50.

———. "Vingt-deux lettres de Jules Verne à son frère Paul." *Bulletin de la Société Jules Verne* 69 (1984): 3–25.

SECONDARY SOURCES ON JULES VERNE AND HIS WORKS

Bibliographies and Bibliographical Studies

Angenot, Marc. "Jules Verne and French Literary Criticism, I." *Science Fiction Studies* 1.1 (1973): 33–37.

———. "Jules Verne and French Literary Criticism, II." *Science Fiction Studies* 1.2 (1973): 46–49.

Butcher, William. "Jules and Michel Verne." In *Critical Bibliography of French Literature: The Nineteenth Century*, ed. David Baguley, 923–40. Syracuse: Syracuse University Press, 1994.

Compère, Daniel. "Le Monde des études verniennes." *Magazine Littéraire* 119 (1976): 27–29.

Decré, Françoise. *Catalogue du fonds Jules Verne*. Nantes: Bibliothèque Municipale, 1978. Updated by Colette Gaillois in *Catalogue du fonds Jules Verne (1978–1983)*. Nantes: Bibliothèque Municipale, 1984.

Dehs, Volker. *Bibliographischer Führer durch die Jules-Verne-Forschung / Guide bibliographique à travers la critique vernienne, 1872–2001*. Wetzlar: Phantastische Bibliothek, 2002.

Dumas, Olivier, et al. "Bibliographie des oeuvres de Jules Verne." *Bulletin de la Société Jules Verne* 1 (1967): 7–12. Additions and updates: *BSJV* 2 (1967): 11–15; *BSJV* 3 (1967): 13; *BSJV* 4 (1967): 15–16. Rpt. in Dumas, *Jules Verne*, 160–67. Lyon: La Manufacture, 1988.

Evans, Arthur B. "A Bibliography of Jules Verne's English Translations." *Science Fiction Studies* 32.1 (Mar. 2005): 87–123.

Gallagher, Edward J., Judith A. Mistichelli, and John A. Van Eerde. *Jules Verne: A Primary and Secondary Bibliography*. Boston: G. K. Hall, 1980.

Gondolo della Riva, Piero. *Bibliographie analytique de toutes les oeuvres de Jules Verne*. Vols. 1 and 2. Paris: Société Jules Verne, 1977, 1985.

Margot, Jean-Michel. *Bibliographie documentaire sur Jules Verne*. Amiens: Centre de Documentation Jules Verne, 1989.

Raymond, François, and Daniel Compère. *Le Développement des études sur Jules Verne*. Paris: Minard, Archives des Lettres Modernes, 1976.

Biographies

Allott, Kenneth. *Jules Verne*. London: Crescent Press, 1940.

Allotte de la Fuÿe, Marguerite. *Jules Verne, sa vie, son oeuvre*. Paris: Simon Kra, 1928. Published in English as *Jules Verne,* trans. Erik de Mauny. London: Staples, 1954.

Avrane, Patrick. *Jules Verne*. Paris: Stock, 1997.

Born, Franz. *The Man Who Invented the Future: Jules Verne*. New York: Prentice-Hall, 1963.

Clarétie, Jules. *Jules Verne*. Paris: A. Quantin, 1883.

Costello, Peter. *Jules Verne: Inventor of Science Fiction*. London: Hodder and Stroughton, 1978.

Dehs, Volker. *Jules Verne*. Hamburg: Rowohlt, 1986.

Dekiss, Jean-Paul. *Jules Verne, l'enchanteur*. Paris: Editions du Félin, 1999.

——. *Jules Verne, le rêve du progrès*. Paris: Gallimard, 1991.

Dumas, Olivier. *Jules Verne*. Lyon: La Manufacture, 1988.

——. *Voyage à travers Jules Verne*. Montreal: Stanké, 2000.

Jules-Verne, Jean. *Jules Verne*. Paris: Hachette, 1973. Published in English as *Jules Verne: A Biography*, trans. Roger Greaves. New York: Taplinger, 1976.

Lemire, Charles. *Jules Verne*. Paris: Berger-Levrault, 1908.

Lottman, Herbert R. *Jules Verne: An Exploratory Biography*. New York: St. Martin's Press, 1996. Published in French as *Jules Verne*, trans. Marianne Véron. Paris: Flammarion, 1996.

Lynch, Lawrence. *Jules Verne*. New York: Twayne, 1992.

Martin, Charles-Noël. *La Vie et l'oeuvre de Jules Verne*. Paris: Michel de l'Ormeraie, 1978.

Robien, Gilles de. *Jules Verne, le rêveur incompris*. Neuilly-sur-Seine: Michel Lafon, 2000.

Soriano, Mark. *Jules Verne*. Paris: Julliard, 1978.

Teeters, Peggy. *Jules Verne: The Man Who Invented Tomorrow*. New York: Walter, 1992.

Vierne, Simone. *Jules Verne*. Paris: Balland, 1986.

Other Selected Critical Studies

Alkon, Paul. *Science Fiction before 1900*. New York: Twayne, 1994.

Angenot, Marc. "Jules Verne: The Last Happy Utopianist," in *Science Fiction: A Critical Guide*, ed. Patrick Parrinder, 18–32. New York: Longman, 1979.

——. "Science Fiction in France before Verne," *Science Fiction Studies* 5.1 (Mar. 1978): 58–66.

L'Arc 29 (1966). Special issue devoted to Jules Verne.

Arts et Lettres 15 (1949). Special issue devoted to Jules Verne.

Barthes, Roland. "Nautilus et Bateau Ivre." In Barthes, *Mythologies*,

90–92. Paris: Seuil, 1957, 1970. Published in English as "The
Nautilus and the Drunken Boat," trans. A. Lavers, in Barthes,
Mythologies, 65–67. New York: Hill and Wang, 1972.

———. "Par où commencer?" *Poétique* 1 (1970): 3–9. Rpt. in Barthes,
Nouveaux essais critiques, 145–51. Paris: Seuil, 1972.

Bellemin-Noël, Jean. "Analectures de Jules Verne." *Critique* 26 (1970):
692–704.

Benford, Gregory. "Verne to Varley: Hard SF Evolves." *Science Fiction
Studies* 32.1 (March 2005): 163–71.

Berri, Kenneth. "Les *Cinq cents millions de la Bégum* ou la technologie
de la fable." *Stanford French Review* 3 (1979): 29–40.

Boia, Lucien. "Un Ecrivain original: Michel Verne." *Bulletin de la Société
Jules Verne* 70 (1984): 90–95.

———. *Jules Verne: les paradoxes d'un mythe.* Paris: Belles Lettres, 2005.

Bradbury, Ray. "The Ardent Blasphemers." Foreword to Jules Verne,
Twenty Thousand Leagues under the Sea, trans. Anthony Bonner,
1–12. New York: Bantam Books, 1962.

Bridenne, Jean-Jacques. *La Littérature française d'imagination
scientifique.* Lausanne: Dassonville, 1950.

Buisine, Alain. "Circulations en tous genres," *Europe* 595–96 (1978):
48–56.

———. "Repères, marques, gisements: à propos de la robinsonnade
vernienne," *Revue des Lettres Modernes* 523–29 (Apr.–June 1978).
Special issue devoted to Jules Verne.

Bulletin de la Société Jules Verne (1967–2000). Edited by Olivier Dumas.
The official publication of the Jules Verne Society in France and one
of the best sources for up-to-date and reliable information on Jules
Verne.

Butcher, William. "Crevettes de l'air et baleines volantes." *La Nouvelle
Revue Maritime* 386–87 (May–June 1984): 35–40.

———. "Graphes et graphie." In Butcher, *Regards sur la théorie des
graphes,* 177–82. Lausanne: Presses polytechniques romandes, 1980.

———. "Hidden Treasures: The Manuscripts of *Twenty Thousand
Leagues.*" *Science Fiction Studies* 32.1 (Mar. 2005): 132–49.

———. "Long-Lost Manuscript." *Modern Language Review* 93.4 (Oct.
1998): 961–71.

———. "Mysterious Masterpiece." In *Jules Verne: Narratives of*

Modernity, ed. Edmund J. Smyth, 142–57. Liverpool: Liverpool University Press, 2000.

——. "La Poésie de l'arborescence chez Verne." *Studi Francesi* 104 (1992): 261–67.

——. "Le Sens de *L'Eternel Adam,*" *Bulletin de la Société Jules Verne* 58 (1981): 73–81.

——. "Le Verbe et la chair, ou l'emploi du temps." In *Jules Verne 4: Texte, image, spectacle,* ed. François Raymond, 125–48. Paris: Minard, 1983.

——. *Verne's Journey to the Center of the Self: Space and Time in the Voyages Extraordinaires.* London and New York: Macmillan and St. Martin's, 1990.

Butor, Michel. "Homage to Jules Verne." Trans. John Coleman. *New Statesman* (July 15, 1966): 94.

——. "Le Point suprême et l'âge d'or à travers quelques oeuvres de Jules Verne." *Arts et Lettres* 15 (1949): 3–31. Rpt. in Butor, *Répertoire I,* 130–62. Paris: Editions de Minuit, 1960.

Cahiers du Centre d'études verniennes et du Musée Jules Verne (1981–96). Edited by Christian Robin.

Carrouges, Michel. "Le Mythe de Vulcain chez Jules Verne." *Arts et Lettres* 15 (1949): 32–48.

Chambers, Ross. "Cultural and Ideological Determinations in Narrative: A Note on Jules Verne's *Cinq cents millions de la Bégum.*" *L'Esprit créateur* 21.3 (Fall 1981): 69–78.

Chesneaux, Jean. "L'Invention linguistique chez Jules Verne." In *Langues et techniques, nature et société 1,* ed. J. M. C. Thomas and Lucien Bernot, 345–51. Paris: Klincksieck, 1972.

——. *Jules Verne: Un Regard sur le monde.* Paris: Bayard, 2001.

——. *Une Lecture politique de Jules Verne.* Paris: Maspero, 1971. Published in English as *The Political and Social Ideas of Jules Verne,* trans. Thomas Wikeley. London: Thames and Hudson, 1972.

Compère, Daniel. *Approche de l'île chez Jules Verne.* Paris: Lettres Modernes, 1977.

——. "Le Bas des pages." *Bulletin de la Société Jules Verne* 68 (1983): 147–153.

——. "Fenêtres latérales." In *Jules Verne IV: Texte, image, spectacle,* ed. François Raymond, 55–72. Paris: Minard, 1983.

———. *Jules Verne, écrivain.* Genève: Droz, 1991.

———. *Jules Verne: Parcours d'une oeuvre.* Amiens: Encrage, 1996.

———. "Poétique de la carte." *Bulletin de la Société Jules Verne* 50 (1979): 69–74.

———. *Un Voyage imaginaire de Jules Verne: Voyage au centre de la Terre.* Paris: Lettres Modernes, 1977.

Compère, Daniel, and Volker Dehs. "Tashinar and Co.: Introduction à une étude des mots inventés dans l'oeuvre de Jules Verne." *Bulletin de la Société Jules Verne* 67 (1983): 107–11.

Costello, Peter. *Jules Verne: Inventor of Science Fiction.* London: Hodder and Stroughton, 1978.

Davy, Jacques. "A propos de l'anthropophagie chez Jules Verne." *Cahiers du centre d'études verniennes et du Musée Jules Verne* 1 (1981): 15–23.

———. "Le Premier Dénouement des *Cinq Cents Millions de la Bégum.*" *Bulletin de la Société Jules Verne* 123 (1997), 37–41.

Diesbach, Ghislain de. *Le Tour de Jules Verne en quatre-vingts livres.* Paris: Julliard, 1969.

Dumas, Olivier. "La Main du fils dans l'oeuvre du père." *Bulletin de la Société Jules Verne* 82 (1987): 21–24.

Escaich, René. *Voyage au monde de Jules Verne.* Paris: Plantin, 1955.

Europe 33 (1955). Special issue devoted to Jules Verne.

Europe 595–96 (1978). Special issue devoted to Jules Verne.

Evans, Arthur B. "The Extraordinary Libraries of Jules Verne." *L'Esprit créateur* 28 (1988): 75–86.

———. "Le Franglais vernien (père et fils)." In *Modernités de Jules Verne,* ed. Jean Bessière, 87–105. Paris: PUF, 1988.

———. "The Illustrators of Jules Verne's *Voyages Extraordinaires.*" *Science Fiction Studies* 25.2 (July 1998): 241–70.

———. "Jules Verne and the French Literary Canon." In *Jules Verne: Narratives of Modernity,* ed. Edmund J. Smyth, 11–39. Liverpool: Liverpool University Press, 2000.

———. "Jules Verne et la persistence rétinienne." *Cahiers du centre d'études verniennes et du Musée Jules Verne* 13 (1996): 11–17.

———. "Jules Verne, visionnaire incompris." *Pour la Science* 236 (juin 1997): 94–101.

———. *Jules Verne Rediscovered: Didacticism and the Scientific Novel.* Westport, Conn.: Greenwood, 1988.

———. "Jules Verne's English Translations." *Science Fiction Studies* 32.1 (Mar. 2005): 62–86.

———. "Literary Intertexts in Jules Verne's *Voyages Extraordinaires*." *Science Fiction Studies* 23.2 (July 1996): 171–87.

———. "The 'New' Jules Verne." *Science Fiction Studies* 22.1 (Mar. 1995): 35–46.

———. "Science Fiction in France: A Brief History and Select Bibliography." *Science Fiction Studies* 16.3 (Nov. 1989): 254–76, 338–68.

———. "Science Fiction vs. Scientific Fiction in France: From Jules Verne to J.-H. Rosny Aîné." *Science Fiction Studies* 15.1 (1988): 1–11.

———. "Vehicular Utopias of Jules Verne." In *Transformations of Utopia*, ed. George Slusser et al., 99–108. New York: AMS Press, 1999.

Evans, Arthur B., and Ron Miller. "Jules Verne: Misunderstood Visionary." *Scientific American* (Apr. 1997): 92–97.

Evans, I. O. *Jules Verne and His Works*. London: Arco, 1965.

———. "Jules Verne et le lecteur anglais." *Bulletin de la Société Jules Verne* 6 (1937): 36.

Fabre, Michel. *Le Problème et l'épreuve: formation et modernité chez Jules Verne*. Paris: Harmattan, 2003.

Foucault, Michel. "L'Arrière-fable." *L'Arc* 29 (1966): 5–13. Published in English as "Behind the Fable," trans. Pierre A. Walker, *Critical Texts* 5 (1988): 1–5; also as "Behind the Fable," trans. Robert Hurley, in *Aesthetics, Method, and Epistemology*, ed. J. Faubion, 137–45. New York: New Press, 1998.

Frank, Bernard. *Jules Verne et ses voyages*. Paris: Flammarion, 1941.

Gilli, Yves, and Florent Montaclair. *Jules Verne et l'utopie*. Besançon: Presses du Centre Unesco de Besançon, 1999.

Gilli, Yves, Florent Montaclair, and Sylvie Petit. *Le Naufrage dans l'oeuvre de Jules Verne*. Paris: Harmattan, 1998.

Gondolo della Riva, Piero. "A propos des oeuvres posthumes de Jules Verne." *Europe* 595–96 (1978): 73–82.

———. "A propos d'une nouvelle." In *Jules Verne*, ed. Pierre-André Touttain, 284–85. Paris: Cahiers de l'Herne, 1974.

Haining, Peter. *The Jules Verne Companion*. London: Souvenir, 1978.

Harpold, Terry. "Verne's Cartographies." *Science Fiction Studies* 32.1 (Mar. 2005): 18–42.

Hernández, Teri. J. "Translating Verne: An Extraordinary Journey."
    Science Fiction Studies 32.1 (Mar. 2005): 124–31.

Huet, Marie-Hélène. *L'Histoire des Voyages Extraordinaires: Essai sur
    l'oeuvre de Jules Verne.* Paris: Minard, 1973.

Jensen, William B. "Captain Nemo's Battery: Chemistry and the Science
    Fiction of Jules Verne." *Chemical Intelligencer* (Apr. 1997): 23–32.

Jules Verne écrivain. Nantes: Bibliothèque municipale de Nantes, 2000.

Jules Verne et les sciences humaines. Colloque de Cerisy. Paris: UGE,
    "10/18," 1979.

Jules Verne—filiations, rencontres, influences. Colloque d'Amiens II.
    Paris: Minard, 1980.

Ketterer, David. "Fathoming *20,000 Leagues under the Sea*." In *The
    Stellar Gauge: Essays on Science Fiction Writers,* ed. Michael J. Tolley
    and Kirpal Singh, 7–24. Carlton, Australia: Nostrillia Press, 1981.

Klein, Gérard. "Pour lire Verne (I)." *Fiction* 197 (1970): 137–43.

——. "Pour lire Verne (II)." *Fiction* 198 (1970): 143–52.

Lacassin, Francis. "Du Pavillion noir au Québec libre." *Magazine
    Littéraire* 119 (1976): 22–26.

——. *Passagers clandestins.* Paris: UGE, "10/18," 1979.

——, ed. *Textes oubliés.* Paris: UGE, "10/18," 1979.

Lengrand, Claude. *Dictionnaire des "Voyages Extraordinaires" de Jules
    Verne: Cahier Jules Verne, I.* Amiens: Encrage, 1998.

Livres de France 5 (1955). Special issue devoted to Jules Verne.

Macherey, Pierre. "Jules Verne ou le récit en défaut." In Macherey, *Pour
    une théorie de la production littéraire,* 183–266. Paris: Maspero,
    1966. Published in English as "The Faulty Narrative," in Macherey,
    A Theory of Literary Production, trans. G. Wall, 159–240. London:
    Routledge and Kegan Paul, 1978.

Magazine littéraire 119 (December 1976). Special issue devoted to Jules
    Verne.

Margot, Jean-Michel. *Jules Verne en son temps.* Amiens: Encrage, 2004.

——. "Jules Verne, Playwright." *Science Fiction Studies* 32.1 (March
    2005): 150–62.

Martin, Andrew. "Chez Jules: Nutrition and Cognition in the Novels of
    Jules Verne." *French Studies* 37 (Jan. 1983): 47–58.

——. "The Entropy of Balzacian Tropes in the Scientific Fictions of
    Jules Verne." *Modern Language Review* 77 (Jan. 1982): 51–62.

———. *The Knowledge of Ignorance from Cervantes to Jules Verne.* Cambridge: Cambridge University Press, 1985.

———. *The Mask of the Prophet: The Extraordinary Fictions of Jules Verne.* Oxford: Clarendon, 1990.

Miller, Ron. *Extraordinary Voyages: A Reader's Guide to the Works of Jules Verne.* Fredericksburg, Va.: Black Cat, 1994.

Miller, Walter James. "Afterword: Freedom and the Near Murder of Jules Verne." In Jules Verne, *Twenty Thousand Leagues under the Sea,* trans. Mendor T. Brunetti, 448–61. New York: New American Library, 2001.

———. *The Annotated Jules Verne: From the Earth to the Moon.* New York: Crowell, 1978; rev. ed., New York: Gramercy, 1995.

———. *The Annotated Jules Verne: Twenty Thousand Leagues under the Sea.* New York: Crowell, 1976.

———. "Jules Verne in America: A Translator's Preface." In Jules Verne, *Twenty Thousand Leagues under the Sea,* trans. Walter James Miller, vii–xxii. New York: Washington Square, 1965.

Miller, Walter James, and Frederick P. Walter, eds. and trans. *Jules Verne's Twenty Thousand Leagues under the Sea.* Annapolis, Md.: Naval Institute Press, 1993.

Minerva, Nadia. *Jules Verne aux confins de l'utopie.* Paris: Harmattan, 2001.

Modernités de Jules Verne. Edited by Jean Bessière. Paris: PUF, 1988.

Moré, Marcel. *Nouvelles Explorations de Jules Verne.* Paris: NRF, 1963.

———. *Le Très Curieux Jules Verne.* Paris: NRF, 1960.

Moskowitz, Sam, ed. *Science Fiction by Gaslight.* Cleveland: World, 1968.

Noiray, Jacques. *Le Romancier et la machine: L'Image de la machine dans le roman français (1850–1900).* Paris: José Corti, 1982.

Nouvelles recherches sur Jules Verne et le voyage. Colloque d'Amiens I. Paris: Minard, 1978.

Pourvoyeur, Robert. "De l'invention des mots chez Jules Verne." *Bulletin de la Société Jules Verne* 25 (1973): 19–24.

Raymond, François. "Jules Verne ou le mouvement perpétuel." *Subsidia Pataphysica* 8 (1969): 21–52.

———, ed. *Jules Verne 1: Le Tour du monde.* Paris: Minard, 1976.

———, ed. *Jules Verne 2: L'Ecriture vernienne.* Paris: Minard, 1978.

————, ed. *Jules Verne 3: Machines et imaginaire.* Paris: Minard, 1980.

————, ed. *Jules Verne 4: Texte, image, spectacle.* Paris: Minard, 1983.

————, ed. *Jules Verne 5: Emergences du fantastique.* Paris: Minard, 1987.

————, ed. *Jules Verne 6: La Science en question.* Paris: Minard, 1992.

Renzi, Thomas C. *Jules Verne on Film: A Filmography of the Cinematic Adaptations of His Works, 1902 through 1997.* Jefferson, N.C.: McFarland, 1998.

Revue Jules Verne (1996–2005). Founded by Jean-Paul Dekiss. A scholarly journal sponsored by several Verne-related organizations located in Amiens and Nantes, including the Centre international Jules Verne (Amiens) and the Musée Jules Verne (Nantes), among others. As of November 2004, they have published seventeen issues.

Robin, Christian. *Un Monde connu et inconnu.* Nantes: Centre universitaire de recherches verniennes, 1978.

————, ed. *Textes et langages X: Jules Verne.* Nantes: Université de Nantes, 1984.

Rose, Mark. "Jules Verne: Journey to the Center of Science Fiction." In *Coordinates: Placing Science Fiction,* ed. George E. Slusser, 31–41. Carbondale: Southern Illinois University Press, 1983.

————. "Filling the Void: Verne, Wells, and Lem." *Science Fiction Studies* 8.2 (1981): 121–42.

Schulman, Peter. "Introduction and Notes." Jules Verne, *The Begum's Millions.* Middletown, Conn.: Wesleyan University Press, 2005.

————. "Eccentricity as Clinamen: Jules Verne's Error-Driven Geniuses," *Excavatio* 16, nos. 1–2 (2002): 274–84.

————. "*Paris au XXème siècle*'s Legacy: Eccentricity as Defiance in Jules Verne's Uneasy Relationship with His Era." *Romance Quarterly* 48 (Fall 2001), 257–66.

Serres, Michel. "India (The Black and the Archipelago) on Fire." *Substance* 8 (1974): 49–60.

————. *Jouvences sur Jules Verne.* Paris: Editions de Minuit, 1974.

————. "Le Savoir, la guerre, et le sacrifice." *Critique* 367 (December 1977): 1067–77.

Slusser, George E. "The Perils of Experiment: Jules Verne and the American Lone Genius." *Extrapolation* 40.2 (1999): 101–15.

————. "Why They Kill Jules Verne: Science Fiction and Cartesian Culture." *Science Fiction Studies* 32.1 (Mar. 2005): 43–61.

Smyth, Edmund J. "Jules Verne, SF and Modernity: An Introduction."
In *Jules Verne: Narratives of Modernity*, 1–10. Liverpool: Liverpool
University Press, 2000.

———. ed. *Jules Verne: Narratives of Modernity*. Liverpool: Liverpool
University Press, 2000.

Stableford, Brian. *Scientific Romance in Britain, 1890–1950.* London:
Fourth Estate, 1985.

Suvin, Darko. "Communication in Quantified Space: The Utopian
Liberalism of Jules Verne's Fiction." *Clio* 4 (1974): 51–71. Rpt. in
Suvin, *Metamorphoses of Science Fiction*, 147–63. New Haven: Yale
University Press, 1979.

Taves, Brian. "The Novels and Rediscovered Films of Michel (Jules)
Verne." *Journal of Film Preservation*, no. 62 (April 2001): 25–39.

Taves, Brian, and Stephen Michaluk Jr. *The Jules Verne Encyclopedia.*
Lanham, Md.: Scarecrow, 1996.

Terrasse, Pierre. "Jules Verne et les chemins de fer." *Bulletin de la
Société Jules Verne* 14 (Apr.–June 1970): 116–21.

Touttain, Pierre-André, ed. *Jules Verne*. Paris: Cahiers de l'Herne,
1974.

Unwin, Timothy. "The Fiction of Science, or the Science of Fiction."
In *Jules Verne: Narratives of Modernity*, ed. Edmund J. Smyth,
46–59. Liverpool: Liverpool University Press, 2000.

———. *Jules Verne: Le Tour du monde en quatre-vingts jours.* Glasgow:
Glasgow University Press, 1992.

———. "Jules Verne: Negotiating Change in the Nineteenth Century."
Science Fiction Studies 32.1 (Mar. 2005): 5–17.

———. "Technology and Progress in Jules Verne, or Anticipation in
Reverse." *AUMLA* 93 (2000): 17–35.

Vierne, Simone. "Hetzel et Jules Verne, ou l'invention d'un auteur."
Europe 619–20 (1980): 53–63.

———. *Jules Verne, mythe et modernité.* Paris: PUF, 1989.

———. *Jules Verne, une vie, une oeuvre.* Paris: Ballard, 1986.

———. *Jules Verne et le roman initiatique: Contribution à l'étude de
l'imaginaire.* Paris: Editions du Sirac, 1973.

Weissenberg, Eric. *Jules Verne: Un Univers fabuleux.* Lausanne: Favre,
2004.

ADDITIONAL MATERIALS RELATING
TO JULES VERNE'S *The Begum's Millions*

Berri, Kenneth. "*Les Cinq cents millions de la Bégum,* ou la technologie
de la fable." *Stanford French Review* 3 (1979): 29–40.

Chambers, Ross. "Cultural and Ideological Determinations in Narrative:
A Note on Jules Verne's *Les Cinq cents millions de la Bégum*." *L'Esprit
Créateur* 21.3 (Fall 1981), 69–78.

Chevrel, Yves. "Questions de méthodes et d'idéologies chez Verne et
Zola: *Les Cinq cents millions de la Bégum* et *Travail*." *La Revue des
Lettres Modernes* 523–29 (1978): 69–96.

Evans, I. O. "Introduction to *The Begum's Fortune*." In Jules Verne, *The
Begum's Fortune,* 5–7. New York: Arco Publications, 1958.

Gondolo della Riva, Piero. "De qui est 'France-Ville'?" *Revue Jules
Verne,* no. 7, n.s. (1er semestre 1999): 19–25.

Grousset, Paschal. "La Conclusion originale des *Cinq cents millions de
la Bégum*." *Bulletin de la Société Jules Verne,* no. 123 (1997): 39–41.

Lacassin, Francis. "Le Communard qui écrivit trois romans de Jules
Verne." *Europe: Revue Littéraire Mensuelle* 595–96 (1978): 94–105.

Leibovici, Solange. "France-Ville et Stahlstadt: Hygiénisme et analité
dans un roman de Jules Verne." In *Twelfth International Conference
on Literature and Psychoanalysis,* ed. Frederico Pereira, 165–72.
Lisbon: Instituto Superior de Psicologia Aplicada, 1996.

Leiner, Wolfgang. "*Les Cinq cents millions de la Bégum*. Utopie und
Deutschlandbild im Roman Jules Verne." In *Texte, Kontexte,
Strukturen: Beiträge zur französischen, spanischen, und hispano-
amerikanischen Literatur: Festschrift zum 60. Geburtstag von Karl
Alfred Blueher,* ed. Alfonso de Toro, 5–16. Tübingen: Gunter Narr
Verlag, 1987.

Martin, Andrew. "The One and the Many." In Martin, *The Mask of the
Prophet,* 55–77. Oxford: Oxford University Press, 1990.

Martin, Charles-Noël. "Préface." In Jules Verne, *Les Cinq cents millions
de la Bégum,* vii–xvii. Lausanne: Editions Rencontre, 1968.

Minerva, Nadia. "Debris d'un discours morcelé: Jules Verne à la lisière
de l'Utopie." *Cahiers International de Symbolisme* 95–97 (2000):
55–69.

Sadaune, Samuel. "Jules Verne: Des *Cinq cents millions de la Bégum* au

Rayon vert, ou la démystification de l'idée traditionnelle de 'progrès.'"
Bulletin de la Société Jules Verne, no. 130 (1999): 14–21.

Sudret, Laurence. *Nature et artifice dans les Voyages extraordinaires de
Jules Verne.* Villeneuve d'Asq: Presses Universitaires du Septentrion,
2002.

Terrasse, Pierre. "A propos des *Cinq cents millions de la Bégum:* Un
modèle de Jean-Jacques Langévol." *Bulletin de la Société Jules Verne,*
no. 31 (1974), 184–88.

Wagner, Nicolas. "Le soliloque utopiste des *Cinq cents millions de la
Bégum." Europe: Revue Littéraire Mensuelle* 595–96 (1978): 117–26.

Weissenberg, Eric. "Jules Verne et les Prussiens." *Bulletin de la Société
Jules Verne,* no. 144 (2002): 9–16.

JULES GABRIEL VERNE   A BIOGRAPHY

Anonymous engraving, c. 1880

Jules Gabriel Verne was born on February 8, 1828, to a middle-class family in the port city of Nantes, France. His mother, Sophie, née Allotte de la Fuÿe, was the daughter of a prominent family of shipowners, and his father, Pierre Verne, was an attorney and the son of a Provins magistrate. Jules was the eldest of five children. In addition to his three sisters — Anna, Mathilde, and Marie — he also had a younger brother, Paul, to whom he was very close. Paul eventually became a naval engineer.

As a child and young man, Jules was a relatively conscientious student. Although far from the top of his class, he apparently did win awards for meritorious performance in geography, music, and Greek and Latin, and he easily passed his *baccalauréat* in 1846. But his true passion was the sea. The shipyard docks of nearby Île Feydeau and the bustling commerce of the Nantes harbor never failed to spark Jules's youthful imagination with visions of far-off lands and exotic peoples. Legend has it that he once ran off to sea as a cabin boy aboard a schooner bound for the Indies, but his father managed to intercept the ship before it reached the open sea and to retrieve his wayward son. According to this story, Jules (probably after a good thrashing) promised his parents that he would travel henceforth only in his dreams. Although this charming tale was most likely invented by Verne's familial biographer, Marguerite Allotte de la Fuÿe, it nevertheless exemplifies the author's lifelong love for the sea and his yearnings for adventure-filled journeys to distant ports of call.

Young Jules also loved machines. During an interview toward the end of his life, he reminisced about his early formative years: "While I was quite a lad, I used to adore watching machines at work. My father had a country-house at Chantenay, at the mouth of the Loire, and near the government factory at Indret. I never went to Chantenay without entering the factory and standing for hours watching the machines. . . . This penchant has remained with me all my life, and today I have still as much pleasure in watching a steam-engine or a fine locomotive at work as I have in contemplating a picture by Raphael or Corregio" (qtd. in Robert H. Sherard, "Jules Verne at Home," *McClure's Magazine* [Jan. 1984]: 118).

Intending that Jules follow in his footsteps as a lawyer, Pierre Verne sent him to Paris in 1848 to study law. The correspondence between father and son during the ensuing ten years shows that Jules took his studies seriously, completing his law degree in just two years. But his letters home also make quite it clear that Jules had discovered a new passion—literature. Inspired by authors such as Victor Hugo, Alfred de Vigny, and Théophile Gautier and introduced (via family contacts on his mother's side) into several high-society Parisian literary circles, the young Romantic Verne began to write. From 1847 to 1862, he composed poetry, wrote several plays and a novel entitled *Un Prêtre en 1839* (A Priest in 1839, unpublished during his lifetime), and penned a variety of short stories that he published in the popular French journal *Musée des familles* to supplement his meager income: "Les Premiers navires de la marine mexicaine" (1851, The First Ships of the Mexican Navy), "Un Voyage en ballon" (1851, A Balloon Journey), "Martin Paz" (1852, Martin Paz), "Maître Zacharius" (1854, Master Zacharius), and "Un Hivernage dans les glaces" (1855, Wintering in the Ice). Some of his plays were performed in local Parisian theaters: *Les Pailles rompues* (1850, Broken Straws), *Le Colin-Maillard* (1853, Blind Man's Bluff), *Les Compagnons de la Marjolaine* (1855, The Companions of the Marjoram), *Monsieur de Chimpanzé* (1858, Mister Chimpanzee), *L'Auberge des Ardennes* (1860, The Inn of the Ardennes), and *Onze jours de siège* (1861, Eleven Days of Siege). During this period, Verne also became close friends with Alexandre Dumas père and Dumas fils and, through the former's intervention, eventually became the secretary of the Théâtre Lyrique in 1852.

In 1857 Verne married Honorine Morel, née de Viane, a twenty-six-year-old widow with two daughters. Taking advantage of his new father-in-law's contacts in Paris and a monetary wedding gift from Pierre Verne, Jules decided to discontinue his work at the Théâtre Lyrique and to take a full-time job as *agent de change* at the Paris Stock Market with the firm Eggly et Cie. He spent his early mornings at home writing (at a desk with two drawers—one for his plays, the other for his scientific essays) and most of his days at the Bourse de Paris doing business and associating with a number of other young stockbrokers who had interests similar to his own.

When not busy writing or working at the stock exchange, Verne spent the rest of his time either visiting his old theater friends (he took trips with

Aristide Hignard to Scotland and England in 1859 and to Norway and Denmark in 1862—the former resulting in a travelogue called *Voyage en Angleterre et en Ecosse* [Journey to England and Scotland]) or at the Bibliothèque Nationale, collecting scientific and historical news items and copying them onto note cards for future use, a work habit he would continue throughout his life. As at least one biographer has noted, the long weekend sessions he spent in the reading rooms of the library may well have been partly motivated by a simple desire for peace and quiet: in 1861 Verne's son Michel had just been born and greatly annoyed his father with his incessant crying.

It was during this time that Verne first conceived of writing a new type of novel called a *roman de la science*. It would incorporate the large amounts of scientific material that Verne accumulated in his library research, as well as that gleaned from essays in the *Musée des familles* and other journals to which he himself occasionally contributed. It would combine scientific exploration and discovery with action and adventure and be patterned on the novels of Walter Scott, James Fenimore Cooper, and Edgar Allan Poe. Poe's works in particular, which had recently been translated into French by Charles Baudelaire in 1856, strongly interested Verne for their unusual mixture of scientific reasoning and the fantastic (he later wrote his only piece of literary criticism on Poe in 1864). Verne's efforts eventually crystallized into a rough draft of a novel-length narrative, which he tentatively entitled *Un Voyage en l'air* (A Voyage through the Air).

In September 1862, Verne was introduced to Pierre-Jules Hetzel through a common friend of the publisher and Alexandre Dumas père. Verne promptly asked Hetzel if he would consider reviewing for publication the rough draft of his novel—a manuscript that, according to his wife, the author had very nearly destroyed a few weeks earlier after its rejection by another publishing house. Hetzel agreed to the request, seeing in this narrative the potential for an ideal "fit" with his new family-oriented magazine, the *Magasin d'Education et de Récréation*. A few days later, Verne and Hetzel began what would prove to be a highly successful author-publisher collaboration. It lasted for more than forty years and resulted in over sixty scientific novels collectively called the *Voyages extraordinaires—Voyages dans les mondes connus et inconnus* (Extraordinary Voyages—Journeys in Known and Unknown Worlds).

Shortly after the publication and immediate commercial success of

Verne's first novel in 1863 — now retitled *Cinq semaines en ballon, Voyage de découvertes en Afrique par trois Anglais* (Five Weeks in a Balloon, Voyage of Discovery in Africa by Three Englishmen) — Hetzel offered the young writer a ten-year contract for at least two works per year of the same sort. Not long after, Verne quit his job at the stock market and began to write full time.

Following Verne's historic meeting with Hetzel, the remainder of his life and works fell into three distinct periods: 1862–86, 1886–1905, and 1905–25.

The first, from 1862 to 1886, might be termed Verne's "Hetzel period." During this time, he wrote his most popular *Voyages extraordinaires*, settled permanently with his family in Amiens, purchased a yacht, collaborated on theater adaptations of several of his novels with Adolphe d'Ennery, and ultimately gained both fame and fortune.

Other notable events in Verne's life during this period include:

- Hetzel's rejection of his second novel, *Paris au XXème siècle* (Paris in the 20th Century), in 1863 as well as an early draft of *L'Ile mystérieuse* (The Mysterious Island) called *L'Oncle Robinson* (Uncle Robinson) in 1865;
- the publication of his nonfiction books *Géographie de la France et de ses colonies* (1866, Geography of France and Its Colonies, coauthored with Théophile Lavallée) and the three-volume *Histoire des grands voyages et des grands voyageurs* (1878–80, History of Great Voyages and Great Voyagers);
- the unparalleled success of the novels *Voyage au centre de la terre* (1864, Journey to the Center of the Earth), *De la terre à la lune* (1865, From the Earth to the Moon), *Autour de la lune* (1870, Around the Moon), *Vingt mille lieues sous les mers* (1870, Twenty Thousand Leagues under the Sea), *Le Tour du monde en quatre-vingts jours* (1873, Around the World in Eighty Days), and *Michel Strogoff* (1876, Michael Strogoff), among others;
- a brief trip to America in 1867 on the *Great Eastern*, accompanied by his brother Paul, and visits to New York and Niagara Falls — subsequently fictionalized in his novel *La Ville flottante* (1871, A Floating City);
- receipt of the *Légion d'honneur* just before the outbreak of the Franco-Prussian War in 1870;

- the death of his father, Pierre Verne, on November 3, 1871;
- the purchase of his third yacht, the *Saint-Michel III,* in which he sailed to Lisbon and Algiers in 1878, to Norway, Ireland, and Scotland in 1879–80, to Holland, Denmark, Germany, and the Baltics in 1881, and to Portugal, Algeria, Tunisia, and Italy in 1884 (and, while in Italy, supposedly invited to a private audience with Pope Leo XIII);
- in 1879, the publication of *Les Cinq cents millions de la Bégum* (The Begum's Millions) in collaboration with Paschal Grousset, a.k.a. André Laurie, Verne's only combination utopia/dystopia, which featured his first "mad scientist," Herr Schultze;
- in 1882, his move to a new, larger home at 2 rue Charles-Dubois, Amiens—the famous house with the circular tower, which is today the headquarters of the Centre de Documentation Jules Verne d'Amiens.

The second phase, from 1886 to 1905, might be called Verne's "post-Hetzel period." During this time, Verne worked with Hetzel's son, Louis-Jules, who succeeded his father as manager and principal editor of the Hetzel publishing house. Verne also entered into politics: he was elected to the municipal council of Amiens in 1888, a post he would occupy for fifteen years. But this period is especially notable because of a gradual change in the ideological tone of his *Voyages extraordinaires.* In these later works, the Saint-Simonian pro-science optimism is largely absent, replaced by a growing pessimism about the true value of progress. The omnipresent scientific didacticism, a trademark of Verne's *roman scientifique,* is more frequently muted and supplanted or replaced by romantic melodrama, pathos, and tragedy. And the triumphant leitmotif of the exploration and conquest of nature, which seemed to undergird most of Verne's earlier novels, is now most often abandoned—replaced by an increased focus on politics, social issues, and human morality. This dramatic change of focus in Verne's later works appears to parallel certain personal adversities experienced by the author during this period of his life. For example:

- serious problems with his rebellious son Michel (e.g., repeated bankruptcies, costly amorous escapades, divorce from his first wife, difficulties with the law, etc.);
- severe financial worries, forcing Verne to sell his beloved yacht in 1886;
- the successive deaths of three individuals who were very close to him:

his longtime mistress and friend Mme Duchesne (Estelle Hénin) in 1885, his editor Hetzel in 1886, and his mother in 1887;

- an attack at gunpoint on March 9, 1886, by his mentally disturbed nephew Gaston, who shot Verne in the lower leg, leaving him partially crippled for the rest of his life.

Verne's personal correspondence from this period also reflects his growing pessimism. In a letter dated December 21, 1886, to Hetzel fils, for example, Verne confides: "As for the rest, I have now entered into the blackest part of my life." A few years later, in 1894, the author tells his brother Paul: "All that remains to me are these intellectual distractions. . . . My character is profoundly changed and I have received blows from which I'll never recover."

Whatever the underlying reasons may have been for this change—the absence of Hetzel père's editorial supervision, Verne's awareness of certain disturbing trends in the world at large (e.g., the growth of imperialism and the military-industrial complex), or the sudden flood of tragedies in his personal life—it is evident that many of Verne's post-1886 *Voyages extraordinaires* tend to portray both scientists and scientific innovation with a heavy dose of cynicism and/or biting satire. And, in contrast to the intrepid "go where no man has gone before" scientific explorations, which characterized most of his earlier and most popular works, the later novels now often foreground, in whole or in part, a broad range of political, social, and moral concerns: among other themes, the potential dangers of technology in *Sans dessus dessous* (1889, Topsy-Turvy), *Face au drapeau* (1896, Facing the Flag), and *Maître du monde* (1904, Master of the World); the cruel oppression of the Québécois in Canada in *Famille-sans-nom* (1889, Family without a Name); the evils of ignorance and superstition in *Le Château des Carpathes* (1892, The Castle of the Carpathians); the intolerable living conditions in orphanages in *P'tit-Bonhomme* (1893, Lit'l-Fellow); the destructive influence of religious missionaries on South Sea island cultures in *L'Ile à hélice* (1895, Propeller Island); the imminent extinction of whales in *Le Sphinx des glaces* (1897, The Sphinx of the Ice); the environmental damage caused by the oil industry in *Le Testament d'un excentrique* (1899, The Last Will of an Eccentric); and the slaughter of elephants for their ivory in *Le Village aérien* (1901, The Aerial Village).

During his last years, despite increasingly poor health (arthritis, cataracts, diabetes, and severe gastrointestinal problems) as well as continuing family squabbles because of his son, Michel, Verne continued diligently to write two to three novels per year. But, with a drawer full of nearly completed manuscripts in his desk, he suddenly fell seriously ill in early March 1905, a few weeks after his seventy-seventh birthday. He told his wife Honorine to gather the family around him, and he died quietly on March 24, 1905. He was buried on March 28 in the cemetery of La Madeleine in Amiens. Two years later, an elaborate marble sculpture by Albert Roze was placed over his grave, depicting the author rising from his tomb and stretching his hand toward the sky.

The third and final phase of the Jules Verne story, following the author's death and extending from 1905 to 1919, might well be called the "Verne fils period." During these years Verne's posthumous works were published, but most of them were substantially modified—and, in some instances, authored—by his son, Michel.

In early May 1905, Michel, as executor of his father's estate, published in the Parisian newspapers *Le Figaro* and *Le Temps* a complete list of Jules Verne's surviving manuscripts: eight novels (titled and untitled, in various stages of completion), sixteen plays, several short stories (two unpublished), a travelogue of his early trip to England and Scotland, and an assortment of historical sketches, notes, and the like. Hetzel fils immediately agreed to publish six of the novels that were originally intended to be part of the *Voyages extraordinaires* as well as Verne's short stories, which were grouped in the collection published in 1910 as *Hier et demain* (Yesterday and Tomorrow). Another remaining novel in the series, *L'Etonnante aventure de la mission Barsac* (The Amazing Adventure of the Barsac Mission), was published first in serial format in the newspaper *Le Matin* and later as a book by the publishing company Hachette—who had bought the rights to Verne's works from Hetzel fils in 1914.

In recent years, these posthumous works have become the topic of heated controversy among Verne scholars: how much and in what ways did Michel alter these texts prior to their publication? After a close examination of the available manuscripts (now housed in the Centre d'études verniennes in Nantes) by Piero Gondolo della Riva, Olivier Dumas, and other respected Vernian researchers, it now seems indisputable that Michel had a much greater hand in the composition of Jules Verne's posthumous works than had ever been suspected:

- *Le Volcan d'or* (1906, The Golden Volcano): fourteen chapters by Jules; four more chapters added by Michel as well as four new characters;
- *L'Agence Thompson and Co.* (1907, The Thompson Travel Agency): in all probability, almost entirely written by Michel;
- *La Chasse au météore* (1908, The Hunt for the Meteor): seventeen chapters by Jules; four added by Michel;
- *Le Pilote du Danube* (1908, The Danube Pilot): sixteen chapters by Jules; three added by Michel as well as at least one new character and a new title;
- *Les Naufragés du Jonathan* (1909, The Survivors of the Jonathan): sixteen chapters by Jules; fifteen added by Michel, along with many new characters, episodes, and a new title;
- *Le Secret de Wilhelm Storitz* (1910, The Secret of Wilhelm Storitz): rewritten by Michel to take place in the eighteenth century instead of at the end of the nineteenth; a different conclusion was also added;
- *Hier et demain* (1910, Yesterday and Tomorrow): most of the short stories appearing in this collection had been substantially altered by Michel; one of them, "Au XXIXème siècle: La Journée d'un journaliste américain en 2889" (In the 29th Century: The Day of an American Journalist in 2889), attributable mostly to Michel, and another, "L'Eternel Adam" (Eternal Adam), mostly by him as well;
- *L'Etonnante aventure de la mission Barsac* (1919, The Amazing Adventure of the Barsac Mission): the supposedly "final" novel of the *Voyage extraordinaires* was written entirely by Michel from his father's notes for a novel to be called *Voyages d'études* (Study Trip).

Scholarly reaction to Michel's rewrites of his father's manuscripts has been decidedly mixed. Some have called Michel's intervention in Verne's posthumous works an inexcusable betrayal of trust and a financially motivated scam that dealt a damaging blow to the integrity of Verne's *Voyages extraordinaires*. In an attempt to set the record straight, from 1985 through the 1990s, the Société Jules Verne in France arranged for the publication of Verne's original manuscripts of several of these works. Other scholars disagree and have pointed out that Jules Verne encouraged Michel to publish his own fiction under his father's illustrious name; that during the final decade of his life when his eyesight was rapidly failing, Jules often asked Michel to "collaborate" with him (as secretary-typist) to help bring several of his later novels to publication; and that Michel's sometimes radical modifications of Verne's posthumous works often improved their readability—an enhancement that would assuredly have received his father's wholehearted approval. The debate continues to this day.

With Michel's death in 1925, the final chapter of Verne's literary legacy was (for better or worse) now complete. Ironically, in April of the following year, a pulp magazine called *Amazing Stories* first appeared on American newsstands. It published tales of a supposedly new species of literature dubbed "scientifiction"—defined by its publisher, Hugo Gernsback, as a "Jules Verne, H.G. Wells, and Edgar Allan Poe type of story"—and its title page featured a drawing of Verne's tomb as the magazine's logo. The popularity of *Amazing Stories* and its many pulp progeny, such as *Science Wonder Stories* and *Astounding Stories,* was both immediate and long lasting. As the term "scientifiction" evolved into "science fiction," the new genre began to flourish as never before. And the legend of Jules Verne as its patron saint, as the putative "Father of Science Fiction," soon became firmly rooted in American cultural folklore.

ABOUT THE CONTRIBUTORS

Arthur B. Evans is professor of French at DePauw University and managing editor of the scholarly journal *Science Fiction Studies*. He has published numerous books and articles on Verne and early French science fiction, including the award-winning *Jules Verne Rediscovered* (Greenwood, 1988). He is general editor of Wesleyan's "Early Classics of Science Fiction" series.

Stanford L. Luce is professor emeritus of French at Miami University in Ohio and author of the first American Ph.D. dissertation on Verne (Yale, 1953). He has published extensively on Céline and has translated, in addition to *The Begum's Millions,* several Verne novels including *The Mighty Orinoco* and *The Kip Brothers.*

Peter Schulman is associate professor of French and international studies at Old Dominion University. He is the author of *The Sunday of Fiction: The Modern French Eccentric* (Purdue University Press, 2003) and the coauthor of *Le Dernier livre du siècle* (Romillat, 2001). He has also coedited several books of essays including *The Marketing of Eros: Performance, Sexuality, and Consumer Culture* (Die Blaue Eule, 2003) and *Rhine Crossings: France and Germany in Love and War* (State University of New York Press, 2005). He is currently working on a translation and critical edition of Jules Verne's *The Secret of Wilhelm Storitz* for the University of Nebraska Press.